STARTING OVER AT SUNSET COTTAGE

LISA HOBMAN

Boldwood

This edition published in Great Britain in 2021 by Boldwood Books Ltd.

Cover Design by Alice Moore Design

Cover Photography: Shutterstock

Every effort has been made to obtain the necessary permissions with reference to copyright material, both illustrative and quoted. We apologise for any omissions in this respect and will be pleased to make the appropriate acknowledgements in any future edition.

A CIP catalogue record for this book is available from the British Library.

Paperback ISBN 978-1-80280-220-7

Large Print ISBN 978-1-80280-222-1

Hardback ISBN 978-1-80280-878-0

Ebook ISBN 978-1-80280-221-4

Kindle ISBN 978-1-80280-223-8

Audio CD ISBN 978-1-80280-215-3

MP3 CD ISBN 978-1-80280-216-0

Digital audio download ISBN 978-1-80280-219-1

Boldwood Books Ltd
23 Bowerdean Street
London SW6 3TN
www.boldwoodbooks.com

For Mum, Dad, Rich & Gee.
You're the stars in my sky and I love you more than words.

1

'So, that's it then, Flick?' Jim MacDuff raised his arms in exasperation. 'You're leaving? You've completely given up on us after six years of marriage?' He was past trying to convince Flick that they could make a go of it, work things out, get through this and come out the other side stronger. The past few months had been one argument after another, and Flick had spent less and less time at home. The thought of being single again at twenty-nine both pained and dismayed him.

'It's for the best, James. And please don't call me Flick.' She sighed. 'It's not my name. Not any more. I grew up.' She snorted derisively. 'It's good in the adult world you should visit sometime, you might like it.'

Jim shook his head, sadness oozing from every pore. 'Aye, well you'll always be Flick to me. And I'll always be Jim. What's with all this Felicity and James rubbish anyway?' His accent always became stronger when he was angry. This was one of those occasions when the true Scotsman in him pushed through. The battle may have been lost but he would go down fighting. His chest heaved as he tried to calm the storm raging beneath his skin.

He almost didn't recognise the woman standing before him in their bedroom, her fitted, designer clothes complete with neat gold chain and matching earrings, and a shoulder-length, smooth, sleek hairstyle. Such a contrast to the girl he fell in love with at university. Back then she was all flowing blonde waves, strings of colourful beads and long, floating skirts. She had stood out in her boho chic and she was softer then, in every way. Now, however, she could blend into any corporate stock photo.

She rolled her eyes. 'As I said James, *Felicity* is my name... Flick was left behind at university. She was doe-eyed, foolish, and rash... Look, there's no point going over old ground.' She pulled the handle up on her wheeled suitcase. 'I'll be staying with Polly and Matt for a while whilst I figure out my next move. I'll come for the rest of my things soon.'

Matt had once been Jim's closest friend, they had met at university and had immediately clicked, but that friendship had somehow fizzled out as Matt's relationship with his girlfriend Polly, from their same university, had blossomed. The lost friendship saddened Jim.

Flick went on, 'Nilsson-Perkins have offered to help find me a new place to rent in Islington so I can be closer to the main gallery.' She wandered over to him and placed her hand condescendingly on his arm. 'It's for the best, James. I think you know that deep down.'

He locked his gaze onto her cold eyes, his chest still rising and falling at a rapid rate. 'For whom is it best, eh? For me? I don't think so.' His voice cracked as he shook his head. He stared intently and for a brief moment she seemed caught in his gaze. He thought he saw her shield begin to melt, but she shook her head and looked away.

Turning back to him she shrugged her shoulders, a sad smile playing on her lips. 'It was inevitable when you think about it. We're from two different worlds... We want completely different things, James.' Her voice softened as she squeezed his arm. Her blue eyes, that were once full of love, were glacial.

She wheeled her case towards the bedroom door and turned back to face him one last time. Her eyes were glassy with unshed tears now and Jim was relieved to see some, albeit small, expression of human emotion from the woman he had witnessed slowly becoming impassive, detached and aloof.

'For what it's worth, James, I do love you. You were my first love and so I probably always will. I just feel like...' She paused. Clenching her eyes closed as if to find the strength to carry on speaking, and several tears escaped. 'Like maybe we're not good for each other. We've grown apart. I'm ambitious and you... you want babies and the white picket fence thing. I'm just not ready. In fact, I'm not sure I ever will be. In a way, I'm doing you a favour.' A sob escaped her throat as she spoke. 'This way at least you get to meet someone new and have children and do all the family things that I'm just not capable of.' She sounded to Jim as though she was trying to convince herself.

His lower lip began to tremble. 'I don't want anyone else... just you. For *ten years* of my life, it's only been you.' He clenched his jaw. 'What I don't get, is that we were on the same page when we moved in together and even more so when we got married. I don't understand how things changed.'

Her nostrils flared and she angrily wiped at her eyes. '*Things* didn't change. *I* did. Like I said, I grew up.' She shook her head. '*You* haven't changed and therein lies the problem.' She snorted. 'Sorry, Jim but it's true. In all these years you've kept the same hairstyle, the same clothing, and the same laid-back attitude. You always said you wanted to be a writer but after a couple of published articles you seem to have given up. You're working on a novel you'll never finish, you still work in the same second-hand bookshop, you still keep that ancient Land Rover, even though it's totally inappropriate for London, and you still take that bloody dog everywhere you go!'

He crumpled his brow. Even though the rest of her words had stung, he couldn't get past the part about the dog. 'Jasper's your dog too.' It hurt him to hear the faithful canine being referred to in such an inanimate way.

Ignoring his protestations, Flick added, 'Look at yourself. Seriously, you're not a student any more, James. You're stuck in the bloody nineties, the decade you were born in for goodness' sake. It's ridiculous. And maybe I want more, huh? Like my mum says, I deserve someone who makes an effort!' Her voice gained an octave as her emotions finally began to get the better of her.

Jim widened his eyes in horror. 'Whoa! Now just hang on there, lassie!' He held up his hands and his stomach knotted at her stabbing words as they sliced his heart. He stepped towards her. 'I don't care what Penelope's been saying. I *do* make an effort. Just because I'm in no way materialistic, like your mother, doesn't mean I don't care. She cares more about status symbols than she does about love. And I love you, Flick. I always have. *You* are my world! I don't need *things*, Felicity. I need *you!*' His heart ached as it bombarded the inside of his chest. 'I've done everything in my power to make you happy. I don't know what else I could've done. And for the record, I'm not the one who's given up here!' He raised his voice too, finally giving in to the pent-up frustration he'd been harbouring.

She gave a heavy sigh. 'We want different things. Accept it. Move on... *please!*' She opened the door, and he made a grab for her. She swung around and crashed into his arms. Without thinking he took her face in his hands and kissed her with all the passion he could muster. To his amazement, she didn't slap him; she kissed him back. Dropping her suitcase, she seemed overwhelmed by desire, anger, passion, lust, whatever the hell it was. She grabbed at his dark, shaggy hair as he ran his hands through hers, desperate to express his love for her, desperate to make her change her mind.

He moved from her mouth to her neck, his kisses urgent. Her head rolled backwards, and she moaned, grabbing at his T-shirt and pulling it over his head in one swift, aggressive movement. Before either could realise what they were doing or how they'd got there, they staggered backwards and tumbled, wrapped around each other, onto the bed. Their lips locked as their tongues danced and probed each other's mouths.

He rested his forehead on hers and looked deep into her eyes where tears had begun to escape and cascade, relentlessly, down her face, soaking through her hair. 'I love you, Flick. I love you so, *so* much... don't leave... *please* don't leave,' he breathed. His vision blurred as the tears in his eyes threatened to spill over.

* * *

As his breathing calmed, Jim kissed her and smiled, stroking her face tenderly. He caught her tears with his thumb. 'I knew you still loved me. I knew it couldn't be the end of us. I just knew it, Flick.' He smiled lovingly, his lip trembling again with overwhelming emotions fighting for release.

He manoeuvred to lay by her side and held her close to him. 'We'll work this out. You and me, Flick. We can get through anything. It's always been you and me,' he whispered as he stroked her cheek and kissed her again, deeply, passionately.

She pushed him away, releasing herself from his arms and touching her swollen lips where his had just been. She grabbed her clothing from the floor and stood, dressing quickly, as she looked down where he still lay. 'I'm so sorry, Jim... Nothing's changed. I'm still leaving.' Her wavering voice broke as she whispered the painful words he didn't want to hear.

His heart plummeted and he sat upright. 'What? I... I don't understand.' He quickly rose to his feet yanking his jeans and T-shirt back onto his body. So many emotions battled and stirred inside of him. So many questions.

He shook his head, his heart now pounding so hard he thought it would burst from his chest, and he asked again, 'What do you mean *nothing's changed*?' He pointed to the now crumpled bed. 'We... we just made love, Flick. I don't understand. Why would you do that if nothing has changed? It has to mean something?'

With a crease of regret visible between her brows and a look of deep, deep sadness in her eyes, Flick touched his face, tears leaving trails down her own cheeks. 'Oh James... it was just... such a beautiful way for us to end things... it was just goodbye, that's all.' Gently, she stroked his cheek, picked up her case and left.

He stood for a moment, stunned, trying to figure out what the hell had just happened. An uncomfortable silence fell over the house and he was momentarily paralysed as if time was standing still. Hurt and angry, he wondered how the hell she could be so damn cruel; to ignite him with a spark of hope and then extinguish it so callously.

Eventually, after what felt like an age, he recovered the use of his legs and walked over to the window. He looked down on to Bushberry Road below with its row of Victorian terraces opposite that mirrored the one they rented, and observed Flick throwing her case into the back of the silly little convertible she was so very proud of. She was all designer suits, first-class flights, champagne dinner meetings, and sports cars, now she was moving up in the world of art sales. Well, at least she fit in well with her new crowd, if not with him, he thought bitterly.

She looked up to the bedroom window and their eyes met. He saw her begin to raise her hand to wave but she stopped as if deciding the gesture was somewhat inappropriate, given the circumstances. She gave a sad half-smile, climbed into the driver's seat and drove away.

Jasper, the black Labrador, padded into the room, walked over and nuzzled Jim's hand. It was as if he knew his master's heart was breaking. Jim scratched the Labrador's head and crouched down so that his face was level with the affectionate animal. 'She's gone, lad. She's really gone. It's just you and me now.' His voice broke and the dog pawed at him. He sunk his head into Jasper's fur and it was then that he was overcome with emotion. It was then that he began to sob.

* * *

Jim was grateful he had booked the weekend off work but on Saturday and Sunday there were a few unwelcome comings and goings from the house. He made the effort to stay out of the way when Flick's new friends came to collect more and more of her personal belongings. They didn't speak much to Jim when he was there. They hardly made eye contact. He hid away at the kitchen table on his old laptop, typing notes up for the final chapters of his debut novel. Despite Flick's comments, he was determined to start submitting the historical fiction book to agents and publishers very soon. The actuality of Flick's possessions gradually dwindling saddened him. After all, the more items she removed the less chance there was of reconciliation.

He had gradually lost contact with his friends from university as they had gone off round the world to begin various careers. Jim and Flick had made new friends as a couple – art-world friends. Except when it really came down to it, he discovered they were his friends by proxy. These people didn't even have to choose sides. They were already on one.

Flick's.

If he was honest, however, the fact didn't concern him too much. He had always found her friends a little too arty farty for his liking. He preferred straightforward and down-to-earth people.

Flick and her friends were always discussing topics he couldn't really care less about. They'd sit for hours talking about the work of modern artists, like Diamond Stingily and Lucia Hierro, making comparisons with the more traditional artists, like Claude Monet, Gustave Courbet, and Salvador Dali.

Jim had often sat staring into space and had mused that one day he would write a book about his random thoughts that formed as they all talked as a collective while he sat on the sidelines; an audience of one to some pretentious chat show where every panellist thought their opinions mattered the most. In his humble, layman's opinion, art was just an expression of the inner workings of someone's mind and was all subjective anyway, so what did it matter? If you liked it, you liked it, enough said. He was an intelligent man, but he never volunteered any content to the lengthy and rather tiresome debates. There would simply be no point.

After what had turned into the worst weekend of his life, Monday morning hadn't come around soon enough. Jim loved his job. He had worked at The Book Depository on Lower Clapton Road, Hackney, for what felt like an eternity, and even before working there, it had been his favourite place to visit. He would sit in the tired old wingback armchair with a dust-covered, tattered old book and a cup of coffee from the machine. He had spent hours in there and had come to know the owner, Charles, quite well. When he had discovered Charles' surname was Oswald he had laughed out loud and complimented Charles on his choice of name for the shop. Charles had appreciated that Jim really *got* him.

Eventually he began to mind the shop on occasions when Charles had nipped for lunch or to the bank, and so one day Charles simply decided to make it an official arrangement. The pay wasn't immense, but it wasn't minimum wage either. Charles was flexible about Jim nipping home to let Jasper out, and every so often, the black Lab would accompany him to work and fall asleep in the back, so Jim couldn't complain and wouldn't have wanted to.

* * *

Even for a Monday morning in February, the twenty-five-minute walk to work was pleasant and soon he was once again surrounded by two of his favourite things: the delightfully fusty smell of old books and coffee.

On seeing Jim, Charles' face scrunched as if he'd encountered something rather unpleasant. 'Bloody hell, Jim, are you all right? You look bloody terrible, old chap.' Charles was a very well-spoken and dapper man in his early fifties. He always wore a colourful bow tie and a tweed jacket with elbow patches, much like an old English professor. He used the word *bloody* in almost every sentence. At first it amused Jim, then it irritated him, and now, years on, he was completely immune to it.

'Not great, if I'm honest Charles, no. Um... Flick left me on Friday.' His lip began to quiver again – as it had on so many occasions over the almost never-ending weekend – and he bit down on it, slumping into the wingback chair and fighting for composure.

Charles gasped and his hands came up dramatically to cover his cheeks. 'Oh, bloody hell, my dear chap, are you sure you should be here? I can manage today if you'd rather be at home.'

Jim held up his hand. 'No, no, it's fine. I'm better off being busy, I think. No point wallowing in self-pity all alone, eh?' Jim tried to snap himself out of the drop in mood.

Charles fidgeted as if wanting to make some kind of physical gesture but struggling to know what to do. 'No... quite... quite. Well, if you need anything...' He paused as he seemed to be calculating his next words. 'And in my opinion, old chap, it's her bloody loss.'

Jim forced a smile. 'Thanks, Charles, I appreciate it. Tell you what, I'd love a coffee if you're making one, eh? I'll go splash my face with some cold water and dump my bag in the back.' He stood and headed for the rear of the shop.

His friend and boss nodded fervently. 'Certainly. Bloody good idea. I'll get onto it.'

The day passed without real incidence and Jim was happy to be thumbing through the latest batch of antique finds that Charles had procured during his recent trip to a Parisian book fair. Amongst the finds had been a rare first edition of *Wuthering Heights* by Emily Brontë. Jim had enquired as to how much the book had cost, but Charles had answered by simply wincing and shaking his head. *Ouch*, Jim had thought. The book was one of a select few, which were locked in a cabinet not to be touched by just anyone. One had to prove the funds were available to purchase such a rare and delicate piece, prior to being granted permission to handle it, and even then, white cotton gloves were insisted upon.

At the end of his shift, Jim said goodbye to Charles and made his way slowly back home. His legs and heart apparently unwilling to thrust him back into the home no longer occupied by his wife. The one saving grace was knowing there would be an excited welcome waiting from his canine best friend.

When he had walked through the door, put down his bag and finally calmed his over-zealous ball of fur, Jim took out his mobile. He hadn't looked at it all day; there had been no point seeing as his only real friend was Charles, and he'd been with him all day. He noticed a missed call from a number he didn't recognise. Hesitantly, he retrieved the voicemail that had been left, and immediately regretted it when he heard Flick's voice.

'James, it's Felicity... listen... I've been talking to my friend Rory and... well... he's a lawyer, as you know... He says we can get a relatively smooth divorce... We can claim irreconcilable differences... That way we can both move on... you know, quickly and permanently... I know this is hard, James... it's hard for me too.' She paused and Jim thought he heard her crying. 'Anyway, I'll leave that thought with you. Take care, James... I hope you're okay.' Her voice broke and the line went dead.

It felt much too sudden and was not the news he wanted. Her words cut him deep to his core and the physical pain was almost overwhelming. He crumpled onto the couch as the word echoed around his mind.

Divorce.

That was that then. It really was over. He leaned forward and rested his head in his hands, his elbows on his knees.

Divorce.

2

On the surface of it all, Flick was handling things remarkably well, but *only* on the surface. She still couldn't help wondering how much of this was her own doing and how much was the influence of her mother, Penelope. Her mother had never really liked James. She didn't *dislike* him per se. She just didn't like him for *her* Felicity.

Conversations had tended to take the same format whenever the topic of Jim came up at home. *'Felicity, darling, you have such potential. You have goals and ambitions. Jim has... Well... there's...'* Her mother would wave her hand and feign being unable to think of a *single thing* her then-boyfriend had going for him.

Flick was very much aware that Jim wasn't from the wealthy background she had been fortunate enough to be born into, yet it had never bothered her. Well, not at first. But clearly her mother had been fixated on the fact from day one, and her constant chipping away at the things Flick had once loved about him – his laid-back attitude, his lack of desire for the latest gadgets, his inherent lack of need to clamber his way to the top of a corporate ladder – had been bound to have an effect one way or another. She now realised that the last thing she wanted was to disappoint her mother.

Since university Flick had shone in her field of Art Procurement and History, she'd been headhunted by a prestigious gallery to work in sales, and everyone had said she would go far. She was painfully aware that her mother had hoped her *silly fling* with Jim would simply fizzle out after graduation, but much to her evident chagrin, it had grown and grown.

Jim MacDuff was a very intelligent man, an erudite scholar in fact, just like Flick, but whereas, he had been admitted to Oxford via a scholarship to study English Literature, art history student Felicity Johnston-Hart came from a long line of Oxford fellows, her father included. It was the expectation that she would simply follow in their footsteps.

* * *

On hearing the news of the break-up, her mother had insisted that Flick should come home to Cobham in Surrey to stay with her parents. She wouldn't hear of her newly single daughter staying with friends. She maintained that her precious girl needed to be around family at such a difficult time.

Penelope was nothing if not persistent.

After the break-up on Friday, and a fitful night of little sleep, Flick had driven to her parents' house on Saturday morning. She was exhausted, and as she walked through the door of her family home, and into the arms of her doting father, she decided she would be calling in sick on Monday, perhaps Tuesday too. She needed time to recover. And perhaps to convince herself she hadn't just made the worst mistake of her twenty-nine years.

Sunday and Monday went by in a blur of tears and regret, and Tuesday was the first time she ventured downstairs before lunchtime. On her arrival in the pristine kitchen, she found her mother to be in rather high spirits. Flick, on the other hand, was not.

Her mother's sing-song voice greeted her as she entered the room. 'Good morning, darling. How lovely to see you so early.'

Flick glanced at the clock on the wall that told her it was eight-thirty. 'Morning, Mum.' She yawned and stretched. Her eyes felt sore and puffy, and she had recoiled on seeing her pale, drawn features in the mirror before she came downstairs. She slowly lowered herself onto one of the wooden chairs at the kitchen table and rested her chin on her hand.

Her mother began to fuss over her as usual. 'Are you feeling better, dear?' It was a stupid question, but Flick didn't bother to comment on the fact. Her mother filled the silence when Flick didn't answer immediately. 'I heard you crying quite late into the night again, and you know how I worry. So, are you? Feeling better, I mean?'

Of course, she wasn't bloody feeling better. She was broken-hearted from the events of the previous few days and no amount of tea and sympathy would remedy that.

Since her arrival back at her family home, Flick's mother had assured her, over and over, that it was all for the best. That it was better to end the marriage now than wait until she was too old to move on. Maybe she was right. After all, James just didn't fit in with her lifestyle now. He hated her friends, knew nothing about art – apart from the knowledge she had imparted – and he had no ambition. None. Not a jot. He was simply happy to write stories and read dusty old books. The stupid thing was he'd graduated with a First from Oxford. The world had been his oyster at that point, but it was almost as if he had done all that studying just to prove to himself that he could. After that, he was done trying, done achieving.

Dragged from her thoughts, Flick remembered her mum had

asked her a question. 'I'm not great, Mum, to be honest. I feel drained. Completely enervated.' She sighed deeply as her mother poured tea into a china cup and put it on the table before her.

'There's no wonder, darling. You should maybe call in sick for the rest of the week. Catch up on rest, perhaps,' her mother suggested.

'No, I can't. Daniel Perkins has emailed to say there's a meeting with the Tate this afternoon. It's a really big deal, Mum. He wants me to be there.' She sipped the tea and winced when it was too hot. 'They want me to go out to Chicago to see some potential pieces for the gallery. Daniel has recommended me as the best dealer for the job at Nilsson-Perkins. If I call in sick again, I'll look like a flake.'

Her mother's face brightened. 'Perhaps Rory will take you out tonight to cheer you up?' Her mother adored Flick's lawyer friend, deeming him a much more suitable match for her. Flick rolled her eyes and didn't answer.

Her dad walked into the large kitchen where the two women were sitting, and Flick was grateful that the discussion was over before it started.

'Good morning, poppet.' Her father, Edgar, kissed Flick's head affectionately. 'How are you bearing up?' He gave her a knowing look and she burst into tears. 'Oh, poppet, don't cry. You can always go back to him. You know he would take you back in a flash. Tell him you've made a terrible mistake.' Her Father took her hand and stroked her hair.

'Oh, don't be so ridiculous, Edgar!' Her mother chimed in. 'What on earth would she do a silly thing like that for?' She stood to leave the room. The two were obviously still at loggerheads over the situation.

'Because she clearly still loves him, Penny, that's why!' His frustration with his wife's cold demeanour was evident. 'Can't you see what you've done?' he continued. 'You've put all these silly ideas in her head, and she's started to believe you! She adores Jim. She always has but you couldn't let her be happy with him, could you?' He squeezed Flick's hand as she sobbed.

Flick sat upright and pulled herself together. 'No, no, Dad, Mum's right. James is just not the right man for me any more. I need to get over him. I need to focus on work. In fact, I was just telling Mum, I'm going in today.' Her father opened his mouth to protest but she held her hand up to stop him. 'It's almost an hour and a half to Islington from here, so I need to go get ready. They know why I've been off and have been great about it, but I don't want to take advantage.' She paused, plucking up the courage to say her next words. 'I think perhaps staying with Polly will be better for me, too, if I'm honest.' She smiled sadly. 'Not that I don't appreciate you having me home. It's just not as far to travel to Islington from Camden Town and I need to be in work. I need to keep myself occupied.'

She looked to her father and then to her mother. Neither spoke. Their conflicting opinions on the matter momentarily silenced. She rubbed her hands over her face to rid herself of the tears and donned a fake smile, stood, and left the room. As she walked down the hallway she paused as she heard her father speaking.

'I hope you're satisfied with the mess you've caused, Penny. You've meddled once too often in their relationship. I honestly don't understand why you couldn't just let her be happy and be in love. I can't support you in this. Frankly, I think it's unforgiveable.'

She heard her mother gasp at her father's harsh words and then the heavy, stomping footsteps that followed and told Flick that her mother had seen fit to storm out of the kitchen.

Flick's stomach knotted at the thought of her parents fighting over this and she turned to walk back towards the kitchen but stopped, deciding she'd had enough confrontation to last her a lifetime.

3

Almost a year had gone by since he'd split with Flick, but Jim knew it was time to stop waiting. Time to start his life over. He could no longer hang around London waiting for Flick to realise she had made a mistake. The divorce had been finalised months ago and he had moved out of the rented house they had shared as a married couple. He had been staying with Charles until his plans were completed but today, he would stop by to visit his old friend, and ex-father-in-law, one last time prior to making his journey to start his new life back home in Scotland.

Even after all this time, Flick's father Edgar was still struggling with the break-up. 'I just don't get it, Jim. It's breaking my heart to see this happening to the two of you.' He rubbed his temples and shook his head.

Jim tried his best to smile but struggled under the weight of emotion in the air. 'I know, Ed, but I can't keep banging my head against a brick wall. There comes a point where you know you're being stupid. You just have to admit defeat.'

'She's a silly, silly girl. She'll regret this. I know her, Jim. She will. One day when you've moved on and met someone new, she'll realise what she had.' Edgar patted his arm affectionately.

Jim looked down at his hands, unable to respond. How could he? What could he possibly say?

After a long, thoughtful pause he spoke. 'I didn't want any of this, Ed. I honestly don't know what I did wrong. I supported her. I was there for her. We were saving to buy a house you know. I reckon we could have afforded one. I was willing to put all my inheritance into bricks and mortar that were ours. She just wouldn't commit. I really thought we both wanted the same things.' He shrugged. 'I think we did at first.'

'I know, son. I remember how excited she was when you got engaged. She lit up when she looked at you. I wish she could think for herself and not listen to...' Edgar's words trailed off as if he felt he had said too much.

'Listen to whom, Ed?'

'Oh, nothing. Don't take any notice of me.' Edgar's lip trembled. 'I was looking forward to grand kiddies.'

Jim squeezed his arm. 'Aye... I know... I know. We had a pregnancy scare once, a couple of years back.'

'What do you mean?' Edgar sat upright as this news.

Jim began to explain the events of that horrible July day...

* * *

'So, what does it say?' Jim was almost boiling over with excitement. Flick remained taciturn as she stared at the little white stick, her hand shaking.

After a while she blinked as if coming out of a trance. 'Erm... it has a cross... I think that means it's... positive.' Her eyes welled up with what Jim presumed were happy tears.

He grabbed her in a bear hug and showered her with kisses.

'Oh, Flick! We're going to be Mummy and Daddy!' He spun her around.

She yelled, 'Put me down!'

He immediately placed her back on her feet. He was a little surprised at her tone but put it down to the shock of the news. She'd come round.

But she just stared at the stick in her hand.

'Flick, staring at it won't change it, sweetheart.' His voice wavered as sadness at her reaction washed over him.

She shook her head as tears escaped and cascaded down her flushed cheeks. 'It can't be right... it can't be... I can't be pregnant, Jim. Not now. There's too much going on. We've not bought a house... My career is going well... You're still at The Book Depository, which pays next to nothing... We're not ready.' She shakily sat on the side of the bath, her eyes staring into space once again.

Jim gripped at his hair and for a moment tilted his head back and stared at the ceiling. 'How can you not be happy, Flick? We're married. I adore you. This wee bairn will get spoiled by its grandparents. I'll be the best dad—'

'Stop it, Jim. Please. I can't think straight. I can't do this. Not now!' She stormed out of the bathroom, pushing past him, and slammed the door to their bedroom.

After the bathroom incident, Jim didn't sleep well and neither did Flick. She went downstairs very early and after a while he heard her talking. He pulled on his shorts and walked down to the lounge where she sat, phone in hand.

'Yes, yes, I have a urine sample ready from this morning. Yes... okay... uh-huh... okay... okay, see you at nine. Thank you... bye.' She hung up.

Jim sat beside her. 'What was all that about?' He rubbed her back gently.

'I've made an appointment at the doctors. I need to get this confirmed officially, Jim. Then I can decide what to do.'

'Then *you* can decide what to do? What do you mean *decide what to do*? We'd prepare to have a baby, surely there's no other decision involved?'

She lifted her gaze to meet his. 'Jim, this is my body. And my career. I have to make sure that I'm ready for this.' She was calm as she spoke, her tone low and disconcertingly quiet.

Jim tried to smile. 'Hang on... there's are a lot of *I* in there... What about me? Us? And what, exactly, are you saying? Are you saying that there's a chance you'll get rid of our baby?' He stood and paced the floor, a knot of anguish balled in his stomach.

Flick lowered her head. 'I'm saying I'll have some decisions to make.' She wrung her hands in her lap.

Jim stopped in his tracks and turned to face her. 'Oh... oh *you'll* have some decisions to make, eh? You, not us? Oh right... right... I get it. I get no say in this? My child, *our* child, and I get no say?'

'Don't raise your voice at me, Jim. This is hard enough as it is.'

He flung his arms in the air in exasperation. 'What's hard? We wanted kids. This is a no-sodding-brainer!' What was she thinking?

Flick stood. 'We wanted kids *eventually*. This is too soon. And I will not speak to you whilst you're acting like this. I'm going to get ready for my appointment.' She stormed back upstairs into the bathroom and locked the door.

He followed her and shouted through the barrier she had put between them. 'Well, I'm coming too! I need to be a part of this, Flick. You can't shut me out!'

'Whatever, Jim,' she mumbled.

The doctor's surgery was overflowing with people coughing and sneezing. Flick sat silently staring at her hands. Jim watched as myriad emotions made their mark upon her face. *She should be excited. I just don't get this.* He was about to take her hand in his when her name was called. They both stood and, desperately needing the contact, he placed his hand at the small of her back as they walked through to see the doctor.

'Good morning, Felicity. What can I do for you today?' The female doctor beamed at them both but didn't address Jim.

'I took a pregnancy test yesterday, which was positive. I... I thought I ought to get checked properly to make sure.'

The doctor's smile remained in situ. 'Oh yes, wise to do so. Did you bring an early morning urine sample?'

Flick handed over a small bag with a little container in it. The doctor opened a long, white plastic package, about the size of a biro, then took out and dipped the end of the implement into the sample.

'It doesn't take long. I'll give you a quick once over whilst we wait.' The doctor proceeded to check Flick's blood pressure and pulse. 'You seem fit and well, which is good news.'

After a few more minutes of Jim scrunching his hands anxiously, feeling somewhat invisible, the doctor checked the test.

The doctor's smile faded. 'I'm very sorry but the test is actually negative.'

Jim sat upright, confused.

Flick let out a huge puff of air as if she'd been holding her lungs full. 'Right, well that's that then.' Her voice was back to its normal breezy self.

'Hang on... that can't be right? The one yesterday was positive,' Jim barked.

'I know, Mr Johnston-Hart. And it is very rare to get a false positive. More likely to get a false negative but in this instance, it *is* a false positive. Your wife is not pregnant.'

He scowled. 'It's MacDuff. Jim MacDuff... and you said yourself false negatives are more frequent, so what if yours is wrong?' He was clinging on to the last shred of hope, although he had no clue why, considering Flick's reaction.

She smiled over her shoulder as she washed her hands. 'I'm very sorry Mr MacDuff, but you can always try again.' Her tone was patronising and made the hairs on his neck stand on end. He stood and stormed out of the surgery, not stopping until he reached the Land Rover.

Flick followed him, trotting along on her stilettos. She opened the car door and climbed in awkwardly, muttering under her breath how she hated the car.

'Don't you think you were a bit harsh on Dr Jacobs in there?' she spat as he sat there, white knuckled, holding on to the steering wheel and staring straight ahead.

'No,' he growled back through gritted teeth.

'Jim, it can't be helped. We have plenty of time. No need to get so stressed.' Now *she* was patronising him, making him bristle.

After a long silent interlude, Jim found the words he wanted to say, however hurtful. 'The fact that it was negative after I got my hopes up was painful, but what's even more painful is that *you* thought the prospect of carrying my baby so abhorrent that you would have had *decisions* to make.' His eyes stung and he bit the inside of his lip, determined not to let his sadness take over.

'Jim, it just isn't the right time. My career is going so well—'

'Your bloody career? Is that what's more important to you than us creating a new life?' His stomach knotted with hurt and anger as he turned to face her.

'Please don't be angry, Jim. Clearly you're more ready for this type of thing than I am.' She gave a half-laugh, fuelling Jim's pain.

'More ready for *this type of thing*?' he repeated, his voice cracking as an angry tear escaped, much to his chagrin.

Flick softened. 'Oh, Jim… I don't know what to say. I love you so much, but I'm not ready to be a mother yet. And yes, I was relieved to find the test was negative. I'm so sorry. Please don't be upset with me.' She leaned over to him and kissed him, wiping away the errant tear with her thumb.

He breathed in sharply. 'Well, at least I know where we stand on the issue now.' He couldn't look her in the eyes.

She squeezed his thigh. 'We have plenty of time, sweetheart. You need to find a better job and we need to save up for a house. It's just not the right time.'

He swallowed hard. 'Maybe not. But it scares me to think about what you would've done if the test had been positive, Flick.'

She turned to face the front, making no attempts to answer, which in effect gave him the answer he was afraid of hearing.

He started the car and they drove home in silence…

* * *

Edgar shook his head in frustration over what he had just heard. He was clearly as confused as Jim had been over Flick's reaction to a possible pregnancy.

'I had no idea about any of that. She kept it very quiet,' he whispered croakily. 'You'll make a wonderful father one day, Jim. I'm just so sad that it won't be my grandchildren you're fathering.' The emotional old man squeezed Jim's arm.

Jim couldn't bear to see Edgar cry over this ridiculous situation. 'I'd better be off, anyway. I have a long drive and I really should get on the road.' He paused, then threw his arms around his ex-father-in-law.

Edgar reciprocated the strong embrace and patted Jim's back. 'Keep in touch, eh? Maybe not straight away, I know you'll be busy getting set up. But drop me a line every so often, even if it's that wretched electronic mail, although I do so prefer handwritten letters, but however you do it, let me know how you're getting on. You're still family as far as I'm concerned.' Edgar's eyes sparkled with moisture as he placed a firm hand on Jim's shoulder.

Jim headed for his Land Rover and opened the door. He called to his dog, who also seemed reluctant to tear himself away. 'C'mon Jasper! C'mon boy!' The Lab somewhat hesitantly jumped into the vehicle and Jim slammed the door.

He looked back to Edgar who was now wiping escaped tears from his haggard face with the back of his hand. Jim's heart squeezed as he watched the old man he had known, and been fond of for many years, trying to deal with the fact that his daughter's marriage had collapsed, and that he'd been helpless to stop it.

Jim smiled. 'You know, Ed, I just want her to be happy. I hoped I could be the one to make her so, but perhaps she deserves more than I can offer,' he said in the hope of making things easier for the old man.

Edgar was having none of it. 'Pish tosh! She's so hellbent on succeeding in that damned career of hers, and listening to those who should know better, that she's forgotten how to think for herself!' He was clearly angry about his daughter's life choices.

Jim couldn't find the words to make an acceptable answer. So instead, he simply said, 'You take care, Ed. I'll write when I get sorted. I'll send some photos too. Perhaps you could come and visit?' He knew there was little chance of Edgar making the journey hundreds of miles from his country pile in Cobham, to the Scottish Highlands, but he at least wanted to make the gesture.

'Yes, yes, dear boy. That would be marvellous.' Edgar nodded but Jim was unclear as to which part he was agreeing with and didn't want to ask.

'Say goodbye to Penny for me. I'm sorry I missed her.' In all truth, he wasn't sorry in the slightest. His ex-mother-in-law was not his biggest fan and he wasn't allowed to call her Penny. She preferred Penelope and made a point of saying so whenever Jim tried to be a little more familiar. He had no doubt where Flick got it from.

'I will, Son. I will. You drive carefully. Make sure you have plenty of breaks. And don't drive if you feel tired!' Bless him. Such concern. A kindred spirit. Unlike Penelope. Jim had simply never been good enough, rich enough, or posh enough for her liking. 'And get writing, son. You've plenty of books in you just waiting to spring forth. Make this fresh start the new beginning of your new career as an author.' Jim had always loved that they had writing in common. Edgar had always told his son-in-law that he believed him to be a potentially best-selling author and that Jim just needed the right setting and the right encouragement. He now hoped that Scotland would give him that.

* * *

He climbed into the driver's seat and gave a final wave before setting off down the long driveway. When he was nearing the gates, he saw a familiar little convertible coming towards him. He slowed when he realised it had pulled over. He did, too, and then stopped. The driver of the car climbed out, long lean legs first, followed by slender body and pretty face complete with stern, serious expression.

Jasper wagged his tail as Flick made her way to the driver's side of Jim's car. She reached into the vehicle petted the dog who had now climbed into Jim's lap.

Once she had finished greeting the black Labrador, she turned her attention to Jim. 'I didn't expect to see you here... You're finally going then?'

Jim took the question as rhetorical. He mused at how, in that moment, she looked harder and more severe than he had ever imagined possible. Her blonde, blunt cut hair resting at chin level, unlike when they had first met. Her designer sunglasses were perched atop her head and she squinted in the sunlight of the cold winter morning. She had an air of superiority about her now that belied her true self.

'Aye, I'm all packed up and ready for the off.' He forced a smile but didn't feel it inside.

'You'll be relieved to get on with your new life now I suppose. The decree absolute came through months ago. I'm surprised you've waited this long,' she stated matter-of-factly.

Jim shook his head, the curve of his mouth taking a downturn. 'Aye well, I had plenty of things to sort out. And I didn't want to leave Charles in the lurch, so I waited until he found a suitable replacement and I found the right place to move to. I wasn't in a rush like some people.' He felt sadly resigned now.

'I'm sure Charles would've managed fine without you. He was fine before you came along. Moving on is the thing we both need.'

Why was she so determined for him to leave? After a pause, he looked back to her and said, 'Flick, we've been apart for ages now, and yet you still manage to make it sound like you're escaping some horrible, despicable fiend of a man.'

She seemed to squirm under his gaze. 'I don't think you're despicable at all.' She shrugged. 'You and I both know that we didn't work. It's over. We can continue to get on with our respective lives.' She pulled invisible lint from the sleeves of her smart winter jacket, avoiding eye contact.

Jim realised he was flogging the proverbial dead horse yet again. 'I'm sad you have such negative memories of our marriage. I, contrary to what you may think and feel, will remember our time together with fondness, and signed those divorce papers with a stab of regret and sadness in my heart.' He put the car into gear and drove away without giving her the opportunity to have the last word.

He leaned over and scratched the top of Jasper's head. 'How did we end up here, eh, Jasper? I really wish I knew.' He began his journey northwards, the sound of 'Beautiful Day' by 3 Colours Red resonating around his beloved car.

4

———

Although he was raised in Scotland, Jim was by no means heading home. Dumbarton, place of his upbringing, held no pull for him now with his parents gone. Having been so devoted to each other, his mother had passed away only weeks after his father suffered one final stroke. They had put every penny they could aside for their sons. The brothers discovered after their parents' deaths that this was the reason for their frugal existence. The modest town house they inherited, on top of the savings, had meant that Jim could buy himself a place, albeit small and a little run down. Although the money had always been intended to set him up in a home with Flick, he'd saved it for years not daring to dip into it lest it be swallowed up on minor frivolities. But that home – their home – clearly was never meant to be.

The choice of his new location, Shieldaig in the West Highlands, was more of an escape. He had visited as a child with his family when they were on holiday, but he didn't remember too much about it. His memories were all in the family photos he'd kept. He just knew that it was a peaceful, almost undiscovered place, certainly more his pace of life than London. And because he had no memories of Flick there, he knew he could start over.

Wipe the slate clean.

There would be nothing around each corner to remind him of what a mess he had made of things. He could reinvent himself if he so wished. Not that he would do that. He wasn't pretentious. That had been part of the problem really. He couldn't pretend to be anyone, but himself, and that hadn't been good enough. He'd come to realise, in recent years, that Flick was out of his league. But he also knew that he wasn't a bad person. Other than a failed marriage he had nothing to be ashamed of. He had loved his wife more than life itself. He'd tried so damned hard to fit in with her life and all its glamour. But he simply wasn't that good an actor.

His brother, Euan, had escaped too. He had emigrated to Australia to be with the woman of his dreams whom he had met two years ago, whilst travelling through Europe.

Jim was slightly envious of Euan's relationship with Aisha. She was very easy going and fun to be around. Every bit the beach babe, she had a petite frame, sun bleached curly hair, and eyes as green as the brightest emeralds. Euan had always been into sports and had excelled in football at school. He had been travelling around Europe with some of his football team mates when he was introduced to Aisha in a bar in Germany by one of his friends.

Euan was due a visit to the UK. He had promised Jim, during their phone call a few days before, that he would be back at some point this year and would be bringing Aisha back with him.

'It'll be great to see you, bro! I can't wait! I'm looking forward to seeing where you end up living now that you're rid of Cruella de Vil!' Euan chuckled. He had always seemed to like Flick but in recent years that clearly had changed.

'Euan, please don't call her that,' Jim said flatly.

'Hey, why the hell are you defending her? After what she did to you, I think you could be forgiven for calling her a lot bloody worse!'

'Aye… well, it won't change anything, so what's the point?' Jim's voice was a low resigned rumble.

'Look, bro, I'm a fair distance away, I know that, but I'm only at the end of the phone, okay? You call me if you need to talk.'

'Aye, I know. Thanks… Love you, bro.'

'Aye and I love you too, you ugly beggar!' Euan chuckled and hung up.

* * *

Jasper slept as Jim drove through the towns and cities of middle England and on up through the industrial landscape in the north of the country. He breathed a sigh of relief when he finally drove across the border into Scotland. It was early evening and the Borders were aglow with the low winter sun. The snow-capped Cheviot Hills dazzled on the horizon as the sun glinted on the bright, glistening canvas, spread over them like a crisp white blanket. It truly was a stunning sight.

Thankfully, the weather had been rather kind and the snow had not yet arrived in earnest. He was sure that this would most likely change once he had reached his new home. This was the worst time of year for getting snowed in, after all.

As night fell the journey was drawing to its conclusion. There had been several stops for Jim to stretch his legs and for Jasper to do his necessary doggy business. Service station coffee had most definitely improved, Jim mused as he drank his third of the journey.

The moonlit Highlands in winter – what a sight to behold. The rugged, stony outcrops sparkled with a light dusting of snow, like icing sugar on a slice of rocky road cake. The temperature had dropped, and the sun had given way to the bright-white full moon.

Myriad stars were visible like diamonds strewn across black velvet. It really was beautiful. He could clearly make out The Big Dipper and Orion as he drove. He had to keep reminding himself to look ahead at the road so that he could drive straight; the sky was such a glorious distraction. The road, however, was empty, apart from Jim's Land Rover and the odd motorbike or car, giving his surroundings a particularly lonely and eerie atmosphere.

He was beginning to feel exhausted and was thankful that tonight would not be the time he officially moved in. He had managed to get a removal firm that would hold his furniture overnight, meaning he could, at least, get a decent night's sleep at a bed and breakfast prior to the gruelling day to come. He had located a dog-friendly establishment where Jasper was allowed to sleep on the floor beside his bed. This was a relief as he didn't fancy having to make his best friend sleep in the car on a clear night like tonight when the temperature was certain to drop well below zero.

It was very late when Jim arrived to check in to the bed and breakfast on the outskirts of Dingwall and he quickly snuggled up for the night, exhausted after the long drive. Sleep came easily, but Jim was plagued by dreams of his ex and their failed marriage. The fitful night's sleep ended at six o'clock when he gave up the fight and climbed into the shower.

* * *

After a delicious, and much-needed, full Scottish breakfast of succulent Lorne sausage, salty bacon, haggis, fried egg with a runny yolk – just how he liked it – and a tattie scone, he made his way to collect the keys for his new place.

The estate agent congratulated him on his new purchase and handed over a small bunch of keys.

He made a comment that stuck in Jim's mind. 'So, Mr MacDuff, it's the end of one chapter and the beginning of a whole new book, eh?'

Jim had smiled and nodded. He was right. This was a fresh start, albeit thrust upon him in many ways. He had to grasp the opportunity with both hands, otherwise he would fail at this, too, and he couldn't let that happen. And talking of books... well... maybe he would give that a go too.

He pulled up the Land Rover outside the little whitewashed building on Main Street facing Loch Shieldaig. Sunset Cottage was double-fronted and extremely pretty, if a little on the small side. It had everything he needed: two bedrooms, in case Charles or his brother came to visit, a dining kitchen, a cosy lounge, and outside stood a small adjacent building that he would convert to a little coffee hut so that he could make a little money when tourists came by. The small campsite behind the house was something he hadn't initially bargained for, but at least he would be kept busy.

His furniture would be arriving a bit later, so he had the opportunity to check that the place was ready. He carried a box of cleaning products into the little house, Jasper following close behind sniffing at everything in a bid to familiarise himself with his new surroundings.

The house smelled of damp due to the fact that it had been standing empty for quite a while. It had been several months since he had first seen and offered on it and even though it had been a low offer the owners had been desperate to sell.

The lounge had a lovely open fire that he decided would get plenty of use. It quickly became apparent that the owners had cleaned everything prior to Jim's arrival, which saved him a major job, however, he decided to clean the kitchen himself, and besides, it would keep him busy until the removals firm came to reunite him with his belongings.

The day whizzed by and was a blur of comings and goings. Piles of boxes appeared in every room and Jim set about opening each clearly labelled box and setting his personal effects in their new and rightful places.

By six in the evening, the place was beginning to resemble a home. Jasper lay out on the rug in front of the roaring fire that Jim had made a priority. Most of the boxes were now broken down and had been placed outside the back door. He had resolved to burn them the following day, wind permitting.

Whilst putting his clothes away in the built-in cupboard in his low-ceilinged bedroom, he came across a box of photographs. He was already feeling melancholy and so figured it wouldn't hurt to look through them. He sat on his bed and took out a packet as Jasper appeared and lay at his feet. With each glossy image Jim travelled back to happier times.

He chuckled at photos of the fancy dress party they had attended a few years earlier at Polly and Matt's house. They had gone as Sid and Nancy. Both had worn wigs and Flick had put on far more makeup than usual. She looked totally different, but then again, so did he. He'd pulled off the sneer perfectly and had scared a couple of elderly ladies as they'd walked down Belmont Street. Flick had nearly peed herself laughing when the two old ladies scarpered as quickly as their stockinged legs and shopping trolleys would carry them. They had almost fallen into a heap through the door when they'd arrived at the party and Flick had made a mad dash for the loo.

The next packet contained photos of a holiday to Majorca. The photo of Flick in her little white bikini reminded Jim of the passion they had shared on that holiday, before she had become distracted by her career. It had been one of the best trips of his life. As he stared at the photo he was reminded of their time on the beach.

* * *

'Are you coming in? The sea's quite warm once you get used to it!' Jim shouted to his gorgeous girl as she lay in her white bikini on a sun lounger reading a book. She removed her sunglasses and placed her book on the sand, then stood and with elegant grace, slinked towards the water's edge.

He was transfixed.

The inward, sweeping curve of her waist was his favourite part of her body, and when she walked, and her hips swayed with her natural rhythm, he gave a deep sigh. How had he ended up so damned lucky?

'God, you look good enough to eat,' he growled as she made her way towards him.

'Happy feasting,' she purred.

He threw his head back and groaned. 'Och, you'll be the death of me.'

'Hmm, I can think of worse ways to die,' she told him as she slipped into the water.

Her breath appeared to catch at the sudden chill, and she made her way over to him. She slid her arms around his neck and kissed him passionately.

He pulled away and gazed into her eyes. 'I'll never tire of this... of *you*. I want you... right here... right now, and forever.'

She kissed him again. 'I'm not going anywhere,' she whispered with a sultry smile.

* * *

Back to reality and a stinging sensation behind his eyes broke Jim's reverie. 'Oh Jasper... this is doing me no good at all, boy.' He took the dog's face in both hands and looked into his chocolate-brown eyes. Jasper licked his nose and Jim rubbed his companion's face roughly. 'C'mon lad, let's go for a wee walk, eh?' Jasper's ears pricked up at the mention of his favourite word and the pair made their way to the front door.

The view from the cottage was beautiful. It was definitely something he wouldn't get bored of quickly. The two friends, man and canine, walked together taking in their new surroundings. The majestic, rocky mountain backdrop was the stuff of Sci-Fi movies, yet the place was undeniably grounded. The little piece of garden across the road that belonged to his cottage was in dire need of a tidy up and beyond that was a shingle beach that led to the loch's edge. As they walked Jim took in the vista of the small tree-covered, uninhabited island just off the coast and wondered, with intrigue, about its avian inhabitants.

The cottages lining the loch were all built in a similar way: single or one-and-a-half-storey, low and hunkered down against potentially inclement weather threats. All had whitewashed exteriors, but each one had its owner's little personal touch, from wind chimes hanging by the door to the colour of the window frames. It had the feel of a seaside fishing village.

The sky was a vivid cornflower blue, but there was a distinct winter chill to the air. Jim found the pub and a little shop with an exterior that had seen better days. He called in and picked up some bread, milk, biscuits and a bottle of red wine. The shopkeeper was an elderly gentleman who introduced himself as Malcolm McLeary after Jim said he was the one who had bought Sunset Cottage.

'Have you a wife and family with you, Jim?' the old man had asked.

'Sadly no, Malcolm. Maybe one day though, eh?'

'Aye, wonderful place to bring up wee bairns, Jim, this place.'

After chatting briefly to the old guy, Jim and Jasper made their way back to the cosy cottage to warm up their extremities. The frost-filled air had a mean bite to it and both males were feeling the effects. As they sat on the rug together staring into the flames, Jim absentmindedly stroked Jasper's smooth, glossy coat and sighed. Jasper wagged his tail.

'I really wish I could go back in time, Jasper. I would do things differently. I don't know what exactly, but I'm sure I'd figure it out. Then you and I wouldn't be sitting here without her, boy.' Jasper's tail beat out a rhythm on Jim's leg, as if he understood every word. He licked Jim's hand as if by way of reassurance. 'Aye, lad... if only time machines had been invented, eh?' He turned back to the dancing, crackling flames and reminisced about the year that changed his life. The fateful year he had met his true love, his soul mate.

His Felicity.

5

'Earth to Jim! Come in Jim! Jim! What on earth are you staring at?' Matthew Clinton-Jones poked his relatively new friend's arm. Jim was no longer partaking of the debate that the rest of the freshers were locked in.

'Sorry, what's that?' Jim didn't take his eyes off the subject of his focus.

'We've been discussing who we think will win the Booker Prize this year. My money's on *White Tiger*. What do you think? Jim? You've been staring into space for the last ten minutes, are you stoned?' Matthew, soon to be known as Matt, followed Jim's line of sight. 'Wait a minute... you're staring at that blonde girl, aren't you?! She is rather gorgeous, I have to say.'

Matthew was from a very well-to-do family who were mainly practicing GPs or surgeons, but Matthew had plumped for reading English Literature with a view to becoming an English professor. His floppy dark hair and round-rimmed spectacles made him look the part, even before his time. His accent was an acquired taste, but Jim was slowly realising that you shouldn't judge a book by its accent... or something like that.

Jim didn't take his eyes off the blonde girl as he nodded. 'Aye, you're not wrong. She looks a bit lost. Think I'll go over and see if she needs any assistance.' He rose, and without looking back to his stunned friends, wandered across the dining hall and over to where the pretty but terrified-looking girl was crouched, shuffling a stack of papers. She looked up and blushed beetroot red as he approached.

'Hi, are you okay there?' At that moment, the papers the girl was fiddling with did a somersault into the air and landed scattered like oversized snowflakes all around her.

'Oh, for goodness' sake!' she exclaimed, dropping her head into her hands and looking even more flustered.

Jim immediately kneeled to help her pick them up. 'I'm Jim,' he informed her as they gathered up the errant items. 'And you are...'

'I'm... I'm Felicity... My friends call me... erm... Felicity... not that anyone wants to be friends with boring old me. I wish I'd stayed at home.' Her bottom lip began to tremble.

Jim smiled. 'Oh, come on, it's early days, Felicity. Freshers' week. We haven't even started lessons yet, remember. Don't be so hard on yourself.' He patted her arm trying to reassure her and her face coloured again. He laughed. 'Keep blushing like that and your legs will go dead through lack of blood supply.'

Felicity relaxed and looked up at the man who had come to her aide. Realising how melodramatic she was being, she sighed. 'Sorry, I just feel a bit like a fish out of water.' She smiled.

She sat back for a moment whilst he worked to gather the last few sheets.

He was a nicely built young man. His hair was shaggy, dark brown, with a natural-looking wave but not in an untidy way, and it fell almost to his shoulders. Mother wouldn't approve at all. She smiled as the errant thought crossed her mind. He wore jeans and a scruffy-looking T-shirt with *Foo Fighters* emblazoned on its front and an image of a group of men. The middle one bore a striking resemblance to her new friend. Jim's arms were quite muscular, and he looked like he hadn't shaved in a while. Not what one would normally expect from an Oxford scholar.

'Hey, don't worry about it. It'll get easier.' He seemed to be trying his best to reassure her again. 'Look there's a party tonight for the freshers in the refectory. Kind of a 90s retro, throwback thing. Just my kind of music really, I grew up with it. Should be some good craic, why don't you come with us?' He gestured towards his friends.

A feeling of dread washed over her at his words, and she wondered what kind of place she'd come to.

She shot to her feet and backed away slightly, wobbling from the head rush of standing too quickly. 'Oh, n-no thanks. I don't do crack... or any drug for that matter. I should go. Thanks for the offer though.' She felt the colour drain from her face as she reached out for her papers.

Jim burst out laughing. 'No! Not crack! Craic! It a Scottish-ism... it means it'll be a wee laugh. Lots of fun? A good night?' She had completely misunderstood his turn of phrase.

Felicity felt her cheeks flaming as relief swept through her and embarrassment took over. 'Oh gosh I'm so sorry.' She was horrified by her own mistake. 'I didn't mean to insinuate... I didn't mean...'

He raised a hand and grinned. 'Hey, don't sweat it. It's fine. Look, I'm in room twenty in the old quad, overlooking the meadow. If you fancy going with me, you know, so you don't have to enter alone, just give me a knock around six-thirty, okay?' He scribbled the details down on a scrap of her paper and handed it back to her.

She smiled, relieved that he hadn't taken offence at her misunderstanding and naiveté and her stomach fluttered. 'That's sweet of you, thank you. Thank you very much, Jim.'

He gave a heart-stoppingly handsome smile before turning to

head back to his friends who appeared to be engrossed in a debate, arms flailing, and voices raised.

Felicity went back to her little room and sat on her bed, trying to decide what to do. She stood at her easel – one of the first things she had made space for – looking at her latest sketched-out canvas intently, as if the answers would just jump out of it. It was no use; she just didn't know what to do. She was inexperienced with the opposite sex as it was and really didn't know what made them tick.

If she called on this Jim fellow, would she look desperate? Needy? On the other hand, he had invited her so would it be rude not to show up? She grabbed her wash bag and decided a shower would clear her mind. She was relieved that Daddy's connections had helped land her an en-suite room. The advantages of being the daughter of a former Oxford fellow were several-fold it seemed. It would have been horrid to have to share with total strangers. It was bad enough to be sharing cooking facilities, let alone showers.

She blow-dried her hair shaggily and pulled on a pair of jeans and a baggy sweater that fell off one shoulder. She made sure to put a vest top on underneath so as not to be too provocative. She smeared a little gloss on her lips and wrapped her Oxford scarf loosely around her neck. That was it, she was ready.

Taking a huge breath and mustering up as much courage as she could, she made her way down the stairs and over to Jim's block. She located his room, checked her watch, *six twenty-five,* then knocked lightly almost hoping he didn't answer so that the decision would have been made for her. He opened the door. *Dammit!*

* * *

Jim couldn't help the grin that took over his face at the sight before him. He had expected her to be late, in true female fashion, or to simply not turn up at all. His respect for her grew as she stood there looking simply gorgeous.

'Oh, hi. Felicity, right?' She nodded and he smiled at how she anxiously twisted the tassels of her scarf between her fingers. 'Want to come in for a quick drink before we go? I think we'll be too early if we go now.'

He stood aside and gestured for her to enter and she inhaled deeply as if having second thoughts but then stepped into his tiny room.

He removed the cap from a bottle of beer and handed it to her, cringing. 'Sorry, I've no champers.' He hoped his laugh made her feel at ease.

She shrugged and glanced around her. 'Oh, that's fine. I quite like Bud.'

He watched as she picked at the label and an awkward silence descended. He riffled through his mind, grasping for conversational topics that may interest this stunning young woman.

In his periphery, he saw her eyeing his guitar and hoped this may be something they had in common. 'Do you play at all?'

She pursed her lips and shook her head apologetically. 'Sadly, no. I wish I did, but I spent so much time painting at home that I never really made time to learn.'

His interest in this shy, gorgeous girl was just growing and growing. 'So... you paint? What do you paint?'

'Whatever takes my fancy really... I like to observe scenes on train journeys, car journeys, and so on... Then I sketch what I remember seeing through the glass onto canvas... then I paint.'

Wow. Just... wow. 'So, are you working on anything right now? I'd like to see your work sometime if you'd be up for showing me.'

Felicity blushed and fiddled with her bottle some more. 'I'm not that good. I don't tend to show people... apart from my parents.'

'Ahem, isn't art supposed to be subjective? And shared?

Shouldn't the viewer be the one who decides whether it's good or not?' he teased.

A crease appeared between her brows. 'Well... I... I suppose but—'

'So, what are you working on right now?' He was determined to knock down her defences. She was so painfully shy.

The red in her cheeks grew stronger and he felt a surge of guilt as she sat down, avoiding his eyes. Eventually she spoke. 'It's just a scene that I saw through the car window on the way up from Surrey. Just fields and trees with some ponies. Nothing special.'

'Aye well, I think you should let me have a look. I bet you're selling yourself short.' He hoped he had encouraged her. She sat silently and continued to pick at the label on her bottle.

Idiot, now you've scared her off.

They sat for a while in an awkward, heavy silence until Jim couldn't bear it any longer.

He coughed and tapped his fingers on his bottle. 'Aye... aye... well... err... ooh, hey, look we should give you a nickname!' He was full of bright ideas. This wasn't one of them. 'Aye, I reckon Felicity is too... *proper*... you know? Too... serious.' He scowled at her to exaggerate his comment.

Felicity's nose scrunched and she seemed to ponder his words. 'Do you think so? My mum used to hate nicknames, so I've always just been plain old Felicity. If I'm completely honest I hate it. It's very formal. I think you're right.' She straightened her spine. 'I quite like the idea of being a little rebellious.'

Jim spotted a glint in her eye. 'Aye? Well then... let me think... ooh, I've got it!' A flash of inspiration came from goodness knows where. 'Flick! We'll introduce you to everyone as Flick! They'll all think you're cool and interesting and not at all posh!' He winced as he wondered if he had overstepped the mark.

A stunning smile spread across her face causing her eyes to

crinkle a little at the corners and she nodded. 'Flick? Hmm, I quite like that.' She stood up and held out her hand to Jim. 'Hiya, I'm Flick... Flick Johnston-Hart... pleased to meet ya.' She made a mock introduction in a bad cockney accent as Jim stood there guffawing.

He shook her hand and blurted out, 'Watcha, Flick, I'm Jim.' He also failed miserably to mimic the accent, resulting, somehow, in a cross between Geordie and Welsh.

Epic fail.

'Flick' burst into fits of laughter. 'Good grief, Jim! You're worse at that accent than I am, and I usually talk like I have plums in my gob!'

She was beginning to relax. And it made Jim's heart rate quicken with excitement. She was such a sweet girl and insanely cute.

When their laughter had naturally subsided, Jim stepped a little closer. 'I like you in that scarf.' He flicked the knitted, standard issue Oxford garment up in the air playfully. She giggled and wrapped it around her neck with a flourish.

They headed out for the party at around seven-thirty, laughing as they walked. They had covered just about every subject known to man in the short time they'd been chatting. Jim had learned all about Felicity's dad, well-known biographer Edgar Johnston-Hart, and her middle-class upbringing, whilst Jim had told her about his hometown of Dumbarton and how – thanks to his educational merits – he had received a scholarship to attend Magdalen College at Oxford University.

Flick was bright-eyed and enthusiastic when she spoke of her dad. He sounded like an amazing man, someone who Jim was sure he could get along with like a house on fire. Her mother, on the other hand, sounded rather like the Ice Queen from the *Chronicles of Narnia*.

* * *

When they arrived at the busy refectory, Jim held the door open for
Flick and she hesitantly walked under his arm, chewing nervously
on her lip.

The space was large and quite austere with arched windows
that reached almost to the beamed ceiling. The woodwork and
flooring were a deep, rich mahogany and it was evident that the
room hadn't changed much over the years.

There were tables and chairs arranged close to the panelled
walls and a band was set up at one end on the stage.

The delicious, herby aroma of Italian food wafted through the
air and made Flick's stomach growl. Jim waved to his friends and
walked her over to introduce her to them, his hand protectively at
the small of her back.

Matthew, Charlie, Clara, Stubbs, Polly, Melodie, Stefan, she
repeated over and over in her mind after the introductions had
been made.

The group were very friendly and Flick – as she had been introduced – immediately began to relax. They all came from similar
backgrounds to hers, which meant they had much in common.
Unlike Jim who apparently hadn't quite noticed he was, in some
ways, an outsider.

The band began to play and included a lot of cover versions of
songs that Flick knew. Jim was clearly into music and he sang along
to almost everything that was played. The group of newly
acquainted friends jigged about chatting loudly over the noise.

Flick watched as Jim moved in time with the music. There was
something extremely sensual and sexy about him. And for a
ruggedly handsome, unsuspecting, tall, long-haired man he could
really move.

The band began to play a slow melodic number, announcing it

to be a cover of Pearl Jam's 'Black'. She had never heard it before but the fact that it sent shivers down her spine told her she definitely liked it. The words were heart-breaking but beautiful. She vowed to listen to more by the band, especially as, judging by his T-shirt, Jim obviously liked them.

She smiled as he closed his eyes and swayed, the coloured lights from the stage highlighting his almost shoulder-length, dark-brown hair, turning it from red to blue to green. He was incredibly handsome, and she noticed shivers traverse her spine once again, though this time it had nothing to do with the music.

Her gaze travelled from his forearms and followed the line of his tendons as they transitioned into the muscular biceps under his T-shirt sleeves. Another faded shirt, this time with the words *Pearl Jam* and *Ten* on the front. Just then he opened his eyes and caught her watching him. Horrified, she widened her eyes and immediately averted her gaze.

Jim lowered his head and spoke directly in her ear. 'You okay? You look a wee bit shaken.'

She snapped her eyes up to his and nodded fervently. 'I'm fine. I'm fine,' she protested rather too much.

Jim smirked. He had caught her watching him and was silently excited. Why wouldn't he be? She was incredibly attractive. Her long blonde hair fell in waves down her back, and he longed to place a gentle kiss on her exposed shoulder and slender neck but knew he wouldn't dare be so bold.

She had the curves of a goddess, too. In no way skinny, just as he liked. He wondered what it would feel like to run his fingers through that luscious hair as he kissed her rosy lips. He gulped his drink down hoping to quench the fire blazing inside him as his fantasy took flight.

The band was taking a break and No Doubt's 'Don't Speak' came over the PA system. He glanced over at Flick again, plucking up the courage he needed to ask the question on the tip of his tongue.

'Oh, sod it,' he muttered. 'Flick... would you like to dance?' He gestured towards the space in the middle of the room that had become a makeshift dance floor.

'Erm... okay?' Her acceptance came out as a question and she took his hand. He led her to the dance floor where other couples had begun to congregate. Sliding his hands around her waist he pulled her a little closer and her hands rested at the crook of his elbows as he gazed down into her eyes. A shot of heat ran through him as she slowly moved her hands up his arms until they were clasped at the back of his neck and she took the final step to align their bodies.

Jim lowered his head and rested his forehead on hers, his eyes closed. Being this close to him felt somehow right, like she was meant to be in his arms. The closest she had come to this before was when she had kissed Adam St. John on the doorstep when his father had returned them home from the cinema. Her mother had caught them and been very upset.

'You most certainly *do not* kiss a boy on your first date, and especially not when you're sixteen years old, Felicity!' her mother had chastised. 'What kind of girl are you?! Think of the reputation you'll have once he goes back to boarding school and tells his friends!'

'Oh, for goodness' sake, Penny, leave the poor girl alone!' Her father had done his best, as always, to defend her.

Flick was pulled back to the present when Jim began singing along with the track as he held her tight against him. She lifted her gaze to meet his and he smiled warmly down at her. Their noses were almost touching, and her heart was pounding so much she was sure he must be able to feel it too.

Slowly, he lowered his face towards her but paused as if waiting for her to pull away. When she didn't, he gently brushed her lips with his. She inhaled sharply but didn't stop him. His lips were soft, and his stubble lightly scratched the edges of her mouth causing tingles to grace her skin.

Despite the fact they had only just met, she had wanted him to kiss her, but there was no way she would have made the first move. Now that he had, she gained the courage to reciprocate the kiss, and he seemed encouraged by this as his hand moved up her back until he reached her hair. Her body shivered with delight and her heart rate increased further. He held her to him and her insides turned to jelly, her legs weakened. Heat rushed to parts of her body she wouldn't have expected from a simple kiss. But then again there was nothing simple about this kiss. She broke away from him and locked onto his gaze.

His brow furrowed; a look of guilt washed over his features. 'I'm sorry, Flick... I-I just got carried away.'

She watched his expression cloud with regret, but she didn't want that at all.

Keeping her hands around his neck and stroking her fingers through the long strands of his hair, she shook her head. 'No, Jim, please don't be sorry... I-I think I had to just check...'

He scrunched his brow. 'Check what?'

'That I wasn't dreaming.' She smiled and tiptoed to meet his lips with hers once again and she felt him smile against her mouth. She parted her lips to invite him in so his tongue could dance with hers, and he scooped her up into his arms leaving her feet dangling just over his shoes. She gave a little squeal of delight as he spun her around. *Wow... literally swept off my feet*, she thought gleefully as he swayed her to the music.

At the end of the night, Flick was aglow with the events of the evening. Jim had been by her side all night and they had kissed several more times. He offered to walk her back to her room and she accepted.

6

___

As they walked back to halls and chatted, Jim tentatively took Flick's hand and laced his fingers with hers as they made their way across campus. 'So did you enjoy the craic then, Flick?' He smiled as he teased her about their earlier misunderstanding.

'Yes, the craic's been great.' She laughed, mimicking his accent and blushing as she did so. He grinned and shook his head at her attempts and squeezed her hand. They walked in silence for a few moments.

He suddenly stopped and pulled her to him. 'Can I ask you something?'

'Yes, erm... sure you can.' Her response was quiet, and she could hear the quiver in her own voice. Her gaze darted around, anywhere but to meet his.

He held her chin gently between his thumb and finger to halt her movements and tilted his delicious mouth up at the corners. 'Do I make you nervous?' He frowned a little but still held a half-smile.

She tilted her face to one side, finally meeting his inquisitive gaze and trying to appear playful and confident despite her pounding heart. 'I-is that the question you wanted to ask? I... thought it would be something different.'

He laughed. 'Oh... no... no. Sorry, that wasn't the question. That was a preamble.'

Flick liked his deep, raspy laugh. It seemed to come from somewhere in his boots and vibrate through his body.

She pursed her lips before answering, 'Well, I am a little nervous but not because of anything bad. I'm just... a little bit shy.' She dared to hold his gaze and her breath caught. Even under the campus lighting she could see he had the most amazing brown eyes, like melted caramel.

'Don't be nervous. I don't bite... Well, not on weekdays,' he whispered and raised his eyebrows cheekily.

'So, what did you actually want to ask?' She hoped she knew the answer.

'I wanted to ask if I could see you again?' He lowered his face until their noses were touching, and her heart relentlessly pounded at her ribcage.

'I was hoping that's what you were going to ask.' She breathed. Her mouth met his for another mind-blowing kiss that was even better than the last. When they broke apart, he held out his hand and she weaved her fingers in his once again.

He grinned. 'Shall I take that as a yes then?'

'You shall.' She hoped her smile said it all.

Just like a perfect gentleman he walked her right to her door and made sure she got inside.

She hesitated and took a deep breath. 'Do you want to come and look at my latest sketch?' The words rushed out of her body as if desperate to escape.

'Hmm, so you're inviting me in to see your etchings, eh?' His impersonation of Sean Connery made her giggle.

'Hardly. It's just the one sketch and it's a bit rubbish really. I just—'

He placed his fingers on her lips. 'I was teasing, Flick. And yes, please, I would love to. Just to see the sketch and then I'll go.' He stepped inside and walked over to her easel. 'Oh yes, I see what you mean. It's totally rubbish.' He teased again.

She hit him playfully on the arm. 'Thank you, but you could have been nicer.'

He held out his arms in exasperation and shook his head. 'Flick, this is beautiful. The attention to detail is... amazing. I can't believe you did it from memory. I have no idea why you doubt yourself so.'

She smiled and nervously tucked her hair behind her ear. 'Thank you. Like I said, it's just what I see through the glass... nothing fancy.' She was almost giddy at his compliment. 'I'm glad you like it though.'

He walked back to the door, pulled her into his arms and kissed her again. 'Goodnight beautiful and talented, Flick,' he whispered placing one last kiss on her nose.

'Goodnight... handsome and sweet, Jim.' The heat in her cheeks rose again. She closed her door after him and then collapsed on her bed with a huge sigh of contentment and a smile as wide as the Thames on her face. She had a pretty good idea what she was going to dream of that night.

Work at university was harder than she had imagined, but for the next few weeks after that initial date, Flick spent every possible minute with Jim. Their friendship deepened and their relationship was secure and special but not yet intimate. They were part of a large group of friends and all socialised together – mostly when they were supposed to be studying.

Matthew caught up with Flick and Jim as they walked back to halls. 'You guys up for a club on Friday night? We're thinking of heading into Oxford to the tastefully named Razzles!' He snorted.

Jim's arm was loosely draped around Flick's shoulders and he looked for her acquiescence. She nodded.

'Sounds like good craic, Matty. Aye. Reckon we could make that!' Jim kissed the top of Flick's head.

Flick's cheek warmed as she smiled at Jim's loving gesture. He had been the perfect gentleman since that first kiss. Never expecting too much of her. They spent a lot of time alone, but things never progressed beyond kissing, albeit passionately. He had only touched her breast once, but she had recoiled at the sensation and he had apologised profusely for pushing her too quickly. He hadn't done it since, and she regretted that fact so much. She was an adult now, for goodness' sake, but thanks to the beady eye of her mother she had never got past first base with a boy. And, by definition, even first base was a little iffy. She was ready to change all that now. She just needed to find a way to convince Jim.

Friday night came around, and Flick and Polly were getting ready in Flick's room. The two had forged a nice friendship on the fact that both were quite shy. Polly had long, fiery red curls that cascaded down her back. She used them as a veil, too, hiding behind them most of the time.

'Flick, can I tell you a secret?' Polly took a swig from the bottle of wine she had been glugging for Dutch courage.

Flick pulled on a long, tie-dyed skirt, camisole and a lace top as she listened to her friend. 'Of course, Pol. I won't tell.' Flick grabbed the bottle and took her own gulp of courage. She needed it for what she had planned.

Polly blushed a bright red that clashed with her hair colour. 'Ahem… erm… I have a massive crush on someone.' She slapped her hand over her mouth and widened her eyes.

'Really?' Flick was intrigued now and dropped to her knees before her friend. 'Who? Tellmetellmetellmeeeee!' She patted Polly's leg as if trying to slap the info out of her.

'Matty,' she blurted. 'He is *so* gorgeous. I love the way he swipes his hair back off his face and pushes his glasses up his nose with his finger… He's like Hugh Grant in *Four Weddings and a Funeral*, have you seen it? Oh and his hands… oh, what I'd like him to do with those hands.'

Flick gasped. 'Polly!' She burst out laughing at her friend's brazen wantonness. The two girls fell about in fits of almost-hysterical laughter when there was a knock at the door and they both froze.

Their laughter ceased.

Polly's face drained of colour. 'Oh, shit! Do you think they heard?' She clapped her hand over her mouth again, making Flick giggle uncontrollably.

Matty and Jim had agreed to call for the girls at eight o'clock and it was now five past. *Dammit!*

Flick grasped her friend's shoulders trying not to giggle. 'Oh, god! Just act normal, Pol. Normal!'

Her friend stared back in horror. 'Normal… yes… I can do normal.' Polly burst into hysterics again and collapsed on the bed.

Eventually they calmed themselves down and answered the door.

Jim rolled his eyes but there was a wide smile on his face as if he'd heard them giggling. 'Bloody hell, Flick, what took you so long? And what's so funny?'

The girls exchanged knowing looks and stifled any further

giggles as best they could under their alcohol-induced giddiness. 'Oh... just a bit of girl talk,' Flick informed him dismissively.

Matty, as Matthew had now become known, went a delightful shade of crimson as soon as his gaze locked on Polly.

His nervous stutter came out with a vengeance. 'H-hi, P-Polly. You l-look l-lovely.' He gazed at the buxom redhead, who almost melted on the spot.

Polly's giggles were gone. 'So do you, Matty... just lovely.' She turned to give Flick and Jim an enormous grin when Matty took her hand in his.

When they arrived at the club the atmosphere was buzzing. It seemed that ninety per cent of Magdalen College was out for the craic. The DJ played decent music, despite the club's somewhat corny name and Jim and Flick spent most of the time on the dance floor wrapped around each other – even when the songs were fast paced.

The end of the night came around too soon and at one in the morning, the gang of friends walked back to their dorms. Some of the group had been a little too eager with the beer and were singing rather loudly, tempting the wrath of the hierarchy without seeming to care. Stubbs and Clara were the two worst culprits. They had all the musical intonation of a pack of howling banshees.

Jim chuckled and shook his head. 'Some of this lot won't be seeing the light of day tomorrow.'

Matty and Polly had stopped and were locked in a smouldering embrace.

'Oh, bless them. They finally got together,' Flick said, looking over her shoulder as Jim turned to see what she meant.

'Aye, thank goodness for that. Maybe he'll stop rambling on about her hair and her eyes and her lips.' Jim mimicked Matty's posh accent and swooned, as Matty had apparently been doing.

Flick smiled in their direction. 'Really? Oh, that's so sweet.'

* * *

They arrived at her door and Jim pulled her close. He lowered his head and kissed her deeply, exploring her mouth with his delicious tongue and sending shivers tingling across her skin.

'See you tomorrow then, sweetheart?' he breathed as he rested his forehead on hers.

Her heart rate increased, and her palms were sweating as she began to speak. 'Would you like to come in? F-for coffee?' She cringed as she stumbled over her words.

Jim smiled enthusiastically. 'Oh... I'd love to. Could do with a cup really. Clear my head a bit. Oh, and to see how you're doing with your painting.' He followed her in.

It wasn't quite what she had in mind and as soon as they were inside, she grasped at him, crashing her mouth into his and grabbing at his clothing.

'Whoa, hey! Flick, what are you doing?' He gasped, grasping her shoulders and stepping back.

She stepped away too as the heat of embarrassment rose from her chest to her cheeks.

Somehow, she summoned up a little of the courage she had felt earlier. 'Jim, I... I... Come on, courage Felicity,' she told herself out loud. 'Jim, I want you... naked.' She lifted her arms up in the air and allowed them to flop back to her sides. 'There I said it. If you don't feel the same, then we have a serious problem.' Her chest heaved as adrenalin coursed through her veins and her heart tried to escape through her chest.

He gaped open-mouthed, as if at a loss for words. Then suddenly as if a realisation had hit, a sweet smile spread across his gorgeous face. He stepped towards her and his expression changed again.

His eyes became darker as he reached to stroke her cheek with his thumb. 'We don't have a problem, Flick.' He spoke quietly and huskily. 'I've wanted you since the first time we kissed... no, even before that. I just got the sense that you may be... ah... a virgin and didn't want to take advantage of you. Things had to be on your terms.' He tucked her hair behind her ear.

Heat rushed through her body. 'Well... I'm sick of being a bloody virgin. I want to experience things. I want to experience sex... with you... now.' She grabbed at his checked shirt, desperate to convey her feelings but worried it was all coming out wrong.

He stopped her movements with his hands. 'There is a slight problem, then.'

Her heart sank and she flared her nostrils trying hard not to cry. 'Oh? Do I want to hear this?' She closed her eyes and gulped.

He took her face in his hands and lightly brushed her lips with his. 'I don't want just sex, Flick. I want us to be a permanent thing and so I want to make love to you. However cheesy that sounds, it's the truth.' His voice was soft. She realised she was holding her breath and was feeling a little lightheaded.

The air rushed from her lungs as she absorbed his words.

She placed her hands over his. 'That would suggest... that you, kind of... love me... Is that what you mean, or am I getting this all completely wrong?'

He took a deep breath and paused for a moment. 'I think I've loved you since that morning you were trying to do origami with all your paperwork.' He chuckled and her cheeks heated at the memory. She had felt so stupid on that day and was a little over-whelmed to hear that he had fallen for her then.

She was trembling now. 'Oh... wow.'

He lowered his face and kissed her again, their tongues teased and tasted each other. She ran her hands through his hair, and he pressed his body against hers.

Stepping away slightly, he eased her denim jacket from her

shoulders and slipped her pretty lace top over her head, followed by the camisole underneath. Her chest rose and fell rapidly as she gazed up into his eyes. He crouched before her and slid the skirt down her thighs. Then he stood and held her at arm's length looking at her, all of her, standing there before him in her white lace underwear.

'Wow... just as beautiful as I imagined,' he breathed as his eyes scanned her body.

Stepping into him, she nervously pulled his shirt down his arms and discarded it with the other clothes. His T-shirt was next to go, exposing his sculpted chest and defined abdominals, the kind she had only ever seen on posters.

On seeing him naked she froze, shaking. She had no clue what to do and was terrified of making an idiot of herself, or of ruining things for Jim.

He pulled her into an embrace. 'Hey, you're cold.' She wondered if he could feel her heart pounding against him. 'Shall we get into bed? Warm you up?'

She nodded silently, feeling in complete awe of his form. They climbed into the limited space, and he lay beside her propped up on his elbow. He trailed his finger down her cheek and placed his palm over her heart. 'Are you okay? If you're having second thoughts—'

'N-no... no second thoughts.' She lifted her hand and pulled him towards her.

7

The university years seemed to fly past in the blink of an eye and before they knew it, they were graduating. Living heavily subsidised in halls had made life easier for Flick and Jim and had meant that they could save what little extra money they had earned at part-time bar jobs.

'I can't believe we've done it! We've finally finished! It's all done. Goodbye education, hello big wide world!' Polly's melodramatic spinning and swooshing of her arms in her robes made everyone laugh. The gang of friends were standing around taking photos whilst their parents chatted and compared notes. Jim's parents hadn't been able to make it due to his dad's rapidly failing health. Flick knew he was disappointed but totally understood how the journey down to Oxford from Dumbarton would takes its toll.

It had been an exhausting and emotional day. Flick had sent her parents off for some R and R at their hotel and she informed Jim that she was going back to her room to pack up the last of her belongings. They had secured a small, two-bedroomed terraced house to rent in Hackney and would be moving in straight after graduation, much to her mother's disappointment. Jim had lined up some ad-hoc work as a freelance proofreader and Flick was starting work at a gallery on the outskirts of London.

'Come up in about twenty minutes, honey bun, and you can help me load the car up before we set out for dinner with my mum and dad.' Flick winked at Jim and squeezed his bottom before she wandered off through the university grounds reminiscing about the wonderful times they had all shared there. It had been a difficult few years but fun all the same.

Her room was all but cleared, her painted canvases wrapped and piled up carefully with the rest of her belongings. Jim had insisted her art would be adorning the walls of their new place and she rolled her eyes but secretly loved that he was so proud of her.

She had already helped him pack his room the day before and it had taken longer than either of them had expected because they had ended up looking through some old photos of his family holidays in the stunning Scottish Highlands. She was amazed by the beauty of the remote places he had visited with his parents and younger brother. They were the types of places she could sit, admire and paint for hours. Sitting and painting a view, whilst it remained before her instead of painting from memory, would be a novelty. She hoped one day he would take her there and then maybe those paintings could adorn their walls, too.

* * *

After saying a fond farewell to his friends, Jim made his way up to Flick's dorm room for what would be the last time. He knocked on the door and opened it to find a stack of boxes.

'Flick? Am I to take these down to the Landy?' he asked, poking his head around the makeshift wall only to find his girlfriend reclining on her bed, naked apart from her mortarboard and standard issue, striped, Magdalen College scarf.

When they had both had their fill and were completely sated, gazing lovingly at each other as their breathing calmed, Jim decided it was time to put his own surprise into action.

He leapt from the bed. 'Sit up and close your eyes,' he commanded.

She giggled at his bossiness. 'Why?' She was clearly in a playful, stubborn mood.

'Just do it!' he demanded as he fumbled around in the pocket of his discarded jacket.

She perched herself on the end of the bed – the scarf still in place around her neck.

'Keep them closed!' he demanded again. She was giggling uncontrollably so he added, 'You cannae open your eyes 'til you've calmed down.' But he, too, was trying not to laugh.

Pursing her lips, she finally managed to quell the giggles and sat, eyes closed, back straight.

Jim took a deep, calming breath. 'Okay, you can open them now.'

She opened one eye, and then both eyes wide. 'What the—?' she gasped.

Jim was kneeling in front of her, holding out a diamond ring in his shaking hand. 'Now, I know this is a bit unorthodox... and I'm a tad naked... but I wanted to remember this moment for the rest of my life.' He gulped and swallowed hard, but the huge grin on her face encouraged him to continue. 'I only intend on doing this once in my lifetime and... so it had to be special.'

He cleared his throat before continuing. 'Anyway, I had a wee word in your dad's ear earlier and I have his blessing... I'm not sure he told your mum but... sorry... so... Felicity Johnston-Hart, I've loved you since the moment I first set eyes on you. And I'm sorry for doing this whilst you're naked too... although let me just say that you are the most stunningly gorgeous woman on the face of the

Earth right now... I've never loved you more... S-sorry, I digress...
ahem... I was going to do it later... at... at dinner but seeing you like
this... beautiful... wearing my favourite outfit yet... I had to do it
now... Flick... Felicity... will you marry me?' His words came out in
such a rush he became quite lightheaded and almost passed out
when he had finished.

She gaped at him as he kneeled there in his vulnerable state. He
hoped she could see the sincerity in his eyes and not be too
distracted by how ridiculous he must look before her.

His heart pounded harder, the longer she stared at him. He
pleaded at her with his eyes, suddenly wondering if he had made a
terrible mistake. He dropped his gaze momentarily along with his
hand. When he lifted his head again, she had covered her mouth
with her hand and tears had escaped the corners of her glistening
eyes.

Oh, no, this isn't good. 'Flick?'

She shook her head. 'Oh Jim, I'm so sorry. I ruined that whole
thing. I was just a bit... *stunned.* And I thought you were joking.'

He shook his head fervently. 'No... I've never meant anything
more... but I think maybe I shouldn't have—'

She wiped at her eyes. 'Ask me again.'

He scrunched his brow. 'Sorry?'

Her eyes softened. 'Ask that important question again, please,
Jim.'

Hope began to rise inside of him, and his stomach flipped.
'Erm... okay...' Taking another deep breath, and this time feeling a
little calmer, he spoke more steadily. 'Felicity, I've loved you since
the day I met you. You make me so very happy, and I want to share
my life with you. I want to be with you forever. Please will you make
me the happiest man alive? Felicity, will you marry me?'

'Oh, yes, Jim! Yes!' She threw her arms around him and they
tumbled back on the bed to start all over again.

8

The lead up to the wedding had been fraught. Flick's mother had insisted, on more than one occasion, that she was rushing into things with a man who was '*ill prepared to look after her with his silly and useless part-time job*' and had even made comments tantamount to a refusal to attend, but thanks to Flick's father, Edgar, Penelope had relented and eventually taken a back seat.

Flick had been heartbroken at her mother's unwillingness to be happy for her but in the great scheme of things, and in her flush of love for Jim, she had pushed it to the back of her mind. Her best friend, Polly, had accompanied her on the search for the perfect dress – a role that should have been filled by her mother. But Penelope's constant bursts of emotion on any mention of the impending nuptials meant that Flick couldn't contemplate her mother being there.

As the wedding got closer, Flick began to dread her mother standing up when the Vicar asked if anyone had any objections. Her other concern was that Jim's loud and lairy brother, Euan, had been given the role of best man. Jim insisted that he had been given strict instructions to behave himself. She could only hope that he would.

The most important day of her life arrived, and Flick descended the wide, sweeping staircase at her family home.

Her father stood, dewy-eyed as he waited. 'Oh, poppet, you look... you look... radiant!'

Seeing her dad so wrought with emotion only served to make tears well in her eyes too.

She knew at that moment that she had definitely chosen the right dress. It was floor length and fitted to accentuate her curves and there was a long train to the back. The lace-up bodice was strapless to show off her décolleté, and the front sparkled with tiny diamantes. She had chosen pink roses – a symbol of gratitude and joy – tied simply with white ribbon. Her hair was smooth and sleek, in a low bun off to one side and dotted with crystals. To complete the look, she wore a silver tiara with real diamonds that her father had insisted upon for his 'adorable princess.'

The popular village church of St Andrew had been booked for the wedding ceremony, thanks to the connections of one Edgar Johnston-Hart. The beautiful building wasn't huge, but it held a special place in the hearts of the family, and Flick could think of nowhere else she would rather marry her darling Jim.

The service was booked for noon on a chilly September Saturday, but Flick couldn't feel the cold. She was too excited. Thankfully, the sun made an early appearance and set a warm glow about the place, even though no one could feel the benefit of its radiating heat, just the colours made it feel warmer.

The bridesmaids wore long, flowing, dusky-pink gowns and carried white and pink roses, tied with white ribbon. All four were friends of Flick's from school and university.

The white Rolls Royce had already taken the bridesmaids and

Flick's sobbing mother to the church, and it now returned to take her on her way to becoming a married woman.

There had been much debate about her name and whether she would take Jim's as her own. Her mother was totally against it. She did make one valid point, however, that the Johnston-Hart name carried a certain amount of weight and that *her Felicity* was already building up a reputation using her maiden name as an art dealer at Art and Soul, a small but well thought of gallery on the outskirts of London.

Flick knew that Jim was hurt about the name thing. He'd wanted her to be Mrs Felicity MacDuff, but after a lot of cajoling by her mother, Flick agreed that it would be best for her to keep her own name. Jim had acquiesced, albeit reluctantly. He said it was simply because he desired her happiness above all else.

She had hugged him and insisted, 'It's not as if I won't wear a ring, for goodness' sake, Jim, and I will be *Mrs* Johnston-Hart.' And so that was that. Mrs Felicity Johnston-Hart she would become. She couldn't be happier. Sadly, when it came to the name choice, Jim could have.

'I now pronounce you, husband and wife.' The Vicar concluded the beautiful ceremony, and Jim couldn't wait to kiss his new bride. Flick beamed from ear to ear as he took her in his arms. The congregation applauded and cheered as the newlywed couple shared their first passionate embrace as Mr and Mrs. They walked down the aisle hand in hand, with eyes only for each other, only breaking away to shake hands with well-wishing guests.

Flick's mother continued to sob and dab at her eyes with a lace hanky.

The reception had gone smoothly, Euan had only seen fit to mention a few embarrassing stories of Jim from their childhood, and one in particular that had involved superglue, a model of the Millennium Falcon and a trip to A&E, had even made Flick snort her champagne.

The honeymoon Jim had planned was an exciting dual destination holiday. Florida's Disney World for the first week, where they met all the famous characters and tried every single ride on his insistence, saw Jim have a roaring time reverting to his childhood. They left with bags full of soft toys and lots of wonderful memories.

The second week was spent in a beautiful villa at Naples Beach. The house was a one-storey white building with a stunning, landscaped outdoor pool. The interior floors were tiled in white marble, and the furniture was plush and luxurious in shades of cream, beige, and white. It was like a little piece of heaven.

They spent the week by the pool, lounging lazily and eating fresh fruit. When they weren't by the pool they were locked in passionate embraces in every possible place around the villa. It was magical. The large whirlpool bath had been their favourite place to devour each other, and they had spent almost every evening in there. Jim had joked that they would wash their golden tans away if they weren't careful.

The image of Flick in her skimpy red bikini and huge sun hat would be emblazoned on his mind forever and it was a memory he knew he would never tire of. Her long tanned legs stretched out before her, and her curves visible for Jim's eyes only.

The return home from their honeymoon was tinged with the sadness of leaving their little cocoon for two, but Jim was excited at beginning their new life as a married couple. Once they had slept off the time difference, they began the enjoyable task of opening their gifts.

Their wedding list had been split between the most prestigious stores in London – Flick's idea. Although certain people had completely ignored the list, buying the most bizarre gifts imaginable. They laughed hysterically at the matching bedside lamps adorned with shells and plastic fish.

'Charity shop!' they had said in unison.

The weird ornament of a bull was a puzzler. The book entitled *How to Let Go When Things Don't Work Out* had no gift tag but was completely inappropriate, given the reason for the gift. Surely it was a practical joke? Although Jim had his suspicions as to the giver.

* * *

Monday came and it was back to work for Flick. She was excited about going back. There had been several new and exciting artists invited to show their works at Art and Soul, thanks to Flick, and she was looking forward to seeing how it was all going. As the newest member of the team, she was determined to make a good impression, and so far, it seemed to be working.

She bent to kiss Jim, as he lay naked in their bed while she got ready. He grabbed her arm and pulled her onto him.

'Awww, Flick, come back to bed... I want you,' he groaned sulkily.

She wore her favourite, sexy, sharp suit – partly because she knew it would drive Jim wild – and she had braided her blonde, wavy locks in one long strand down her back.

He pouted up at her. 'Another day won't matter, surely?'

'Jiiiiim, I have to go.' She tried to pull away. 'We've had our fun this morning... now it's time for me to go bring home the bacon.' She giggled.

They had agreed it was time for him to begin hunting for a 'real job' as spending any more time as a freelance proofreader wasn't what either of them wanted. The money was good but the work wasn't regular and so it didn't feel like a secure income.

He kept insisting he wasn't good at job hunting, however, and he had been visiting The Book Depository in town so often he had become like the old wingback chair – part of the furniture of the place. He had regaled Flick of the fact that he and Charles, the owner, had started to have a laugh and a joke like old friends. He had even helped answer the telephone one morning whilst Charles had been busy.

'I will get a job, I promise.' Jim kissed Flick's shoulder as she leaned on him.

'I know you will when the right thing comes along. But until then, I expect you naked waiting for me when I get home.' She kissed him on the forehead.

He groaned and flung himself back onto the bed and she rushed out the door before he could try to convince her otherwise. Only because she knew she wouldn't take much convincing.

* * *

After he had showered and dressed, Jim headed for The Book Depository. He vowed to himself that he would have an hour there and then he would go to the Job Centre. Although just the thought of it was enough to put him in a bad mood for the day.

It was late September following the honeymoon and there was the nip of autumn in the air. After a short walk, he arrived at the shop at around ten to find Charles in a flap about some book delivery that had gone completely belly up. He walked in as Charles was trying to sort the matter out on the phone.

Charles barked at the person at the other end of the line, 'I'm bloody annoyed though, Simeon! This can't keep bloody happening! I'm up to my bloody eyes in it, old chap! I simply cannot keep accepting books I haven't bloody ordered!'

A man walked into the shop and began to browse the shelves of dusty old books, but Charles continued with his call. Jim stepped from foot to foot feeling he should do something to help but not knowing if he would be overstepping the mark.

Suddenly, the customer approached him. 'Erm, excuse me. I'm looking for a first edition of *The Velveteen Rabbit*. Would you happen to have a copy? I know it's a long shot but it's my wife's favourite book and it's our tenth wedding anniversary. I want to get her something special that she'll treasure, and I'd love to get her that particular book. But I would really rather have a first edition. It'd be all the more special.' The man rambled at Jim completely unaware that he wasn't an employee.

Jim cringed. 'I'm sorry mate, but I don't actually work here... It's Charles... there... who you need to speak to.' He gestured towards the flailing shop owner whose complexion now matched his crimson bow tie.

Charles placed his hand over the mouthpiece of the phone. 'Jim, you're hired! Start now!' he snapped in a loud, hoarse whisper at the bewildered Scotsman. It had come up in conversation a while ago that he was looking for work, but this was unexpected.

A grin spread across Jim's face almost splitting it in two. 'Oh... oh, right... great!' He grabbed the set of keys and a pair of white gloves from the cash desk and turned to address the customer. 'Right then, sir. First edition... *Velveteen Rabbit*... I think we may have just the thing.' He showed the relieved customer to a cabinet where all the first editions were kept and unlocked it.

The customer left with a huge smile on his face, but it was nothing compared to the one on Jim's as he realised he had just, inadvertently, acquired his dream job and made his first – *very* lucrative – sale.

Charles hung up the phone and let out a huge sigh. 'Some bloody people should bloody well learn to do their bloody jobs properly!' he shouted. Jim stood there with his grin still fixed in place. Charles regarded him for a moment before he burst into fits of laughter. 'I have never seen anyone so bloody happy to be working in a dusty old bookshop. Welcome a-bloody-board, Jim. And thank bloody goodness you didn't bloody say no!'

'Not a bloody chance!' Jim joined in the laughter. 'Right, what d'you want me to do first, boss?' he asked Charles, who was dabbing tears from his eyes with a navy and red spotted handkerchief and still spitting out a chuckle every few seconds.

'Oh... I don't know... I've never had an employee before. Shall we have a coffee and discuss your terms?'

'Good plan. I'll get right on it,' Jim chimed enthusiastically as he walked over to the machine, which stood on an old, dark wood table in the corner of the room.

The shop wasn't huge but consisted of two rooms filled with second-hand and antique books; there were shelves upon shelves of books, floor to ceiling, all crammed to the top. The smell was a damp and fusty one, but Jim loved it. Each and every book had its own history, and he liked to imagine how many people had read each one; how many different owners each had had; how each person had come to own and then let go of each book; and how each book had affected each reader. It really was a fascinating place.

There were two ancient-looking armchairs; one was an old beaten-up wingback chair, something akin to that which you would find in a Gentleman's club. It was once bright gold and burgundy when its tapestry fabric had been brand new. Now, however, it was frayed, and the pattern had rubbed off in lots of places. Jim loved it because it was incredibly comfy and had char-acter befitting such a treasure trove where any bibliophile would feel right at home. It was as if a thousand people had all imprinted themselves on the chair, making it squashy and moulded perfectly to the right shape. The other was an old leather armchair which creaked and groaned when sat upon. It, too, was a comfy chair but not quite the same as *his* chair, as he now called it.

Charles had reluctantly joined the 21st century and bought a computerised cash register system but it was hidden behind a rack of shelving, away from view, as if Charles was ashamed of its very presence in the shop. Admittedly, it wasn't quite as pretty as the old antique push button thing that was purely for display these days, but it certainly made life easier and was much quieter to use.

Jim called at the little supermarket near home and picked up some chicken, salad, French bread, and a bottle of wine to celebrate his good news. He arrived at home before Flick, who walked in at six looking exhausted. Dinner was ready and Jim had laid the table placing candles in the middle. It all looked very romantic just as he intended, and her eyes lit up when she saw what he'd done.

'Jim? What's all this?' she asked hugging him tightly.

'I've got good news.' He could hardly contain his excitement as he spun her around in the small hallway.

'What? What is it?!' She grabbed on to him, pulling at his shirt. 'Tell me!'

He ushered his beautiful wife towards the stairs as he spoke. 'Go get changed into something comfortable before I forget my news and I ravish you instead. When you come down to eat all will be revealed.'

Whilst she was gone he sat at the little table in their lounge-come-dining room, tapping his fingers in eager anticipation of her return. She re-joined him and as always took his breath away. Even makeup free, wearing her pale blue, checked pyjama bottoms and a grey off the shoulder sweater she was the stuff of dreams. Her feet were bare, and her long, corn-coloured, wavy hair was scrunched up on top of her head accentuating her sensual long neck.

Wow, he thought, *just wow*.

'What? Why are you looking at me like that?' she asked, a blush spreading up her chest and into her cheeks as he stared.

'Flick… you're simply exquisite,' he breathed.

She gasped at his words and immediately came to straddle him on his dining chair, kissing him as she did so.

'Okay, handsome, what's your exciting news?' she asked as she stared lovingly into his eyes and brushed her fingers back through his hair.

'Weeeell…. I got me a job!' He grinned.

Her eyes widened. 'Really?! That's fantastic! I didn't even know you had any interviews lined up. You kept that very quiet. Is it in the City? Wa-wa-wait… let me guess! Is it with a publishing house? Nononononono… is it with a Literary Agency? Oh, I give up! Tellme-tellmetellme!' She bounced up and down on his lap.

Worry that he was about to disappoint her hugely niggled inside of him. He had graduated with a First from Oxford and had such potential, after all.

Everyone said so.

'Erm… no… none of those.' He sighed.

She scrunched her face in apparent confusion. 'Okay, so where?'

He cringed a little. 'Well, you know that I go to that little book-shop… The Book Depository?'

'Yesss?' The confusion didn't leave her features.

'Well, Charles the owner just gave me a job completely out of the blue! Isn't that great?' He was now trying to convince them both.

She rolled her eyes and tapped his arm playfully. 'Oh, right. Sorry I thought you meant a *job*-job. I didn't realise you meant a steppingstone. You had me all excited then, silly. But that's great, sweetie. It's a more regular income even if it is lower. And it'll certainly put you on for a while whilst you're looking for something permanent,' she chimed, kissing him on the nose and climbing off his lap.

'Hmm... yes... I suppose it will,' he mumbled, not daring to tell her that, besides becoming a bestselling author, this was all he had ever wanted.

9

Several years passed and Jim was happily ensconced in his job at The Book Depository. Flick had stopped hounding him about the career ladder as her own climb was happening rapidly. The latest rung had been achieved when a prestigious gallery had head-hunted Flick and Jim couldn't have been prouder.

'It is with great pleasure, therefore, ladies and gentlemen that I introduce to you, our newest team member and exceptional art critic, buyer, and discoverer of unique talent, Felicity Johnston-Hart.' Applause rumbled around the room as Flick took the micro-phone from Franco Nilsson, her new employer.

'Many thanks, Franco. This has been quite a year, to say the least.' She smiled at her captivated audience. 'I was delighted when Julian Forster was awarded the Carlson Art Prize as it meant that all our hard work had paid off. Julian is a most talented and prolific artist, and I was proud to be the one who discovered him and presented him to the world. Julian will now go on to display at the Tate and has been offered space at Le Louvre for a short time to see how his work is received there.

'When Franco Nilsson and Daniel Perkins made contact with

me and offered me the position of International Art Dealer here at this most prestigious of companies, I jumped at the chance. I'm happy to say that the proprietors of Art and Soul gave their blessing and full support to this next chapter of my career. I'm very excited to be embarking upon such a wonderful journey here at Nilsson-Perkins and look forward to encouraging you all to buy art in the near future.' A chuckle from the audience was followed by applause.

Jim stood at the back, observing proceedings from a safe distance. He had worn the grey suit Flick had chosen for him at some expensive designer shop. He had protested about a tie and she had, thankfully, relented. So, there he stood, shaggy, shoulder-length brown hair, neatly pulled back into a ponytail, stubble trimmed to designer level, waistcoat fully buttoned, jacket open, white shirt open at the collar. He felt trussed up like a Christmas turkey. It wasn't his favourite look, but he had done it for Flick.

He listened as she spoke eloquently about her new role and her excitement over the fact that one of her hand-picked artists had won such a prestigious award. He felt proud but detached. Flick had been spending more and more time away. Paris. Chicago. Milan. Not bad for someone who hated flying. He was happy for her and outwardly supported her every venture. He just felt like he was becoming a square peg in the round hole of her new life.

He glanced around the gallery. Its walls were adorned with the most amazing and striking pieces of modern art. There were some more traditional pieces, too, but just like Jim they seemed out of place.

Thankfully, the music chosen for the evening's festivities was eclectic just like his own taste. Debussy's 'Clair De Lune' began to play over the P.A. system as Flick walked towards him, her hips swaying. Everyone in the room could have disappeared, he wouldn't have noticed.

She slipped her arm around his neck and kissed his cheek, whispering in his ear and making him shiver with desire. 'Hello, handsome, look at you all sexy.'

He returned the favour. 'You don't look too shabby yourself, darlin'.'

She blushed. Her wavy, blonde locks had been replaced with a more severe style: shoulder-length and straightened within an inch of its life with her newly purchased, ceramic hair straighteners. Her fitted black shift dress accentuated her womanly curves and the teardrop-shaped cut out showed just the right amount of cleavage to send Jim's mind racing whilst remaining classy for this, her first work function.

They arrived home after what had been deemed a very successful launch of Flick's career with the very highly regarded Nilsson-Perkins international art dealers and gallery owners.

Their journey home was silent. Jim couldn't bring himself to voice the worries that had taken up residence in the forefront of his mind. The last thing he wanted to do was to rain on her parade.

Once inside the house, the lamps illuminated, and the door closed on the night, Flick slipped her arms around his neck. 'Jim, sweetie, what's wrong? Look at me, Jim,' she urged.

He raised his face. Her eyes mirrored the sadness he knew his must show.

'Flick... I'm... I'm so scared,' he admitted.

She frowned. 'Of what? I don't understand.' She stroked his face and kissed him gently.

'You have this new job and you'll be jetting off all over the world. How will I keep up? Will I still be enough for you?'

Suddenly, she looked perturbed. Not in the least bit compassionate. 'What kind of question is that? I don't know where all this is coming from. When have I given you such an idea that you won't be? I thought you'd be happy for me.'

He realised she hadn't answered his question. 'I *am* happy for you. Of course, I am, sweetheart. I am so proud of you. I'm just worried that I won't fit into your new life. That you'll get tired of me… a lowly book salesman.' He smiled as he rested his forehead on hers, hoping for reassurance.

It never came.

'Jim, this is beyond ridiculous.' She snorted, freeing herself from his grip. 'I'm going to take a shower. Open a bottle of champers, please. There's one chilling in the fridge,' she called back to him as she made her way up the stairs.

Jim's heart sank.

* * *

Flick had worked quite a few late nights since beginning her new job a month earlier. Jim had done his best to just ride it, not to get stressed and certainly not to lay a guilt trip on her.

She was living her dream and he wanted her to be happy. This job seemed to go some way to fulfilling her creative side. Although he had noticed that she painted less and less, a fact that concerned him greatly. Painting was a part of who she was. It had always been her passion. Her job, however, seemed to take her away from the one thing that sparked her desire to study art in the first place.

Jim's twenty-seventh birthday rolled around, although he didn't really care that he was getting older. Age was just a number after all. What he did care about was the fact that he was probably going to be spending this one without his wife. It was already seven in the evening and she wasn't home. She hadn't called but he hadn't prepared dinner on the off chance that she was going to take him somewhere as a surprise. It was a long shot, but he could hope.

He had dozed off on the sofa when the door opened bringing a cold draft into the small room. Flick breezed in carrying a white plastic bag, and along with her came the aroma of Chinese food. She was gripping a bottle of wine under her arm.

She bent to kiss Jim where he lay and handed him the shopping. 'Take these to the kitchen, sweetie.' And then she turned and ran back out to the car.

Jim clambered off the couch and walked through to place the food on the kitchen countertop. When he arrived back in the living room Flick had returned.

'Sit on the couch and close your eyes. No peeping!' she insisted. So, there was a surprise. His stomach fluttered as he followed her instructions and a huge grin stretched across his face.

He heard Flick walking in and whispering, 'Shh... shh,' as she did.

Was there going to be a party? Was he going to open his eyes to a hoard of people yelling, '*Surprise*!'? The suspense was killing him.

Flick crouched down in front of him. 'Tadaaaa!' Excitement tinged her voice.

He fluttered open his eyes and before him was a large white box with holes punched in the lid. He slowly removed it and gazed inside.

'Happy birthday, sweetie.'

Jim's heart skipped. 'Oh, Flick, he's gorgeous. Thank you so much.'

He scooped up the little black Labrador that wriggled and jiggled in his arms. He held the little bundle to his face and the dog licked him and immediately proceeded to pee.

Jim held him away from his body. 'Oh, no, Flick get the back door, quick!' he burst out laughing and she joined in as she jumped up and ran to the kitchen with Jim and his new friend in hot pursuit. By the time they reached the back garden the pup had finished, and they watched him skipping around the small outdoor space, sniffing at everything and falling over his giant paws.

The little dog gambled back to Jim who bent to scratch his belly.

'So, what are you going to call him?' Flick asked.

Jim knew immediately. 'Jasper. It suits him, don't you think?'

She squeezed his shoulder. 'Oh, I think it's a lovely name.'

Back inside the house Flick began to serve out the Chinese take-away she had brought home with her. The aroma made Jim's mouth water and he realised he was ravenous. So was Jasper, judging by the way he sniffed the air. Flick produced a tin of dog food from the takeaway carrier and handed it to Jim.

'I hope that's for the dog and it's not our appetiser.' Jim winked.

She chuckled. 'Best feed him now, eh, before he has your Chicken Satay.'

Jim slipped his arms round his wife's waist. 'Aw, Flick this is the best gift I've ever received. He's just gorgeous. Thank you so much.' He kissed his wife lovingly before feeding his new little friend.

* * *

Valentine's Day was a washout. Jim was waiting by the phone and had been for hours. Flick had been in Chicago on business for almost a week, and although she had called a couple of times, the conversations had been short and not so sweet. Today, however, he was expecting a longer call. He missed her like crazy and hoped she was missing him but sadly the recent calls hadn't helped to quell his insecurities.

At around nine, the phone finally rang. He reached over from his position on the arm of the couch and grabbed the handset. 'Hey, sweetheart. H—'

'Hey, Jim. We've just had the most amazing meeting with a phenomenal artist at the Art Institute of Chicago. It's looking like we may get the UK rights to her work! Isn't that fantastic?' She blurted out without even saying hello.

Jim's knee bobbed up and down and his jaw clenched. He felt heat rise in his cheeks. 'Hi, Flick... Oh, hi, Jim... I miss you so much... Yes, I miss you too, Flick, and wish you were here.' He snorted sarcastically.

'Aw, sorry, sweetie. I'm just so excited. Anyway, I can't talk long. We're going sightseeing at five before we head out for dinner and I need to get sorted. I know it's only three in the afternoon, but you know how long it takes me to get ready. Can you believe I've been here a week and I haven't even been to the Loop yet?' She laughed.

Jim did not.

He heaved a deep sigh. 'Look, Flick, I was hoping we could talk. You know... properly. I miss you so much it hurts.'

'Oh, I'll be home before you know it and then you'll be sick of the sight of me! Anyway, I really must dash. I really must shower and change, or I'll be late. Love you, sweetie, bye.'

'Oh... so you really meant you couldn't talk long then. Okay... bye.' His heart sank as he hung up without reciprocating the breezy 'I love you' and regretted it immediately. He was angry and hurt. He threw the handset onto the sofa and slumped down into the seat.

Jasper came and placed his head on Jim's lap and he scratched him behind the ears. 'At least *you* love me, eh, lad?'

To top it off, his birthday was approaching again and even with her being home late for last year's celebrations, he was wishing it could be the same as the last one. At least she was at home then. This was going to be the first one, since they got together, that he would definitely be spending without her. She was due home two days after his birthday.

This year there would be no surprise gift in a box with holes in it, and instead of spending a romantic evening with his wife, he would be spending it with Charles. They were going to the cinema to see the Coen brothers' film *Hail! Caesar*, which wasn't really a film that appealed to Charles – he was into Film Noir and this was the closest thing there was out – but it was either that or *How to Be Single*. Jim had to draw the line somewhere considering this birthday was already sad enough as it stood, without watching a movie that felt too close to home.

* * *

Jim's birthday arrived and so did a card from Flick. At least she had managed to get it to him on time. He spent the day making notes for his book and later, reluctantly, he met Charles at the cinema.

'Hello old chap. It's bloody freezing. Good thing we can warm up with some Indian food later. I've booked us a table at the Taj Mahal for after the film. It may not be romantic but at least you're not alone, eh?'

Jim smiled and followed his friend inside. Charles insisted on buying the largest bucket of popcorn available, along with chocolates, nachos, and jelly sweets. The majority of which were gone by the time the film started. Silly, really, considering they had a table booked for dinner.

After the movie, they moved on to the Indian restaurant and once again Charles insisted on paying. 'No, Jim. Put your bloody money away, old chap. My bloody treat. If a chap can't treat his best bloody friend on his birthday, when can he?'

'Best friend? Aw, Charles, mate.' Jim hugged his friend, feeling quite touched at his words.

Following their meal, with stuffed bellies and light hearts they headed to the Nags Head for a few beers. A few beers turned to many beers and Charles got quite tipsy. Jim found drunken Charles hilariously funny, although he was by no means sober himself. They stumbled out of the pub after being chatted up by too rather scary looking, overly made-up older women and as they waited for a taxi at the nearest rank they could stumble to, Charles made a confession.

'My dear, Jim.' Jim chuckled at the fact that Charles remained posh even when inebriated. 'Jimmy, Jimmy, JimJim.' His chuckle became a laugh. 'Be serious Jiminy. Listen, you are my beshtest friend... didjoooo know hathat?' Charles slurred.

'I did not know that until earlier tonight, my old pal... but I dae now!'

They swayed as they chatted in their nonsensical way, Jim's Scottish accent thickening with the effects of the alcohol.

Charles jabbed a finger towards Jim. 'Ohhh yes. Beshtest friend in the whoole world. In fact, I am so best friends with you, I'm gonna tell you a sheecret.' Charles looked around conspiratorially and leaned on Jim for support. 'I don't like ladies, Jim... nononono.' He wagged his finger vehemently. 'I like men. I am what one would call a hhhomosexshalll.' The revelation surprised Jim a little, although he had always wondered. 'But don't worry... nononono, don't you worry... you're not my type.' He patted Jim's shoulder.

Rather affronted at his admission Jim's mouth fell open. 'Eh? Whaddya mean I'm not your type? What's wrong wi me?' The brusque and rather offended Scotsman had pushed his way to the front of Jim's mind. 'I'm a good catch me, you know,' he informed Charles.

Charles waved a hand in front of Jim's face. 'Oh, yesss, yesss, I bloody know that old boy... don't be hoffended. I just like you asafriend... thass all. Hafriend. And besides... I would be wasting my time because I know that you're... erm... heter... hetrara... hetooosesh... you like girls. Especially on account of the fact being that you are married, as well too.' He nodded, rambling on.

'Aye... that I do... that I am, my friend. Fair comment... fair comment. Well, one girl actually.' Sadness suddenly washed over him. 'But, to tell you the truth, I think she's going off me, Charles, and it makes me hurt in here.' Jim pointed to his chest. Hearing himself admit this openly made him rapidly sober up and he wished he could suck the words back in. Maybe that way they wouldn't be true. The pair stood in silence after their session of openness and waited for a cab.

Jim arrived home to the rented house on Bushberry Road at just after midnight. He took his mobile out of his pocket and noticed a missed call from Flick. He cursed himself for forgetting to take it off silent after the cinema. Thankfully, there was a voicemail, so he hit play.

'Hi Jim... it's Flick. I'm sorry I didn't ring earlier but I've been so busy. Anyway, I'm sure you've had a wonderful night out with Charles. I'm guessing you'll be home around one in the morning, so I'll call you at one. Okay? Bye.'

No 'I love you'. Great. He went into the kitchen and drank a pint of water to try and fend off the hangover that would undoubtedly hit at some point in the not-too-distant future.

He made a pot of fresh coffee and took it back into the living room, determined he would stay up and wait for her call at one.

He woke with a start and looked at the clock. Two forty-five. She hadn't called. With a heavy heart and a pounding in his skull he took himself off to bed.

10

The second Hogmanay since his move back home to Scotland was destined to be a washout. Charles had spent the first one with him and had made sure it was an event filled with laughter and far too much whisky. This year, however, the threat of impending blizzard conditions had put paid to his visit. So, in a bid to stave off the loneliness that tended to strike at this time of year, he had invited his neighbours and friends from the village round on the spur of the moment, expecting most of them to be unavailable. It turned out the threatened snow had meant lots of cancelled plans for them too, however, and his invite had been the highlight of the day.

Ironically three of his closest friends were artists like his ex-wife. Miranda, Jilly and Max and his partner Phil, all brought food, lovingly and artily displayed on platters, which was unexpected but welcomed. Jasper sat by the buffet table Jim had set up in the kitchen, just waiting for something delicious to fall to the floor.

'How's the new book coming Jim?' Max asked as they stood in the living room where Jim's iPod was playing a track list of Scottish music, and The Proclaimers were singing of being on the way to happiness.

'Aye, I've been wondering that too,' Phil interjected.

Jim shrugged. 'To be honest I haven't had much time to write recently. The Coffee Shack is taking up most of my time.'

Max stuffed a haggis bonbon in his mouth and chewed thoughtfully for a moment. 'Aye well, crack on lad. Your last one was a belter and some of us are waiting with bated breath to see what happens next.'

'He's a sucker for a happy ever after aren't you, Max?' Phil said with a nudge.

Writing a novel based on his own experiences hadn't been something Jim had ever anticipated, and of course his Shieldaig friends had no clue that *Through the Glass* was almost autobiographical. It had been cathartic to write, and he had self-published under a pseudonym. So far, the book had been quite successful, and he had been asked on several occasions about a sequel. But therein lay the problem. His own story had ended, so whatever he wrote from now would have to be solely fictional. He wasn't sure he had the imagination to take his protagonists – Jack and Fiona – into a future he hadn't got to experience.

Jim wasn't sure how to answer his friend but thankfully Miranda saved him from having to make something up on the spur of the moment.

'It's almost midnight folks!' Miranda announced as she turned off the music and switched on the TV. 'Has everyone got a drink?'

Jim went round topping up glasses as the countdown began.

The mention of his book had made him pause momentarily, and wonder what Flick was doing at that precise moment. Was she with another man? Was she happy? A sudden feeling of melancholy took over and he shook his head as the countdown reached four. He wouldn't look backwards. Hogmanay was about looking to the future, and he had plenty of that ahead of him.

'Three, two, one! Happy new year!'

The friends drank a toast and put down their glasses, linked arms and sang a rendition of 'Auld Lang Syne' that made Jasper bark and howl. Jim hadn't laughed so much in a long while and it felt so good. Poor Jasper, however, wasn't so keen on the singing and during the second verse he left the room, escaping to the safety of the kitchen.

Jilly flung open the front door. 'Look! Fireworks!' The friends took to the pavement and watched as the hills behind Sunset Cottage lit up with a multitude of colours and sparkles. Miranda and Jilly both kissed his cheek and Max and Phil hugged him in that *slap-your-back* way that almost choked him.

Nah, the future is where I'm looking, Jim told himself as the next lot of whizzes and bangs illuminated the sky.

The sky over Shieldaig was the tell-tale pink that occurs before heavy snowfall, and even though it was only nine in the morning, Jim had already lit the fire. It was Saturday which meant the Coffee Shack was scheduled to be open at ten, so he sat by the fire eating his porridge with Jasper beside him and stared into the flames as they danced.

Someone knocked at the door.

'Blimey, Jasper, the postie's early today. Must be getting it done before the snow comes, eh, lad?' He placed his porridge bowl on the coffee table and went to answer the door.

On opening it, he got the second biggest shock of his life – the first being his wife's request for a divorce... oddly enough she was involved in this shock, too.

'What the hell are you doing here?' His greeting was far from cordial and Jasper gave a high-pitched yip. Did he recognise her?

Flick stood shivering on the doorstep her eyes rimmed with red. 'C-can I c-come in please, Jim? It's important,' she pleaded.

Reluctantly, he stepped aside so the Ice Queen could enter his cosy little cottage. The weather outside a fitting fanfare for her unexpected arrival. As she walked past him into the living room, the cold, biting air from outside followed her as if it emanated from her very being.

She crouched as Jasper jumped up at her and she nuzzled the dog's fur. 'Hey, sweet boy. I've missed you so much. Yes, I have.' Jasper's whole body wagged, and Jim felt a little betrayed by the canine.

Brushing off the ridiculous thought, he shuddered. 'You could've called to let me know you were coming, Felicity. I mean, I have no idea why the hell you're here. You're miles away from home.' He was speaking to himself really.

She stood. 'Be honest, Jim, you wouldn't have agreed to see me if I had called.'

She had a point. 'Do you... do you want a coffee?' he asked, completely befuddled as to why his ex-wife had driven for almost ten hours to turn up on his doorstep without prior notification.

'Y-yes, please. Brrrrrr.' She shivered. 'This is a sweet place. Completely different to Bushberry Road.' She followed him into the kitchen.

He forced a smile. 'Thanks. It's small but perfectly formed, as they say.' He poured freshly brewed, steaming coffee into a mug for Flick. 'So, I'm Jim again, am I?' he asked, confused.

'It suits you better,' she stated with a sad smile.

It's taken her long enough to figure that out. They wandered back through to the living room and sat beside the fire, silently. Jasper laid at Flick's feet and she scratched his head, hunched as if the weight of the world was dragging her down.

Finally, Jim could wait no longer. 'So... to what do I owe the unexpected... erm... visit?' He would have said *pleasure* but considering he had spent almost the last three years getting over their divorce it wasn't a word he could associate with Flick any longer. She had caused him so much heartache. He couldn't go there again.

Her lip began to quiver, and her eyes glistened with welling tears. 'I... I'm sorry to just turn up... I'm afraid I have some bad news, Jim, and I couldn't tell you over the phone. I just couldn't do that.'

Jim put his cup down and slid to the seat beside her on the sofa. 'Hey... hey, what is it? What's wrong?'

'It's Daddy, Jim... He passed away just before Christmas... He'd been ill but had kept it quiet. We had no clue how bad things were.'

The news hit Jim like a blow to the gut. He inhaled sharply and ran his hands through his hair. It explained why Edgar's letters and emails had dwindled.

She twisted her fingers in her lap and glanced up briefly. 'He had been secretly receiving treatment for his illness when he was supposed to have been out playing golf, but he didn't want Mum fussing over him.' A sob broke free as the tears overflowed from her closed eyes and spilled down her face. 'And he didn't want to worry me. But I should've guessed. I should've done more.'

Jim stood and leaned on the fireplace. 'Why... how... I don't...' His stomach clenched into a knot and nausea washed over him. Edgar had been like a father to him. He had written several letters over the past year and had received light-hearted replies regaling Jim with details of the latest book he was working on. The last letter had been full of facts about George Leigh Mallory, the subject of his latest biography. It was the beginning of December when he had received the last letter. There was no mention of illness. *None*.

Flick stood. 'I shouldn't have come here... You're right, I should've called you... I should've—'

Jim turned around and pulled her into his arms. 'Hey, hey, shhh... c'mon, it's fine that you're here. I just wish I could've helped... or at least been there for you.' He stroked her hair as she sobbed, his own eyes stinging with unshed tears.

* * *

Flick relaxed into Jim's arms. It felt good to be there again. She had missed the feeling of being loved, *really* loved. Even though she knew that there was no way he could possibly love her now. Not after everything she had put him through.

'Felicity... I just want to ask you something.' He pulled her away from his body and peered into her eyes, his were showing signs of regret and pain. She gazed up at him, blinking through the blur of her tears. She had been doing a lot of crying lately, especially on the journey here. It probably showed. Jim's next question caused her stomach to knot. 'Why wasn't I invited to attend Edgar's funeral?'

She stepped away, her own guilt and regret twisting her insides as she dropped her gaze to the floor. 'I'm so sorry, Jim. I wanted to speak to you... to tell you what had happened, but Mum... she insisted that you were kept away. She said it was too far for you, and that you wouldn't have come anyway.'

'Hang on. You know how much I loved him. Both of you know that. You know I would've moved mountains to be there! How could you let her keep me away? What's her problem with me? I don't get what I ever did to her.' The volume of his voice rose exponentially with his evident anger. His fists clenched by his sides.

'Jim, I tried to convince her,' Flick pleaded. 'Honestly I did. But she was adamant. And she was grieving. I couldn't argue, Jim. That's why I'm here now.'

His chin trembled. 'Well, you can tell her a big bloody thank you from her favourite ex-son-in-law for taking away my chance to say goodbye to someone I loved!' His anger-filled voice cracked as his tears flowed freely now. Flick broke down again. She was a jelli-fied mess. Her whole body shuddered with every pain-filled sob.

Jim regretted shouting at her. It wasn't really her fault. Her mother had, yet again, interfered in their lives. He couldn't comfort her now though. He didn't feel able. He just watched for a few minutes as she let all her sorrow pour out.

Once she had begun to calm, he walked to the window where he looked out towards the loch. The snow had begun to fall heavily and in the short space of time since Flick had arrived the road had completely covered. Unless she left immediately, it rendered her stranded. Looking over to the little island in the distance he could see that visibility was low, so realistically leaving now wouldn't even be an option. Plus, he could hardly kick her to the curb whilst she was in this state.

Great.

Now what would happen? The snow had been predicted, but he'd had no clue it would get so deep so fast. He let out a long huff and shook his head as a combination of grief, anger and disbelief caused him to clench his jaw hard.

Flick stood and joined him at the window and threw her arms up in exasperation. 'Oh, shit! What am I going to do now? I can't drive in this!' Her hands rested on her hips and she shook her head. 'This is just perfect. *Perfect.*' Her voice began to wobble again.

Jim continued to stare out of the window watching the glis-tening flakes floating down, down to the water, pavement and road below creating a sparkling white canvas as they settled.

Eventually he spoke. 'Where were you supposed to be staying?' His voice was devoid of emotion, and he didn't turn to face his ex-wife.

'I stayed over on the way up but hadn't booked anywhere for tonight,' she whispered. 'I figured I'd just speak to you and then set off back home... maybe stop off if I got tired.'

'Well, I'm afraid it looks like you won't be going anywhere.' He turned to face her. 'You can either stay here in ma spare room or you can walk down to the pub... They have rooms there.' He made no attempt to convince her either way.

Frankly, at this point he didn't much care.

She began to ramble, 'Do you have to be somewhere? Do you have anyone who's expecting you? I don't want to keep you from anything. I can stay at the pub if that's better. I don't want to cause you any problems.'

He clenched his jaw as he briefly glanced sideways at her. 'Look, Felicity, I said you can stay. If you want to stay, then stay. I've got to go next door and open up the Coffee Shack. I'm late opening as it is.'

He left her standing by the window, grabbed his Arran sweater, scarf, and coat and pulled on his boots. 'I'll leave Jasper here with you. Make yourself at home. I only open until two on Saturdays throughout winter, but I doubt there'll be much demand today, so I'll be back later.' He walked out of the house, closing the front door behind him.

* * *

Flick stared at the door. Jim had been so cold towards her, but she couldn't blame him for that. She had just broken his heart all over again. She was good at that, almost to the point of it being an art form.

Jim's cottage was pretty and homely. The open fire gave the living room such a warm, cosy atmosphere. The stairs ascended from this room, and the kitchen-diner was to the right of the stairs.

He had decorated the place simply but tastefully and she was impressed with his choices, which made her wonder why he hadn't had much input in decorating the home they had once shared.

After bringing her bag in from the car and making the decision to stay the night, she went upstairs to locate the spare room. Jasper followed closely behind. He too appeared to be intrigued as to why she was there.

At the top of the stairs, she opened a door to find what was clearly Jim's room. The large, brass-framed, double bed dominated the space. The bedding was striped in pale blue and crisp white and a thick, sumptuous cream throw blanket was draped along the edge of the bed. The curtains matched the duvet cover, and the walls were a fresh, clean white. She scanned the room for photographs and clues as to what he had been up to in the last few years but there was nothing to give any hints.

On a chest of drawers in the corner of the room, she spotted a collection of frames, so she wandered over to take a closer look. There were old photos of Jim and his parents, more recent ones of Jim and his kid brother, Euan. There was one of Jim and a mystery woman, and right at the back, Jim and Flick. It was a photo taken at university on graduation day. They were laughing and holding each other. Seeing the photo brought a swell of emotion, and she left the room as quickly as she could.

The next room was a bathroom. There was a roll top bath complete with a large handheld shower attachment. He had gone all out to make a luxurious room to relax in. It really was beautiful, and she was taken aback at his attention to detail. She had always thought *she* was the artistic one. Perhaps she never really knew him at all.

The final door was the spare room. There was a white-framed double bed with apple-green and white spotted bedding. It was fresh and bright without being overly feminine, or masculine, for that matter. She placed her bag on the floor and lay down on the bed, suddenly feeling drained, both physically and emotionally. She covered her eyes with her arm and began to sob again. The rest of the bottled-up emotion of the past few weeks overspilled and her body shuddered. Jasper had followed her and sat expectantly beside her head. She rolled over to face him and he tried to lick her nose.

'Oh, Jasper... Why has it all gone so horribly, horribly wrong?' She nuzzled his fur and began to cry again. Eventually she cried herself to sleep with Jasper on the floor beside her.

'Flick... erm... Felicity...'

She awoke to find Jim standing at the foot of the bed and sat bolt upright. 'Oh, heck, Jim, I'm so sorry, I must've dozed off.' She rubbed at her sore eyes.

His expression remained impassive. 'No need to apologise. Nothing's spoiling. You look like shit though.'

Ouch. 'Gee, thanks.'

He had never spoken words like that to her before and even though she was sure there was an element of truth in them, it hurt.

He walked back to the door and with his back to her he said, 'I've made coffee if you want some. And I've made some food, too, if you're hungry.' He didn't turn around but kept on walking and headed downstairs.

A terrible sinking sensation squeezed at her stomach. He really didn't want her here.

After she had washed her face and freshened up, she made her way down to the kitchen where the aroma of something delicious tantalised her taste buds. She salivated and her tummy growled in anticipation.

Jim stood at the stove ready to dish out the food. 'I made a steak pie. I hope you like that. If not, I can rustle you up a sandwich.'

'Oh, yes, pie. That's lovely, thanks.' She smiled and sat down at the little beaten-up old table which stood against the opposite wall to the white pot sink. 'I'll get out of your way as soon as the snow clears, Jim. I... I don't want to impose.'

'Aye, well... you'll not be going anywhere for a few days. I've been listening to the local news. The roads are blocked. The snow's been pretty heavy all afternoon. There are severe weather warnings throughout this part of Scotland. And they're saying don't travel unless it's an absolute necessity.' He didn't smile or show any emotion at all for that matter and Flick felt increasingly unwelcome and uncomfortable. Anxiety and anger built inside of her. Why was he being so cold? What was the point?

She slammed her hands on the table and stood to face him. 'Look, Jim. I know this is not ideal and I'm the last person you want in your house... and in your life... but I can't help the fact that I'm stuck here! I don't like it any more than you do. So, would you just stop being so damned glacial towards me? I can't deal with it right now! I know I hurt you. I can't take that back. I wish I could, okay? I hate feeling like this! It's awful but I can't deal with you treating me like some evil bitch, Jim! It's not fucking fair! And I hate swearing and you've made me swear!' she screamed at him, her arms flailing as she went towards him, hellbent on slapping him, pent-up anger and frustration seeping out of every pore.

He caught her by the wrists before she had the chance to make contact with his face. 'Have you finished?' he asked calmly, still holding her wrists but not tight enough to hurt her.

Her chest heaved as if she had just completed a marathon.

He held her gaze, his eyes steady and his face too close to hers for comfort. She began to calm down as tears cascaded, leaving cool, glistening trails down her heated face.

She sobbed. 'I'm so sorry... please forgive me... for everything, Jim. I'm such a mess. I'm sorry for everything... so, so sorry.' She rested her head on his chest and clung on to his shirt.

Quite unexpectedly he encircled her in his arms and let her cry for what felt like an eternity. Being in his arms felt like being home. Something which she knew there was no point acknowledging. He smelled of the same cologne that he always used to wear. He was still a creature of habit in many ways.

Jim stroked her hair. Having her here was unsettling. This was his place. There had been no memories of her here and that was a good thing.

Not any more though.

She looked great, beautiful in fact, despite the puffy eyes and dark circles. Her familiar perfume filling his nostrils and striking him with melancholy as he was almost transported back in time to when he was meant to hold her in his arms. He stamped on the train of thought, bringing himself reluctantly back to the present.

She shuddered in his arms.

He hated to see her cry, always had. 'C'mon, let's eat, eh? Before it gets cold,' he whispered.

She lifted her face from his chest. There was a huge wet patch of tears and mascara where she had been pressed against him.

She giggled. 'Whoops, sorry about that, I think you may need to wash your shirt.'

He looked down and smiled in return. 'Aye, looks that way.'

They ate in silence for a while. Jim got up only to grab a bottle of red wine and two glasses.

He poured them both a large measure. 'Don't know about you,

but I reckon we need this,' he said as he held up his glass to take a large swig.

Smiling, she did the same. 'So, what have you been up to since we last saw each other? Have you met anyone special?' *Why the hell am I asking that? I don't want to know!* He frowned at her as if to ask her the same question she was asking herself. But after thinking for a few minutes, he turned the question on her.

'Why, have you? You know, met someone?'

She smirked at his avoidance of the question. 'Not since Rory.' She pushed her plate away.

He huffed. 'I knew it.'

'What do you mean?' She scrunched her face.

'I knew you'd end up with him.' He pushed his own plate away now, his expression stern and serious. 'He was exactly your type. Well, your *mother's* type for you to be exact.'

'Jim, nothing happened until after you and I... until after... it was after we had split.'

'So, you say you've not met anyone since Rory? What happened with him?'

Felicity began to recount the not-so-pleasant details of her affair with Rory Fitzsimmons, which began a year after the break-up, the affair that, in effect, gave her a taste of her own medicine.

And it was a bitter medicine to swallow.

11

Sitting at her desk in the back office, Flick heard Franco Nilsson, the gallery owner, greet a client. 'Good afternoon, Mr Fitzsimmons. Are you on the lookout for another piece?'

'Ah, good afternoon, Mr Nilsson.' Flick recognised the name and the accompanying deep voice, and she peeped around the wall. The man continued, 'No, actually I'm on the lookout for your rather stunning International Art Dealer.'

'Am I to presume you mean Ms Johnston-Hart and not our intrepid Daniel Perkins?' Franco laughed at his own joke.

Mr Fitzsimmons simply ignored him and carried on. 'Is she in?' His lip was curled up in disdain as if he felt he was being deliberately delayed.

As he finished his question, Flick made her way, purposefully, towards the front of the gallery, carrying her briefcase and a file. Her heart began to beat a little faster when she saw Rory standing in the gallery. Rory was everything she wanted in a man – or so she thought at that particular point in time. He was tall, good-looking, ambitious, wealthy, and intelligent and to top it off, he had a very prestigious career and an Aston Martin.

Rory was a university rugby star and successful lawyer at Jenkinson-McLeary Solicitors. She had heard that he was hoping to make partner in the firm at a young age and that he worked long hours to ensure that he was first in line should the opportunity present itself. He was five years her senior and had made her acquaintance whilst purchasing artwork for his home and office from her former place of work, Art and Soul.

He had followed her to Nilsson-Perkins gallery to purchase more artwork. Back then she'd thought perhaps he had a crush on her. Why else would he follow her to another gallery when Art and Soul had some wonderful pieces to tempt him? She had always thought Rory handsome and charming. He was tall, around six foot five she guessed, a whole lot taller than she, and around four inches taller than Jim. He had neatly cropped, dark, almost black hair. And with his stature and presence he dwarfed Flick and she quite liked it.

There had been a few coffee dates in the year since she split from Jim, but Rory had not made any attempts to kiss her nor ask her out officially. He had hinted that he wanted her and had given her many compliments but seemed reluctant to take things any further.

She had put it down to the fact that she was still legally married at the time –well that's what she had hoped it was. He had offered her advice about divorce just after she had left Jim when he took her out for coffee on her request for his assistance. She had wondered for a while how she would feel underneath him in bed and now that her divorce was final, she hoped perhaps his attitude would change. Flirting with him had always been fun, exciting in fact. Even her mother approved.

'Rory! To what do I owe this unexpected pleasure?' She beamed at him from across the large, bright space.

He gave her a lascivious grin. 'I was just in the area, so I thought

I'd come and insist on taking you out for a celebratory dinner.' Under normal circumstances she would think him arrogant, but this wasn't just anyone. This was Rory Fitzsimmons. No, she needed to make this one work. Her mother had met him at the gallery and had not stopped talking about him since.

She laughed. 'I have nothing to celebrate, it's not my birthday for two months... but funnily enough, I've just finished work. I'm on my way back to Polly's.'

'Ah well, you deserve to celebrate your decree absolute now that you're a free woman. Dinner is courtesy of yours truly. We'll go now.' He was very insistent, but she liked that. It made a refreshing change for a man to be so decisive and forthright.

Flick blushed and tucked her hair behind her ear, realising that Nilsson was still observing their exchange. 'Okay, sounds good. Where shall we go?'

'There's a delightful little Italian around the corner. Bella Roma? My friend Sal is the owner. I've booked a table for... ooh around about now,' he said looking at his watch. Flick made a bet with herself that it was an expensive designer watch, a Breitling perhaps or a Hublot. She would check later.

'Oh? And what if I'd have said no?' she teased.

'Don't be ridiculous. I knew you'd say yes, of course.' *Hmm, okay a little arrogant*. She didn't comment aloud.

They made their way round to the Italian after dropping her brief-case and file at her car. Rory guided her into the restaurant, placing his hand at her lower back. Sal greeted them personally. He was a very handsome man with a goatee and floppy black hair. He seemed friendly and made Flick feel welcome.

They chatted easily throughout their meal. And she managed to check out Rory's watch. Judging by the Breitling logo on the face she guessed it must have cost as much as her car. Whilst they were finishing their drinks, Rory grazed her fingers with his own and gazed into her eyes. This could be the night. Please let this be the night, she prayed silently.

Rory chatted briefly with Sal at the end of their meal, and they said their goodbyes. Sal waved to her and gave the expected, '*Ciao Bella!*'

When they reached Rory's car, he pulled Flick into an embrace. 'Right then, sexy. I want to get you home.' The hunger visible in his eyes made her tingle. 'I've wanted to kiss you for absolutely bloody ages, but you were with that John idiot, and as much as I hated him, I wasn't prepared to share.'

That made Flick uncomfortable. 'His name is Jim, and he isn't an idiot—'

He gave a small smile. 'He let you go, didn't he? That makes him a prize idiot in my book.'

A confusing combination of emotions fought in her mind. She was both flattered and affronted at the same time, but his body was pressed up so close it was hard to think.

He reached down to squeeze her bottom. 'Now, come on. I want you in my bed.'

Crikey. He's forward all of a sudden. 'But... my car—'

He stopped her mouth with a very full-on, passionate kiss, which took her by surprise, but her legs weakened all the same. One hand held the back of her head and the other slid to her lower back, pulling her into him.

Gosh, so demanding.

'Come on, sexy. You'll be staying at my place tonight,' he insisted, thrusting his pelvis into her suggestively.

She giggled like a teenager, eventually feeling rather silly, but the promise of what was to come hung in the air between them and she couldn't help feeling excited.

Her car was locked safely in the compound behind the gallery, so she climbed into the passenger seat of Rory's Aston Martin. He reached over and squeezed her thigh. Shivers traversed her body and she felt heat rise quickly up her chest and to her cheeks.

They arrived at Rory's stunning Georgian home in Holland Park and Rory came round to open her door for her. *Such a gentleman.*

Once inside the hallway of the house he closed the door and immediately grasped her in a strong embrace once again, pushing her up against the wall and invading her mouth with his tongue. She could hardly breathe and pushed him back. He released her and she gasped, her chest heaving.

Rory was breathless, too, and a frown creased his brow. 'What's wrong? Have I got the wrong end of the stick here?'

'No... no... you just... surprised me. Can we take things a little slower, Rory? I don't mean to be a tease. It's just that I haven't slept with anyone since Jim, so it's been a while.'

'Who said anything about sleeping?' He smiled and scooped her up in his arms. She gave a squeal as he did so. He chuckled at her reaction and proceeded to carry her up the first staircase.

She had wanted this to happen but had expected there to be a little romance first. A little wooing perhaps. 'Rory! What are you doing?' She found him physically attractive, and she did want to have sex with him, but he was a lot more dominant than she had anticipated, considering he had been a perfect gentleman until her divorce was final. But as he carried her, he nibbled on her neck and she somehow lost the ability to think straight.

'I think we should remedy your situation. Don't you?' He kissed her and smiled as he placed her back on her feet in his bedroom.

'I... I mean...'

He pouted. 'You do want me don't you, Felicity?' He proceeded to kiss her neck. 'Or should I stop? I can stop if you want me to. Do you want me to?'

She was suddenly lost in sensations she hadn't experienced in too long and the pleasure radiating through her body fogged her mind. 'No, don't stop,' she breathed.

* * *

She awoke at eight the following morning, naked in Rory's bed. She stretched, feeling the ache in every muscle of her body. He had been very attentive. Completely different to Jim, but perhaps that was a good thing – not that Jim hadn't been attentive. But anyway, the last thing she wanted was to be remembering Jim every time she made love with Rory. Although, calling it *making love* was perhaps a little optimistic. She hoped he had different levels of intensity, otherwise she may struggle to function normally if their fledgling relationship made it past the starting blocks.

Rory walked into the bedroom carrying a tray of coffee, croissants and pains au chocolat. He was completely naked. She sensed that, without a doubt, he was very comfortable in his own skin.

He placed the tray on the bed as she let her gaze roam over his body. He hadn't looked as she had imagined. He was broad and had fairly muscular arms and shoulders, which was to be expected as a former rugby player, but he was a little soft around his middle. He wasn't sculpted like Jim. Jim's abs were defined, and his biceps were strong and rounded, and his pecs... *Dammit! Why am I doing this to myself*? She shook her head to remove the unwanted invasion of images and pulled the sheet up over her breasts.

Rory sat on the bed beside her and scratched the stubble that had formed overnight on his chin. 'I think you should move out of Polly's and come to live here,' he announced, out of the blue.

Flick inhaled sharply as if she had been stung. 'I'm sorry, *what*?' She could have sworn he had just suggested that she move in with him.

'Well... it's silly for you to live at Polly's really. It's clear there's something here, between us. I'm not one to mess about when I know what I want.'

'I... think it's a bit too soon, Rory. Don't you? You can't just ask me to move in because you *think* there's something here.' She scrunched her brow and shook her head. 'We need to get to know each other. Let things build and grow.'

'Things *are* growing,' he said with a lascivious grin. When she didn't smile, he rolled his eyes and pulled her into his lap. 'Come on, I'm joking around. I really do think we have something special though. I've wanted you for ages and I think you've quite fancied me, too.'

She sighed. 'I do find you attractive Rory, but I'm not some possession you can just claim. You can't just demand that I move in. I want to be treated with respect. I know I slept with you rather quickly, and I have to say maybe I was a bit rash in doing so, but—'

'Don't do that, Felicity, don't say you regret it. It was amazing. *You* are amazing. You can't blame me for trying to keep you, can you?' He pouted again and fluttered his eyelids. He resembled a cute puppy, and she couldn't stay angry.

'I won't move in right away. Let's see how this goes, okay?'

He pushed the tray across the bed and laid her back. 'We'll talk about it later. Now, how about we work up an appetite for all the pastries I've bought especially for you?'

* * *

Against her better judgement, and only two weeks after their first date, Flick arrived at Rory's home with her suitcases. He hadn't let up on it and his insistence that there was something serious between them had been encouraging. What tipped the scales in his favour was her mother.

Penelope had almost had kittens, she had been so excited to hear her daughter had been asked to move in with such a wealthy, handsome, well-to-do man. She had thought it terribly romantic and immediately began trying to convince Flick of the same. She encouraged her to throw caution to the wind and pointed out all the wonderful things about the man, especially all the ways he was better than Jim. Eventually Flick had been worn down by both Rory and her mother, and one morning after breakfast, she had told Rory she would move in.

Expecting him to be overjoyed, she was a little shocked and tried to put out of her mind the fact that he said, 'I knew you'd give in eventually.' Laughing heartily as if he had won a bet. He could be brash and crude and he drank a lot, but he bought her flowers, cooked her delicious meals, and bragged about her talent as an art dealer at every opportunity he got, so she told herself that he was right for her. She resolved to make it work.

Perhaps she could change him?

On that first night he had helped her bring her bags in and had left her to get settled whilst he ordered a takeaway, and opened a bottle of his favourite wine, a nice, expensive, vintage Rioja. Only the best would do for Rory.

In bed that night he had pulled her into his arms, kissed her on the nose affectionately, and whispered, 'Night-night, wobbly arse. Welcome home.' It was such a sweet gesture that she smiled and cuddled into him, choosing to ignore the comment about her bottom.

And so, it went on.

* * *

She spent an awful lot of time on her own during the evenings and that was saying something considering she worked late herself. Some nights he didn't roll in until midnight, stinking of whisky.

Needing something to occupy her time, she began painting again, setting up a makeshift studio in one of the many spare bedrooms. She really enjoyed reconnecting with her own art; and discovered how right Jim had been when he had told her a couple of years before that she wasn't herself unless she was painting.

She started work on a piece that just came to her. It wasn't a scene she had memorised through the glass like the others she had painted in the past. This was a place she could see in her mind's eye. It felt familiar yet almost invented simultaneously; it was a place that she hoped one day to discover was real, so she could visit. A peaceful, beautiful place where she could sit and breathe in the fresh air whilst feasting on the scene before her. But for now, she would settle for putting the scene on canvas.

'Hi, wobbly arse! I'm home!' he shouted as he came in from the office at almost midnight one August evening.

She knew he'd been drinking as she had asked him not to call her that, but he always slipped up when wine or whisky had been consumed. She refused to let his pet name make her paranoid, although she often wondered why he had chosen that particular one.

She was still painting in her makeshift studio and he came in and stood behind her as she worked on the piece. 'Hmm, not bad… not bad. Not as good as the stuff you sell in that gallery of yours but a nice little try all the same.' She gasped. *Patronising, insulting bastard.*

He bent to kiss her neck and she clenched her jaw. The realisation that this was *really* not working, finally sinking in. There was no tenderness. In his opinion, showing emotions was for *poofs and mummy's boys*, as he so eloquently put it. She had realised a while ago that she wasn't getting what she had hoped for out of the relationship, but all she could think of was her mother's face lighting up every time they visited.

And boy did Rory know how to charm Penelope.

'What do you say we take this to the bedroom, wobbly arse?'

'I'm sorry Rory but we need to talk. Can you stop doing that please.' She reached back to stop his groping, but he ignored her and advanced further causing her to lose her balance. She lurched forward into her easel, the paintbrush still in her hand. Landing on all fours, her paint-covered hands squelched, slap-bang in the middle of her freshly painted canvas, smearing the wet paint and putting a hole in it.

It was completely ruined.

He laughed and dropped to his knees behind her. 'Whoops! That one's for the bin I think, darling.'

She hit out behind herself. 'You've ruined it! You stupid idiot! You've ruined my painting!' She pushed him back and stood up, tears welling in her eyes. He stood, too, staring aghast at her. She shouted, 'You idiot... I can't believe it... all that work... all those hours... you bloody idiot!' She shook her head as sobs broke free.

His eyes widened and he stepped towards her, hand raised, ready to strike. She closed her eyes and waited for the impact but when it didn't happen, she opened them again to find him glaring at her.

'Just who the hell do you think you're speaking to?' he asked through a clenched jaw, anger oozing from every pore. 'And why are you so wound up over a few bloody crap blobs of paint? It's not like you're an artist for god's sake! It was a pathetic effort, and you know it.'

He really didn't know her at all. He had made no effort to do so.

All he had wanted was a woman to have sex with and to have on his arm at parties. He had no clue about her passions, about what made her tick. And the fact that he had raised his hand to her, even though he didn't follow through, was the final straw.

She gritted her teeth. 'I'm going to collect my things and go,' was all she could muster up the courage to say, scared he would actually hit her if she were to say anything else.

He snorted. 'Oh, come on, wobbly arse. I didn't hit you. I stopped myself,' he declared proudly as if she should admire him for it. 'And you've got to admit you were out of fucking line back there!'

He followed her up the stairs into the bedroom.

Tears of anger and frustration at her own stupidity were streaming down her face now. She wiped her hands on some toilet roll to get rid of the excess paint and grabbed her suitcase from under the bed.

'I didn't hit you,' he repeated. 'Is it because of the name? Because it's not meant as an insult, you know. I like your arse.' She didn't respond so he continued to fill in the silence. 'Is it because of your painting? I'm sorry, okay? I didn't mean to hurt your feelings. I just know what I like when it comes to art, that's all. But it was a good try. Maybe we can get you some lessons? I'm happy to pay for that if you'd like.'

She clenched her jaw and inhaled a calming breath before she turned and saw a furrowed brow and eyes filled with regret, but it was simply too late.

She sniffed as her lip trembled. 'Rory, please just leave me to pack.'

He pulled the tie from around his neck and threw it onto the bed, slumping onto the mattress. 'You're such a moody cow. Do you know that? I mean, it was one bloody attempt at painting, and it got damaged by accident and look at you, all *boo hoo hoo, you ruined my crappy little painting*,' he mocked like an errant child.

She shook with anger. 'Rory, please... just leave me alone.'

'No, I won't leave you alone.' He sounded like a sulking school-boy, whining because he'd been told to tidy his room. 'I invited you to share my home... I gave you a room to do your hobbies in for god's sake! And this is how you repay me? By leaving?' He huffed. 'Well, that's just bloody charming. Is this how you show gratitude, eh?'

She stopped what she was doing and turned to face him. 'Gratitude?' She snorted derisively. 'Rory, I have lived here for almost a year and a half. A year and a half of my life that I will never get back. In that time, I've spent more time with Madge, your cleaner, than I have with you. You come home late, smelling of alcohol and cigarette smoke and expect me to just part my legs for you, whether I'm in the mood or not. You never take me out. You never tell me you love me, in fact, I don't think you have a clue what love is. AND YOU CALL ME WOBBLY ARSE FOR CRYING OUT LOUD!' she shouted at him.

'I've just told you it's a term of endearment!'

'You belittle the one thing I have had a passion for since I left Jim. And then to top it off, you push me into one of my pieces, ruining it beyond recognition, almost slap me, and then mock me for being upset!' She turned and began shoving items of clothing, footwear, and toiletries into her case again. Her voice was loud, and she knew she sounded strung out. 'I'm an intelligent woman! I can't believe I stuck this out for so long.' She laughed dryly at herself. 'I'll have someone call for the rest of my stuff as soon as possible.' She stomped past him and down the stairs collecting her car keys from the hall table.

'That's it... you just sod off! You leave everyone, don't you? Don't stick to anything! Yeah well, I can get laid wherever and whenever I bloody want so you'll be easily replaced!' he shouted after her.

She stopped in her tracks and with as much venom as she could muster, she shouted back, 'Is that so? Well, for your information, you fat pig, it helps if you know what to do with your actual prick. It's no use just acting like one!' She slammed the door behind her getting away from there as quickly as she could.

12

Once Flick had finished regaling Jim about the delights of her failed relationship with Rory Fitzsimmons, he sat in a stunned silence. Hearing about her being treated so horrendously made his insides churn. He didn't quite know what to say and so saying nothing seemed to be the best option until he could figure it out.

Eventually, he huffed out a long breath. 'Shit... I can't believe he almost slapped you.' He shook his head trying to allow this new information to sink in. 'It's a good thing I didn't know about it at the time. I'd have killed the bastard.'

Flick gave a half-smile. 'I was just glad to get away from him. I was such a fool... I thought I loved him, but I was simply starstruck by the material things. The huge house, the Aston Martin, the fine wine, the...' She sighed. 'We never even took a holiday together. The whole relationship was a joke, and they were all just things... things to make a statement, status symbols. I think Rory is just destined to be a perennial sexist, a chauvinistic bachelor. He had no feelings for anyone but himself. Well, not until I left, and he realised that he did actually love me in his own way. He used to call me at Polly's telling me he would kill himself if I didn't go back to him. Apparently, he was going to jump off London Bridge.'

'And what did you say to that?' Jim enquired, frowning.

She smirked and covered her eyes with her hand. 'I asked him if he'd like me to give him a push.'

Jim burst out laughing. 'Ahhh, such compassion... I love it!'

She joined him in laughter. 'Well, you know... he was a big bloke... He might have needed a bit of a push outwards to stop him hitting his head on the concrete on the way down! Less messy that way!' They both fell about laughing uncontrollably at the rather macabre discussion.

Jim chatted with Flick late into the evening until she began to yawn. After her brutal honesty about her relationship, he wondered if maybe he should tell her about his, but he decided it could wait for another time.

'Hey, you look exhausted, Felicity. You should get to your bed,' he told her as he placed their empty glasses in the sink.

She yawned again and rubbed her eyes. 'Mmm, I think so.' She stood to make her way to the stairs but turned. 'You've stopped calling me Flick.' Her voice was tinged with sadness.

He nodded and shrugged. 'Aye... just like you wanted. I've had to change a lot of things over the past couple of years, eh?' He realised he'd almost acquired the ability to switch off the outward expression of his emotions – but then again, he had learned from the best, hadn't he?

She rested her head on the doorjamb as she kept her pain-filled eyes locked on him. 'Yes... yes, I know you have. It's just that... I kind of miss being called Flick.'

Not knowing how to respond to that, he turned to continue with the dishes. 'Aye, well, goodnight, eh?' He was willing her to go to bed. He needed this conversation to be over.

Thankfully, she took the hint and went to bed.

Once the dishes were done, Jim stepped out into the sub-zero temperature with a very reluctant Jasper in tow. He pulled his woolly hat down further over his ears and zipped his coat right up as far as it would go. Snowflakes drifted from the inky-blue sky and congregated with the rest at his feet. The scene of the lochside street before him was reminiscent of a Christmas card with the amber glow of the streetlights, and he smiled. He really did love the place.

'C'mon, Jasper. I know it's cold, pal, but a dog's gotta do what a dog's gotta do.' He scratched the dog's head and began to walk, hoping that the cold air would clear his head of the fog, sadness, and perplexity that he was now plagued with, thanks to his unexpected visitor.

Jasper obediently followed close behind, stopping every so often to sniff the air. Jim paused momentarily and looked out over the water. The distant mountains were enveloped in snow and the little whitewashed cottages in the village were now camouflaged against the thickening achromatic covering. Although it was nighttime, the snow reflected the moonlight, making it feel much earlier in the day. The icy air nipped at his skin and numbed his senses.

Flick lay awake replaying her last days of married life and how she had treated Jim. There really was no wonder he was struggling to be cordial now. She had put him through so much and sadly, it was too late to realise the error of her ways.

Full of regret and with the heaviest of hearts she allowed warm tears to fall as she rolled onto her side wondering if, and how, she could possibly make amends.

* * *

Jim awoke to the smell of bacon drifting up through the floor-boards. His stomach grumbled appreciatively. It was clear that Flick was trying to make herself useful. He stretched and lay there for a few moments longer until there was a light knock on his door.

The door was pushed open slightly, but she didn't enter. 'Jim? Erm… I made breakfast,' she whispered.

'Aye, it smells delicious. I'll be down in a minute, Felicity.'

'Okay… I made fresh coffee too.' She was silent a moment. 'I'm afraid the snow's still really bad.'

'It tends to stay awhile when it settles in. No bother. You'll just have to stay as long as the snow's here.'

What other choice did he have than to make it as amenable for them both as possible? There was no point in suffering through a negative atmosphere. It wouldn't change things.

'Thanks, Jim… I appreciate it.' Out of the corner of his eye he watched through the crack in the door as she rested her head on the frame for a few seconds. It appeared that she had more to say but she clearly thought better of it and walked away, returning to the kitchen.

A few minutes later, after pulling on a T-shirt and jeans, Jim walked in and was greeted by a plate of chunky bacon sandwiches. *Perfect*. His stomach made its desire known with another loud growl and he pulled up a chair and sat.

He cleared his throat. 'Thanks for this, Felicity. I don't expect you to wait on me whilst you're here though, you know.'

'Hey, it's the least I can do. Tuck in and enjoy.' She smiled, taking a bite of her sandwich.

There was a strange atmosphere hanging between them. It almost felt like they were still married and were on a mini-break in a little Highland cottage instead of being thrust together under duress.

She chewed thoughtfully for a while as he watched her discreetly. It was obvious something was preying on her mind.

Eventually she opened her mouth to speak. 'So... I told you about my failed relationship with Rory. What's your story since we split?'

Jim raised his eyebrows. 'Whoa! Don't hold back, Felicity... ask away!'

She frowned as though regretful, and a twinge of guilt dug at him. He was frustrated that she had even asked as it wasn't really a subject he felt comfortable talking about with her. He sat silently chewing for a number of minutes, trying to figure out what to say.

Flick gathered the courage to look at him. Instead of the usual impassive mask, however, was a look of frustration... or confusion... some unreadable emotion. A distinct line creased his brow and his lips, when not moving to chew, were in a fixed line. She wanted to take the question back and was on the verge of apologising when he spoke.

'There is someone. Well, there was,' he finally admitted. Flick's heart sank. He continued, 'She's not from around here. She travels around with a band. She plays the fiddle. They've stayed up on the campsite out back a fair few times. Mainly through the summer. Her name's Heather. We get along really well, but we've never... ahhh... you know... we're not *together* as such.'

Flick nodded trying her best to process the new information without showing her true feelings. Feelings she had no right to own. 'Oh... right. Where is she from?'

'She stays in the Borders. Near Jedburgh. It's a fair trek really and that's why we only see each other when she comes up with the ceilidh band. I've got my work here and she spends most of her life on the road. They've done a few functions in the hotel along the way. The band is quite well-known and very successful. They travel all over Europe in fact.'

'Oh, gosh. That's amazing.' She sipped on her coffee and contemplated what else to say. 'What's she like, Heather?' She wasn't really sure if she truly wanted to know but was too intrigued not to ask.

He scratched his chin. 'Ahhh, she's quite petite, slim, long dark hair, naturally wavy. Very pretty. Blue eyes.' Jim looked almost wistful as he spoke. He drifted off into a kind of trance.

Flick wondered what he was thinking about…

* * *

'Hi, Heather. Have you guys got everything you need up there?' Jim asked the guest as she walked down from the small campsite at the back of his cottage.

'Aye, Jim. We're all sorted. We're not playing until tomorrow night so we're going to have a barbeque if you'd like to join us?' She smiled, her azure eyes sparkling with warmth as she spoke.

It was a warm August evening and perfect weather for cooking outside. Jim and Heather had known each other since he'd taken over the campsite and the band had visited for the first time. There was a definite spark of attraction between them, but both were shy. Heather inherently so, which was surprising considering her profession, but Jim's was an acquired shyness since his failed marriage had knocked his confidence. He was often bemused as to why the band didn't stay at the hotel, but it was good for business, so he never asked the question.

The band laughed and chatted as they stood around the brick barbeque that Jim had installed not long after moving into the cottage. It was the perfect addition to his little campsite. The heat from the barbeque was welcomed now it was late evening and the temperature was dropping. Jim and Heather sat drinking bottled beer on the log bench also constructed by Jim, who had acquired many hands-on skills since the move. Heather shivered audibly.

'Hey, I heard that. Here you go.' Jim slipped off his jacket and placed it around her shoulders.

She smiled gratefully pulling the jacket around her.

'Thanks, Jim. You're so sweet. Why are you not married?'

The question was meant to be rhetorical but regardless of the fact, Jim opened up and explained all about Flick and the divorce. Heather listened intently. It felt good to talk about things with someone who was removed from the situation.

Heather shook her head in disbelief. 'Wow. I'm surprised that happened to you. You're such a nice guy. It doesn't seem fair.'

Jim smiled at her comments. Why couldn't things between him and Heather be easier... less complicated. And why couldn't the distance be less? Eventually Jim decided to call it a night and Heather accompanied him down to the house where the small shower block was situated.

'Thanks for the jacket,' she said handing it back to him. As he took it, their fingers grazed, and he took her hand.

Holding on to her for a moment, he weaved his fingers into hers and sighed. 'I wish you didn't live so far away.'

She cocked her head to one side giving a half-smile up at him. 'Oh? Why's that, Mr MacDuff?'

He stroked her cheek. 'I just... I think... never mind.' He shook his head realising there was no point elaborating.

Heather placed both hands on his chest and tiptoed so that her face was just below his.

He gazed down at her, lowering his head until their lips were almost touching. 'Heather, how could this work? You live so far away, and you travel so much I would never see you and—'

She placed her hand on his lips. 'Shhh, Jim. Some things are just not meant to be, no matter how much we'd like them to happen. So... just kiss me.'

With that, he lowered his lips to meet hers. Her hands slipped up around his shoulders and his found her waist. The kiss was light but wonderful and over far too soon.

Heather turned and walked back towards the campsite, looking over her shoulder and smiling at him, her long, chocolate-brown hair floating, almost in slow motion as she walked. In that moment, she reminded him of Arwen, the beautiful elf from *The Lord of the Rings*, and his heart ached just a little knowing that she would never really be his.

* * *

Flick cleared her throat and then spoke to bring Jim back to her from wherever he had drifted off to. 'You seem to really like her. Don't you think you'll find a way to make it work?'

'No. It wouldn't be fair to tie her down. She's not a homebody like me.' He smiled as he spoke, his eyes tinged with sadness. 'But I will say one thing.' He looked directly at Flick now. 'Although I know I won't ever be with Heather, she's given me the hope that there can be someone else.' He exhaled loudly. 'When you and I split, I felt that I could never love anyone else. Never let anyone else get close. Heather made me realise that I could. That it's possible. There's hope for me yet.'

Flick felt her eyes sting with tears. She hated herself for making him feel he couldn't love again. Although, hearing him speak about being with someone else cut her in a way she wasn't prepared for. But it was always a possibility that he would have moved on. She had. Albeit temporarily.

Jim glanced over and saw a pained look in Flick's eyes. He never intended his words to hurt her.

He had to try and break this melancholy that had descended over them. 'Anyway, enough of that. Look, I'll have to work whilst you're here and it's looking like you may be here a few days. I cannae leave the shack closed, I'm afraid. It's a lifeline for some of the villagers and I cannae let them down. What are you going to do during your time here?'

'Well, I have my laptop and so I could maybe do a little work, send some emails, do some research.'

Jim laughed at this remark. 'I hate to break it to you Felicity, but I'm afraid the Wi-Fi is down just now. It tends to happen when there's a heavy snowfall. They're working on installing updated equipment, but it hasn't happened yet. So, it's back to old-fashioned pen and paper for now, I'm afraid. I don't tend to use the internet much anyway so it doesnae bother me. I have email but I've never been into tweeting, squawking or booking faces and the like.'

Flick laughed. 'Good grief, Jim! You're in the dark ages. Social media is huge! How do you find out what's going on in the world?'

He laughed too. 'There are such things as newspapers you know.' He shook his head. 'Nope. I say I'm in the *peaceful* ages.' He never got why people felt the need to connect with total strangers when there were real people, real friends in his life. 'Seriously though, what are you going to do? You'll be bored stiff, knowing you. You don't like the same books as me so that's a no-no.' He pondered for a moment. 'Hey, I know! Why don't you paint? You can do it in the kitchen, or the living room. I don't mind.'

'Oh, yeah, because there just happens to be a branch of Atlantis Art Supplies up the road.' She snorted, evidently thinking his idea utterly ridiculous given their location.

He shook his head. 'Felicity, you're in the Highlands now, don't forget, artists on every street. Leave it with me.' He gulped down the rest of his coffee and grabbed his coat. 'Back in a wee while.' He disappeared out of the front door before she could protest.

* * *

Flick stared after him in bemusement. She hadn't painted in earnest since Rory and the debacle of the ruined canvas. She hadn't admitted this to Jim, however. Whilst she was left alone, save for the pair of big brown eyes attached to the panting head resting on her knee, she thought back to the scene she had been painting that fateful day. She could recall the colours and shapes and began to imagine reproducing it. With this, her excitement started to build.

Whilst Jim was gone, she wandered around the house and examined the books on the shelves in the living room. It was so cosy in there with its log burner and gnarled railway sleeper mantle. The walls were painted a warm buttermilk colour complemented by the thick, gold and burgundy tapestry curtains. *Judging by the weather I bet these are a godsend*, she mused as she held the textured fabric between her fingers. His artwork consisted of architectural drawings of various random buildings that she had never heard of. She had to admit, however, that they made very interesting viewing. The detailing was incredible and gave a real feel of what each must look like. What surprised her the most was seeing one of her own small, framed paintings hung on the wall in the kitchen. She hadn't expected him to have kept anything, let alone to have displayed it.

Jasper lay upon the thick pile of deep red rug gazing up at her. Every so often he would wag his tail expectantly, but Flick was too busy gazing into the crackling, dancing flames and thinking back to another time, a time when she and Jim had spent Christmas in a little cottage by the sea in Lincolnshire. She was so completely mesmerised by the flames and caught up in the memories that almost an hour later, Jim's return made her jump, snatching her back, rather cruelly, from her reverie.

He stumbled in, arms full of treasures and brought along with him a freezing cold draft of air, which diffused through the ground floor quicker than she could pull her cardigan zip up.

He beamed at her. 'Look what I got!' He sounded like the Jim she remembered from uni – excited and giddy, and she scrambled to her feet from the squishy, old, gold-tapestry sofa to his side, to examine the haul.

His mood was contagious, and she clapped her hands enthusi-astically. 'Good grief, Jim. How many artists do you know?' Her jaw dropped as he placed the goodies on the sofa. There were canvases, brushes, acrylics, water colours, palettes, an easel, all good quality too.

He clearly knew some very generous people. 'Quite a few. Miranda Helliwell just along the road, sells her art in galleries throughout the area. Max West just a little further along, and then along the other way, Jilly McDougal – she's an amateur but bought all the best stuff when she started. All very nice people, all wanted to help.'

Flick was lost for words. 'Wow,' was all she could manage. She could feel her heart begin to pound as she thought about getting started. How well thought of he must be here. He deserved no less.

Jim smiled widely as he saw the flames ignite in Flick's eyes. He knew that look. He knew that hunger and had seen it in her a million times before. He knew she must miss this, miss painting. After all it was a part of who she was; he had always said so. His heart swelled as he watched her. The expression of sheer delight on her face was reminiscent of the Flick he knew way back, and it made him happy to know he had helped put it there.

He rubbed at the hair on his chin. 'Look... I have an old pair of dungarees and a T-shirt that you can borrow to wear whilst you paint. They're scruffy as hell, but I only ever wore them for gardening or decorating. They're yours if you want them.'

She flung her arms around his neck and kissed his cheek. 'Oh,

Jim, thank you!' He froze. 'This means so much to me. I can't really explain, but... thank you.' As she clung to him, the smell of her deliciously familiar perfume drifted into his nostrils again, clouding his judgement and mocking him for days gone by.

He lifted his arms to hug her back, but instead patted her back like he would an old friend. 'Aye well, get set up whenever you're ready.' He released himself from her grip. 'I'll be off next door. Lots to do.' He smiled awkwardly and left her to begin.

13

The Coffee Shack had begun as just that, a place to grab a coffee to go, popular with tourists passing through but over the last year, it had expanded and become the village store when the actual village store closed due to the owner's ill health. Jim stocked all the essentials needed for such a situation as the current weather. He stood outside looking out over the snow-covered street. It was strange how the thick blanket had dulled every sound, making it audibly quieter. It didn't feel quite as cold now. The snow had not only insulated sound but had acted as a duvet to the lochside village, too, although it wasn't warm enough for the snow to melt away. Not yet.

He opened the shack and switched the heat on full. A steady stream of customers filed in throughout the morning. During a lull, Jim stood before the heater rubbing his icy hands together. The radio was playing old tracks in the background, and when he heard the lyrics of 'Distance' by Christina Perri and Jason Mraz floating around the small space he stopped to listen. He closed his eyes and absorbed the poetry for a few minutes, feeling a lump form in his throat. Distance from Flick was something he had both enjoyed and endured in recent years, but that had all changed now.

He opened his eyes as one of his friends, Jilly McDougal, breezed into the shack with a pink nose, forcing Jim to swallow the lump and put on his customer-friendly mask.

The friendly middle-aged woman pouted at him. 'Hi, Jim. Please tell me you have some kindling left.'

'Hi, Jilly. You're in luck. I only have a couple of bags. Everyone must be making the most of their open fires with the snow and I haven't had a chance to stock up since the weather turned.' He lifted a net bag and passed it over to her.

'No wonder! And my fire at home is a true godsend in this weather. It's blowing a draft under every door in my house. Oh, by the way, did your lady friend like her art supplies?'

Jim felt his cheeks warm at her choice of words. Lady friend. 'Aye, she did, Jilly. Thanks ever so much for your help with that.'

'Oh, good. If it puts a smile on that handsome face of yours, I'm all for it.' Jilly blushed a little. 'Bye, Jim.'

'Bye, Jilly. Thanks again.'

Once she had gone, he quickly checked on his stock levels. They were getting lower by every hour he was open. Switching the coffee machine on, he quickly counted the number of packs of powdered milk, candles, matches, and bags of kindling he had left. There was nothing he could do about it. There was no way out of, or into, the village at that moment. Luckily the villagers all rallied around a neighbour in need.

As he was placing out the last of the bread, Flick walked in, Jasper following closely behind. Jim was surprised she wasn't inside the cosy cottage starting a masterpiece.

'Hi... what are you doing out?' he asked as he stacked the remaining loaves. He noticed she was wearing one of his thicker coats. She was buried inside it as if it were eating her alive. He smirked a little.

She frowned at him. 'What's so funny?' He didn't answer so she shook her head and continued. 'I thought Jasper and I could go for a walk. It looked so pretty out. I'll start my painting later.' She glanced around. 'Wow, nice little shop. I had no idea you had diversified. I thought it was just coffee and tea.'

'Na. It evolved. The villagers needed it and so I obliged.' He poured her a coffee to go and handed it over.

'Ooh, thanks.' She wrapped her hands around the paper cup and its corrugated cardboard insulator sleeve. 'I borrowed a pair of Wellington boots and a few pairs of socks. I hope that's okay?'

He looked down at her giant man feet and couldn't help but laugh. She looked at her feet, too, and blushed her famous cerise-pink, giggling. She looked adorable.

She sipped the steaming coffee carefully. 'You really seem settled here. It's obvious you care a lot about this place, and its people.'

He spoke without turning to look at her. 'Aye. It's all I ever wanted. To be myself and to be relaxed in my surroundings.' He baulked as the words left his lips, an immediate stab of guilt niggling at him for the dig about their past. He hoped she hadn't noticed.

'You never liked London, did you, Jim?' she asked in a small voice.

Dammit, she noticed.

He turned to her now, making his eyes stern. 'London was fine. We had each other and I loved my job at the bookshop.'

She nodded. 'Yes. Yes, you certainly did.' She smiled sadly and set out, calling Jasper to her side.

That sinking sensation happened inside him again. He really would have to *try* to be less abrasive with her.

* * *

As Flick walked, the snow crunched beneath the Wellington boots, which felt like barges on her feet. Jasper cavorted in the snow like a pup, his stubby legs disappearing with every touchdown and his tail wagging frantically as it collected tiny snowballs. The sky was a bright cornflower-blue, but the hue was deceptive, a direct opposition, in fact, to the icy temperature making her breath into clouds of humidity.

Although the cold made her lungs sting, she couldn't help but breathe deep. The air may have been icy, but it was fresh. There wasn't a hint of smoke or engine fumes to fill the spaces where natural, crisp air belonged.

Happiness flowed through her as she watched children playing at the opposite side of the road. Their snowman was dressed in all of their parents' finery, and Flick wondered how much of it had been taken without permission.

On several occasions, she had to duck to dodge snowballs as they were thrown from one side of the street to the other between rival gangs of friends, laughing and shouting. Each time was followed by, 'Sorry, lady!' to which she waved, a gesture to inform them that she wasn't bothered by their game playing.

A woman was walking towards her with a yellow Labrador, and she smiled as she approached Flick.

'Ahhh, hello there! I'm guessing you must be Felicity, Jim's friend?' the older, grey-haired lady said as they were about to pass; the dogs greeting each other like old friends.

'Yes... yes that's right. How did you know?' Flick was intrigued.

'Well, for one, you have Jasper, and for two, you're wearing what I'm presuming are Jim's clothes!' She laughed, her eyes examining Flick's oversized attire.

She looked down at the sleeve ends where her hands would normally be. 'Oh, yes of course! And you are...'

'I'm Miranda. Jim called to see me earlier to borrow some art supplies for you.'

'Oh, yes. Thank you so much. You've been so kind. Too kind to a stranger such as me.'

Miranda waved a gloved hand. 'Oh no, no, any friend of Jim's is a friend of mine. You'll find that with everyone here. He's very well thought of.' She smiled. 'We all just wish he'd find himself a wee lady and settle down, have bairns, you know?' She winked, clearly unaware of her status as Jim's ex-wife. 'Aye, well, best be off, Jess needs her walk and I need to get back to my painting.' She turned away but stopped. 'Come over for coffee and a wee chat whenever you like. Jim will direct you. It'd be good to talk arty things with a fellow artist.' She smiled and carried on.

'I will... thank you.'

Flick made her way back to the Coffee Shack. She could see Jim in the distance standing outside chatting to one of the villagers. Since her arrival, she had noticed that he looked so much more relaxed than he had done during the last year of their marriage. He looked younger and more bohemian. Before, he was in the realms of designer stubble but now he sported a neatly trimmed full beard. His hair was still thick and in shoulder-length, shaggy layers, but it was smattered with tiny flecks of grey now.

He looked so comfortable in his chunky jumpers and scruffy jeans. He wore them well. He had always been a very attractive man and the attraction was still there, unfortunately. He had filled out, too, but she had noticed that it was all muscle when he had removed his jumper the day before and exposed a little of his torso, causing her mouth to dry and her heart to skip.

He looked up and waved.

* * *

Jim watched Flick tramping towards him in her oversized clothing. 'Nice stroll?' he asked as his neighbour walked away complete with a bag of kindling.

'Yes, very bracing. Had to dodge a few snowballs.' She laughed. There was the smile he remembered from years ago, and that almost musical, infectious laugh. Her features had relaxed. She pursed her lips for a moment as if unsure of something. 'Were you planning anything for dinner? If not, I thought maybe I could treat you to a nice meal at the hotel?'

He thought about it for a second. What harm could it do? They were adults, admittedly with a complicated history, but nevertheless they were past all that, weren't they?

'Oh, erm. Aye... aye okay. That'd be nice. They have a good menu. I don't eat there often. No point with it just being me.' He shrugged. 'Anyway, I'll be home in around an hour, so why don't you go get yourself showered and ready. You may still have to wear my Wellies. Snow's quite deep... and you look so fetching.' He chuckled. He couldn't help but tease.

Flick's cheeks coloured pink. 'Hey, cheeky!' She hit him playfully. 'I'll go and get sorted and see you soon.' Jasper dutifully followed her next door to the cottage.

* * *

Thankfully, when they arrived at the Shieldaig Hotel, the fire was already roaring, giving a cosy, amber glow to the bar area. They hungrily perused the extensive menu in silence and once their food was ordered, Jim brought a bottle of Pinot Noir over from the bar.

A kind of shyness fell on the pair as they sat together in romantic surroundings but without the romantic attachment.

Flick sighed, suddenly, as they sipped their wine. 'Where did it all go wrong, Jim?'

Jim was perplexed at her choice of conversational topic. 'You want to talk about that now?'

She shrugged. 'It's on my mind I suppose.'

Jim pondered a moment before speaking. 'I didn't fit into your world.' He shook his head as a twinge of sadness tugged at his heart. 'And you wanted to find someone who did. I wanted you to be happy, so I let you go.' Jim gave his harsh but real verdict in a nutshell.

She visibly cringed at his matter-of-fact admission. 'So, you take no responsibility?' she asked, a line of frustration etched between her brows.

He rolled his eyes and then locked them on her. 'Aye, well, I suppose I was to blame for the fact that I didn't fit into your world. But I loved you, Felicity. More than anything. It just... wasn't enough for you.' He took a gulp of his wine, as the fire's radiating heat became a little too much.

She twisted her glass between her fingers. 'You had so many possibilities ahead of you though, Jim. You graduated with a First from Oxford, for goodness' sake. Why didn't you do something with it? Where was your ambition?' She shook her head. 'I got so frustrated by your lack of ambition.'

He clenched his jaw. 'Felicity, you seem to forget that you had enough ambition for both of us. Wasn't it enough that I supported everything you did? I never missed a function. I even wore suits!' He laughed incredulously. 'All I wanted was to love you and have you love me enough. I guess it wasn't meant to be, eh? Like you said back then.'

She tilted her head, and her frustrated expression was replaced by regret. 'I did love you. I was crazy about you. But...' She moved her gaze to the tablecloth. 'I think I listened to my mum too much.'

You got that right, sweetheart. 'Your mum? Aye, she wasn't my biggest fan, eh? And still isn't by all accounts.'

Flick scoffed. 'Yeah, well, she's a total fraud.'

'What do you mean by that?' Jim was intrigued by the biting statement.

She inhaled deeply through her nose as if to summon courage. 'Something I found out at the will reading. Something she had kept from me all these years.'

Jim leaned forward unable to hide his interest. 'Which was…?'

'Her name. The stupid woman changed her name just to impress.'

Jim placed his elbows on the table. 'Eh? Sorry, I don't follow?' But before she could go into any detail their food arrived.

Flick smiled at the waitress. 'Oh, lovely. Smells delicious and I'm famished.'

'Enjoy.' The young woman smiled back. 'Hi Jim, how's Jasper?'

'Hi Sally, oh, he's fine. He's missing you. Be sure to pop round and see him soon, eh?'

The young woman blushed and tucked a stray strand of mousy-brown hair behind her ear. 'Oh, I will. Been a bit busy lately with my studies but I'll pop round,' she told him and then left them to their meal.

'Gosh, do you know everyone?' Flick asked.

He stabbed a piece of steak and held it to his mouth, with a raise of his eyebrows he said, 'It appears so.'

Once they finished their meal they headed back out into the freezing cold evening, to the cottage. Flick bent to supposedly fiddle with her boot but instead grabbed a handful of snow and threw it straight at Jim's head. It hit with a thud and splattered into his hair.

He laughed, bending to seek his own ammunition. 'Whoa! You little swine!'

She dodged and caught him square on the back of the head with her second snowball.

Picking up a huge handful of snow he ran towards her. 'Right, that's it! This is war!'

She tried to run away but slipped and landed on her bottom in the snow, thanks to the ridiculously large Wellington boots she was wearing. When Jim's ice-cold missile struck, she let out a squeal as snow slid down her back under her oversized coat and stuck to her hair.

Acting far too sure of himself he began to guffaw but slipped too, landing half on top of her, and they both laughed hysterically, gasping for air as they lay in the snow-covered street.

They made eye contact and suddenly their position wasn't so funny. She searched his eyes as he breathed out puffs of breath, which clouded as the warm hit the cold.

Slowly his smile faded. He closed his eyes tight and leaned closer. Flick held her breath, feeling sure he was going to kiss her.

But instead, he rested his forehead on hers and sighed, clenching his jaw. 'Come on. Let's get in where it's warm,' he whispered.

He clambered to a standing position and held out his hand to pull her up. Feeling surprisingly disappointed, she took his hand and was immediately pulled to her feet. They brushed the snow from their clothes and made their way inside, both dashing upstairs into separate bedrooms to change, and emerging at the same time in their dry clothing.

'I'll open another bottle of wine, eh?' Jim said as he headed towards the stairs.

She followed him down and curled up in the old armchair beside the fireplace. 'Jim... this chair is the same as that scratty old thing Charles had in The Book Depository,' she called through to the kitchen.

'Aye… that's because it is the scratty old thing from The Book Depository.' He smiled as he walked back into the room. 'It was my parting gift from Charles. He said it wouldn't look right without me sitting on it.' He chuckled.

She felt a lump lodge in her throat and bit her lip to abate the threatening tears. 'Awww, that's so sweet.'

Jim poured them both a glass of wine and sat on the floor in front of the blazing fire. Jasper came and spread himself across his legs.

'Earlier, you mentioned something about your mum but didn't finish telling me. Do you not want to talk about that any more?' he asked tentatively, afraid that perhaps she had changed the subject deliberately.

'Hmm. She drives me to distraction, Jim. Honestly, I let her influence me far too much when I was younger.'

He cringed. 'I'm sorry but I have to agree with you there. I hope you don't mind me saying this, but she really was impressed by status and *things*… possessions. Your dad was completely different. So accepting. To be honest, I often wondered how they stayed together so long.' Jim let the words fall from his mouth and then regretted them. 'Shit, Felicity, I'm sorry I shouldn't have—'

Her face became flushed with anger. 'Shouldn't have what, Jim?' She laughed bitterly. 'Shouldn't have spoken the truth?'

He was all ears now. 'What did she do to you that's so bad?' Clearly Penelope had irked her daughter in some way, and badly it would seem.

'Well, she always used to tell me that I could do better… you know, when you and I…' She swallowed and held up her hand. 'Jim, I didn't agree with her.'

He raised his eyebrows. 'Hmm. Not at first, eh?'

'That's just it. She used to go on and on about social standing and making something of myself. She's made it her life's work to ensure that I get the very best. Including boyfriends. She turned her nose up at anyone who wasn't Oxbridge educated or about to be Oxbridge educated. She used to instil in me how important it was to be seen in the right places, to wear the right clothes, to have the right car, the right job. She even insisted I keep my own name when you and I married.'

Jim shook his head. 'I knew she was behind that.'

She laughed without humour reflecting in her eyes. 'Well, it turns out that Mrs Posh-Knickers lied all along about her own upbringing! She always told me that my grandparents were wealthy but died in mysterious circumstances, and that's why she never received her vast inheritance.'

He took a sip of his wine. 'Aye, that's what you told me.'

'Well, on the day of Dad's will reading it became very clear that Penelope...' She made inverted commas in the air. 'Wasn't all that she seemed.'

Jim scrunched his face. 'I... I don't really get what you're—'

'Janet.'

He held out his hands in utter confusion. 'Felicity, what are you talking about? Who is Janet?'

Her face flushed and her chest heaved. 'Janet is my mother, Jim!' She lifted her glass with shaking hands and took a large glug of the red liquid. 'She lied all along. About... *everything*!'

He rubbed his forehead. 'You're going to have to explain. I'm sorry, I'm just confused.'

'Not half as confused as I was. Right, where do I start? Probably the beginning, eh? Okay, so she was born in the East End of London to a very poor family. She was christened Janet Mason. When she was seventeen, she went on a job interview in the centre of London at a hotel and got the job as a receptionist. On accepting the job, she began telling people that her name was Penelope Brandon. She met Dad at the hotel when he was a guest. She lied to him, too.' Flick shook her head as she spoke the incredulous truth.

'She told Dad, and me for that matter, that cock and bull story about my grandparents when it turns out they both died quite young and left her nothing because they *had* nothing. There were no suspicious circumstances at all. She had basically disowned them through shame. She was ashamed of her own parents because they were poor, Jim. How sad is that? How cruel? Dad never met her parents. I have no idea how she managed to pull off the story for so long about being so wealthy.'

Jim gaped in shock. 'How the hell did you find all this out?' He couldn't quite take it all in.

'The solicitor, who was a very good friend of Dad's, had found it out when he was doing the paperwork for the will. He called her Janet at the reading and the colour drained from her face. Of course, I wondered what the heck was going on so afterwards I asked for an explanation. She broke down and told me everything. She cried and kept insisting she was sorry. But then she acted as if everything was wonderful, and she felt better for getting it off her chest. Bloody great!' Flick snorted derisively.

'Off her chest and onto my mind. Honestly, Jim I was so, so angry. I feel like I don't know my own mother. She lied to me all those years and then tried to make *me* into *her*. And it nearly worked. Thanks to her I lost my marriage... and... my...' She covered her face with her hands and her shoulders began to shudder as pent-up anger and frustration connected to the ridiculous situation began to overflow. 'You weren't just my husband, Jim... You were my best friend.'

Jasper jumped up as Jim moved forward to comfort her. He held her wrists, pulled her hands away from her face and locked onto her desolate gaze. She threw her arms around his neck and he cradled her, allowing her to cry. Her anguish was palpable as she shook with violent sobs that racked her body and he stroked her hair.

Eventually, when she had calmed, he held her face in his hands and wiped away her tears with his thumbs. 'Hey, you've been through such a lot lately. I'm angry with her, too. I'm angry that she put us in this situation. It was a horrible thing to do. No mother should do such a thing. But she's still your mother and I guess deep down she thought she was doing the right thing. Don't let yourself get bitter and twisted about this, Flick, eh? It's not worth the stress. Just rise above it and move on. We both need to do that.'

'Jim?'

'Yeah?'

'You called me Flick.'

He closed his eyes for a second. 'Oh, sorry, I mean *Felicity*.'

She managed a small smile. 'No, I liked being Flick. Hearing you call me that takes me back. You know, to when you and I were actually okay.'

He let out a deep sigh. 'Aye, that's a long while ago, eh? But that's just it, Flick. We can't go backwards, only forwards.'

'Oh, dammit. I've just remembered. I have something for you. The whole reason I'm here.' She jumped up from her chair and hurried upstairs, returning soon after with a large, brown, padded envelope.

Jim looked on in bemusement. 'What the heck is that?'

She sat back in the chair. 'It's for you. It's from Dad. It was in the will that I bring it to you... personally.' She sniffed.

He took the package. 'What is it?' Whatever it was. it was sealed very well.

In a wavering voice, she told him, 'It's an incomplete manuscript. The last one he was working on before he passed away. He wanted you to have it. The solicitor said Dad wanted it to be delivered by hand.'

Jim held the precious envelope with both hands. 'That's… really sweet. I have a little piece of him right here now. That's…' He stared at it, emotions washing over him and the sting of tears becoming apparent in his eyes. 'I'll treasure it… always.'

Overcome with mixed emotions and unwilling to set them free in front of his ex-wife, Jim made his excuses and went to bed.

The manuscript lay unopened at Jim's bedside. He was touched by the gesture and would cherish this gift. He would keep it sealed until he felt better equipped to read it. There were too many things going on right now. He drifted into a fitful, dream-filled sleep.

14

Jim opened his eyes and looked to his right. Flick was stroking his bare chest delicately with one finger and watching him intently. When their eyes connected, she pulled herself up to him and kissed him gently on the lips.

'Hey, sleepyhead... I've been waiting for you to wake up.'

Confused, Jim tried to speak but she stopped him with a much deeper kiss. It felt good to be with her again, like this. The room was glowing, bathed in the bright, early morning sunlight.

Flick slipped off her white cotton nightie and moved to straddle his torso. She was so beautiful in this light...

'Jim... Jim... Jim!'

His eyes snapped open, and he sat bolt upright. It had been a dream. *Dammit!* He had let her get inside his head. *Not good. Not good at all.*

Flick spoke through his closed door. 'Jim, are you okay? You were moaning in your sleep and I was worried.'

'Erm... yeah... yeah, I'm fine thanks... just a nightmare!' *Huh, I got that damned right.*

'Oh... okay. It's nine o'clock. I'm making coffee. The sun's out.'

He cleared his throat and rubbed his hands roughly over his face. 'Aye, thanks. I'll be down in a wee while,' he replied.

He took a cold shower and tried his best to rid himself of the images from his dream. When he was done, he dried and dressed slowly, delaying the inevitable face to face meeting with the subject of his fantasy, and eventually made his way downstairs.

Flick was by the window. *Oh great.* The sight of her made things worse. She was standing in front of her easel with his dungarees loosely falling off one shoulder, and a pale-pink, cropped vest top underneath. It was the type she used to wear for working out, and he could see the curve of her waist. *Oh god*, he moaned inwardly. He had always loved that part of her body, that feminine curve. She already had paint on her cheek.

He had to leave the room.

He clenched his jaw and made his excuses. 'I'm just getting my coffee,' he called, his voice breaking as he spoke. He felt like a silly teenager lusting after his art teacher or something equally as ridiculous. *C'mon man, pull yourself together! She's your ex-wife, remember? EX!*

When he had gathered himself, he went back to the lounge to peer over her shoulder and look at the painting.

'Wow, that's really beautiful, Felicity,' he said, genuinely impressed at the familiar looking scene on the canvas. He had called her Felicity again and it felt so damn formal. But she had made it that way and anyway it was probably best to keep the familiarity at bay.

'Do you think so? It's the same scene I painted that time at Rory's... you know, the one he destroyed?'

'Oh right. It looks...' He shook his head, 'really familiar.'

She smiled as she stood back and tilted her head, keeping her eyes on the canvas. 'No. It's an imaginary place. I've had it in my head for a long while and I felt I needed to paint it. I wish it were real. I'd love to climb into the view.'

He stared at it for a while, trying to figure out why the scene on the canvas pulled at him so. 'I'm not opening up today, so I thought I would take Jasper for a walk. Leave you to your painting,'

She turned to face him and gave a breath-taking smile. 'Okay, that's fine. I really want to get it done this time. I don't think it'll take me long now I've made a start. I'm so passionate about it. It won't leave my head until I get it done.'

He raised his hand up with the intention of wiping away the paint splodge from her cheek but changed his mind. 'You've got some paint...' He gestured to her face.

She laughed and wiped at her cheek. 'Oh... that's always happening. I get a bit carried away.'

In that precise moment, Jim's heart ached. She looked more beautiful when she was painting than at any other time. Her eyes sparkled with life and vitality and her face glowed. She really was exquisite. He'd always thought so. They shared a glance for a few moments, but Jim broke the spell by turning away.

'I'll... ahem... be off now. Leave you in peace.'

Flick's heart sank. She saw something in his eyes but couldn't decipher it. She wanted more than anything to make amends for how she had treated him. She would love to be his friend again. But would he let her?

As he walked along the edge of the loch, Jim noticed that the snow was beginning to turn to slush. The day felt warmer, and this would all mean the end of Flick's little sojourn to Shieldaig. He felt a pang of sadness but knew that it was for the best really. It had to end sometime. He had to return to normality. He didn't have to like it, but he knew it was going to happen.

He trudged through the snow for hours and was no longer feeling the cold. There were a few villagers out and about and he had a couple of chats along the way which, together with the stunning surroundings, reiterated the fact he already knew – that he was meant to be in Shieldaig. As he walked back to the cottage, he saw a snow plough in the distance, and the children were out in force waving at the welcome visitor, who was about to create a lifeline to the world beyond their little village. This would mean schools would re-open and he would be able to receive stock deliveries for the Coffee Shack once again.

When he returned home, he found Flick even more bathed in paint than she had been when he'd left. The fact amused him. He was amazed at how she had managed to cover herself in splodges but had not allowed a single drop to fall on the carpet or furniture. There was something a little too comfortable about her being here and it irked him to think so.

'You're back. Did you have a nice walk?' She didn't look up from the canvas.

'Aye, very fresh. Fancy a coffee?' he asked as he removed his cold outdoor garments and Jasper resumed his usual place on the rug in front of the fireplace.

'Oooh, yes please! I'm gasping. I haven't stopped since you left. It's coming along nicely,' she called.

Jim came back through whilst the kettle was heating. And he gasped when he saw the portrayal of the stunning vista on the canvas before him.

'Wow, Felicity... it's... it's stunning... truly beautiful.' Her paintings always took his breath away and made him feel quite emotional. This occasion was no different. He swallowed the lump in his throat and walked quickly back to the kitchen.

As he leaned on the countertop, he recalled the first time he had seen one of her completed pieces...

* * *

Thursday evening had come around quickly.

Thursday was their night, a night when Flick and Jim spent some time alone together. They had only been an official couple for a few weeks, and everything was still in its rosy glow of lust, passion and new love. Jim had been to collect fish and chips from the van that stopped just off campus and it smelled delicious. He tapped gently on Flick's door.

'Hi, you.' She smiled at him as he leaned in for a sensuous, lingering kiss. He brushed her hair back from her face and chuckled at the stunning vision before him. 'What?!' She feigned hurt.

'You do make me smile. You've paint on your nose, chin and forehead. In fact, you even have it in your hair.' He kissed her again.

'Oh, it always happens.' She smiled. 'I get quite carried away! Anyway, come and see.' She pulled him by the arm and led him to the easel over by the small window. 'Ta daaaaaa.' She waved jazz hands, proud of the painting before her.

Jim stood open-mouthed as his gaze strolled over the canvas. The painting was of a man and woman, not unlike themselves, kissing by a tall leafless tree in a wintery-looking meadow. Although the subject matter could've been construed as somewhat cheesy and clichéd, the brushwork was stunning and the sentiment, much to Jim's surprise, brought a lump to his throat.

'It's beautiful, Flick. The people look familiar,' he said, stepping close behind her and kissing her neck.

She shivered. 'You think so? Can't think why,' she purred, slipping her arms up behind her and around his neck. 'The scene is one I saw through the window on the train when we went to London last weekend but the people...' She turned and kissed him again.

Suddenly, he nipped her bottom playfully, making her squeal. 'C'mon, I'm starving, and I mean for food for once!' He laughed as he handed her the fish and chips, wrapped in paper, their mouth-watering, salty and vinegary aroma wafting through the small space.

Shaking himself back to the present again, Jim poured boiling water on the instant coffee granules in the mugs for himself and his ex-wife, and he pondered awhile on the painting of the couple by the tree in the meadow. He had no idea what happened to it. He didn't have it. He'd be intrigued to find out where it was now. Or maybe that would do him no good whatsoever.

15

The following day brought bright blue skies and sunshine. It wasn't exactly tropical, but it was enough to almost complete the thawing process. Flick's painting was just about complete, and Jim knew that she would be leaving soon. Considering that fact produced mixed emotions all over again. On the one hand, he could resume the status quo that existed prior to this intrusion; on the other, he *would* resume the status quo that existed prior to this intrusion. The direction of his thoughts concerned him.

He needed her gone.

When he had showered, and made his way downstairs, she was standing in front of her easel making some additions to her canvas.

Her eyes lit up when she saw him. 'Hey... sleepyhead! I've been waiting for you to wake up.' Her words produced a flashback to his vivid dream from a couple of nights before and he gulped, lost in his thoughts for what felt like an age, as he pictured her naked in bed. He shivered and shook his head as if shaking away a snowfall. She frowned. 'You look like you've seen a ghost.'

He cleared his throat. 'Erm, no. Sorry, just waking up, I

suppose,' he stuttered as he tried to shrug her comments off. *A ghost? No. But a vision of the past, most definitely.*

She chatted as if all was normal, as if she had just somehow slipped back into his life. 'I'll make coffee, if you like? Then I thought maybe we could take Jasper for a walk. I'll cook tomorrow night, but I thought maybe we could eat at the pub again tonight?'

The snow on the roads had all but gone meaning access to – and therefore exit from – the village was clear. What was she playing at? He still couldn't find it in his ruptured heart to trust her.

'It's okay, I'll cook tonight,' was his feeble response. The pub setting had been too romantic. Why couldn't he just ask her to leave? After all, she did have a life and a job to go home to.

They sat drinking coffee and staring at the scene on the canvas as if it was an actual vista and they were sharing it on top of a hill somewhere. Myriad thoughts raced through his mind and he struggled to organise them rationally into any semblance of normality. He felt it best, therefore, to remain taciturn.

He could see that she kept glancing sideways in his direction. She, too, appeared to be feeling the same awkwardness. She opened her mouth to speak but as she did the phone rang. Jim jumped up to answer it. *How does the phrase go? Saved by the bell?*

'Hello?' He scrunched his face at a voice yelling down the line. It was so loud the whole of Shieldaig could probably hear it!

'It's Penelope. Have you got my Felicity there? I demand to speak to her. What have you done with her? You've kidnapped her, haven't you? You beastly man!'

'Whoa... whoa! I've done no such thing! Yes, she is here, but she chose to come here. She is an adult, you know.'

'She wouldn't come there of her own volition. Not without telling me first!'

'Oh, just shut up, will you? I'll put her on.' He thrust the receiver at Flick who, with a bemused expression, took it.

* * *

'Hello?'

'Felicity? Darling! I've been so, so worried. Why on earth are you *there* with *him*?' Her mother sounded almost hysterical.

'Mum, stop being so melodramatic. I came here to do what I should have done before Dad's funeral.'

'You shouldn't be there! You know what will happen. He'll brainwash you into going back to him!' Penelope's hysteria increased and so did Flick's annoyance.

'You're being ridiculous. I know you're upset but this was something I had to do. It was in Dad's will. I didn't tell you because I knew how you'd react.' She could feel the crease between her eyes deepen. 'And anyway, how did you get this number?'

'I had to practically beg Charles from that smelly old bookshop to give it to me!'

'Oh, great. Poor Charles.' She covered the receiver and whispered to Jim, 'You had better call Charles. Mum's been harassing him, I'm afraid. Sorry.'

Jim shook his head and his nostrils flared. No wonder really, poor Charles didn't need this.

Flick continued to listen to her mother ranting about the huge mistake she had apparently made in travelling to Scotland where there is no mobile signal, and how Jim would no doubt twist things to try and make her stay. On several occasions, she held the receiver away from her ear as the volume became too intense.

Eventually, Flick's temper got the better of her. 'Mother! Just stop! You of all people cannot talk about being manipulative and twisting things! You wrote the book on deceit. And for your information I have had my mobile switched off because I knew you'd be hounding me once you found out. Oh, and Jim and I are not getting back together. Not that it would be anything to do with you if we were. I was snowed in here. The snow is melting now, and I'll only be here a couple more days. Satisfied? Actually, quite frankly, I don't care whether you are, or you aren't. This is my life! Do you hear me? Mine! I intend to live it by my rules from now on! Goodbye.' She pressed the hang up button and threw the phone onto the sofa with such a force that it broke.

With her chest heaving, she covered her mouth. 'Oh, shit!' Her eyes widened in horror. Jim stared at his broken handset. 'I'm so sorry, Jim!'

* * *

Jim shook his head and left the room, followed closely by his shadow, Jasper. He jogged upstairs to use the handset in his room to contact Charles, but the landline rang again before he could dial.

'Ignore it!' Flick called to him, 'It could be her again!'

He ignored her and answered. Before he could say hello, a stressed and concerned voice wavered down the line. 'Oh, Jim, old boy, are you okay? I tried to call earlier but it was bloody engaged for ages! And I can't find your mobile number anywhere.'

Jim sighed. 'It's okay. I'm okay.'

'Did Dragon Lady call? She called here, and when I wouldn't give her your number, she bloody turned up in the bloody shop and made a right old bloody scene in front of customers! I was bloody horrified, old chap.'

Jim rubbed his eyes as he shook his head. 'Shit, I'm so sorry you had to go through that, Charles. It was unfair of her to involve you.'

'No, no. It's fine. Is Felicity up there with you? Or has she got it wrong?'

Jim sat on his bed with his back to the door. He rested his elbow on his knee and his head on his hand. 'Aye, Charles. She's here but it won't be for much longer though. I can't handle this any more. I had no memories of her here and that was so good for me, but now... Her being here is too... too... *hard*, you know?'

* * *

Flick's heart sank as she heard Jim's words. She had climbed the stairs to see who was calling and to rescue Jim from her mother if necessary.

He clearly wanted her gone. She understood why but his words stung like shards of glass in her chest. She made her way back downstairs and sank into the sofa. Leaning forward, she placed her head on her folded arms and let tears trickle, unfettered, down her face. She felt lost, desolate almost. This was not how things should have gone.

He eventually came downstairs so she wiped her eyes and gave him a sad smile as he stood looking down at her where she sat.

'Look, I think I'll gather up my things and leave. The snow has pretty much gone... and...'

He nodded. 'Aye... the road was clear of snow yesterday. You could've gone then.' His tone was harsh.

It felt like the first time she'd left him. Only this time she was reluctant. Her heart twinged in her chest, a real physical pain that made her reach up and rub the area.

Jim winced as if he realised he had been too hard on her. 'Look, you may as well stay until tomorrow, eh? We'll have that meal and you can get an early start in the morning.'

Jasper approached the pair reticently and Jim crouched down to fuss him.

Flick's eyes began to sting once again with the threat of more tears. She desperately wanted to stay awhile longer, but couldn't express this to Jim, who had clearly concluded that she had outstayed her welcome.

If only she could stay a couple more days... maybe then she could get him to forgive her? But how? She had no clue when she thought about it. The scars ran far too deep. She rued the day that she had ever listened to her mother. Jim had been her best friend for so long and she had lost that. Whenever anything good had happened in recent years, Jim had been the first person she'd thought about calling. Thought about, but never actually plucked up the courage.

She stood, thinking it best to say something. 'Jim... I...' Her lip quivered as she searched for the words that might go some way to express how she felt. But the words failed her.

She shook her head and Jim left the room.

16

Flick retreated to the guest room and lay on the white-framed double bed glancing around her. She decided that if she lived here – which wouldn't be happening – she wouldn't change a thing about this room with its apple-green bedding and driftwood picture frames. It saddened her that she felt so at ease... at home even. She switched on her mobile and sure enough there were a gazillion voicemails from her mother. Each more frantic than the last. She deleted them all and the text messages begging her to call then she dialled Polly's number.

'Hey, you. Your mum's been ringing me. I lied and told her I had no clue where you were. I hope that was the right thing to do.'

'Hi Pol. Thanks for that. I'm sorry to put you in that position.'

'It's okay. How are things going? How did Jim take the news about Edgar?'

Flick sighed. 'Not great. It really hurt him that he wasn't able to say goodbye.' Her chin trembled as she spoke. 'I hate myself Polly. Why didn't I just defy my mother? What right did she have to keep Jim away? I feel so awful. He's been pleasant and we've reminisced a little but... I've hurt him so much.'

'Oh, sweetie, I'm so sorry. Maybe going up there wasn't the right thing. I know your dad insisted upon it but he's not here to know, is he? You have to look after yourself and your heart.'

'I know. I just held on, you know? Anyway, I've only myself to blame. The snow is almost gone so I'll be heading home soon. I probably won't ring again. Not much point when there's nothing to tell.'

'Okay, honey. Take care and drive carefully. Love you.'

'Love you too. Bye.'

Once her call had ended Flick laid back and closed her eyes.

When things had settled down, there was a knock on the door.

'Yes?' she called.

'I'm taking Jasper out again. Do you maybe, erm, want to come?' Jim replied through the closed door.

'Oh, no. No, it's okay,' she croaked and cleared her throat. 'I... I don't want to get in your way any more than I have, Jim.'

There was a light thud as if he had rested his head on the door. 'Look, I want you to come. I have something to show you,' he insisted.

She sat upright, a smile pulling at her lips for the first time since the incident earlier. 'Oh! Okay. Give me five minutes.'

He went quiet and she figured he had left her to get ready.

She pulled on her jeans and sweater, then the socks that she had borrowed, and stifled a giggle at how ridiculous her size four feet looked in something belonging to a size ten. She grabbed her mobile and stuffed it in her jeans pocket and ran her fingers roughly through her unruly hair.

* * *

The late afternoon sun was low and cast that familiar amber glow over the picturesque little village. Jim and Jasper headed up the lane leading away from their street and Flick followed.

The snow had been melting and mixing with the mud causing a dirty grey slush to form. The gentle breeze was bringing the blood to the surface of Flick's cheeks and nose, making her look flushed. Her hands remained in the pockets of her oversized, thick, fleece-lined coat and every so often, Jasper stopped and glanced back as if to check on her, wagging his tail almost in encouragement as they trudged the muddy, sloping ascent. *Soft old thing*, Jim thought.

'Jim... where... are... we... going?' she panted.

'We're nearly there. I just thought it was important to show you while the light's good.' He hadn't really answered her question.

Eventually he stopped walking. 'Look.' He gestured out before him when she reached his side.

She inhaled sharply as she looked out. 'Jim! It's... it's my painting!' Her hands covered her mouth, and her eyes were wide like saucers as she looked over the valley below them. Snow still covered most of the sheltered areas, but the trees were positioned almost identically to her supposed imaginary view.

'Isn't it breath-taking?' Jim turned to her. His heart pounded and his head was filled with a million different emotions all vying for the surface.

'Oh, Jim. It's... Wow.' Her words came out in a breathy whisper.

They stood side by side, looking down to where the trees lined a little loch. The mountains in the distance created the perfect backdrop to the vista, their rocky surface still dusted in a sparkling white, frosty layer.

Jim nodded and smiled and without turning to face Flick he said, 'I know how it happened now... Many years ago, when we were packing to leave uni, you and I went through my old childhood photos. I came here with my mum, dad and Euan on holiday when I was about eight. My dad took the photo and I always treasured it. I'd completely forgotten about it and always wondered why I was so drawn to this place. I haven't looked through those photos since you and I did all those years ago. I can't believe it stuck with you, too, but clearly it did. You painted it, Flick.' He paused to glance at her.

Tears glistened in her eyes as she listened, and realisation appeared to dawn on her. There was something distinctly magical about the place, otherworldly even.

Jim took a lungful of the crisp, wintery air. 'I come up here in the good weather usually. Flask of coffee, blanket, and a good book. I read for a wee while and then sit and drink my coffee, just staring at the view. I haven't been up for a while thanks to weather but... It's the closest thing to paradise I can think of.'

He turned his head slightly and smiled warmly. 'When I saw your painting, I couldn't figure it out, but then I came up here with Jasper and I realised. It's... it's like you'd been here before. But then again you have, in a way. We shared the memory back at university and you couldn't get the place out of your mind, you said so. We'd both just forgotten why that was.'

He turned now to look at her fully and she turned to face him with anticipation in her wide eyes as if she was wondering what would happen next. He stepped towards her but then something flashed through his mind. He couldn't do this. Not again. His heart wouldn't take it. He turned away, his jaw clenching, as he tried to get a handle on his emotions.

At that moment, Flick's mobile phone rang. 'Oh, good grief, who would have thought I'd get a signal up here?' she mumbled. 'I only switched it on to delete the messages from Mum.' She looked blankly at the handset in her hand. 'I don't even know why I brought it out with me to be honest. I've enjoyed the peace and quiet.'

Jim gestured towards the buzzing handset. 'Aren't you going to answer it? It might be important.' He knew his voice was flat. He'd shut down again and was back to the emotionless state that he'd managed to maintain for most of the past few days.

Self-preservation.

'Oh, right. Yes, I suppose I should.' She lifted the handset to her ear. 'H-hello? Felicity Johnston-Hart speaking.' She stepped a few feet away, but Jim inadvertently listened to the one-sided conversation.

'Oh, hi Franco. Yes, I'm feeling much better, thank you. Really? Oh, my. That's incredible! I can't quite believe it. It's just so sudden... I know... yes, an amazing opportunity. Oh, yes most definitely... I see... yes... oh, right. So, when do you need to know by? Gosh... so soon? Okay, leave it with me. Yes, I'll be home in the next day or so, weather permitting... Thanks Franco... see you soon, bye.' She hung up and looked over to Jim. The colour flushing her cheeks only moments before had paled significantly.

'Are you okay?' Jim asked, keeping his face blank, an expression-less mask.

She frowned. 'Yes. Yes, fine. Just got some thinking to do, I suppose.' She stared off into the distance once again.

Jim was intrigued now. 'Oh? How come?'

'I've been offered a job in Chicago. Starting in a month.'

His heart sank. 'Chicago? Wow, that sounds like a fantastic opportunity.' He tried to sound bright, breezy, and positive but failed miserably.

'Yes. Yes, it's fantastic. But... I have just two days to think about it.' She turned to Jim again. 'It's not long, eh?'

He could tell her smile was forced, and he could see pain in her eyes. In fact, the enthusiasm she should have been feeling just didn't manifest itself in her expression.

He cleared his throat. 'No, no it's not long at all really. But you've always dreamed of working in Chicago. Right back when you first joined the art world it was always a dream of yours. What is there to consider?' He knew what he wanted the answer to be, but the answer never came. She just stared blankly at the view.

After a few silent moments, he touched her arm. 'We should get back and eat. You've an early start in the morning, eh?'

She nodded. 'Yes, we better had.'

They walked slowly back towards home. Jasper covered twice the distance, running away and then back to them again, his tail wagging frantically.

* * *

Back at the house, Flick went to the spare room to pack the rest of her belongings, leaving Jim to concoct something that smelled delicious in the kitchen. When she was finished, she wandered down and leaned against the doorframe. 'Mmm, something smells good,' she said as she watched him working.

He smiled back over his shoulder. 'Aye, I made us a nice beef stew with a hint of red wine. It'll be ready in around an hour.' He looked more relaxed now. His dark hair was deliciously shaggy, and he wore his favourite Pearl Jam T-shirt with his tattered old black jeans that had almost faded to grey. His feet were bare. She watched his sculpted arm muscles as he stirred and chopped.

He hadn't lost his draw for her. She still found him so very attractive. It was almost an invisible pull that had only faded temporarily with distance but was back with a vengeance in the close confines of the cottage. She allowed herself to hope that when she left it would fade again.

But deep down she knew that wouldn't be likely to happen.

* * *

The table was set, and the wine bottle stood in the middle, a little of its contents sacrificed to the stew. Just as Jim put the plates on the table, the lights went out.

Flick jumped. 'What's happening?' Her voice wavered, and if Jim wasn't mistaken, he'd have sworn she sounded scared.

He chuckled. 'Don't tell me you're still afraid of the dark, Felicity?'

'No, of course not,' she snapped. 'I just can't see what I'm eating, that's all.'

In spite of her protestations, Jim knew the truth and he had a huge grin on his face. It was wrong to find pleasure in her discomfort, but thankfully the lack of light meant she couldn't see.

'It's just a power cut. Hang on, I have some candles... here... somewhere.' He fumbled around in a drawer. 'Ahhh, gotcha.' There was a crackle and suddenly the faint glow of candles began to brighten the room. He placed tea lights on every surface. 'Thank goodness for IKEA, eh?' He chuckled again. 'It's funny, whenever I go to that place, I always seem to come away with a bag of tea lights or a few pillar candles. Now I know why.'

Flick giggled. 'Gosh, I thought I was the only one who did that.' She looked around the room. 'This is nice, actually, the candlelight,' she said as she sipped her wine.

'Aye. It's kind of... ah, never mind.' He shook his head.

'Kind of what?'

He shrugged. 'Och, I was going to say romantic but, I don't know, didn't feel like the right thing to say.'

Her responding smile was tinged with sadness. 'Ah.'

He decided to gloss over the awkward pause that hung in the air. 'Sooo, any more thoughts on the new job? How did it come about anyway?'

'Apparently, the guy who was heading up the new gallery in Chicago, a guy called Chester Withers, turns out he's had a kind of nervous breakdown by the sound of it, poor thing. It must be the stress. To be honest though, from what I'd heard, he'd been losing his touch. His last few acquisitions weren't up to standard, and Franco was unhappy but couldn't really do much. Anyway, when Chester got too bogged down with the stress he walked, or he was fired, I'm not that sure. Anyway, Franco wants me to take over as soon as possible.'

'And if you say no?' Jim chewed on a mouthful of beef as he spoke.

'Don't know. I suppose they'd advertise. Someone would snap it up. I'm very lucky to be offered the position.'

'Franco clearly has faith on your abilities,' Jim offered, positively.

'Oh, yes. There's no doubt about that.' She cringed at her response and added, 'Yikes, did that sound terribly conceited of me?' Her fork was halfway to her mouth.

He winked. 'Aye, but you're allowed.'

Flick reached over and hit his arm playfully. 'Hey!'

After a few more minutes of eating in silence, Flick pushed her plate away. 'That's it, I'm full to bursting!' She patted her tummy as she leaned back in her chair. 'It was delicious. Thank you.'

'Aye, it was rather good, wasn't it?'

Flick giggled. 'Now who's the conceited one?'

'Touché.' He laughed. 'Come on, let's go sit by the fire. I'll do the dishes in the morning when I can see.'

The pair retired to the lounge where the fire and the addition of a few tea lights created a cosy atmosphere. They sat in silence with the remainder of the bottle of wine in their glasses. The flames were quite hypnotic in their dance around the large lump of wood they surrounded.

Jim watched Flick as she focused on the fire. Her loose, knitted top had slipped down off her shoulder revealing her collarbone and the curve of her slender neck where a familiar pendant sat. He felt an aching deep inside and reached out, absentmindedly, to touch it.

She turned quickly to look at him evidently shocked by the tender contact. 'Jim?'

'You're still wearing my heart after all these years.' He gazed into her eyes. They looked like they were on fire as the flames were reflected back at him. He placed his glass on the table beside him and took her glass from her hand, placing it next to his. Without stopping to think things through, he took her hands in his and kissed them both. She inhaled sharply as his eyes stared deep into hers.

He leaned forward until their mouths were almost touching, anticipation building deep in the pit of his stomach. Her breathing had become a series of short inhales and exhales. He knew she felt it, too, whatever the hell it was.

Before he had time to consider the consequence of his actions, he kissed her. His hands slipped into her hair and she returned the kiss with as much fervour as it was being given, breaking away only to remove her top. He stifled the groan bubbling up from within and pulled her to him kissing her urgently this time and feeling her softness against his hard chest.

* * *

Flick's body ached for his touch as it had since she'd arrived at his door a few days ago. He didn't disappoint her. There was a hunger in his eyes that she had missed so, so much.

She tugged his T-shirt over his head and stroked her hands down his torso. His body was still the most sensual thing she had ever touched, smooth skin over taut muscles. Effortlessly, he laid her back and removed her remaining clothing until she was lying there before him, waiting, anticipating, hoping.

His own clothing was soon discarded. Neither said a word. Their eyes remained locked unless one or the other was closing them to revel in the ecstasy of their caresses.

Now do you see, Jim? Now do you get it?

Being with him again was so good. Amazing, in fact. She felt like she was home.

* * *

Jim collapsed onto her and she clung on to him. It had felt so good, so very right despite how wrong it had been. A sinking feeling set in and he knew immediately he had made a terrible mistake.

Such a fool. A lustful, idiotic fool.

This wasn't meant to happen. They were over a long time ago. His feelings didn't count. They never had. And he couldn't stand to go through losing her again. It had taken years to get over her and – who was he kidding – he never really had.

* * *

She held him as he lay there, his heart pounding against hers. She was desperate for him to realise how she felt, and she hoped that now she'd made it clear. This was where she wanted to be, in his arms. This was the only place she had ever been truly happy. If only she could voice it, say the words.

The fire had begun to die down as they lay there, still saying nothing. She stroked her fingers lazily up and down his spine as he remained motionless.

But he shifted and stood suddenly, clearly unable to make the eye contact that had been so direct only moments before.

He pointed awkwardly towards the stairs. 'I'm going to take a quick shower and then I... I think I'll turn in,' he announced.

She tried to ignore the uncomfortable knot churning within and pushed it away. They had just shared such intimacy for the first time in years. Of course, it would feel strange.

She forced a smile. 'Okay... I'll be up soon.'

When he had left the room, she gathered her items of clothing together and slipped them back on. Her muscles ached in the best imaginable way. She never thought that being with him again was remotely possible. And she had never expected that it would feel so right. She had hoped but never really expected it. But he had instigated it so there was hope. Wasn't there? It must have meant something, surely?

She finished off her wine and blew out the candles. The cottage wasn't a scary place, but she really didn't like the dark. Much the same as she really didn't like flying. The thought of taking the job in Chicago preyed on her mind for a few moments until she pushed that aside too.

She tiptoed upstairs, and finding that Jim was out of the shower, she climbed into it and was enveloped by a cocoon of steam. Once finished, she travelled along the short hallway, opened the door, and slipped into bed.

Beside Jim.

17

When Flick awoke, she was alone.

She heard Jim clattering about downstairs and guessed he needed a hearty breakfast after the night before. Her delectable memories of their shared night returned to her as she stretched. She refused to think there could possibly be any other reason for his absence.

Once she had washed and dressed in a comfy sweater and jeans, she jogged lightly down the stairs to where he stood at the sink finishing off the dishes from their wonderful evening together.

Slipping her arms around his waist she kissed his shoulder. 'Good morning, you,' she whispered, nuzzling into him. 'I see the power's back on.'

'Oh, good morning, Felicity,' he replied rather stoically. She felt him tense under her embrace and he stood frozen as if afraid to move. 'I've made some porridge. It's keeping warm on the cooker.' He pointed in the direction of the stove. 'There's syrup, or I have jam?'

'Oooh, yummy. Thank you.' She felt his eyes on her as she almost skipped over to the cooker and dished some of the gooey mixture into the bowl that he had left out for her. She drizzled golden syrup on top and sat down at the table. 'So, did you sleep well?' She grinned.

His face remained the usual impassive mask. 'Aye, I did, thanks. Erm, what time are you setting off?' he asked avoiding eye contact. He dried his hands and took a sip of the coffee in his mug.

She stopped eating and looked up at him. 'Oh... I... erm... Oh,' was all the response she could manage. She bit her lip as confusion and embarrassment washed over her whole body, followed by hurt. She felt her cheeks heat.

Jim rubbed his forehead. 'It's just that it's eight o'clock now, and I think you should get a good run at it, you know, so you don't get caught in traffic.' He appeared unsettled by her reaction.

A familiar stinging sensation needled at the back of her eyes. 'Yes, yes. I suppose I should get going.' She stood to leave the room, but her chest hurt and dizziness filled her head.

Jim's face was filled with concern. 'Are you okay? You've gone pale.'

She nodded vehemently. 'Yes, I feel a bit dizzy that's all. I think I stood up too quickly.'

Jim nodded his understanding. 'Well, finish your porridge. You can't leave on an empty stomach, eh?'

'Suddenly, I'm not that hungry any more.' She left the kitchen and returned upstairs to her room.

She sat on the edge of the bed. A mixture of anger, pain, and sadness knotted her insides. He didn't get it. But how could he? He was so bloody dense! Maybe it had meant nothing to him? Anger began to rise from deep within her as she grabbed her things together and then stomped downstairs, dragging her bag behind her.

Jim was standing in the living room, leaning on the mantle when she entered the room. He looked up and met her gaze. She couldn't read the emotion she saw there. Was it regret? Was he about to ask her to stay?

Staying as calm as possible, she kept eye contact. 'Right, I'll be going. You don't have to put up with me any longer,' she stated coldly.

His smile didn't arrive at his eyes. 'It was no bother really.'

She bent to cuddle Jasper; her heart ached at the thought of leaving him too. She hadn't realised how much she'd missed him until she'd seen him again; she stroked his soft fur.

'Bye, my lovely friend. Thank you for not hating me,' she whispered as tears blurred her vision.

She stood and turned to leave but stopped with her back to Jim. 'Just answer me one thing, Jim. Why did you make love to me last night?' Tears of anger combined with pain welled in her eyes again.

Jim was silent for a moment. 'You were leaving anyway, Felicity. You have a life to go back to. And... isn't... isn't that how you and I say goodbye?'

She turned to look at him. A crease of genuine confusion deepened on his face. She gasped as the realisation of what he had done hit her like a ton of bricks.

Revenge. Of course. It was revenge.

How cold and calculating could a man be?

'You bastard,' she whispered. 'I never thought you were the kind of person to keep score. You've been waiting for this opportunity, haven't you?' She was physically shaking and the threatening tears overflowed but she didn't care any more.

He held his hands up in surrender and stepped towards her. 'No... no, Flick. That's not—'

'Save your breath, James,' she interrupted, uninterested in any pathetic explanation he had to offer. 'That's how you want to play it? Fine. I'll be sure not to think of you when I'm in Chicago. I mean, why would I waste my time?' She opened the door and stormed out without looking back.

* * *

Jim stood frozen to the spot. He was completely baffled. What the hell just happened? He couldn't understand her reaction.

She didn't still *love* him... did she?

No!

She had left *him*. She only came here out of guilt and some obligation to her father! Last night was about history and pent-up feelings of lust. It was about goodbye, not love.

He snapped to his senses and was determined to stomp to the car and have this out with her.

She left me, for god's sake! How dare she act like I'm the one in the wrong?

When he arrived at the curb, she was halfway up the road, driving much too fast. He watched until she was out of sight and then he went back inside and slumped onto the sofa. Jasper wandered over and rested his chin on his knee.

'I just don't get it,' he told the dog who stared up at him as if he understood his pain. 'She left *me* and now I feel like shit? I just don't understand, Jasper. We both wanted that intimacy last night. I've been dreaming about her, for goodness' sake. I could tell she wanted it, too. Just sex, that's all she wanted. She made it clear when she left me the first time that she was no longer in love with me,' he rambled at the dog who looked on with his ears back as if unsure how to react to his master's loud voice. 'Who am I kidding eh? It's never just sex with her. I've spent all this time convincing myself I'm over her but I'm an idiot who's been lying to himself. I just don't get her reaction. She can't still have feelings for me. She's just grieving.' A horrible thought struck him. 'Oh god... Did I take advantage? Is that what was wrong with her? I would never do that deliberately. Surely she'd know that.'

Jim wandered around all day trying to figure out what on earth had got into Flick. He vacuumed, scoured, scrubbed, stripped the beds, and did several loads of laundry. Still, he couldn't figure out a plausible reason for her behaviour, other than the horrid one that had made him feel awful. *It's not as though she came here to win me back.* He snorted at the thought and decided to take Jasper for another long walk to clear his head.

The snow was all but gone. But it was a bitterly cold day. Jim and Jasper walked up to the viewpoint he had shown to Flick. Sadness enveloped him as he looked out across the valley. She had left the painting propped up against the wall in his bedroom. She obviously didn't want it after what had happened. But it was beautiful. He wanted to hang it but felt sure that he would be overtaken by emotion whenever he looked at it. Just as he was then, looking out at the real thing.

He returned to the house after an hour and a half of brisk walking in the cold January air. The living room was chilly. After he had built a fire, he went upstairs to change into his joggers and a sweater. Maybe lifting weights would help?

Before he made his mind up, he spotted the brown, padded envelope on his nightstand. Picking it up, he examined it. His name was written in Edgar's own handwriting and had evidently not been opened since Edgar himself had sealed it.

Jim took the package downstairs with him and placed it on the coffee table. He chewed on his nails and stared at it for a while until curiosity got the better of him and he carefully opened it up.

Inside, the contents were neatly tied with a red ribbon, rather like the legal documents of a solicitor. There was a thick wad of paper, which he presumed was the manuscript of the incomplete book on George Leigh Mallory. Underneath the ribbon was an envelope addressed to Jim, again in Edgar's handwriting. Jim slid his finger along the seal and took out the contents. Awash with emotion, he began to read.

Dear Jim,

If you are reading this, I am no longer with you. I instructed my solicitor that no one, but no one must open this letter, except for you. My dear boy, I can only apologise for the fact that, no doubt, you were excluded from my send-off by my wife. It pains me to be sitting here knowing that this will undoubtedly be the case. She has some ridiculous notion that you are bad for my girl. How one could surmise such nonsense when one only must know you to understand how much you cared for (and probably still do) my Felicity.

Please forgive Felicity. For she, too, has the ridiculous notion that my busybody of a wife knows what is right and wrong for her. The well-known phrase 'Mother knows best' sticks in my craw, old boy, I can tell you. The day you were forced out of my family was one of the saddest in my life and as my illness took over me, my one real pleasure, apart from seeing my daughter, was awaiting your wonderful letters and emails. You have a way with words, son.

This brings me on to the manuscript enclosed. Now I know you want none of the fame and fortune of becoming a well-known writer, even though your talent is beyond that of many published writers I have read, and so I present to you an opportunity to, ironically, become my ghostwriter. I would very much like for you to finish the manuscript and forward it to Geoffrey Haddington, my editor, who has been instructed to await your contact. If you choose not to take this opportunity, however, know that my opinion of you will not deteriorate. I regard you with the highest esteem and always have. Please remember that.

Now, on to my main reason for writing to you from beyond the grave. Hmm, that's a strange thing to write when I am still here! Anyway, I digress. Felicity has not been the same since she jettisoned you from her life. I can only liken it to a light being switched off. Her eyes don't sparkle the same any more. She's lost her… how do you put it? Va-va-voom! I must say that's a word I never thought I would write! Anyway, I'm digressing again!

A week ago, after I had been honest with Felicity about my illness and the fact that I wouldn't be around for very long we had a heart-to-heart. I asked her to be truthful about your break-up. Jim, she broke down and sobbed. She cried for about fifteen minutes and I just held her. When she had calmed herself down, I asked her again. I would like to share with you what she said.

Felicity felt that she had something to prove to her mother. She felt that she had to be a successful, wealthy woman who was going places. The crazy thing is that I already saw that in her. But her mother, who has always been critical, had standards that she set, which were impossible to meet. I know things about Penny that would make all of that seem a little ironic but I'm sure they will come out soon enough, if they haven't already. Penny, for reasons known only to herself, didn't feel that you fit in with this inflated sense of importance she had for material things; and quite rightly too. You are far better than that.

Felicity confessed to me that you were her soul mate. You were her best friend. She convinced herself that these things were not important. She did so because her mother's manipulation tactics had worked. I cannot tell you how sad and angry this makes me. I sincerely hope that Penny can live with herself for the damage she has caused to the child she loved so desperately.

Despite all this, I, too, must admit to being a fool for love. No matter how much my wife meddles and interferes I cannot help but love her and I know that she loves me too, deeply. I know, also, that she wants the best for her daughter. She is just misguided as to what that entails. I have spoken to her recently about you and think she may be realising what she has done. This has made her angry. But this anger, whilst outwardly expressed in a way that hurts others, is only dealt with as such because to turn it in on herself would destroy her. The guilt she feels is eating away at her and she has no idea how to deal with it. I'm sure she will have protested at Felicity coming to see you, through pride, if indeed Felicity even told her.

Now, what I'm about to impart came directly from Felicity's own mouth… She still loves you, Jim. I will write that again in the hope that it sinks in. Felicity still loves you. She has remained in love with you all along. She just pushed the feelings down until she, too, believed they were gone. Her heart is broken. She realises now that she made a terrible mistake in letting you go but she will not and cannot bring herself to tell you of this as she feels sure that she has hurt you to a level that is beyond the powers of forgiveness. And so, I'm doing so from wherever I have gone. I know you can forgive her because I have forgiven Penny. When you love someone as much as this, it is all you can do.

Now, I requested that Felicity should deliver this package to you personally if you had not been allowed to attend my funeral. If she has, in fact, delivered it and she is still with you when you read this letter, then please don't be upset with her if you were not informed about my passing until after the funeral. I can assure you it will not have been her decision to not invite you. If she is still with you, I would like you to take a look deep into her eyes and see the truth.

You are meant to be together.

If Felicity is no longer in Scotland, I would like you to seriously think about what I have told you. Ask yourself if you can forgive this misguided young woman and if the answer is yes, I want you to get in that battered old Land Rover of yours and drive down to London to take back what should never have been broken asunder.

She feels that you and she have some connection that goes deeper than 'normal' love. She dreams of you often and a place where you and she stand looking out over a valley surrounded by trees and mountains. It sounds very much like some of the places you have described in your beautiful letters to me, Jim. You are two souls that are incomplete without one another.

Please, for the sake of you both, go to her. You will never be complete with another and I think you know this deep down.

I will close now as I'm feeling rather tired and emotional. It pains me to know that I may never see your smiling face again, Jim. But know this. I have loved you since my daughter brought you home. You and I had an affinity just like a father and his son and that is what you have always been to me.

My son.
With much love,
Your Father
Edgar

18

Jim's shoulders shuddered as he sobbed. His face was wet with hot tears. Jasper sat beside him with his head resting on his knee.

The information contained in Edgar's letter both shocked and saddened him. Now he understood why she was so damned upset when she left. He looked like a revengeful bastard. Of course, he did. *Idiot!* That was the total opposite of how he'd felt. He'd said those things to make it easier on her. To take the pressure off. He didn't want her to feel obliged to be with him just because they'd shared one reminiscent night. Why didn't he realise what her reaction meant?

Seeing Flick again had brought all his suppressed feelings to the forefront. He hated the fact, but he still loved her. And now he'd no doubt blown it. There was no way things could work out after his *'that's how we say goodbye'* comment. What a total and utter fool! He hadn't acknowledged his real feelings until it was too late. Any chance there may have been to reconcile with Flick now had died.

The way she looked at me as she left. He groaned. *How could I have been so stupid? So blind?*

There was no point chasing her down. None.

He sat, drumming his fingers, his knee bouncing up and down as it often did when he was frustrated. He re-read the passage over and over where Edgar told him that Flick still loved him. He mulled it over in his mind and then read it again.

In a fit of determination, he grabbed his mobile phone and riffled through the numbers until he reached Flick's – a number he hadn't dialled in years. Did she even have the same one after all this time? Knowing she was meticulous when it came to her business dealings, he doubted she would have changed it. All her clients had her number, after all. He hit dial, knowing she would be on the road but hoping she would answer on handsfree.

He waited. Three bleeps and then nothing. He tried again. Same response. *Dammit! Either she's blocked my number, or she does have a new one.* He had to do something. But what? Time was of the essence as he knew that she would take the job in Chicago now.

He picked up his mobile again and dialled. 'Matt? Hey it's Jim... MacDuff.'

'Bloody hell, Jim, long time no speak. How are you?'

'Yeah, I'm good thanks. Listen... I know it's a strange request, but do you have Flick's new mobile number?'

Matt paused. '*New* number? She doesn't have a new number as far as I'm aware.'

Jim's stomach dropped. *She blocked me.* 'Ah, right. Okay. My mistake. So, how have you been?'

After twenty minutes of chatting to Matt and catching up on his news, Jim hung up the call and dialled his friend.

'Miranda? Hi, it's Jim. I need to ask you a favour. Any chance you can look after Jasper for me? I need to go to London.' Miranda was intrigued but Jim didn't elaborate. She agreed to take Jasper in the next day, so Jim dashed up the stairs and grabbed an overnight bag.

Once done, he picked up the phone yet again. 'Charles?'

'Well, hello, old bean. How are you doing? Has the snow cleared?'

'Yeah, thankfully, it has, and I need to ask you a favour. Can I stay with you for a couple of days?'

'You don't even need to bloody ask, old chap. Your room's waiting.'

'Great! Thank you sooo much.'

'What's happened? Is everything okay?' Concern etched his voice.

'It's a wee bit complicated. But I should be down tomorrow afternoon, I'll explain then.'

'Righty oh, Jiminy. See you then! Ciao!'

Jim hung up, sat back and heaved a sigh. He looked down at Jasper and scratched the top of his canine friend's head. 'Nothing ventured, nothing gained, eh, Jasper?'

Now that he knew she had blocked his number as soon as she had left his house, he had no clue what he would say to her once he arrived in London. In fact, he had no clue whether she would even speak to him. Maybe he should have explained things to Matt and asked him to get Polly to see how the land lay, as he felt sure that Flick would tell her everything. That's what best friends do. But then again, even if Polly said he mustn't come, he would still get in the Landy and head off to London to see for himself.

He decided he would get an early night and rise at around six, drop Jasper with Miranda, pack some sandwiches, and set off. He figured he could make most of the journey without stopping. He resolved that he would only stop if absolutely necessary, that way he could maybe meet her from work, and they could go somewhere neutral to talk things through. That was it. All planned. He breathed a sigh of relief, leaned back, and closed his eyes.

A loud rhythmical knock at his door made him jump up. His

heart leapt. *Shit! Maybe she came back?!* He hurried to the door and yanked it open, almost pulling it off the hinges in his excited rush.

'Ta daaa!' A tall, lanky man threw his arms around Jim.

'Euan!' Jim shouted, hugging his brother back. 'Shit, Euan, why didn't you call? I could've picked you up at the airport!'

'In that ancient old shed you call a car? No thanks! We hired something a lot more civilised, didn't we, Aish?' he asked over his shoulder. The petite frame of Euan's girlfriend stepped sideways and opened her arms out to Jim.

'Hey! Aisha! You look amazing, come here.' Jim scooped her up and swung her around and then pointed to his brother. 'And you, you great heathen, you leave my lovely Landy out of this. She'll go on forever. She's done me proud all these years and there's plenty of life left in her yet.'

Euan punched his brother's arm playfully. 'Yeah, whatever you say! And get off ma woman, you hairy lout!'

'God, it's so good to see you both, come in!' Jim stepped aside as his brother and potential sister-in-law entered his tiny cottage.

'Geez, bro. I'm sure this place gets smaller.' Euan laughed. His last visit had been the year that Jim had moved in and he had been overwhelmed by the size of the property compared to the one he and Aisha shared in New South Wales.

'Aye, but there's only me and Jasper so it does us just fine.' He went through to the kitchen to make coffee for his guests. 'So, how long are you staying?' he asked, cringing as he remembered his letter from Edgar and the plan to chase after Flick.

'We're here for a month, mate! A whole month!' Euan beamed at his big brother.

Dammit. That would mean that Flick would be in the States when they left. Shit, shit, shit! What could he do? His brother had flown all the way around the world to be with him. He couldn't just leave and dash off to London or the USA on a whim. It wouldn't be right.

'That's great.' It *was* great. It was wonderful. He would just have to have a major rethink.

The evening was filled with chatter and catch-ups. The brothers joked around like old times and Aisha listened intently whilst the two regaled her with stories of their childhood in Dumbarton. They told her these stories whenever they got together and so she rolled her eyes frequently and smiled as they carried on regardless.

Euan and Aisha updated Jim on their latest hobby, windsurfing. Jim was slightly envious at that. It was something he had always wanted to try but had never had the courage. As the evening wore on, Jim cooked a large pan of Spaghetti Bolognese and a garlic baguette. The wine flowed and so did the conversation. At around midnight, Euan stretched and yawned. He looked down at his gorgeous girl who lay across him, fast asleep.

'I'm bushed, Jim. I think I'll turn in if you don't mind, eh?'

'Aye, you know where your room is, bro. I'll make breakfast when you get up so don't rush, eh?' The brothers hugged and Euan scooped up his girl like a little china doll and carried her up to bed.

* * *

Jim couldn't sleep. He lay awake almost all night trying to figure out what to do. He could call her at the gallery, but she would no doubt be angry and refuse to speak to him. And anyway, he wanted to see her face and discuss things properly. He would have to wait. It may mean a flight to the USA but so be it. Eventually he drifted off into a fitful sleep.

Sleep didn't carry him away for long and he was in the kitchen making coffee at eight the following morning when he decided to call Charles and explain that his visit was cancelled.

'What was your reason for coming all this bloody way, old boy?' Charles enquired, probably guessing that there was more to this than just a social visit.

'It's a long story, Charles, but to give you the abridged version… Flick brought me an incomplete manuscript as requested by her dad via his will. In the envelope with it was a letter. Edgar said in the letter that Flick still loves me.'

'Bloody hell! Do you think it's true? Or another bloody lie?' Charles asked in his Charles-type way.

'Edgar wouldn't lie. He says she told him I'm her soul mate, that she has always loved me, that she regrets how things ended between us.'

'Well, it was her bloody doing, old chap. You weren't going to bloody chase her down, were you?'

'I wanted to at least talk to her, you know? I need to know if she still feels that way, although after how things ended when she was here this week, I'm guessing I've blown it.'

Charles sighed. 'But Jim, I thought you were over her? You spent so long putting things in place to help you move on.'

'Aye, I know but I can't help myself.'

He went on to explain to Charles what had happened the night before Flick left. How they had ended up sleeping together and about her reaction the next day when he treated it as *just sex*. He felt ashamed as he spoke, realising that this was the first time he had ever done something as callous. It wasn't meant to be that way. He had simply misread every single signal. The stupid thing was he had been completely oblivious to the signals and the looks until now.

Charles sighed. 'Oh, Jim. You bloody fool. I'm sorry but you are.' He was right. He was a bloody fool, for so many reasons. The conversation ended and Jim sat with his head in his hands.

'So, she was here? And she still loves you, eh?' A familiar voice came from over his shoulder making him jump.

Jim didn't bother to hide his annoyance that his brother had been listening in. 'Euan, you scared the crap out of me! How long were you standing there?'

'Long enough, bro.' He pulled out the chair opposite Jim and sat down to face him. 'Look, you've spent the last two years, no, longer, getting over that bitch—'

Jim pointed a finger at his brother. 'Do *not* call her that.' His tone was harsh, and he spoke through gritted teeth.

Euan held up his hands. 'Sorry, sorry. I just can't believe you're thinking of going back to her after what she did to you. She messed with your head and broke your heart. Are you seriously going to give her a chance to do it again? I thought you were over her?'

'Bro, you don't know how I feel. I miss her. I never stopped loving her. I tried, believe me, I did. But she's not someone you get over easily.' Jim rubbed his forehead as he always did when he felt stressed. The brothers sat in silence for a while.

Euan helped himself to coffee and sat back down at the table. 'Jim, please, give it some time, eh? Think this through. I like Flick. She's a great girl, as long as she's not breaking your heart. At first, I was so chuffed for you. She was gorgeous, funny, a talented artist like I have never seen before. Does she still paint by the way?'

Jim stood and without saying another word, went upstairs to collect the canvas from his room. He returned and without speaking turned the piece around to show his brother.

Euan gasped. 'Bloody hell, Jim! That's beautiful. Why is she wasting her time chasing millionaire's money and other artists when she could be getting recognition for her own talents?'

'I have no idea. She loves to paint. I've never seen a sexier, more beautiful woman than Flick when she paints. She lights up. It's a wonderful sight.' Jim sat, clinging on to the canvas.

His mind drifted to her standing by the window where the best light was, easel set out before her, paintbrush in her mouth like a rose in the mouth of a flamenco dancer, hands on hips. He remembered the sensual curve of her bare flesh just peeking out through the side of the over-sized dungarees.

Euan snapped him out of his daydream. 'Whatever happened to all her other paintings? You know? The ones she did when you were together?'

'She left them behind at the house. She didn't seem to care about them. But I did. I kept them. I even brought them here when I moved. Some are under the bed in my room and the smaller ones are in the loft. There was only one that I couldn't find. One she painted of the two of us.'

'What a waste.' Euan shook his head. He was right. So, so right. Flick should be the one whose art was on display in galleries. Someone should be selling her canvases, not the other way around.

'Aye, total waste, bro. But she thinks she's happy doing what she does now. The trouble is, I don't think she really knows what she truly wants, thanks to her mother.' Jim went on to explain all about Penny, aka Janet, and her advice to her daughter.

Euan was aghast. He shook his head. 'Why would you do that to your own daughter? Does her happiness mean nothing to that witch?' Euan didn't particularly hold back.

Jim shrugged and placed the canvas against the wall. 'I think, deep down, she thinks she is doing what's best for Flick. I suppose me being unambitious and in a so-called dead-end job didn't help matters at the time. And I'm not sure things are any better now.'

'Sod that, Jim! You have your own home and a business. Two businesses if you count the campsite. What more does she want? Just because you're not rolling in cash and famous doesn't make you unworthy.'

Jim sighed. 'I know that, and you know that...'

'I just think you should take care, Jim. She's hurt you before. What's to stop her doing it again?'

Jim rubbed at his tense shoulders. 'Nothing, Euan. That's the thing. She could stomp on ma heart again, and I think I'd just go with it if it meant I got to be with her for a little while.'

'You idiot!' Euan smiled, shaking his head. 'You really love her, eh?' Jim nodded. 'Well, do me one thing, okay? Really think this through before you go running after her, eh? Anyway, you have me here now and I'm your real family.' He winked.

Jim leaned over and ruffled his brother's hair like he used to when they were kids. 'Aye, don't have much choice about that one, do I?' Euan whacked his hand away. He still hated it.

19

Flick pulled up outside Polly's late in the evening. Her long journey of almost twelve hours down from Scotland had completely drained her. She had stopped several times when her emotions had got the better of her and tears had blurred her vision.

Throughout the whole journey back to London, she played the past few days over in her mind. No matter how much she thought things through, she couldn't realistically blame Jim for his treatment of her, but his actions still disappointed her beyond measure. Reeling from his words, she had pulled over as soon as she had left Shieldaig and had immediately blocked his number from her phone. Just in case he tried to apologise. It was too late for that.

Once inside Polly and Matt's Georgian town house, she heaved a sigh of relief and dropped her bag by the coat stand. Polly came through from the kitchen, took one look at her, and opened her arms. Flick fell into her friend's warm embrace and began to sob yet again.

'Oh, sweetheart. What on earth happened up there? I've been so worried.' Flick didn't answer right away. Instead, she just poured out all the raw emotion that was left inside her, soaking Polly's cashmere sweater through with warm, salty tears. 'Come on, let's go through to the lounge. Matt, would you bring Flick a glass of wine, darling?' she called to her husband.

Matt brought the glass, squeezed Flick's shoulder knowingly, and left them to talk. Polly handed a rather pretty tissue box to Flick and waited for her to calm down enough to speak.

'Oh, Polly, what have I done to him?' She sobbed.

Polly held Flick's free hand and gently stroked the back of it. 'Sweetie, that's all in the past. Surely, he wasn't still holding a grudge, was he?'

'No, no, he was lovely, for the most part. Distant and guarded, but lovely. He let me stay when I got stranded because of the snow when he could've insisted I went to the hotel along the road. He cooked for me. He even borrowed painting supplies from his friends so that I wouldn't be bored.' She sighed. 'But he clearly has a visceral fear of getting hurt again. There's been no one serious since me. He met someone lovely by the sound of it, but she apparently lived a fair distance away and he used that as an excuse not to take things further. He won't allow anyone to get close and it's my fault entirely.'

'I don't understand though. What went wrong?' Polly tucked a stray strand of hair behind Flick's ear. 'You only went to tell him about your dad and to deliver that package.'

'Oh, Polly, things were going so well. I felt like I was making amends. I apologised. We talked so much. About everything and then last night... last night we made love.' She covered her face with her hands.

Polly eyes widened. 'You did what?!' She didn't attempt to hide her shock, sitting bolt upright as she spoke. 'Oh no, sweetie. But... but how come?'

'I don't really know to be honest. We kind of got caught up in the moment. There was a power cut. I don't like the dark and, well one thing led to another.'

'But Flick, darling, we talked about this. You know how vulnerable you are about Jim. We talked about how you would protect yourself, honey. You're still so deeply in love with him that sex was bound to complicate things.'

'I know. I just didn't think long enough to stop myself. And I wanted to be with him so much. I think that, on some level, I naively thought we'd get back together. That making love to me would make him realise he still loved me too. But then this morning... he repeated back to me the horrible line I said to him on the day I left.'

Polly shook her head. 'Which was what, Flick?'

Flick couldn't look Polly in the eyes now. She hated what she'd said to Jim on that fateful day and hearing it repeated back to her had cut like a knife. But it was no more than she deserved.

She took a deep breath. 'That sex was how he and I say goodbye.' She rested her head in her hands feeling rather ashamed.

'Ah.'

Flick had made her friend aware of *most* of the details behind her decision to leave Jim at the time it happened. Polly had been honest and said that she didn't completely agree that leaving him was the right thing to do, and urged her to rethink, but she'd stood by her and vowed to always be there for her in her time of need.

This was that time. And Flick needed her best friend more than anything.

'I broke his heart so severely, Pol, that he has built these walls up around himself. I've ruined his life and I can't bear it. He was my best friend in the whole world. My soul mate. And I broke him for my own ridiculously selfish crusade.' Tears began to fall freely once again as Flick absorbed the weight of her actions.

A while later Flick awoke with a start. She sat bolt upright when she realised the room was empty. She was covered over in a cream, faux fur blanket on the sofa where she must have fallen asleep. The clock above the mantle told her it was the early hours of the morning, so she switched off the table lamp and made her way outside and to the basement flat that she rented from Polly and Matt.

Today of all days she was happy about the living arrangement that had been in place since she split with Rory. Polly and Matt had been on the verge of advertising the basement flat when Flick asked if she could take it. They were delighted to have someone they knew living beneath them as they had invested a lot of money into the place. But living with Polly and Matt was only ever meant to be a temporary thing, and she had plenty of money to afford her own place. But in all truth, the thought of living completely alone filled her with dread. She couldn't take the loneliness. And having friends around when she needed them, like now, was a blessing.

The little apartment was just right for one with its combined living and dining room. It was all neutrally decorated and there was a modern kitchen with all mod cons. Off the lounge, was a decent-sized bathroom with separate shower cubicle, and through another door was a double bedroom with built-in wardrobes.

Considering Flick's penchant for art, the walls were bare. She had a few photographs of herself with Polly at university, and some of her family but no artwork per se. In her bedside drawer, she kept one framed photo of herself and Jim. It was taken during their first Christmas as a married couple, and their second in their little rented house since leaving university and moving in together right away. It was such a beautiful image, one that she treasured. She had hidden it away in the drawer so that she could avoid the emotions that seeing it evoked, but she knew it was there for the moments when she felt stronger. Even though this was not one of those occasions, she couldn't help lifting it out of the drawer and thinking back to that wonderful, special Christmas time...

* * *

The tree was quite small but stood proudly in the corner of their pretty, little lounge, by the fireplace. They had bought most of their ornaments from Covent Garden. Luckily, they both favoured the more traditional decorations. They agreed on white lights that stayed nice and still so as not to cause migraines or a huge distraction whilst they watched TV or kissed for hours at a time. It looked beautiful.

Flick and Jim sat in front of their tree on Christmas morning opening gifts from friends and family, which were mostly of the couple variety – house gifts such as matching Mr and Mrs mugs, His and Hers robes and towels, sweet little penguin salt and pepper pots, kitsch but cute. Flick had bought Jim a beautiful, leather-bound notebook with his initials embossed on the front for his poetry and book ideas, which he loved. Jim handed a small gift bag to Flick, and her eyes lit up. 'Small gifts are always more exciting,' her mother always told her, 'They usually contain diamonds!' She doubted it on this occasion, as money was tight. But she didn't really care about diamonds.

With the sound of Bing Crosby singing 'White Christmas' in the background, Flick opened the bag and took out the velvet box. She opened it slowly, prolonging the anticipation. Jim chewed on his nails, as if he wasn't sure she would like the contents.

Flick gasped. 'Oh, Jim! It's beautiful!' She flung her arms around his neck and kissed him. 'I just love it. Put it on me. I'll never take it off.' She handed him the silver-coloured chain, which had a simple heart-shaped pendant hanging from it.

As he fastened it around her neck, he said, 'It's white gold you know. Not silver. I couldn't afford platinum, but now you know you will always have my heart.'

Flick turned to face him. 'Jim that is the most romantic thing anyone has ever said to me. I'll treasure it and look after it always.'

As soon as the words had left her lips, he had kissed her tenderly.

* * *

Back in the present, Flick sat alone on her bed in her little rented apartment holding the photo of her with Jim. *Didn't do a very good job of looking after his heart, did you?* She chastised herself regretfully. She trailed her fingers down the image of Jim's handsome face, kissed it and placed the frame back in her drawer.

20

The morning after his brother's surprise arrival, Jim sat drinking coffee in the kitchen. He played over in his mind all the things that Euan had said. His brother was quite rightly against him chasing Flick down. He got it. Totally. But Euan didn't fully understand the way he felt about Flick and the impact she'd had on his life. Euan had said that if it were up to him, his big brother would be convinced that there were plenty more fish in the sea and that he should do himself a favour, go fishing and move on. Jim took it all with a pinch of salt. It was great to have him around, but he couldn't help wishing he could just get in the car or on that plane and go to her. If Euan knew he felt this way, he'd be so hurt and upset. He began to feel a tad guilty for wishing the time past.

Euan and Aisha finally roused from the land of slumber and joined Jim at the kitchen table. They kept whispering and looking at each other. It was clear there was subterfuge afoot. Jim didn't ask. He waited until one of them plucked up the courage to speak.

Euan apparently could hold his tongue no longer. 'Jim, we've had an idea. Tell us to butt out—'

'Butt out.' Jim smiled snidely as he interrupted his brother.

Euan rolled his eyes. 'Okay, I deserved that. Seriously though, I've been thinking, that is, Aisha and I have been talking, and we think you should do something with the paintings. Flick needs a wake-up call.'

Jim scrunched his face in confusion and shook his head in protest. His voice was sharp as he spoke. 'What do you mean? You're not suggesting I throw them away, are you? 'Cause if you are—'

Euan raised his hands in submission. 'No! Don't be daft, Jim! Not at all. Quite the opposite. We think maybe you should try and get them into a gallery. Don't you have any connections with anyone she knows?' Euan looked hopeful. 'Or maybe that gallery she used to work at before? Art and Soul, was it? You know, an exhibition of her own work. Maybe if she sees that she can make it as an artist in her own right, she'll feel able to come back here to be with you. It's the perfect location for an artist.'

Jim contemplated for a few minutes whilst Euan stared expectantly.

After a long silence, Euan spoke again. 'Look, I hope I haven't crossed a line bro, it was just a suggestion.'

The cogs in Jim's mind were almost audibly turning. 'Actually, it may be a good idea.' He rubbed his chin as he thought. 'I could try to find someone...' His words trailed off as he disappeared into his own mind.

Euan smiled at Aisha who slid onto his lap, closing the distance she had apparently been keeping in case fireworks ensued at her partner's suggestion. 'Anyway, I'll leave you to decide what's best to do about it. Like I said it was just an idea.'

Jim straightened his spine and with a wide grin said, 'I never thought I'd hear myself saying this, little bro, but you may have had a brilliant idea for once in your life.'

Euan punched Jim's arm playfully. 'Cheeky sod!' Jim cried out in pain whilst chuckling simultaneously.

After breakfast Euan and Aisha announced that they were going to sample some of the wonderful Scottish fresh air available, and that they were taking Jasper along for the stroll.

Jim decided to rummage through a box of items belonging to Flick that had been discarded at their marital home when she left him for her new life. He was sure there was a little black address book in there. She had purchased an iPhone back then and had copied all the numbers over, rendering the little book useless. He wasn't sure until now why he hadn't just thrown it all out. Maybe things did happen for a reason.

On locating the book, he opened it and thumbed through to the F page. Sure enough, there it was, the telephone number of one Julian Forster, Flick's first protégé in the art world. Jim sat back on his haunches as he remembered his first encounter with the unlikely star...

* * *

'It's all bollocks, you know,' a voice from beside Jim rudely tore him from his reverie.

Rather taken aback by the harsh comments of the stranger, Jim turned quickly. 'Excuse me?'

Waving his arms around at their surroundings, the man continued. 'This. It's all pretentious bollocks. They make it about money.' He gestured in the direction of Flick and Franco Nilsson. 'But all I want to do is paint and have someone appreciate my art.'

Smirking at the truth of the man's words, Jim said, 'Aye, I think I could be inclined to agree, mate.' He nodded and took a swig of his Jack and Coke.

The man held out his hand. 'Julian Forster.'

Jim reciprocated and the pair connected in a firm handshake. 'Jim MacDuff.'

'Aren't you Felicity's partner?' Julian enquired.

'Husband.'

'Ah, but she doesn't have your name,' Julian observed.

Flinching at the comment, Jim took another swig of his drink. 'Long story.'

'Hmm. I bet that's a load of pretentious bollocks, too,' Julian said dryly.

Jim laughed. 'Do you know what? I think you just hit the nail on the head again.'

Julian suddenly perked up. 'Come on, Jim. I say we go and make the most of the free bar.'

'Aye. Why the hell not?' Jim followed the artist as he led the way to the place where Dutch courage could be acquired on tap.

'She used to paint, you know,' Jim offered as he caught sight of his beautiful wife, who was busy networking, smiling, and flirting as she did, without realising it.

'Used to?' Julian's response told Jim that he couldn't imagine painting being something discussed in the past tense.

'Aye, she gave up when all this started.' He took another gulp of his Jack Daniels, neat this time. He hissed as the heat from the amber liquid slid down his throat.

'Shit. How could she give it up? With me it's... it's who I am.' Julian watched Flick too now, shaking his head as he spoke. 'I know you shouldn't let such things define who you are, but with me it... well, it just does,' Julian explained.

'Aye, well, with Flick it's clearly not the case,' Jim concluded.

'Does she miss it?'

'She never talks about it. Not really. It's a shame though. She was bloody good at it. And I used to love watching her paint.' Jim smiled absentmindedly as images of a paint-covered Flick flashed through his mind.

'Huh. What a bloody waste.'

'Aye, you can say that again.'

After that meeting, the two men found themselves at several other gallery and art-world functions together. Finding solace in each other's company they would stand at the bar uncomfortably attired in their suits, drinking and complaining about how plastic some people were.

* * *

Back in his current reality, Jim was trying to formulate the plan for which his brother had planted the seed. Even though he had found a number for Julian Forster, he was in no way sure that Julian would even still have the same mobile phone. People these days seemed to change their gadgets like they did their underwear.

Nothing ventured, nothing gained, he reminded himself as he picked up his phone and dialled.

'Hel-lo?' came the response at the other end.

'Hi, is this Julian Forster?' Jim asked tentatively.

'That all depends on who wants to know,' replied the stern male voice.

'I don't know if you'll remember me, my name is Jim MacDuff. We met—'

'Jim! Of course, I remember you. My partner in the crime of hating all things plastic. How could I forget? How the hell are you?' Julian's voice perked up at the realisation.

'Great, thanks, Julian.' Jim's voice wavered and he cringed at the sound of it.

'No problem. What can I do for you?'

'Look, you know how I told you that Felicity, erm Flick, used to paint?'

'Yeah, I still don't get how she could give it all up to sell other people's work.'

'Well, that's just it. I need to ask your advice. And maybe a favour, too.'

Jim went on to explain about his divorce from Flick, their recent meeting, the letter from Edgar, and that he wanted to ask his professional opinion about the paintings.

'Wow, that's some serious stuff. And you'll never believe this, but I'm in Inverness right now! I've been painting for fun again. London just consumes and digests you until there's nothing left to give. I have to get away every so often to remember why the hell I started painting in the first place. How about I meet you in the city on Friday, and I'll take a look at the pieces?'

'Julian, I would be eternally grateful. Thanks so much.'

'No worries at all. I can see why you love it up here so much, Jim. The Black Isle is stunning beyond words. I've rediscovered my passion for painting Scottish scenery again. I think Flick would be crazy not to jump at the chance to come back. I'll do everything I can to help, don't you worry.'

Julian agreed to meet Jim at Johnny Foxes, a pub he had discovered in Inverness, the following Friday. He asked him to bring a selection of Flick's artwork along for him to look over. It was all set. Jim felt a rush of excitement at the thought of doing this for Flick.

On the return from their walk, Jim filled Euan and Aisha in on his plans to meet with Julian.

Aisha got quite giddy. 'I can't believe you know Julian Forster! *The* Julian Forster!' she squeaked. 'He is so famous in Oz! His artwork is just... transcendent,' she announced, dreamily, to the two baffled men opposite her. She blushed, reminding Jim of how Flick used to do the same, so easily.

He smiled at the memory. 'Aye well, whatever you say, Aisha. I just know he likes to paint nice pictures!' Jim laughed. 'And he sounds keen to help me out on the little mission.'

Friday morning was thankfully dry, making the transportation of Flick's paintings somewhat less risky than anticipated. Jim and Euan loaded up the Land Rover with a selection of Flick's canvases in a variety of sizes. They were mainly landscape paintings of scenes she had painted from memory following car and train journeys.

Her method of painting had always impressed Jim. She looked out through the glass and saw the beauty out there in ways he never could. She made even industrial landscapes beautiful. She had been known to set up her easel and paint what she saw before her, too, but her best works were taken from her mind's eye. That way she could put her own interpretation into the colours and breathe life into the dullest of scenes. Each piece had a personality of its own. Each showed the untapped talent that Flick had quashed and hidden away from view for far too long.

Aisha and Euan hugged Jim as he prepared to leave. He was starting to feel the nervous energy building inside him. 'Phew, I'm shaking like a leaf,' he informed the couple who stood with their arms around each other.

'You'll be fine, Jim. Flick is immensely talented. Julian will see that right away,' Aisha assured him.

'Yeah, and I bet he has loads of contacts. You need to get him on side, Jim.' Euan looked as nervous as Jim felt.

'Don't worry, bro, I intend to make something out of all this. I have to. Wish me luck, guys.'

'Oh, we certainly do.' Euan turned to his girlfriend.

Jim buzzed with nervous excitement as he drove. Time was pressing. He knew that there was a good chance Flick was already preparing to fly to Chicago. And he knew how much she would hate the journey. Regardless of the necessity to fly for her job he was acutely aware at how much it terrified her; of how much courage she had to muster to even get on a plane in the first place.

He arrived at the agreed meeting place right on time. His

palms were sweating as he walked through the doors and scanned the pub for a sign of Julian. Someone waved frantically at him from a corner table. Jim didn't recognise the man with the full beard until he got closer and realised it was, indeed, Julian Forster.

'Jim! Great to see you!' Julian grasped Jim in a manly bear hug, nearly knocking him off balance.

Jim laughed. 'Julian, good to see you, too. I almost didn't recognise you.'

'Yeah, that'll be the fuzz, I guess?' Julian scratched at his hairy chin. 'I got sick of being all clean-shaven and proper so I thought, sod it, I'm growing a beard.'

Jim pointed at his own chin. 'Well, I can't say anything, eh?' They both laughed. The pair agreed that the need to be clean-shaven was not a necessity in this day and age.

'What's your poison? I'll get you a drink.' Julian headed for the bar as he spoke.

Jim sat down at the table. 'Ah, just a juice, thanks. I've got to drive.

Julian returned and placed the drink in front of Jim. 'So, you guys split, eh?' Julian looked saddened at the news. 'Mind you, I have to be honest. I always thought you were a bit of an odd couple.' Jim was a little hurt by his words and it must have shown in his face. 'No, no, don't get me wrong. I'm not saying there was anything wrong with either of you,' Julian backtracked. 'No, it was just a, I don't know, strange coupling. She was so ambitious and clean-cut and you, well, you're so laid-back and... *normal*.'

Jim took a large gulp of his juice. 'Gee, thanks. Is that supposed to make me feel better?'

Julian's eyes showed the guilt he felt for what he had failed to communicate. 'See, I don't really get my point across with words. That's why I'm not a writer like you. I just felt that she kind of overshadowed you back then. You looked like you hated being at the gallery events. Am I wrong?'

Jim paused for thought but conceded that he was quite correct in his assumptions. 'Nah, I used to hate those things. But I loved her, Julian. I would have done anything for her, you know? Still would and that's my downfall. She's my weakness. I think I'd forgotten that until I saw her again and I mucked it up.' He rubbed his hands over his face.

'So now you're trying to win her back?' Julian asked.

'Well, I don't really know what I'm trying to do, to be honest. Things didn't end very well when she left to go back home, and I seem to have misread all the signals. I just... I want her to be happy. It's what I've always wanted.'

'And you think that getting someone to display her work is a way to do that?'

Jim leaned forward. 'Julian, when you see the paintings, I think you'll agree that she can't just leave her talent behind. It's like she's lost sight of who she really is. If I'm honest, I want the girl I fell in love with. And that was the Flick who paints amazing, heartfelt pieces of stunning artwork. Not the woman who jet sets all over the world discovering other artists and selling their work, no disrespect. I wouldn't mind but she absolutely *hates* flying.' Jim looked pleadingly into Julian's eyes. 'I want *my* Flick back, Julian. Or at least I want to try, and then even if it doesn't work out, I know that I've done everything I can.'

Julian nodded, but then after a pause he huffed a long, drawn-out breath, as if preparing to deliver bad news. 'But, Jim, what if she doesn't want to be that person any more? What if she's angry at you for doing this?'

He looked directly into Julian's eyes. 'It's a chance I have to take.' His resolve was firm.

Julian took a large gulp of his drink, placed his half-empty glass down and clapped his hands together. 'Right then, let's have a look at these paintings!' He stood with determination.

The two men stood in the car park perusing the artwork in the back of the Land Rover like they were doing some dodgy, under-handed deal. Jim glanced around nervously hoping that some passer-by didn't see them and call the police.

Julian gasped. 'Bloody hell, Jim. I can see what you mean.' He shook his head. 'This girl is wasting an amazing talent!'

Jim let out a huge sigh of relief. 'You think so?' He bit on his bottom lip and fidgeted, tying his fingers in knots.

A wide grin spread across Julian's face. 'Think so? I *know* so. And I know just the person to show them to.' His expression changed to one of concern. 'The only trouble is our Felicity John-ston-Hart is well-known throughout the art world. If her name is on them or on the exhibition, everyone will know it's her and she'll find out what's going on before we have time to finalise things.'

'She never used to sign the fronts of her pieces. I think that was another sign of her feelings of inferiority. You'll find her signatures are on the back.'

'Well, that's a good start... so all we need to do is decide what name to put down for the artist presenting the exhibition.' Julian looked skyward as if the answers could be found up there.

Jim's brain whirred with ideas. A grin spread wide across his face. 'Flick MacDuff,' was all he said.

21

Chicago was cold. Flick hadn't been prepared for quite how cold it would be. It was Valentine's Day, and the temperature was well below zero, as it had been the last Valentine's she had been here.

Prior to leaving the UK she had held on to the ridiculous notion that Jim might turn up on Polly's doorstep, having seen the error of his ways, and demand that she stay with him. She knew it was unrealistic to wish for such things. But it didn't stop her wishing. When it didn't happen, she accepted the Chicago job and decided this had to be a fresh start.

She had put all her possessions into storage so Polly and Matt could let the basement flat to someone new. They had offered to throw her a going away party, but she graciously declined knowing it would be so hard to say goodbye. She had left her grieving mother in the capable hands of the ladies from bridge club with the assurance that they would get in touch if anything warranted them to do so, but she sincerely hoped that Penelope would be okay.

Everyone presumed New York was the place for art but Flick had always known Chicago was just as important. With its myriad galleries and history of important figures such as Picasso exhibiting there first when he was discovered back in the day, Chicago could certainly hold its own. Nilsson-Perkins had seen the potential, too, opening their first USA gallery on Michigan Avenue, right in the cultural centre of the city.

Once she accepted the promotion at the Chicago gallery, Franco had insisted she fly out early. She had jumped at the chance to escape and get Jim out of her mind once and for all, even though it meant another long flight – something she would happily avoid forever. The gallery looked amazing, and she had settled in okay since making the journey to begin her new position. The only problem was, the *getting Jim out of her mind* part of the whole thing wasn't quite working.

The first couple of days in the big city had been a blur of refamiliarising herself, finding her bearings and meeting her new staff. Everyone had been lovely but a little cautious to begin with. She understood their reticence at welcoming her as Chester's replacement but did her best to be friendly and approachable. Yet here she sat, at her paperwork-covered desk, wishing she had a romantic evening to look forward to.

'Hey, Felicity. You look deep in thought there.' A female voice dragged her from her sadness. She smiled as she turned towards Ella, her personal assistant – formerly Chester's personal assistant. She was a strikingly beautiful brunette with a figure that most women would give their eyeteeth for. And the annoying thing was she was kind of sweet, too.

Ella cocked her head to one side, smiling. 'Penny for your thoughts?'

Flick sighed. 'Oh, I was just depressing myself with the fact that I'm once again in Chicago for Valentine's Day, and I'm totally alone.' She shook her head as if to rid herself of the melancholy. 'Oh, pay no attention to me. I'm just being a sissy.' She forced a laugh.

Ella's eyes were filled with sympathy. 'Not at all. It must be hard being away from your husband.'

Flick mumbled her reply. 'Ah, well, I'm actually divorced from... the love of my life.'

Ella's eyes and mouth widened simultaneously, then she pulled her lips in between her teeth and frowned. Her confused expression was no surprise to Flick.

'If you don't mind my asking, if he's the love of your life how come you're divorced?'

Flick sighed and gave a sad smile. 'It's a very long story and I don't want to bore you when we've only just met. You'll end up thinking I'm dull.' Flick laughed lightly.

'Tell you what, why don't we head across the street for a drink after work? I usually meet some friends there, but they're out of town for Valentine's, go figure. So, it'd just be you and me. We could work on that *we've only just met* issue.' She smiled warmly.

Flick regarded her again and smiled. 'Okay, why not? Thanks Ella. That would be lovely.'

'Great! Shall I come get you at six-thirty? I know you tend to work way past five and I have some stuff I need to get finished, too, so...'

Flick huffed, rubbing her eyes. 'Yes... although it may be a little after that. It's four now and I have lots of things to work through. The acquisitions paperwork has been left in an awful state.'

Ella cringed. 'Is it that bad?' She looked uneasy. 'Can I help with anything?'

'Yes, I'm afraid it is that bad and no, thank you, I need to get this done myself. The figures are just not adding up, and I need to call Franco with a full report by the end of the week. Lucky me, eh?'

Ella gave a friendly, encouraging smile. 'Okay, well if you need anything, even if it's a coffee, just holler.'

'Thank you, I will.'

* * *

Right on cue at six-thirty, Ella came back to Flick's office and tapped on the door. 'You ready yet?'

'Hi. Almost. Give me fifteen more minutes… make it twenty.' It was Flick's turn to cringe. 'Oooh, I'm sorry, Ella it may be more like twenty-five.'

'Hey, don't worry. I'm all done for today, but I have my book. It's really good.' Ella held her hand up in a dramatic gesture to talk behind it. 'It's a little steamy, if you know what I mean. The lead male is sooo hot. Scottish and tattooed. Plus, he's a little rugged and has a potty mouth.' She sniggered. 'So, I think I'll just sit in the break room and wait on you.' She turned on her heel and walked away.

Scottish and rugged, eh? Go figure.

Mick's Bar was bustling when they arrived at seven. Despite its name the establishment was quite upmarket and was viewed as one of the places to be seen around the city. Ella waved to the bartender to get his attention and he came right over.

'Hey, Steve. I'll have my usual. This is Felicity. She's British. It's her first time here at Mick's.' Ella bombarded the man with useless information.

He turned to Flick and his smiled broadened. He had a look of Joey from the series *Friends*, and she half expected him to raise an eyebrow and feed her the line the character was most famous for.

Instead, and much to Flick's disappointment, he lifted his chin in a move of acknowledgement. 'Hey, British. What's your poison?'

Flick felt her cheeks heat. 'Oh… Jack and Coke?' She had no clue what to order and for some reason Jim's favourite drink was what sprang to mind.

'Comin' right up.' He turned to go prepare their drinks. Flick looked towards Ella who was now grinning from ear to ear.

She nudged Flick playfully. 'Is he cute or what?'

Flick couldn't deny that there was something attractive about the man. He was very muscular. His hair was tousled in that *just-got-out-of-bed* way and he did have a very nice smile. But she didn't really care how good-looking he was. He wasn't Jim.

The two women found an empty booth and took their drinks over, claiming it as their own. Flick was relieved to finally be getting to know someone else in the city. It had been beginning to look like the start of a lonely and isolated life for her.

Ella seemed nice and was only a few years younger than her. She seemed like the type of person Flick could be friends with, even if she did look like she had walked off a movie set or the cover of a swanky magazine.

A true Chicagoan by birth and upbringing, Ella knew all the best places to eat, the best places to visit, and the best places to meet eligible bachelors. Flick smiled at her comments about the single men of Chicago and hoped that maybe one day she would be able to meet someone. But right now, the idea of someone new was so far off in the future that it didn't need to take up valuable space in her mind. Her mind was crammed full as it was.

They chatted easily for a good couple of hours. Ella Cole was an only child. She loved art and had studied art history at college much the same as Flick. That was their common ground and for hours they talked about their favourite artists. Flick discovered that Ella had a boyfriend but was reluctant to talk about him, constantly changing the subject back to Flick. At one point, Ella did let slip that her man was quite a bit older than she was and Flick decided that must be why she was uneasy talking about him. Perhaps he was married?

The conversation centred a lot on Flick and her life. Surprisingly, she found it easier than normal to open up about her past with Jim. Ella had decided point blank Jim just wasn't good enough for her. But she didn't know him at all.

Flick had to change the subject. 'So, tell me, Ella, what happened to Chester?'

The former manager of the art gallery had allegedly had some sort of break down, but Flick had met him several times whilst working for Franco and he always seemed so together.

Ella shifted uncomfortably in her seat. 'Oh, you know, work pressures. He let things get on top of him.'

Flick thought she noticed her cheeks colour as she spoke. Perhaps she felt somehow responsible? Poor Ella.

'But he was so controlled. I find it hard to believe he just gave up.'

Ella shrugged but didn't make eye contact. 'Yeah well, he just got so wound up about stuff, that something had to give. I guess it was his health and sanity or his job.'

There was something in the way she spoke that just didn't ring true. They sat in silence for a few moments whilst Flick mulled things over. Eventually she put it down to the alcohol.

Ella quickly changed the subject back to Flick's single status again. 'So, Felicity, are you going to date while you're here?'

Flick stirred the ice around her glass. 'I seriously doubt it for the moment. I really want to get a place to rent and get the gallery organised and then, maybe in a few months, who knows.'

Ella giggled. 'That's a shame, there's a gorgeous guy at the bar who is totally checking you out.'

Flick felt the heat rise in her cheeks again as she slowly shifted her gaze and looked over to where the man sat. He smiled and raised his glass to her. She turned away abruptly.

Ella leaned over the table towards her. 'What's wrong, Felicity? He's a good-looking guy. Just relax and have some fun with it.'

Steve, from behind the bar, came over to their table with two more drinks. 'Ladies. Compliments of the mafia-type dude sitting at the bar.' He smirked as he placed the drinks down in front of the two women.

Flick shook her head. 'Oh. No, no, thank you but please tell him I don't accept drinks from strangers.'

Ella snorted with laughter. 'Oh, come on, Felicity. Live a little.' Felicity felt sure she was crimson by now.

Steve informed her, 'Hey, it's okay, British. Poured them myself. He never got to lay a hand on them, so they're good.'

Feeling somewhat cajoled into the situation, Flick accepted the drink. 'Well, tell him, thank you.' She glanced over to where the man sat again. He was very attractive. Clean-shaven, short, dark, almost-black hair, and olive skin. He looked Italian. He was gorgeous, if you liked that movie star thing.

'Back in a sec,' Ella announced rising from the table.

Flick panicked. 'Where are you going? You can't leave me!'

'I'm going to the restroom. You have to stay here in case someone takes our booth. It's getting busy in here. I won't be long.' She walked away.

Flick looked up to see the handsome man walking towards her. God, he was not only gorgeous, but ridiculously tall and well-built too. *Oh shitty, shitty, shit.* Why did this stereotypical, Italian hunk want to hit on her, for goodness' sake?

'Good evening, I wanted to say thank you for accepting the drink I sent over. It's not something I usually do, and I could see that you hesitated. I don't blame you. You are very sensible, and I apologise if I offended you or worried you in any way.' *Yup... Italian... and gorgeous... and nice. Dammit!* Guilt washed over her as the man turned to walk away.

'Wait.' She spoke before thinking. The man stopped and turned back to her. 'Erm... I should thank you... for the drink, I mean.'

'You are most welcome. I was watching you and felt... drawn to you. Forgive me.' It was a cheesy line but, boy, up close he was rather stunning, as she had presumed he would be. He held out his hand. 'I am Vitale DeLuca... and you are?'

'Felicity Johnston-Hart. Pleased to meet you, Vitale.'

'The pleasure is all mine I can assure you. Are you here on holiday with your husband?' he enquired.

Flick caught herself looking at his lips and inadvertently licked her own. 'N-no... I'm here to work. I... I manage the Nilsson-Perkins Gallery. It's a new role and I haven't been here long.' She gulped as the man slid into the booth opposite her, never taking his gaze from hers.

'I thought as much. If I had seen you before, I would have remembered. *Sei un gioello.*'

Oh god, and now he's talking in Italian... I'm done for. 'I'm s-sorry, I don't speak much Italian.' *Idiot, you don't speak any sodding Italian!*

Vitale smiled wider this time, revealing a set of perfect white teeth. Not fake veneers. No, these were his own, perfect white teeth, sitting in his own delicious mouth, behind those full luscious lips...

'It means you are a jewel... a gemstone.' He cringed and shook his head. 'I must sound like a... what do you call it? Cheese monster?' He bowed his head, his self-deprecation sweet.

His English was remarkably good, and Flick couldn't help but smile. 'Not at all. I've never been called a jewel before.' She realised she was twisting her hair around her fingers. *Oh, for goodness' sake woman, get a grip.* She released the strand.

Looking hopeful and smiling at her reactions, Vitale said, 'I would very much like to take you to dinner. Would you consider this maybe?'

'Oh, I don't know. I'm not looking for—'

Vitale's smile faded. 'No, no. That's fine. I pounced on you the moment your friend left. You are new here and this is the last thing you need. Strangers coming on to you... I understand.' He stood to leave just as Ella returned.

Stupid, stupid, stupid woman. She was mentally beating herself up as guilt washed over her. 'The offer was very sweet. I don't mean to offend you.'

Vitale reached and took Flick's hand. 'Not possible. You have brightened my evening simply by speaking to me. I give you my card.' He released her hand. 'Maybe once you are settled you can give me a call and I can cook for you? Not Italian though. I will not betray my mother's memory. My Italian cooking is terrible. Instead, I will cook for you the best Paella you have ever tasted. I don't know any Spanish people I could offend by doing this.' He laughed and she couldn't help but laugh, too, at his admission.

'That would be lovely,' she replied.

As she took his card from his hand, he held her fingers in his. He smiled warmly, his dark eyes sparkling. 'Until next time. Have a wonderful evening, ladies.' And with that he turned and walked away.

Ella fanned herself dramatically. 'Wowee, lady! He was so freaking hot I thought my panties would melt! Are you going on a date?' She tapped her fingers together giddily.

Flick shook her head. 'No, he asked, but I declined.' *Again, stupid!* Jim hadn't chased after her so she knew she would have to move on eventually.

'Seriously? Are you crazy?' Ella's wide-eyed expression told Flick all she needed to know.

'Yes... I think it's official.' She said putting the card away without looking at it.

22

Jim watched the rental car as it disappeared into the distance. He waved one last time to his brother. Seeing Euan and Aisha together had made him realise just what he had been missing with Flick. A smile spread across his face at the thought of his plans for the exhibition. She had to realise she was meant to paint after this, surely? Shivering, he went inside and closed the door to the sub-zero temperature that had set in once again overnight.

He scratched Jasper's head. 'Come on, boy. I need a cup of Joe after the cold out there.' He walked through the cosy lounge where the fire was just about dying down, and on into the kitchen.

He had made the decision to fulfil Edgar's dying wish and complete his book. His father-in-law had meant so much to him and it was an honour to have been given such an important task. His own historical fiction book had been shelved – oh, the irony – a long time ago in favour of his autobiographical romance. But this was something totally different. Something non-fiction that required research, commitment, and something that would speak to the writer inside of him.

Today was going to be a pretty major step on the technology

front. He needed the boost of caffeine for what would, no doubt, be one hell of a confusing experience. RAM and processor speed, Wi-Fi router this, that, and the other. It was all Greek to Jim, but he had decided that Edgar's book needed to be finished using the most up-to-date equipment if he was going to do it justice at all. His own laptop was rather like a lump of concrete and it took ages to power up. Plus, the battery life was non-existent. It was fine for what he had needed up to now, but not fine for something as important as Edgar's manuscript.

After two cups of fresh coffee, he donned his warm fleece and waterproof walking coat and climbed into the Landy. He set off for the closest retail park – which wasn't that close at all – in search of a new, all-singing, all-dancing, laptop. *Oh... and a printer... of course, I'll need a new printer... and some paper... and something to keep it all in... bloody hell, this is going to be expensive.*

* * *

After being bombarded with overly complicated information and looking at a gazillion different laptops – that all looked identical until they all blurred into one – he exited the store, weighed down with boxes and bags galore. The young male sales assistant clearly knew his stuff, which highlighted the exact opposite about Jim as he was bamboozled with memory sizes, running speeds, and graphics cards.

The young guy – oddly enough called Guy – had gaped at Jim for what felt like an hour when confronted with the news that he had just never been that interested in computers. After being asked what sort of memory he was looking for, Jim restrained himself from saying something ridiculous like, 'I wouldn't mind the memories of Brad Pitt,' and instead looked blankly at the young man. Guy went on to inform Jim that, these days, it was a crime to not have cloud storage. Once again, Jim managed *not* to look skyward and say, 'Doesn't stuff get all wet up there? And won't it fall through?'

Guy had given detailed instructions on how to set everything up when he arrived home and that he needed to call his telephone provider to upgrade his internet connection. He had thrust a business card into Jim's hand, telling him to call if he got stuck, and then he had given him a look of sympathy. Jim felt ancient and about two inches tall but had to admit the information was already a jumble in his mind.

On arriving back at Sunset Cottage, he unloaded his purchases, rolled up his sleeves, and set about the arduous task of joining the 21st century.

Firing up the new laptop was quite exciting. He still loved his old Underwood Champion typewriter and would happily do all his work on that – it was, after all, preferable to the old laptop that he'd bought for university, and still owned. There was something soothing about the click, click of a typewriter and burrr-ing of the winder that made him smile. But these days, it just wasn't practical. So, here he was tapping away at the keyboard of his flashy new laptop, with its touch screen and sleek appearance, feeling quite proud of himself for buying it and not chickening out.

He made a start on Edgar's manuscript as soon as things were set up and gave himself a pat on the back for getting it all to work first time. *In your face, Guy.* He mentally stuck two fingers up at the *barely-out-of-nappies-patronising-to-the-core* sales assistant.

The manuscript pages sent to him by Edgar were wonderful. Jim had always loved the gentle flow of Ed's prose and having this opportunity to write and be published while being able to remain in the background was just mind-blowing. He had gone through the myriad notes with a fine-tooth comb and felt well-equipped to do the work justice. It would keep him occupied while Julian put everything in place over in Glasgow.

* * *

Julian rang later that day. 'Jim! How's it going? You started writing that book yet?'

'Hi, Julian, yeah. I made a start today when I'd finished setting up my new laptop.' Jim couldn't help but smile to himself with pride again.

'Ooh, get you joining the techno-age. You'll be Tweeting next.' Julian chuckled. *Oh no, I bloody won't.* Julian continued, 'Great, great stuff. Anyway, I'm glad you took him up on it. It'll do you good to be writing again. Look, just a quick update. The guy I mentioned at the gallery, Jean-Paul Fabron? Remember? He absolutely loves the paintings, and he has agreed to a three-month exhibition!' The excitement in Julian's voice took it up an octave.

His enthusiasm was contagious, and Jim felt giddiness bubbling up from his boots. 'What? Really?' He sat up straight, silently fist bumping the air and mouthing the words, *Get in!* 'That's fantastic news! Thank you so much, Julian. Thank you.'

'Hey, it's no problem, mate. She's so talented it's worth it to see her get the notoriety she deserves. Now, I need to talk to you about getting her to come over.' Julian's voice became serious. 'I have to be honest; I think it would be best if someone went over to Chicago to speak to her face to face. This is big deal and it's too easy to say no over the phone. But... I think I need to be the one to fly over, Jim.'

Disappointment washed over Jim; his mood plummeted. 'You? How come? I... I wanted to go see her.'

'I know, I know. But I think we need to keep it anonymous right up to the point where she walks in and sees it. I can go over there and pretend to have an amazing find for her. She'd go for that.'

'Aye, I know but—'

'What would you say if you went? That you love her and have taken her most private works and slapped them all over Glasgow to show her just how much? Think about it. What if she's angry? She *could* be. I think that me getting her here is the best idea. Once she sees the exhibition, she'll be bowled over. She couldn't possibly be angry when she sees them up there.'

Jim acquiesced. After all, it did make more sense. But he couldn't help the heaviness he felt over it. 'Aye, okay. So, what's the plan?'

'Right, so here's what I'm thinking. I go over and tell her I've made this amazing discovery, but that I'm keeping it anonymous so that no one else can see the work before Nilsson-Perkins. That I want them to have first refusal, or specifically *her*. She'll go for that. I'll tell her to book a flight and come over so that she thinks she's coming on business. You'll be hiding in the wings, so to speak, when she arrives for her private showing. Et voila! She adores you once she finds out how amazing the paintings look and that you have been instrumental in arranging it all!'

Jim thought for a few moments, his heart already pounding at the plan. 'Okay, so when are you going out?'

'I think next month. The exhibition will start in April, and so she'll have a month to make arrangements and get herself over here. Sorted.'

'And what if she refuses?'

'Not a chance, Jim. I know Felicity of old, mate. She's like a dog with a bone when she sniffs new talent. I only have to think back to how she was with me. Talk about bloody tenacious. She wouldn't leave me alone until I'd agreed to work with her. She's good at her job, Jim, even if she should be painting instead. And I think that I can lay it on thick enough to make her completely intrigued.'

Jim didn't like how much he had been manipulated in one day but had to agree that, in Julian's case, he was right. 'Okay. Great. Keep me posted, eh?'

The call ended and Jim went back to Edgar's book. He made a

call to Edgar's editor to let him know he had taken up the challenge. Geoffrey Haddington had been a long-time friend of Edgar's and was delighted to receive Jim's call.

'I'm so glad you decided to do it, Jim. Edgar thought the world of you, and he was so hopeful that you would take it on, but I was under strict instructions not to bother you if you chose not to. Bless you for doing this.'

'Oh no, don't thank me. It really is an honour. And I thought the world of him, too. I miss hearing from him. But I feel closer to him when I'm working on his book if that makes sense.' Jim felt his cheeks heat at his sentimental admission.

'Perfect sense, Jim. And thanks to you Edgar will live on through this final work. I can tell you with all honesty that he would be so very proud of you. He often spoke of you and how much he missed you being around. I'm sure you know this but... he thought of you as a dear son. And he knew that you would do a good job. Again, thank you.'

The older man's words brought a lump to Jim's throat, but he felt good when the call was over. If he had been in any doubt over completing the book, those doubts had melted away completely now.

23

At the end of their evening, Flick and Ella made their way out of the bar and hailed a cab. Ella was dropped off at her apartment block and then the taxi travelled to the rather plush hotel where Franco had insisted Flick stay for a while until she found somewhere more permanent. It was very elegant and elaborate but it was the kind of place you needed to experience *with* someone. Not alone. And she was oh-so-alone, feeling that ten times more when she arrived back there in the evening and had time to herself. Time to think and reminisce.

She reached the sanctuary of her luxurious and over-the-top suite and unlocked her door with the key card. Falling back onto the plush sofa, she switched on the television, and of course, there it was on the screen, the well-known movie where the girl looks across at the empire state building just as it lights up with a heart and she realises that her Mr Right is probably waiting for her at the top. Jeez, even the TV was mocking her.

Grabbing her bag, she rummaged around in it until she found the card that Vitale had given her. She read it with interest.

Vitale DeLuca, Managing Director,
DeLuca Pharmaceuticals.

Wow. He was a bigwig all right. M.D. of a drug company. Obviously, a drug company that was doing quite well judging by his expensive suit. She took out her mobile and tapped the screen to open the search engine. After typing in Vitale's name, she hit 'search,' but before the internet could enlighten her, the phone died.

'Ugh, where did I put my charger?' she asked the empty room. She located it on the bedside table and plugged in her phone. She contemplated getting her laptop out but decided it was too late in the day, and that there was probably no point seeing as it was doubtful she'd be seeing him again.

She placed the card back in the bottom of her bag as Jim suddenly sprang to mind. Okay, so he wasn't Italian, dark or mysterious. But he was warm, sexy, and hilariously funny. Passionate… yes, he was that, too. She groaned as she realised once again that she had blown it with him.

She resolved to focus on work. Romance was something she could, would, and should live without. Jim was someone she would have to learn to let go of.

Work.

That was the answer.

* * *

Monday morning was bitterly cold. She was beginning to become accustomed to this February, Chicago weather. The skyscrapers went a little way to shielding her from the icy chill, but she still wished she had more appropriate clothing. She resolved that she would have to go shopping.

Shopping in Chicago.

Alone.

Bleurgh. She could ask Ella to accompany her. That would probably be best, as Ella would know the best places to shop. Although after Friday, she was unsure as to how much, other than art, they had in common.

She sat in her office thumbing through some more of the paperwork that Chester had made a pig's ear of. Ella had called and asked if she wanted to join her for lunch, but she had declined.

Sarah, the receptionist who was heavily pregnant, had gone to her prenatal visit, and Kyle, the other gallery assistant, had met his wife and daughter for lunch, and so the gallery had been closed for an hour. Not something Flick would usually do, but on this one occasion, when everything was just so disorganised, it didn't seem to matter too much.

Her head was throbbing, and typically, she didn't have any headache pills with her. She decided to go check the break room and see if there were any in a drawer or cupboard. She hunted through every available cabinet but to no avail.

A door at the other end of the break room had intrigued her for days now. She hadn't noticed it on her last visit, but when she asked Ella what was through there, she was told it was just a stockroom where old, damaged paintings were kept ready for insurance claims. How many damaged items could there be to warrant a whole room?

This was not something that had ever been an issue before. Not something she had heard of. Not something that was needed in the London gallery. It was becoming so very clear why Franco had let Chester go, and she knew that, as the new manager, it would be her job to deal with damages and insurance. *Oh joy*.

She decided, as no one was here to give her lame excuses, that it was time she looked in that storeroom. She wondered what the hell else Chester had done. It had to be him. Ella had seemed sympathetic to him, showing some kind of misplaced loyalty. But Ella was just a nice girl who would do anything for anyone. She must have respected her former boss a great deal. At least she had some admirable qualities, which is more than could be said for the man himself.

She tried the handle, but the door was locked. Incensed that, as the manager of this gallery, there were rooms she couldn't even access, she riffled through drawers looking for a key but her initial search was unfruitful. With her anger increasing she decided that someone must have a key.

Ella wasn't due back for almost an hour, so Flick nervously went to her desk first. No key there. Next, she searched Sarah's desk, and then Kyle's. Nothing. Back to the kitchen, she riffled through the drawer nearest to the door once more. Nothing. One last-ditch attempt found her standing on a chair sliding her hand along the top of the doorframe. And bingo! Sure enough there was a key secreted on the top of the frame amongst the dust bunnies. Why were the contents of this room so protected when they were damaged stock? She took the key down and decided to try the door.

The key fit, and with trepidation at just how much money Chester had seemingly lost for the company, she now dreaded what was behind the mysterious door. She flicked on the light switch and walked in. She gasped, covering her mouth with her hands, as she saw several stacks of paintings. *There must be thousands of dollars of damaged canvas here!* Her heart raced. What the hell had caused this? How could Chester have been so lacking in care? How the hell would she explain this to Franco? How did he not already know this stock existed? And if he did, why had he not informed her?

She flicked through the canvases to see if any could be salvaged. But confusion washed over her. She shook her head and went back to the start. *What the—?* She pulled out canvas after canvas, which showed no damage. Not in any way. So why? She froze when she pulled out two canvases she recognised as pieces by well-respected artist Edward Vincent, who was known for producing valuable one-off paintings. So why were there two canvases here that were identical? And more to the point, why were there two of *this* painting when she had sold the original to a wealthy businessman in London? Looking closer she inspected the signature and numbers denoting that this was, indeed, a one-off. *Oh no! They're copies! Forgeries!* Gathering speed, she flicked through the canvases again.

Copy after copy marked up to be one-off, original pieces. Copies of paintings that were worth tens of thousands of dollars and considering how many of them were here, in this room, it would amount to millions of dollars. *Forgery. Oh. My. God.* Her heart rate increased further and sweat beaded on her forehead. Someone was using this gallery to sell forged artwork. *Shit! This can't be happening!*

She quickly closed and locked the door taking care to leave everything as it was. She needed to think. Who knew about this? Who was in on it? Did Franco know? Surely not. Franco was a genuine man with a passion for originals, especially one-off pieces. There had to be an explanation that didn't include Franco.

She returned to her desk and stared at her phone. Who could she trust with this? She snorted. Of course, Jim would be the only one she would trust with this kind of situation. He was sensible and levelheaded. He would know what to do. She picked up the receiver but immediately put it back down. She couldn't just call him out of the blue. That would be ridiculous after how things had been left between them.

She surmised that Chester was somehow involved but couldn't prove that yet. Considering she was an Oxford graduate from Surrey, this kind of thing was relatively new to her, and she had not one single clue as to how to go about solving such a crime. She was no detective. And she could be implicated in this, too, if the criminal behind it found out she knew. This was not good. *So* not good.

Suddenly, Ella breezed in. 'Hey, there. Brought you a cupcake from the little bakery across the street. They're sooo delicious.' She rolled her eyes as she spoke.

How sweet. Ella had worked here awhile. She would know if dodgy dealings were going on, wouldn't she? Or indeed would she? She had been sympathetic to Chester before. But she was so nice. Maybe she just felt sorry for him? She couldn't possibly be aware.

Ella frowned and tilted her head to the side. 'You okay, Felicity? You don't look so good. You're... real pale.'

Flick rubbed her temples. 'Erm, no. I don't feel too good. I think I have a migraine coming on.'

Ella stepped closer to Flick's desk. 'I have some pain pills. I could bring them to you.'

Flick nodded but it hurt to do so. 'That would be great. Yes, please, Ella.'

Ella disappeared and quickly returned with the tablets and a glass of chilled water. Flick downed two of the capsules and took a large gulp of water. 'Thank you so much.'

'Maybe you should go home? I mean back to the hotel? You look so pale. We can manage here. It's been quiet all day.'

As much as Flick hated to admit it, Ella was right. Plus, she needed to distance herself from her discovery for a while to think. Formulate a plan. She stood and wobbled, the pain in her head causing the dizziness and a wave of nausea to wash over her. She grabbed her bag by the strap, but everything fell out as she did.

Ella crouched to put the items back in Flick's bag. 'Here, let me help you there.' Ella put her arm around Flick's waist. 'Come on, I'll walk you out and hail a cab.'

Flick smiled. 'You're being so lovely. I do appreciate it.'

'Hey, that's what friends are for.' The two women walked towards the exit.

Ella hailed a cab and waited until Flick got inside okay. She instructed the driver where to go and waved goodbye.

'I'll call you later,' Ella told her with the look of concern still in place.

Flick held her hand up in a wave but was struck by dizziness again as she turned her head.

Back in her suite, she sank onto her bed, not really knowing how she managed to coherently pay the driver and make her way up to her room. Migraines weren't something she regularly suffered from, but she knew it could be induced by stress. The events of the day had just about knocked her sideways, but she couldn't think about it now. She decided to let sleep take her and she would think more tomorrow. Thankfully sleep came quickly as the pain pills kicked in and she drifted off.

A phone was ringing somewhere. Flick opened her eyes and carefully sat up as she realised it was her mobile that was making the high-pitched noise. She clambered off the bed and stood. Her head felt much better but there was still a dull ache at the back of her skull that reminded her of why she was there and not at work. The room was dark apart from the light of the lamp in the corner.

She fumbled around and managed to find what she was looking for. 'Hello?' she croaked.

'Finally!' Ella sighed heavily at the other end of the line. 'I was getting so worried, Felicity. I was ready to send for paramedics or something. How're you feeling?'

'Oh... you know... fair to crap.' She yawned.

'Do you want me to come over and look after you? I have nothing planned. I could bring food if you like?'

Bless her. 'No, no, it's fine, Ella. Probably better if I get some more sleep. I feel completely drained.' She rubbed her head again. 'What time is it?'

'It's after eight. I wanted to give you long enough to sleep off the migraine. Do you get them often?' Ella's question stopped Flick for a moment.

'Do you know… I don't remember the last time I had one. It's a long time ago, now.' In reality, Flick knew the last one she had was on the day she left Jim.

'Well, something must have triggered it. I think you should consider seeing a doctor. I can recommend one if you'd like me to. But for now, get some more sleep and stay home tomorrow if you feel bad. Honestly, Felicity, we can manage without you for a couple days.'

'That's very sweet, Ella, but I have a serious job to do at that gallery. I can't afford time off.'

Ella sighed. 'Okay, you're the boss. Sleep well. You have my cell. If you need anything just call, okay?'

'Okay, thanks again, Ella. I really appreciate it.' She hung up.

The next time Flick awoke it was to the sound of her alarm clock. With trepidation, she lifted her head, anxiously awaiting the thud, thud, thud of her headache. Thankfully it didn't happen. Pulling herself to a sitting position, she suddenly remembered what had caused her headache to get so bad in the first place. She let out a long sigh. She really had to think through what to do next about the little stash of art forgeries, and to ensure it was dealt with as soon as possible, but without any innocent parties, mainly herself, being implicated.

She climbed into the shower, turning the dial as hot as she could stand it. Maybe she could scald some ideas into her brain and wash the remnants of the issues down the drain? Neither of those things happened. *Dammit.* She readied herself for work, blow-drying her blonde hair roughly and pinning it up into chignon. She applied a little makeup and put on her charcoal-grey trouser suit.

* * *

When she arrived at the gallery, Sarah was already there, making a pot of fresh coffee. She smiled at Flick as she arrived. 'Good morning, Felicity. Kyle called. He'll be a little late in.'

'Okay. Is everything all right?' Flick enquired.

'His daughter is running a fever and his wife is suffering with morning sickness, so he has to run his daughter to see the paediatrician.'

'Oh dear. I hope she'll be okay.' Flick's concern was fleeting and she felt a little guilty. But she needed to get into her office and formulate a plan.

Ella arrived carrying her staple take-out black coffee and a bran muffin in a brown paper bag. She poked her head around Flick's door. 'Hey. You're looking much better today.'

'Thanks, I feel it. Ella… can I speak with you for a moment?'

Ella's brow furrowed. 'Sure… this sounds ominous. You look serious.'

'Close the door first please,' Flick requested and Ella did as instructed before she walked over to the chair opposite Flick.

Concern was etched on Ella's face. 'Uh-oh… am I in trouble?' She placed her cup and bag on the desk.

Flick smiled as warmly as she could. 'No, nothing like that. I need to speak to you in confidence. A serious matter has come to my attention.'

'Oh? What serious matter?'

'You know the storeroom at the end of the break room?'

'Yesss? The damages den as I like to call it. What about it?'

'I went in to assess how many damaged pieces there are. I'm trying to get a very broad picture of what needs to be dealt with, you understand?'

'Yesss?' Ella's brow was still creased in confusion.

Flick clasped her hands on the desk and informed her, 'I made a rather startling discovery.'

Ella's mouth dropped open and she leaned forward. 'Really? How much damaged stuff was in there?'

'None. Not one damaged thing, Ella.'

Ella's cheeks lost a little colour, and she touched her hands to her face. 'What? I don't understand? Where's it all gone? Chester said it was in there—'

'No, no there were pieces in there. Just not damaged ones.'

Ella shook her head. 'I'm sorry, Felicity. I don't remember Chester dealing with them all before he left. I may be coming across dumb here, but I don't get—'

'Forgeries, Ella.'

Ella's eyes widened like a startled animal. 'I'm sorry? What?'

'I found row upon row of forged pieces. Copies. I know this because there were several copies of *Jagged Heart* by Edward Vincent, a one-off piece that I sold in London to a very private millionaire businessman, and that one *was* the original. I took delivery of it in person from the artist himself.'

'Are… are you accusing me of having some kind of involvement in this?' Ella's face continued its colour-changing journey, this time she blushed cerise, and her eyes became glassy.

Flick shook her head vigorously. 'No! God, Ella no, don't be silly! Not at all.'

Ella heaved a sigh of relief and visibly relaxed. 'Phew! I really thought I was in seriously deep shit for a moment there.'

'No. But I think I do know who is involved.'

Ella narrowed her eyes. 'You do?'

Flick nodded slowly. 'I think it may be Chester.'

Ella laughed loudly. 'Chester? No way! He was so... strait-laced. Honestly. He would never do something like that, Felicity... I swear it.'

Flick leaned forwards. 'Think about it, Ella. He was letting the pressure get to him. He was making lots of mistakes. He was in over his head. I think I need to speak to Franco.'

'No!' Ella spat making Flick jump. 'I-I mean, no, he wouldn't do that.' Desperation filled her voice. 'There must be a mistake. Why don't we do a little bit of detective work? We could figure it out between ourselves, then decide what to do? I'll help. Wouldn't it be better to go to Franco with more evidence than a room full of fakes? We could all be implicated.'

Flick thought about it for a moment. Admittedly, it would be better to go to Franco once they had more evidence. And she couldn't just go accusing someone simply because he was suffering with his health. Perhaps Ella was right? They could do some digging around and see what they could find out.

She sighed. 'Yes, maybe you're right. Maybe we should do a little research? I don't really know where to start.'

'Okay, look, I know Chester. We worked together a hell of a long time. He's a good friend. I could, you know, do a little subtle investigating with him. I could arrange to go see him.'

Flick shook her head vehemently. 'No, Ella. I can't risk you being in any danger.'

'Like I said, I know him very well. He's not a violent man. He's sweet, gentle, and kind. He wouldn't hurt me. I promise you that.'

Flick pondered again. 'Okay. If you're sure you know him well enough.'

'I do. Leave it with me. If he's in on it, I can assure you that I'll be able to tell.' Ella seemed determined to help Flick get to the bottom of this.

'Great. Let me know when you've been in touch with him, okay?'

Ella stood. 'Sure. Is that all?'

'Absolutely. I think that's enough drama for one day, don't you?' Flick rolled her eyes, trying to make light of a very dark situation.

24

As the weeks passed, calls from her mother were becoming frequent. They only added to the weight the art forgeries were pressing on Flick's mind yet somehow the whole situation made her homesick. Only she was homesick for Jim. It was March already and even from this distance, Penelope insisted on giving unwanted advice and repeatedly asked her when she might be returning home. Her mother didn't seem to understand the concept of a permanent job being... well, *permanent*. Although, Flick had to admit that being in Chicago wasn't all she'd hoped it would be so far. Since discovering the stash in the storeroom, Ella had been meeting with Chester to try and wheedle information out of him. Her reports back to Flick were that things were on track, but it was taking so long. Flick wanted things to move much faster as this matter needed to be dealt with and over.

Soon.

'Look, I can't just rush in there and say, "Hey Chester, were you selling fake artwork when you were at the gallery?" He'd run for the hills and then where would we be? If he is involved, we need to be gentle, Felicity. He isn't well and he needs to be treated with kid gloves.'

'I know. I get it. I do. I'm just worried that the longer those things are here, the more chance there is that we could all be implicated too.' Flick shuddered at the thought.

Ella nodded. 'I know. But that's why we need the evidence to stack up. So we're not implicated.'

Flick felt like a schoolgirl sulking because she wasn't allowed to tell a secret. Again, Ella was making sense, but she just wanted the matter out of her headspace.

Flick stood to leave. 'I'd better go. I'll be late for my appointment with the realtor.'

'Are you sure you don't want me to come along? I know the best places to live and if the realtor tries to rent you somewhere gross or in a bad area, I could be there to have your back?'

Flick shook her head and smiled at the gesture. 'I'm a big girl, Ella. I think I can handle apartment hunting.'

Maddison Kennedy met Flick outside the first apartment block. It was an older building but not quite as old as some of the buildings in London. It had character but she just wasn't sure. Although she did need somewhere to live, and soon. She decided it would be best to keep as open a mind as she possibly could manage. After walking up two flights of stairs, Flick realised just how unfit she had become. *Why... is... there... no... elevator?*

'And here we are. Number two fifteen. Come on in.' Flick followed the petite redhead into the flat. She had to stay a couple of steps away so as not to be knocked out by the overpowering perfume that Miss Kennedy wore. 'As you can see, it's open concept, much the same as most of the apartments in the city. It has that old world charm, don't you think?'

'Erm... yes... I suppose so.' *If by old world charm you mean wallpaper that Noah himself could have chosen, wiring of death, and a peculiar smell of cabbage.* She walked around the room. The kitchen area was small and dingy. Someone had painted the cupboards in a dark green for some strange reason. The lounge area had fitted bookshelves, which were probably the nicest thing about the place. There was only just enough room to put a small table by the window.

'Come on, I'll show you the bedroom.' Maddison oozed enthusiasm but Flick guessed that the realtor would no doubt act the same if showing her a cardboard box by the roadside. Occupational hazard.

'Bed*room*? Singular?' Flick enquired.

Maddison's face dropped. 'Ah-huh, that's right.'

'Ah. Therein lies a problem. I need a two-bedroomed apartment. My mother will come to visit at some point, and I don't think I can ask an old lady to sleep on my couch.' Although that idea did appeal just to see the look on Penelope's face. 'And I don't relish the thought of giving up my own bed either.'

'Oh. Okay, let's go to the next place. It's only a couple blocks away. I'll drive us.'

'Great, thanks.' Flick cringed at the thought of being in a close and confined space with *perfume-girl*.

As they left the building, Flick's mobile rang. She excused herself and answered the call.

'Hey, how's the apartment hunt going?' Ella's voice trilled in her ear.

Flick gave a dejected sigh. 'It's not. No luck so far.'

'Well, I have news that may cheer you up!' Ella sounded giddy.

'What news?' *Please let Chester have confessed to everything and be willing to give himself up.*

'You have a visitor waiting here for you,' Ella sang.

Flick's heart jumped into her throat. 'Who? Who is it? Is it Jim?' She was filled with hope.

Ella's voice dropped sympathetically. 'Oh, no, sorry. It's Julian Forster. You know, *the* Julian Forster, famous British artist?'

Flick laughed without any real feeling. 'I know Julian very well, Ella. I discovered him, remember?'

'Whoops, sorry. Anyway, he says there's no rush. He says he'll go across to Mick's and have a drink while he waits for you.'

Flick wondered what on earth Julian was doing in Chicago. His exhibition wasn't until later in the year. 'Tell him I'm on my way.'

Feeling a sense of relief for her nostrils, Flick informed Maddison that an urgent appointment had come up. 'I really should get back. He's flown in specifically to see me, and I can't keep him waiting,' she lied.

She had no clue why he was here. It was a social call for all she knew, but it gave her the excuse she needed to get away from *Miss Perky-Perfume-Pants* and find another realtor. One who actually listened to her clients' requirements and maybe didn't bathe in eau de toilette before leaving the house.

Phew!

They shook hands and Flick hailed a cab to Mick's.

* * *

Fifteen minutes later, after fighting through the bustling metropolis that is Chicago City, Flick walked through the doors of Mick's Bar and scanned the room searching for her friend.

'Felicity!' came a voice from the direction of the bar, and she looked over to see a tousled and bearded man walking towards her.

He was dressed in dark-blue jeans, a lighter blue shirt, and big tan-coloured boots. His signature long black trench coat was unfastened, and he had a striped Edinburgh University scarf draped around his shoulders. In his left hand, he carried a woolly hat that looked far too long to fit any human head.

'Julian! Hi!'

He pulled her into a warm bear hug, towering over her even in her four-inch heels. 'Come on, let's grab a drink. What can I get you?' He kept his arm around her shoulder as they walked over the bar.

She sighed. 'Just a mineral water please. Got to be back at work this afternoon.'

Julian ordered their drinks and guided Flick to a booth towards the back of the bar. The place was surprisingly busy considering the time of day.

When they had made the small talk associated with two friends who haven't seen each other in a while, Flick cut to the chase. 'So, what brings you to *Le Ville Venteuse*?' She giggled at her own terrible French accent.

Julian laughed, too, rolling his eyes. 'Ah, well, therein lies a tale Ms Johnston-Hart. I have something for you.'

She held out her hands. 'Ooh, I love presents. Gimme, gimme.'

'Not so impatient, honey. I can't give it to you directly as such. You have to come and see it.'

She narrowed her eyes at him but kept her smile in place. 'Hang on. Are you being smutty? Because if you are—'

'Good grief, no!' He laughed. 'No offence but my heart belongs thoroughly in the clutches of another. No this is work related.'

Flick sighed. 'Oh. I got excited then.' She took a sip of her iced mineral water wishing it were wine.

Julian raised his eyebrows. 'Don't sound so disappointed. I can assure you, you will love this.'

Suddenly, paying full attention to Julian, she leaned forward across the table. 'I'm all ears.'

'Okay. So, there I am looking through some paintings belonging to a friend when I come across these amazing pieces by an unknown artist.' His eyes sparkled as he spoke.

Flick's interest peaked. She loved to discover new talent. 'Tell me more. I like the sound of this.'

'I knew you would.' He grinned. 'Okay, so I'm not at liberty to reveal the artist's identity yet. She's quite shy, and we feel that until you've seen her work and decided whether you think Nilsson-Perkins will be interested, we should keep her name quiet.'

Flick's face scrunched in irritation. 'That's a bit unorthodox, Julian.'

'Yep, yep, I'm aware of that. But you trust me, don't you?'

'Of course.'

'Right, okay then. What else do you need to know?'

'Well, I've ascertained the tiny detail that the artist is female, so... where is she from? Who are her influences? What does she paint? How old is she?'

'She's from the South of England. Her influences are the greats, Monet, Manet, myself.' He dusted at his shoulders in a boastful manner and with a glint in his eye. 'She paints the most amazing landscapes. But she doesn't just paint the scene. She brings it to life in the most remarkable way. And the way she uses light...' Julian rolled his eyes back as if in some kind of euphoric state. 'I'm telling you, Felicity, she is the next big thing.'

'Hmm. Well, I suppose you should know, having been in that position yourself, eh?' Flick poked his arm playfully across the table. 'She sounds great.' Her eyes glazed over a little as she felt a surge of emotion.

'You okay, Felicity?' Julian sounded concerned and his crumpled expression told her the same.

'Sorry, yes. Just a little melancholy. Things have been a little tough lately and, well, I used to paint. I think I miss it. Being here makes me see that and hearing you talk about this young woman makes me feel a little envious. What I wouldn't have given for someone to have said that kind of stuff about my work...' She waved her hand dismissively and cleared her throat as she shook her head. 'Oh well, what's past is past. Just ignore me. Right, so when do I get to meet her?'

Julian seemed to be stifling a smile. 'That's the thing. She won't fly. I need you to come to Glasgow and see her work.'

She narrowed her eyes. 'But you said she was from the south of England, and why can't she fly? I *hate* flying and yet I still do it. And besides I'm rather busy here. I don't think I have the time to—'

'It's a medical condition,' he blurted. 'Yeah, she's awaiting clearance for flying, but it'll take too long if we wait. And she can't risk trying. And yes, she is from down south, but lives and paints in Glasgow just now. Honestly, you don't want to miss out on her. I swear you'll regret it.'

She eyed him suspiciously for a moment. But his expression was blank. 'Okay. When do I need to come out?'

He exhaled a huge breath. 'Great! Okay, you really need to fly out in April so it's not long. I have the details of the exhibition I'm helping to set up, right here.'

He handed her a piece of paper with details scribbled on it. She cringed. 'Gosh, Julian, you should have been a GP with writing like this!' She laughed and his cheeks flamed.

'Good job I'm an artist then. People only have to be able to read my autograph.'

She rolled her eyes. 'True.'

Julian and Flick spent the next hour catching up and eating a late lunch, which she decided she needed. He was only in Chicago overnight, so they hugged and parted, agreeing to see each other in April in Glasgow.

* * *

Back at her hotel that night, Flick felt lonelier than ever. She contemplated contacting Ella but decided she had leaned on her enough lately. She pulled out a box from her wardrobe that she had made sure to keep with her when most of her other belongings had gone into storage.

It was a box of keepsakes, things of sentimental value, things she knew would make her cry. She didn't look at the contents of the box often. In fact, for her own sanity, she chose to avoid looking inside the box at all costs. She had only brought it to the hotel as the thought of it being piled up in some storage unit made her feel physically sick. They were her memories after all. Little pieces of her heart were hidden in the contents of the box.

Seeing Julian had exacerbated her homesickness. He was a connection with the UK having been her first big discovery and was the only person from her art-world life that Jim had any friendship with. They'd got on well and remembering this made her miss Jim even more. It was silly really. It wasn't as if they were best friends. It was a tenuous link when all was said and done. But it was a link, and it made her heart ache.

Tentatively removing the lid from the box, she looked inside. Folded pieces of paper, photos, movie ticket stubs, and a little teddy bear. She pulled out the first piece of paper.

You are my soul; my love has no destination without you
    You are my breath; I breathe but dust when we're apart
        You are my warmth: chills sear me when you're gone from me.

You are my friend, my love, my passion; you are my heart.

The poem Jim had written for her on their first Valentine's Day apart was the first thing she came across. She'd been in Chicago and he had hidden it in amongst her clothing in her suitcase. She had cried silent tears when she'd read it then; now was no different. She hated that she had been so dismissive of him then when he'd clearly been missing her. She'd been too hellbent on making a good impression with her colleagues and contemporaries. Now, here she was in Chicago without him once more. Only this time he wasn't waiting at home for her return.

25

Jim's eyes were fuzzy, and when he looked at the clock, he was surprised to discover it was eleven in the evening. He had been trying to keep his mind off Julian's visit to Chicago. He said he would call as soon as he could with news, but as yet no call had come through. He was hoping this lack of communication wasn't a negative thing. But he couldn't be sure.

Would Flick see right through the plan and figure out who was behind it all? Would she believe every word that fell from Julian's lips? She had no real reason not to, but she may think it was odd. Who would blame her?

He shut his laptop down and resorted to making a cup of hot chocolate and clearing out the fire grate. It was a very cold March evening and the fire had been on the go most of the day. He had let it die down a couple of hours earlier, thinking he would write for another ten minutes and then go to bed. That hadn't happened and now he could see his breath clouding when he exhaled.

He took Jasper out to find there had been another snowfall. This time it was a light dusting that glittered in the yellow of the streetlights. There had been talk of more snow all week at the

Coffee Shack, but so far it wasn't as bad as had been anticipated. He only hoped that Shieldaig wouldn't be snowed in again anytime soon. He had plans.

The island off the coast glowed a pale silver in the hazy moonlight with its frosty smattering. The water surrounding it was almost still, but Jim could hear the ripples as the gentle, yet chilled, breeze tickled the surface.

Jasper nudged his hand.

'Are you cold too, eh, lad? Come on, let's get back home.'

* * *

Once back in the lamplight of Sunset Cottage, Jim and Jasper huddled under a fleece blanket on the couch. Jim began to doze off. He fought sleep as best he could, but Jasper's gentle snoring lulled him ever closer to the Land of Nod. Every few minutes he jerked his head up after drifting off.

Suddenly the phone rang, and Jim dived towards it, narrowly escaping broken ribs in the process as he landed on the hard arm of the couch and grabbed the landline handset.

'Hello? Julian?' he panted.

'Hi Jim! You sound like you've been jogging.' Julian laughed.

'Hardly. It's midnight here.' He tried but couldn't keep the annoyance out of his voice.

'Yeah, sorry about that. I've just got back to my hotel from seeing Felicity.'

'And?' He didn't even try to hide his impatience.

Julian yelled down the line, 'She fell for it, mate! Woo hoo!'

Jim's breath left his body in one quick huff. 'Thank heavens for that!'

Julian laughed triumphantly. 'Erm, I think you mean thank *Julian* for that.'

'Aye! That as well!' Jim chuckled. 'How did she seem?' *Please say she talked about me non-stop and misses me terribly.*

'She looks amazing, Jim. I won't lie to you. I mean sizzling hot. You're one lucky dude, I tell you. Want to know something funny?'

'Always,' Jim replied

'When I told her about our mystery artist, she got all misty-eyed and said how much she missed painting.'

Jim was shocked but over the moon with that little nugget of information. 'What? Really?'

'Really. She's so talented Jim, but she doesn't even realise it. She just hasn't got a clue.'

'Aye, you're right.' Jim chuckled. 'Honestly, Julian, I can't thank you enough. I really appreciate all this. You're sacrificing a lot for me.'

'Nah. I'm sacrificing nothing. She discovered me and now it's my turn to help her dreams come true. Honestly, I have nothing better to do with my time at the moment. The cash is rolling in nicely and I'm all finished on the pieces for my next big exhibition, so this is giving me something to focus on. And to be truthful, I've found it quite exciting, all this cloak and dagger subterfuge shit. It's a break from my normal routine.'

'Aye, well, it means the world to me, all this.' Jim suddenly felt emotional, so he cleared his throat and said his goodbyes.

He shuffled up to bed despite the fact he was now wide awake. A new flood of adrenaline coursed through his veins and he prayed that he hadn't left things too late. He'd wanted to go to Flick as soon as he'd read Edgar's letter, but then with the arrival of his brother his plans had been scuppered. He'd lost confidence. Simply turning up now that she had gone to Chicago was not an option. She would be in her element there. The last thing he wanted was to fly all the way out there to be shot down in flames. No, this was the best way.

This way he had a life to offer her that would make her come alive again, and he couldn't wait.

* * *

Early evening, Flick sat watching mind-numbing reality shows on the TV in her suite. She was bored and miserable and contemplating calling room service when her telephone rang. Perhaps Ella had come to her rescue again.

'Hello?' she answered in a less than enthusiastic tone.

'Ms Johnston-Hart?' the young man on reception asked.

Well, who else would it be you utter muppet? I'm alone up here. As usual.

'Yes, this is she.'

'Ah, good. There's a gentleman in reception to see you.' Her heart fluttered. Who on earth would be here? Julian was going home. Unless his flight was delayed, or he'd decided to stay to do some sightseeing. The young man spoke again. 'Ms Johnston-Hart?'

'Oh, yes, sorry. Did he give a name?' she asked, puzzled.

'Yes, he says he is Vitale DeLuca.'

Ohmygodohmygodohmygod! 'Oh! Did he say what he wants?' She glanced into the mirror at her reflection. *Hmm, hair in a ponytail, no makeup, yoga pants, and a T-shirt. Great. Very glamorous. Not.* There was a long pause while she presumed the receptionist was asking her visitor what he wanted.

Oh great. Not at all embarrassing then.

'He says he's here to take you to dinner and the table is booked in our restaurant to dine in half an hour. He says he will wait in the lounge while you ready yourself.'

Presumptuous or what?! 'Right. Okay. Please tell Mr DeLuca I'll be down as soon as I can. Oh, and tell him I apologise for keeping him waiting.' She waited as the receptionist relayed the information.

'He says... ahem... you are worth the wait, Ms Johnston-Hart.' Even though Vitale was not in the room, Flick's cheeks heated at hearing his words relayed to her.

'Thank you. Bye.' She hung up and dashed to her wardrobe. Riffling through, she located the little black dress that she had brought along for evenings out. Not that she anticipated needing to wear it at all. She showered quickly, being careful not to wet her hair. Once out and dried she applied a little makeup and combed through her hair.

She slipped into her dress and black stilettos and surveyed her reflection in the full-length mirror. The dress was her favourite, sleeveless and fitted with a slash neck. The little teardrop opening gave just a hint of cleavage, very elegant and not revealing. The fitted style accentuated her feminine curves.

* * *

She grabbed her purse and made her way down to the hotel lobby where she spotted him.

Her breath caught in her throat.

He was standing with his back to her. Very tall and broad-shouldered, black hair neatly trimmed into the back of his neck. He wore stone-coloured trousers that fitted his form very well, and a chocolate-brown suit jacket.

As if he sensed her presence, he turned to her. Under the jacket, he wore a button-down shirt in pale blue. He looked like he had walked there direct from an ad for some high-end aftershave lotion, all casual and sultry. And that megawatt smile... Oh boy, was she in trouble.

He walked towards her, his handsome, panties-melting smile staying in place. When he reached her, he bent to kiss both cheeks.

'Bella... Sei un gioello.' She recognised the phrase he had used last time. 'You really are exquisite, Felicity.' The way he spoke her name with the rich hint of an Italian accent, sent shivers down her spine. She smiled as she felt her cheeks flush again and butterflies tap-dance around her tummy.

Pure. Unadulterated. Lust.

She gazed up at him. 'Vitale. How lovely to see you. What brings you here? We didn't arrange anything.'

'I know. My apologies again. I saw your work colleague... Miss Cole? She was at the bar again and I asked her for your number. She refused to divulge the information but told me you were staying here, and if I wanted to see you, I had to go through the hotel. She must think highly of you. She is protective, *si*?'

Flick smiled. She would have to thank Ella on Monday. 'It appears so. What did you want to see me about?' She fiddled with her hair.

He shrugged. 'I simply wanted to see you. No other reason than that. I couldn't stop thinking about you. It seems you have made an impersonation on me.' He smiled.

Flick couldn't help but giggle. 'I think you mean I made an *impression* on you.'

He rolled his eyes and his tanned cheeks coloured ever so slightly. 'Oh my. Yes, I think perhaps you are correct. I get a little wrong sometimes with my words.'

She smoothed her hand down his lapel, immediately regretting the intimate gesture. 'Not at all. You speak English very well, Vitale.'

'Ah, you are too kind, *bella*. I think we should go. Our table... I hope it is okay that I choose the restaurant here?' He held out his arm and she took it and walked beside him.

The panelled dining room was delightful in its rich, luxurious decor. Crystal chandeliers hung from the ceiling and refracted shards of light around the intimate space. Classical music played in the background, and there was a low mumble of conversation. They were seated at a table for two and a smartly dressed waiter brought over a wine menu, handing it to Vitale.

'Would you like to select a wine, Felicity?' He offered her the menu as her name danced off his tongue in the same beat as her skipping heart.

'No, no, you choose, that's fine.'

He perused the menu and waved the waiter over. 'Could we please have a bottle of the Gosset Brut?' He handed the list back to the waiter.

She clasped her shaking hands on her lap. 'Brut? Are we celebrating?'

'I think we should celebrate your beauty and the fact that you allowed me to take you out this evening.' He leaned his hands on the table and stretched out towards her. It was almost an invitation.

She felt her cheeks heat again. 'Oh, really, Vitale, you do flatter me.'

He waved his hand dismissively. 'Not at all. I simply speak the truth.'

Over dinner they chatted about Flick's job and her passion for art, then briefly about Vitale's business. He didn't give much away about what he did other than he had studied medicine at university in Milan but had chosen not to pursue a career as a doctor. She thought it was a shame and could imagine the female patients feigning illness to be seen by him.

'How did you end up in Chicago?' Flick asked with intrigue.

Vitale sighed. 'I followed my heart. I met a beautiful woman when I was studying. She was taking a year out in Italy. I fell in love. When I graduated, I followed her. We had two wonderful years until she realised she loved me no longer.' He shrugged. 'But by this time Chicago was already my home.'

'Oh goodness, I'm so sorry to hear that.'

He smiled warmly. 'I am not sorry. Because now I meet you.'

Dinner was wonderful, three courses of the most delicious food, alongside delightful company. Vitale insisted on paying the bill and left a generous tip before walking her to the elevator bank.

He lifted her hand and kissed it softly. 'Thank you, *cara mia*, for a most wonderful evening. It has been an absolute pleasure.'

'W-would you like to come up for a night cap?' *Stupidstupid-stupid woman.* She wanted to take back the words, but it was too late. His eyes lit up and she began back-pedalling, 'Obviously, I know you're a busy man and probably have things to do—'

'No, not at all. I made sure this evening was free just for you. I would very much like to come up for a night cap.'

Dammit. 'Okay, great.' No. It really wasn't. It was a colossal mistake.

* * *

Once on her floor she unlocked her suite door and walked inside holding the door open for him. He glanced around. 'Nice place you have here.' He turned to her with a grin on his face.

She returned the smile. 'Why, thank you. I think so, too. I'll get us a drink... brandy?'

Vitale nodded, silently watching her. She went to the oak bureau where the hospitality items were kept and located the small bottle of amber liquid. As she stood there pouring their drinks, he walked up behind her and slid one arm around her waist. He pulled her hair to one side and kissed her neck softly.

Shivers traversed her spine and she felt annoyed at her body's betrayal.

She clenched her eyes closed. 'Oh! When I offered a night cap... I'm afraid I meant just a night cap, Vitale.'

He turned her around in his arms so that she faced him. 'Please forgive me, *bella*. I cannot help it. You drive me crazy with your accent and your beautiful eyes.' He stroked her cheek and gazed at her. 'Please, Felicity, let me kiss you just once.' He bowed his head towards her and paused briefly before taking her mouth with his.

His lips were soft but demanding. His skin moved smoothly over hers, and he groaned as he slid his hands into her hair. She couldn't deny the kiss was rather delicious, but it felt wrong.

Guilt knotted her insides.

Before she could protest, he slipped his hands to her back and began to slowly slide the zip of her dress down, down, down. He caressed her bare back with gentle fingertips, and she gasped, her traitorous body reacting once again against her will.

'*Il tuo corpo è bello... bella... Voglio fare l'amore con te,*' he mumbled huskily as he kissed her. Caught up in the moment and probably because of his Italian mutterings, she began to help him remove his jacket. He pulled it off and threw it over onto the chaise. He slid her dress from her shoulders and gasped when he was presented with her black lace underwear. '*Sei bellissima,*' he whispered.

He crushed his mouth into hers again and held her with one arm at the small of her back whilst he unbuttoned his shirt with the other. He released her momentarily to slip his trousers off.

She clenched her eyes closed again wondering what the hell she was thinking and her mother's words about kissing on a first date rattled around her head. *My god, Penelope would have a coronary right now.*

Scooping her up in his arms, he carried her over to the bed and laid her down hovering over her. '*Sì ... sì ... bellissima.*'

Nervously, she looked up at him. 'I'm so sorry but I have no clue what you're saying to me, Vitale, even though it sounds so beautiful.'

'I am telling you that you are beautiful, and I want nothing more than to make love to you now.' He slowly bent to kiss her again, but she froze. 'Felicity... what is wrong? Are you all right?' He lay down beside her and stroked her cheek.

Her eyes began to sting, and she bit her lip. 'Vitale, I'm so sorry. I can't do this. I can't sleep with you.'

He looked genuinely concerned, which made it worse. 'But, *cara mia*, what is wrong? Did I upset you? I know you said no to begin with, but... but I did not mean for you to feel pressured... you seemed to enjoy—'

A tear escaped as she pulled herself to a sitting position. 'No, you did nothing wrong. You've been lovely. You're a very attractive man and I'm pretty sure I'm completely loopy... but—'

A look of confusion took over his handsome features. 'Loopy? I do not know... what is this loopy, *cara*?'

'Crazy, Vitale. It means crazy. And I must be because I'm here in Chicago, single, and alone, and a sexy, intelligent, Italian hunk of a man is trying to seduce me and here I am crying like an idiot.'

'*Bella*, why is it that you cry? Can I help? Are you unwell?'

God, why does he have to be so effing nice?

She let out an exasperated sigh. 'Vitale, I can't sleep with you because I'm hopelessly in love with my ex-husband. My ex-husband, who doesn't even want me. There I admitted it to a stranger. A complete stranger who desires me and wants to have sex with me!' She laughed derisively. 'I'm totally mental! I must be.' She threw her arms up and looked over at Vitale, who sat there looking sexy and unkempt in boxers and his open shirt with his sculpted, hairy chest on show.

Goodness, he really is delicious.

'He is your ex, yet you still love him?' Vitale continued to look bemused and there was no wonder.

'Yes. I left him years ago. I thought I wanted a different life, but I was wrong. And now he's moved on with his life and doesn't want me any more. It serves me right.'

'*Bella*. Have you spoken to this... this... ex?'

'Jim... his name's Jim, and no I haven't spoken to him because I'm a coward, and he would trample all over my heart, which is exactly what I deserve after how I treated him. I do need to get over him. I do. But I'm just not ready yet. I'm so sorry for wasting your time. Really I am.' She lifted her chin and met with his compassionate gaze.

'Well, I think he must be the loopy one.' He smiled and tucked a strand of hair behind her ear. 'You are a beautiful woman, Felicity. And I want you badly. But I see your heart belongs to another. I would be more than happy to help you get over your ex... but as you say this is not what you desire right now, and so I will step aside.' He lifted her hand and kissed it.

'Vitale, you're so very sweet. And so gracious. I feel terrible and incredibly stupid.' She wrapped her arms around her semi-naked body.

Somehow understanding her discomfort without her uttering a word, he dragged the comforter from the end of the bed and wrapped it around her. 'I will leave now. But if you would like to get out for a little sightseeing or to have coffee, or lunch perhaps, you have my card. Please do not hesitate to call me. And if you should suddenly change your mind, I am happy to help you with your... how you say... exorcising the ex.' He smiled that sexy, wonderful, perfect smile and her heart sank.

For a moment, she wondered if she was passing up a potentially wonderful relationship with an extremely attractive and pleasant man. But she really wasn't the type of person who could just sleep with someone for pure gratification. At that moment in time, she sincerely wished she was.

Vitale dressed himself and Flick pulled on her robe. He kissed her softly on the cheek. He smelled so good, and part of her wanted to pull him back to the bed and take advantage of his offer to help exorcise Jim. But she knew that as soon as things got hot and heavy the reality of her heart would spring to the forefront of her mind once again. And so, she thanked him for a wonderful meal, apologised again and said goodbye.

26

Flick's cell phone rang in the early hours of Sunday morning. Startled, she clambered out of bed and fumbled for her phone.

She finally spoke, out of breath. 'Hello?'

'Felicity, it's Ella. There's been a break-in at the gallery.' Her voice was filled with distress. 'They're gone. The forgeries have been taken.'

Flick sat bolt upright. 'What?! When?' Panic washed over her. 'I-I... what about the other pieces?'

'That's the weird thing, nothing else was taken. I can't call the police, Felicity. If I call the police and they find out that only forgeries were taken, they'll wonder why we didn't report them and we'll look so guilty. We can't report them now. We'd be in so much shit. I don't know what to do. I'm so scared.'

Flick was shaking and her heart was beating so loudly she could hear the pounding in her ears. 'Ella, are you okay? Are you safe?'

'Y-yes. I'm fine. Just a little shaken. We'll need to get someone in to change the locks.'

'Hang on... why were you contacted about this and not me?' Flick asked, puzzled.

'I guess Franco forgot to update the database with the security firm. It's no biggy. Don't worry. I'm fine. Just a little upset.'

'Where are you? I'll come and get you.' Flick rushed the words out.

'No, no, don't do that. I'm home now. The doors are temporarily secured, and the security firm has been instructed to guard the premises. It'll be fine.'

Flick sighed. 'Okay, well if you're sure. I'll be in early and I'll try to deal with this. We'll come up with something, I promise, Ella.'

'The thing that's scaring me the most is that whoever oversaw the forgery racket knows that *we* know something. Why else would they break in now to take the pieces? What if they come after us?' Ella sounded terrified.

'No, no. I think that now they have the paintings they have exactly what they want. Maybe it's over, Ella. I really hope it is.'

'Me too, Felicity, me too. I'll see you soon.'

* * *

Sleep evaded Flick for the rest of the night as she tossed and turned wondering what the hell to do next. Eventually, giving in to her wakefulness, she showered and dressed quickly, leaving the hotel without eating. She arrived at the gallery early to find Ella already inside assessing the damage.

She rushed over and flung her arms around Flick's neck, sobbing. 'Oh, Felicity, I'm so scared.'

'Hey, shhh. It's okay. I'm sure it'll be fine now. I think it's over. Like I said last night, they have what they want. They didn't take any of the other pieces.'

Ella was shaking uncontrollably. 'But what if they come after us?'

Flick placed her hands firmly on Ella's shoulders. 'Ella, you need to calm down. I will figure this out. Why would they bother coming after us? It's not like we really know anything. I'm going to the UK next week to meet a new artist, and I'll think all of this through. When I return, we're going to report this whole thing, first to Franco and then to the police. We'll do it together and back each other up. I just need to think it through.' She bit her lip. 'And maybe if we leave it awhile the criminals will think we're going to do nothing. If they're watching us, they'll see things going on as normal. That way they won't know to expect the police. I need to put everything down in writing and get the facts straight so that you and I are not implicated at all. We need to be kept out of this whole thing, or it could ruin both of our careers.'

Ella chewed on a fingernail. 'Do you think that'll work? If we wait, I mean?'

Flick nodded. 'I hope so. I think so.'

Ella closed her eyes for a moment. 'Okay. Have you booked your flight for the UK and everything? Hotels and a car?'

'Not yet. I need you to do that for me whilst I start compiling a report. Franco knows about the trip, but he doesn't know the reasons behind it as yet.'

'Okay. I'll get on it right away. Will you be flying business class or first class?'

'Oh, I'll just fly regular economy. It'll be fine.' Flick turned towards her office.

'Economy? Ewww. How come?'

'No reason. Just go ahead and book. I'll be fine in economy.' She went into her office and closed the door behind her.

* * *

Being surrounded by wonderful art and discovering new talent used to thrill Flick. The buzz of finding an unknown artist with lots of potential used to drive her. But hearing Julian talk about the painter he had discovered, and how this woman produced pieces with such passion had made her long to paint again. All this talk of forgeries, break-ins, and criminal activity on her doorstep tarnished everything.

Being so far away from everything she loved and knew was difficult, and she had felt like a fish out of water ever since arriving in Chicago. It was such an amazing city, and this had been the opportunity of a lifetime, but all she could think about was Jim and going home. She wanted to be with him. He had loved her once. Maybe if she returned to the UK, she could at least go to visit him and try to make him see that she had changed? She contemplated calling him but every time she picked up her mobile, she was reminded of his parting words and her heart squeezed. This was something she needed to do in person, face to face. It was the only way to show him how she really felt.

There must have been something deep within him, some part of him that still wanted her. She just hoped that it wasn't only a physical pull that remained. She wanted his heart to still desire her, too. The sex between them had always been great. The trust to share their desires and fantasies was something she had cherished until she had been convinced by her mother that sex and love weren't enough. But now she knew, in spite of Penelope's protestations, that career, money, and power weren't all they were made out to be either. Especially if there was no one to go home to at the end of the day.

She had decided, however, that whatever happened now, returning to the UK was the best plan. This was not the type of business you could be a part of if your heart wasn't in it. And her heart was, sadly, no longer in it. Her heart had only one place it wanted to be and that was with Jim.

27

Flick sat in the public area of O'Hare International Airport clutching the little case that held her tickets and passport. She had arrived way too early, as usual, and was plucking up the courage to go to the check-in desk. She felt sick to her stomach just as she did every single time she flew. Ridiculous considering the very nature of her job. *International Art Dealer – pah! Laughable.* This time was worse, however, as she knew that she had to speak to Franco whilst in the UK and inform him of the fraudulent goings on in the Chicago gallery. She hadn't made Ella privy to this latest snippet of information, as she didn't want to cause her any further worry. But Flick now had enough evidence to point the finger at former gallery manager, Chester Withers.

Her palms were sweating, and her heart was presumably choreographing a new version of *Riverdance* in her chest judging by its erratic beat. She glanced around at the eclectic mix of people surrounding her: Businesspeople in suits conversing seriously on mobile phones; parents and young children playing eye-spy games to try and fend off the boredom of waiting; couples saying their heartfelt goodbyes.

Her own heart skipped a beat as she thought about how close to Jim she was about to be. In less than a day, she was going to be in Glasgow to view the new artist's work, so she was going to make time to travel up and see him again or at least to ask him to meet her. There were so many things she needed to say that couldn't be said over the phone. Apologies needed to be made in person. She realised now that he was who she wanted, despite their last encounter. She had to fight for him, prove to him that she had changed. And if it was too late, which she suspected it was, well... at least he would know the truth and she would have the opportunity for closure, knowing that she had done everything she possibly could.

This was going to be her second to last trip back to the UK if things went as she planned. Chicago was not for her. She had once thought it offered her exactly the life she craved. But hearing about this fantastic, new, mysterious female artist had made her yearn for her brushes and canvas. She missed her friends. For goodness' sake, she even missed her mum.

* * *

'Room for a little one?' A familiar voice broke her from her reverie. Looking up she smiled into the face of Ella Cole.

Flick jumped up and pulled her colleague into a death grip hug. 'What are you doing here?!'

'I should be asking you the same. I went by your hotel to check up on you, and they said you had already checked out. Why are you here so damned early?'

'Nerves, I guess. I always do this. I'm always scared that I'll realise I've forgotten something and have to go back. So, if I get here early, I have plenty of time.' Flick's face heated at the admission.

Ella laughed. 'Hmm, that's some twisted logic you got there, missy.'

Flick shrugged. 'Yes, it is, but it works for me. So why are you checking up on me?'

'Well, you sounded kinda worked up about the flight, and about seeing Jim, so, when I found out you'd come here so long before your flight, I thought I'd come keep you company for a couple of hours while you waited to check in. Give you a little moral support.' Ella smiled sweetly and held out her hands in a ta daaaa gesture.

'Oh, that's so lovely. Thank you so much. I could use a friend to keep my mind occupied. I do so hate flying. Come and sit.' Flick sat again.

'Tell you what. Why don't I go and get you something to drink? Calm your nerves a little?'

'Oh, I don't know. It's only just after lunch, and I know it's maybe a little too much information, but I tend to get sick before a flight. So, it wouldn't work anyway.'

'Sure, it would. And you won't get sick because I'm here to take your mind off of things.'

Flick pondered on the thought of alcohol on her already churning stomach. 'I really don't think—'

'Don't forget you have to check in and clear security yet, and then you'll be sitting around for a while or looking around the boutiques before you board. Anything you drink now will relax you for a little while but will have gotten out of your system way before that.'

Flick scrunched her nose, 'Ahh, I just don't feel—'

Ella tipped her head to the side and framed her face with her fingers playfully. 'Look, trust me, I'm a Chicagoan.'

'Oh, okay. Just one then, I suppose.'

Ella clapped her hands theatrically and headed for the bar.

Flick sat, nervously staring up at the screen displaying flights and departure times. Flight nine four two was going to depart right on time at five p.m. She had been sitting here for what had felt like a decade, when in fact, it had only been an hour or so.

Her mother was meeting her at Heathrow in the morning, briefly, before the connecting flight to Glasgow, after insisting that she had missed her terribly, and then guilt-tripping her with, 'But darling, your little artist can wait, I'm your mother. Surely, I'm more important? Surely you can delay your trip to Glasgow for a day for your mother?'

Flick had agreed they could meet in the public area at Heathrow for coffee, but that she only had a couple of hours until her connecting flight. Her mother had sighed and reluctantly agreed, at which time Flick had rolled her eyes. Her mother was going to have to get used to her making her own decisions from now on.

Out of guilt she had foregone her first-class ticket and the sumptuous lounge that went with it – a decision she now regretted – knowing she would be flying back here only to tie up loose ends, before handing in her resignation and flying home again permanently.

Permanently. Her heart skipped once again.

'There you go. Jack and Coke. With ice and a twist, seeing as we're celebrating.'

Flick took the glass from Ella and took a large gulp. 'What are we celebrating?' She already knew the answer.

Ella rolled her bright green eyes. 'Your future with your ex of course! Even though I think you're totally crazy.'

Hearing those words made Flick's stomach do somersaults as the butterflies took flight again. She took another large gulp and shivered as the bitter alcohol hit her throat. 'I know... I just... I love him. I always have. So many things have gone wrong for us. But I need to at least try to get him back.'

Ella's bottom lip protruded in a mock sulk. 'There are so many hot guys in Chicago who would just adore you and your British accent. Chicago guys are the best. You just haven't given them a chance. Take that Vitale guy.' She fanned herself. 'He was so hot. Although I don't suppose he could be classed as a Chicagoan... but anyways, I wouldn't have turned him down!'

'Yes, but that would just be lust and I want—'

Ella interrupted rolling her eyes again. 'Love, yada, yada... love... blah, blah. I get it.' She smiled and leaning over she squeezed Flick's hand. 'Don't worry. It will all be over soon.'

Flick huffed and scrunched her nose. 'Over? Thanks for that vote of confidence.' She gulped her drink again.

Ella giggled. 'You know what I mean.'

A flush of nervous energy rolled over Flick and her stomach lurched. 'Oh god, I think I'm going to be sick, Ella.'

Ella nudged her and teased, 'Oh em gee, you're such a baby!' When Flick glared at her she shook her head. 'I guess a sense of humour is something you don't have right now. Okay, look, you go and... do whatever you need to do in the restroom. You can leave your stuff with me. Try to hold on to your lunch though, okay? It's not good to fly on an empty stomach.'

Flick stood and her stomach rolled again. 'I'm not sure that's going to happen.' Without another word, she ran to the nearest bathroom, her hand covering her mouth. Luckily, the ladies' room was empty. She made it into a cubicle and hurled. Alcohol plus nerves equals a very bad combination. Sweating and panting, she sat back onto the hard, tiled floor. Her head pounded. This was one of the most severe flight panics yet, hardly surprising under the circumstances. *I really should take a fear of flying course.* The cubicle began spinning. Lurching forward, she vomited again as her head swam.

* * *

Jim stood wide-eyed beside a grinning Julian Forster. 'This place looks absolutely amazing, Julian. I can't thank you enough.' He roughly hugged his friend and ally.

The exhibition, *Through the Glass*, was due to open in three night's time. Flick would land at Heathrow early tomorrow and then get a connecting flight up to Glasgow.

Jim couldn't hide his excitement. There was also a little trepidation. What if his plan didn't work? He had hurt her deeply when he last saw her. Then there had been the letter from her father urging him on. She had to still want him. She *had* to.

'Jim, I'm honoured to have helped you, my friend. I really hope this works. You two are just meant to be together.' Julian squeezed Jim's shoulder.

Jim held out his hand. 'Oh god, look Julian. I'm shaking. I'm so nervous. Her flight will be boarding soon. She'll be here in a day! What the hell will I do if she slaps me and walks away for good?' His voice wavered as he almost pleaded with Julian to tell him it would all work out.

Julian turned to face him and placed a hand firmly on each shoulder. 'Look, Jim, you're taking a risk, admittedly. But think about it. Her dad says she has never stopped loving you. And who knows a woman better than her dad, eh?'

Jim pulled in a long, deep, steadying breath. 'Aye... aye... she has to be happy. That's all I want. And look at this place. She has to love this.' He gestured around the room at Flick's artwork as it hung there in all its beautiful splendour.

Julian slapped his back. 'Now, I want you to go back to the hotel. Take a long soak in the tub, chill out for a bit. Maybe even sleep because by the look of you, you haven't done much of that since this whole plan was borne. You know Jasper is safe with your neighbour, so you've only to concentrate on picking up your suit from the hotel reception and awaiting the arrival of your gorgeous, talented girl. And Jim?'

'Aye?' Jim focused on Julian's words like his life depended on it. Because at this moment in time it really did.

Julian's face lit up with humour. 'Trim your fecking beard, man! You look like the wild man of fecking Borneo!'

Flight nine four two was scheduled to land at six tomorrow morning, UK time. Jim checked his watch: Five-thirty.

Right... shower, food, beard, and bed. Not necessarily in that order. Well, apart from bed. And maybe the beard could wait.

* * *

The next morning, Jim awoke and checked his watch again: nine-fifteen. *Great! She should be on her way north anytime now*. He did a little happy dance on the way to his rather luxurious en-suite bathroom in the fancy hotel that Julian had insisted on. 'Jim, you can't have make-up sex in a dump,' he had informed Jim. Quite right. Flick deserved better.

Staring at his reflection, Jim sniggered as Julian's words came back to him. His beard had really gotten long and fuzzy. He would've looked at home as the fourth member of ZZ Top. Trimming it was essential and it was only fair seeing as Julian had shaved his off to look the part. It was the least Jim could do. He set about tidying it back to a more acceptable length. Pleased with the result, he switched on the shower, and when steam filled the room, he stepped in, allowing his muscles to relax as the water encased him in a cocoon of warmth.

He played over in his mind what he would say to Flick when she stepped through the doors of the exhibition. Would she like what he had called it? *Through the Glass* had been the obvious choice considering the subject matter and the circumstances through which it had come about. It was the same reason he had used it for his novel and it reminded him of how she saw the world. She saw beauty in everything. She observed each vista as if it were already a framed masterpiece. He had always admired her ability to memorise a view on a journey and turn into something transcendent. So yes, there was something poetic and fitting about the name.

Naming the artist as 'Flick MacDuff' was the next sticking point. The reasons for the choice were threefold. One, it wasn't her name and never had been, and so if word had been somehow leaked, she would hopefully see it as a striking coincidence. Two, it had a certain ring to it... like it always had to Jim, and three... he wanted the name to be his future. *Their* future.

Once out of the shower, Jim couldn't help but smile at his reflection. His eyes looked brighter already. He felt that familiar nervous energy course through his veins at the thought of seeing her and observing her reaction to her exhibition. His heart flipped. The grin on the face of his reflection made him laugh.

He pointed at the mirror. 'You, mate, are a complete nutcase!' He shook his head and wrapped a towel around his waist. Drying his shaggy hair with another towel, he made his way through to the bedroom.

Picking up his phone to check the time... *again*, he noticed that in the space of the twenty or so minutes he had been in the shower, he'd had three missed calls, all from Julian. He had forgotten he'd set it to silent the night before to ensure he got a good night's sleep. He couldn't see Flick with baggy, tired eyes, now, could he? Sensing the urgency behind the need to ring him three times in quick succession, Jim's heart sank. *Oh shit, has something happened at the gallery? A flood? A break-in?* With shaking hands, he dialled Julian's number, preparing for the news.

Julian answered after only one ring. 'Jim? Have you heard from Felicity?'

Jim scrunched his brow. 'No. Why?'

Julian paused. 'It's weird but... she didn't get off the plane at Glasgow, so I phoned her to see if she had missed her connection, but her mobile number goes straight to voicemail. I called Franco Nilsson, but he says the last he heard she was getting on the five o'clock flight. He was worried so, even though it's early morning over there, Franco managed to get a hold of Ella from the Chicago gallery and she said she saw her at the airport, Jim. She was feeling nervous about the flight but was determined to get on it when Ella left her.'

Jim's heart sank. 'Do you think she changed her mind? Maybe she sussed out what was going on and decided not to come back.'

'I don't know Jim, but it feels off to me. Ella contacted the hotel to see if she had arrived back, but they haven't seen her. Where the hell is she?'

Jim closed his eyes and chewed his lip, he had a feeling he knew what had happened. 'Can you leave it with me for a bit, Julian? I need to make a phone call.'

Julian sighed. 'Sure, yeah. Keep me posted, okay?'

Jim hung up and riffled through his phone for the number he didn't want to dial.

'Hello? Felicity? Is that you, darling? I've been so worried.'

Jim frowned. 'Erm, no, Penelope it's, erm. Jim... Felicity's ex-husband.'

Penelope sighed deeply. 'She's with you, isn't she? Bypassed her own mother to run straight back to you, didn't she?' she snapped.

Confusion washed over Jim. 'So, she hasn't been in touch with you then?'

'Don't be ridiculous, James. She knows how I feel about you. No offence but you're not what I want for my daughter. She has so much ahead of her, and you'll just drag her down. The best thing you can do is send her back to Chicago. Set her free for goodness' sake, you selfish, selfish man.'

Anger flared up within him. 'Hang on a minute, Penelope. You're being very unfair, and you don't know the facts. She—'

'Oh, believe me, I know enough. I know you have some kind of spell over her. I know you—'

'Penelope!' Jim shouted and she stopped speaking. 'Felicity isn't here. She was supposed to be in Glasgow to... to see a potential client but—'

'I know that, James. She told me. And I figured out it was a ruse.'

He sighed and closed his eyes. 'No, Penelope, there was no ruse, not on Felicity's part. But that's beside the point. She hasn't arrived in Glasgow.'

Penelope fell silent for a moment. 'Oh. She... she was supposed to meet me at Heathrow for a coffee before her connecting flight to Glasgow but... She never arrived and her mobile keeps going to voicemail. I'm terribly hurt, James. Why would she not contact me if she had decided not to come?'

Worry niggled at the back of Jim's mind. 'I can't answer that. But she hasn't let Julian Forster know she's not coming either. And no one can get hold of her.'

Penelope gasped. 'Oh, my goodness. Where is she James?'

He shook his head as he felt the colour drain from his face. 'I have no idea.'

28

After making contact with the airline, Jim discovered that Flick never boarded the flight from Chicago O'Hare. No one had heard from her since. The police explained it away as a woman who had decided to take a leave of absence from her life to clear her head, but Jim felt, deep down, that it was nothing of the sort.

With the help of Ella in Chicago, Jim had contacted several hotels and the airport for sightings of Flick, but up to now there had been nothing. Ella reported that she had spoken to all the hospitals in and around the city but to no avail. Jim was sick with worry. Penelope had been in contact over and over, but he had been unable to tell her anything and guilt rankled at him. Even though the woman had openly disliked him, she was looking to him now for support, and for Flick's sake he couldn't sit idly by and leave her alone to suffer.

After almost a twelve-hour drive with a couple of stops off for comfort breaks, he sat in the drawing room of Flick's family home, holding Penelope's hand. He had explained everything, about the exhibition, about getting Julian involved, and about the reason for her trip back to the UK. He'd even admitted to the fact that he wanted Flick back in his life for good. That he loved her with all his heart and that even Penelope couldn't change that. Penelope had listened, but much to his surprise, hadn't commented negatively. She'd simply smiled and said that what he had arranged for her daughter was sweet and thoughtful.

It was the day of the exhibition opening and Julian had taken the reigns. Jim just couldn't face it. Not with Flick missing. Penelope's pallor was that of a corpse. Usually well made-up, she sat, pale and shaking beside him as she sobbed. It was all too much to bear.

He was exhausted both emotionally and physically. He had fought with the worry, which had turned to anger, and then subsequently, to sadness and guilt. *If only I hadn't set this whole thing up. If only I had just left her to her new life.* But what was the point of if only?

Flick was nowhere to be found.

Polly and Matt had been in constant contact, seeing as they too had heard nothing from Flick. Polly insisted this was so out of character for her friend.

'She wouldn't leave without saying goodbye, Jim.' Polly had said, her voice wavering with worry. 'She'd know how much worry that would cause. She wouldn't do that. I know she wouldn't.'

But this left the bitter truth: Flick was missing against her will. What would Jim do if she was never found? He'd lost her once, but this was different. This could mean forever.

And forever was a hell of a long time.

'I'll... I'll make more tea.' Penelope stood in a zombie-like stupor and looked at her hands for a second as if she had forgotten her reason for standing. Confusion played on her features.

Jim stood and placed his hands on her shoulders. 'Penelope, let me... please.' He squeezed lightly to bring her back to Earth. She had clearly drifted off momentarily, maybe to a world where Flick wasn't missing.

As if his small act of kindness had pierced her heart, she let out an anguished cry and collapsed into him. 'Oh, James, I'm so sorry. I'm so, so sorry.' Her tears soaked through the fabric of his shirt as he held on to her to stop her from falling.

'Hey... shhh. It's okay. Don't apologise.' His voice broke on hearing the anguish in hers. 'You've nothing to apologise for.' He stroked the distraught woman's hair.

'No, you're wrong. You are wrong, James.' She raised her voice angrily shouting through her tears. 'I caused this. This is my fault. All of this. Edgar was right.' Her body convulsed and she clutched on to his shirt.

He cupped her face in his shaking palms. 'No, Penelope, no, you're not to blame. I am. I should've just let her get on with her life. She didn't need me confusing matters. She didn't need her paintings on display and me trying to put some pathetic surprise together to win her back.'

The woman straightened up and looked directly into his eyes. 'Jim, listen to me. If I had just let her be, let you both be and let her really love you she would never have gone. She would still be here with us, with you.' She visibly shuddered as she spoke. Her voice had taken on a calm and collected tone as though she was resigned to her guilt.

She called me Jim. He stroked her cheek. 'Oh, Penelope. What's the use, eh? We can't change things if we beat ourselves up. We must forget blame. Please, can we do that?'

She placed her hands over his. 'I don't deserve your kindness, Jim.'

'Of course, you do. All you ever wanted was the best for Felicity. I can understand that. Because it's all I ever wanted, too.'

Penelope lowered her gaze. 'I told her you weren't good enough for her.'

Jim tilted her chin to meet her eyes again. 'Aye, and you were right.' He smiled. 'She deserves so much more than me. But I love her, Penelope. I love her with all my heart.'

'I know you do, Jim. I know. And I only wish that I could have accepted that your love was more important to her than you being a high-flying, big shot executive. Love is what matters. Support, love, and happiness far outweigh the material things in life. You always felt that way. You were right, and I was wrong, especially about you, Jim. I know that now. But it might be too late.' The tears began to fall again, and Penelope's pained sobs made Jim's heart ache.

'No. It's not too late. You and me, we need each other now. We will get to the bottom of this. We will find her.' He clenched his jaw in a bid to fend off the emotion bubbling up from deep inside. 'I want to show you Felicity's true passion. I want you to come to Glasgow and see her work. Will you do that, Penelope?' She nodded.

Thanks to Ella there had been more calls to the Chicago police, and more calls to the hospitals. She was determined to find Flick, too, and was doing everything she could to help. Instead of sitting around, waiting for news, Jim asked Penelope to pack a bag so they could go to Glasgow.

* * *

The journey north was a long, emotionally draining one. Jim had booked them two rooms at one of the best hotels in Glasgow. He was desperate to make this as easy on Penelope as possible. On arrival at the hotel, he called Julian about the exhibition opening.

Julian's voice cracked as he spoke. 'Oh, Jim, it was astounding. The press loved the work. There was such a buzz in the gallery that

I had to keep going out of the room, I was so emotional. She would've been so happy with it. I hope you know that.'

For a moment Jim couldn't reply. The words became caught as anguish and pain constricted his throat. He wasn't ready to talk about Flick in the past tense.

Finally, he said, 'Thanks, Julian. Thanks for everything. I... I... can't wait until she can see it for herself.' Tears needled the backs of his eyes and his chest ached. Penelope placed a hand on his arm, which pushed him over the edge. 'Sorry, Julian, I've got to go.'

He hung up and clung to his ex-mother-in-law. She did her best to soothe him as the raw emotion erupted from his soul like a volcano. His tears spilled like molten lava, burning a trail down his unshaven face.

After what felt like an eternity of letting him cry, Penelope placed hands on either cheek and looked into his eyes. 'James... Listen to me... Jim, look at me.' His sore eyes met with hers. 'I am so proud of you. To have loved my Felicity... *our* Felicity, so much and to have done all this... I want you to know how proud that makes me. Do you hear me?' Her words were his undoing once again.

When they arrived at the gallery, Julian was outside the room in which *Through the Glass* was being shown. There was another round of press firing questions about the mystery artist, the identity of whom had been kept a secret until Jim and Penelope had seen the exhibition. Julian fielded the press away so Jim and Penelope could enter; the pair were not yet ready to face the emotional onslaught of being thrust into the public eye, which would no doubt happen given the unusual circumstances.

Julian eventually broke away from the group and came over to where they stood. He looked tired and drawn – exactly how Jim felt.

He hugged both Penelope and Jim in turn. 'Are you ready to go in? I've kept the room clear today until you've been in.'

Jim looked at Penelope and held out his hand to her. 'Let's go, eh?' He squeezed her hand in reassurance. She nodded, clearly nervous and glassy-eyed. They both took deep breaths as they followed Julian to the large, wooden double doors. He pushed them open and stepped aside with a sad smile.

Jim's breath caught in his throat at the sight that met him. The antique, wood panelled walls were adorned with Flick's beautiful paintings. He'd known they were magnificent but didn't expect them to look as spectacular in this setting as they did. His hand came to cover his mouth as he tried to stifle an anguished sob. He looked over to Penelope who stood open-mouthed, tears tracing glistening lines down her pale cheeks.

Slowly Jim walked over to the beginning of the exhibition. The painting was of the view from a coastal road they had driven along on a weekend away to Devon. The sea rolled towards the sand, and the white horses skipped along with it towards the shore. The tall grasses that edged the clifftop almost looked to be swaying in an imaginary breeze as a pair of gulls hovered overhead.

Next was a mountainous scene painted from a memory of Jim and Flick's honeymoon. The journey had been one they had made on one of the only overcast days. They had driven away from the coast towards the mountains, but the sun had broken through the clouds casting an ethereal glow over their surroundings. It was magical. She had captured the light perfectly and he was only truly seeing this now that it was hung in a gallery, like it should have been long ago.

Piece after piece, Jim and Penelope stared at the paintings created by the woman they both loved so dearly. Sadness that she could not see this most wonderful achievement hung in the air between them as they shared glances filled with pride but tinged with melancholy. Hours were spent simply gazing and absorbing what surrounded them.

The final piece, the painting she had finished so quickly whilst she was with him in Scotland, almost brought him to his knees.

Julian appeared and grasped his shoulders, willing him to stay upright as he stared into the image of that special place that had stuck in her mind for all those years without revealing it's true meaning to her until he had taken her there. He covered his mouth again as another pained sob erupted from within. He glanced at Julian whose eyes had also given way to saltwater.

Images of Flick in her paint-spattered clothing and grinning from ear to ear as she revealed her latest work plagued Jim's mind. How he had kissed her and told her she was the most wonderfully talented and sexy woman he had ever encountered; how she had blushed at his words and nuzzled his neck to hide her embarrassment at the compliments he bestowed upon her.

His whole being ached to hold her again. Penelope came to stand before him and wiped his tears away with her thumbs. Tears he hadn't realised were still falling.

Anger at himself knotted his insides and the pain of loss was almost too much to bear. Why hadn't he realised she still loved him? Why had he sent her away? Why couldn't he go back and change this present agonising reality? Questions that may never be answered but that would plague him for the longest time, and his heart destined to be a scarred canvas that she would never paint on again.

On the return to their hotel, neither Jim nor Penelope had the energy to eat. They parted with an embrace and went to their separate rooms. Jim collapsed, fully clothed onto the bed, emotionally exhausted. He drifted into a sleep filled with dreams of Flick. His Flick.

* * *

The following day, he and Penelope had held a press conference that had been arranged by Franco Nilsson with the Chicago police. It took place by video link. They asked the Chicago public for any information about Flick's whereabouts, and for them to report any sightings. Lastly, they appealed to Flick herself, in case this was just all a mistake.

'You don't have to come home, Flick, if you don't want to. We'll understand,' Jim had said, his vision blurred with tears. 'We just need to know you're okay. You don't even have to speak to either of us. Just phone the police, or whoever you feel comfortable phoning. We love you and we just want to know you're safe.' Their clasped hands were visible on the tabletop in the hope that Flick would see, and be reassured that they were together, that everything between them was fine now.

After the conference, Penelope insisted on taking the train back to Surrey, and Jim had only argued for a few minutes before realising her resolve was strong. He had an ex-wife to find.

Julian had assigned himself to dealing with the press and had become a temporary fixture at the gallery, hellbent on doing all he could to assure that *Through the Glass* was a success. He didn't have to try hard. Flick MacDuff's true identity wasn't going to be released until they had definitive news on the missing woman.

After the long drive and retrieving Jasper from Miranda, with a brief explanation as to what had happened, he arrived back at Sunset Cottage. Before unlocking the door, he stood with his back to the house and gazed out over the water. This was the time of day when the cottage's name came into its own. The sun was descending behind the island out in the loch and the sky appeared to be afire; gold, burnt sienna and pink painted the sky like one of

Flick's pieces and he swallowed the lump of emotion that had formed in his throat. She would've loved this sunset. She would have painted it and captured it forever on canvas if she'd only been able to see it.

As the sun disappeared out of sight, he opened the front door, stepped inside with trepidation, and closed it behind him. The house he had loved since moving in now felt cold and lifeless. With a heavy heart, he walked into the living room he had been hoping and expecting to come back to with Flick. He was going to bring her in, build a roaring fire, and lay her out in front of it. He was going to worship her body like he should have the last time, never letting her go again. But instead, he stood in his home without her.

Even though she had only been here with him for a brief time after Christmas, it had felt right, although he couldn't admit it at the time. But what do they say about hindsight?

Every inch of the place echoed with memories of her. She belonged here, only he had realised too late. If only he hadn't been so harsh. If only he hadn't misread the signs, she would be here with him now. She would never have left. She would never have gone to Chicago and she would never have gone to that damned airport.

Leaning his back against the wall and sliding down with a thump to the floor, he pulled Jasper into him. 'She's left me again, Jasper. But this time I don't know where she is or if she's okay and it's killing me. I need to find her, Jasper… I have to.' He nuzzled the dog's fur and began to grieve all over again.

* * *

The following few days were spent in a numb haze. Jim had to make great efforts to carry out the simplest of tasks. His brother had arrived two days after his return from Glasgow after Aisha's parents had insisted on paying for a flight, even though their daughter had stayed home in Australia.

Euan did his best to look after his older brother, but the fact was Jim had no interest in looking after himself. All he cared about was obsessing over internet searches for Flick's name and calling every person he could think of who might have the tiniest clue where Flick was.

Euan nudged Jim's shoulder as he sat beside him holding out a tray of food. 'Jim, you're going to have to eat, bro. I made you some soup. After you've eaten this, you need to take a shower. You stink, you know.'

Jim took the tray and rested it on his knees. 'Gee thanks, brother. I'm so glad you came,' he replied sarcastically and smiled, but the smile only curled at his lips, not making it as far as his eyes.

Euan patted his brother's shoulder. 'You're welcome. So... food... shower... bed, yes?'

'Aye. Okay,' Jim acquiesced.

Euan began to walk towards the kitchen but stopped and turned to faced Jim. 'Oh, and another thing...'

'What now?' Jim looked up into his brother's concerned gaze.

'Please stop playing that music over and over, okay? I know they're pieces that remind you of her. But it's not healthy. Listen to something else, eh?'

Jim had played Pearl Jam's 'Black' and Debussy's 'Clair De Lune' pretty much on a loop whenever he was cocooned in his room. The lilting melodies and the memories of Flick that they evoked were like a security blanket.

Jim's tone remained steady, but he narrowed his eyes at his brother. 'I'll listen to what the hell I like. It's ma house.'

Euan's eyes were filled with sadness. 'Aye, I know that. It's just... Well for starters, it's doing my bloody head in, and I used to love both tracks... but... you can't bring her back by playing them over and over. You know?'

Jim glared up at him through his matted hair and anger rose within him. He stood, throwing the tray to the floor. 'Don't you think I know that?!' he shouted. He was shaking and his fists were clenched at his sides. 'Don't you think I know that this pain won't go away until I have some answers? Until I know where she is and if she's alive or...' His voice cracked as he pointed to his chest. 'It's a physical, excruciating pain. I lost her once before, Euan. I can't deal with losing her again. Not like this. It's too much! It's not fair!' An anguished sob erupted from his throat and he dropped to his knees.

In two strides, Euan crossed the room and grabbed Jim into a strong embrace. 'I know... I know. Forget I said anything. I'm sorry, Jim, I am. I'm so, so sorry.'

* * *

Jim was awoken from a dream by a strange noise. He sat bolt upright and checked the time. Four o'clock. He realised the strange noise was the house phone. *Who the hell rings at four o'clock in the morning?* An awful thought ran though his mind. Oh shit, something's happened to Penelope.

The ringing stopped as Jim dived out of bed and bolted downstairs. He flicked the light switch on in the living room. Euan stood there holding the phone, shaking his head. Jim's stomach lurched and his heart pounded against his ribcage.

Euan covered the receiver and looked to Jim. His eyes once again filled with concern. 'It's Penelope. Jim, she's screaming, and I can't get a word in. I think she's had some sort of breakdown. She's not making any sense.' He held out the receiver to Jim.

Jim grabbed it. 'Penelope? It's Jim. What is it? What's wrong?'

His breathing was erratic both from running down the stairs and from nervous energy and panic.

'Jim! There was a lead! The press conference! They've called me from Chicago. Oh god, they think they've found her!' Penelope's voice sounded manic, filled with terror, and Jim's heart plummeted inside his ribcage. Had his worst fears come true? Was Flick dead?

He had to remain strong. 'Okay, Penelope, slow down. I think you need to take some calming breaths and explain what's happened.'

Penelope virtually screamed down the line. 'Jim, you're not listening to me! They think they have found our Felicity... alive!'

Jim's legs weakened. He heard a buzzing noise loud in his ears and felt the blood drain from cheeks. He slumped to his knees as Euan stood beside him.

'Jim, you all right, bro? Jim?'

29

Jim sat in the passenger seat as Euan drove him to the airport. His heart rate still hadn't settled, and he had just about pulled holes in his jeans where his nails dug into the denim covering his legs. This morning's conversation played over and over in his mind...

* * *

'Jim, are you there, Jim? You've gone quiet.' Penelope's voice had been filled with concern. 'Jim, are you all right, dear?'

Jim had rubbed his hand over his face and snapped himself back to reality. Anger brewed up inside him. 'Is this some kind of sick joke, Penelope? Is someone trying to play us here? Because this sounds like someone has made a prank call to you.' How could people be so cruel at a time like this? To this poor woman who has lost her daughter?

'No, Jim. It's real. I had a call from a Detective Rand with the CPD. Someone called into the hotline after the press conference to say they had discovered a collapsed female in the ladies' lavatories at O'Hare on the day of the flight. She had no I.D. on her and she was unconscious.' Jim listened intently to every word, trying to decipher whether this was really happening. 'She was taken to hospital where they had a terrible job of trying to find her identity. She had no luggage, and the search at the airport did nothing to resolve that matter.'

Jim's voice was shaky and beads of sweat trailed cool paths down his overheated skin. 'But... what happened to her? I don't understand.'

'I don't know much because they need someone to go and identify her. She's... she's in a coma, Jim, the woman they found. She fits Felicity's description though.' Penelope's voice was croaky and faltering as she spoke. 'She was apparently drugged... Someone tried to kill her.' She sobbed down the line. 'This was done deliberately.'

The words stabbed Jim in the heart and physical pain speared him. His stomach lurched. 'Someone tried to kill her? Why?'

'That's what they're trying to figure out. She wasn't a random target that's for sure. It appears all of her belongings were removed when the culprit left the airport.'

Jim rubbed his hand over his head as the words sunk in. 'Shit... oh god, I'm sorry for swearing, Penelope.'

He heard a faint laugh down the line. 'Oh, Jim, don't worry. I think I even swore a little myself, at the news. You need to get on a flight over there. My passport has expired, so my friend Barbara is going to take me to get a fast track one. I'll meet you over there. Your flight is booked, and you need to be at Glasgow Airport by five o'clock this evening. And I've booked you into the Hilton by O'Hare.'

* * *

Euan broke Jim from his thoughts. 'Earth to Jim? Are you okay, bro?'

Jim cleared his throat and turned to glance at his brother. 'No, I'm seriously not okay. What if it's not her? What if it is her, and she dies anyway? I can't stand this, Euan. It's tearing me apart. I think I'm teetering on the edge of a breakdown here.'

Euan smiled reassuringly. 'I think it's unlikely they would drag you all the way out there if they weren't sure, eh? I'm guessing that you going to identify her is just a matter of clarification. Dotting the "Is" and crossing the "Ts" kind of stuff.'

'Aye, maybe. I'm terrified though. Why the hell would anyone want to kill her? I just don't get it.'

Euan gave his brother's leg a firm pat. 'Me neither. But thank goodness they didn't succeed, eh? Right?'

'Aye, not yet anyway.' Jim's eyes stung from all the crying and lack of sleep he had endured since the terrible news about Flick's disappearance. And now he was just downright confused.

* * *

After landing in Chicago's bustling O'Hare airport, Jim made his way through to the taxi rank outside. He didn't even bother to go to his hotel. He simply directed the driver to the Mercy Hospital where the *Jane Doe* was lying in a bed awaiting official identification. The staff had been made aware of Jim's impending arrival, and as soon as he walked through the doors to the intensive care unit, he was ushered into a side room by the consultant in charge of her care, along with a man in a suit.

'Welcome, Mr MacDuff, please take a seat.' Jim sat on a sofa situated along the wall. The two men remained standing. 'I'm Dr Felix Guzman and this is Detective Niall Rand. We've been dealing with the case of the woman we now believe to be Felicity Johnston-

Hart. Now, we wanted to go over a few things prior to taking you to see her. What lies ahead may be quite distressing for you, and we feel you should know the full extent of her condition.'

Jim listened intently but just wished they would get on with it so he could go to her. 'Yes, yes of course, whatever's needed.' He nodded.

The detective spoke next. 'Okay, so here's what we know so far… The woman was found in the ladies' restroom at O'Hare by a janitor, on the day of flight nine four two, but after the flight had departed. She was covered in vomit and was unconscious. There was no I.D. on her person and no baggage was found in the waiting area. She was brought here by ambulance and was admitted in order that Dr Guzman and his staff could carry out tests.'

Dr Guzman nodded. 'Hmmm, it was a bizarre one, Mr MacDuff. Large quantities of a very strong prescription drug were found in her blood stream. It's a drug that cannot be easily obtained. It comes in liquid form and it's almost without taste apart from a slight bitterness. However, it could be easily disguised. It's a powerful drug and is usually used to treat psychosis. Now, it appears that she may have been given the drug in an alcoholic beverage. The amounts that were found in her blood stream were enough to seriously harm her, but considering she had vomited a lot, possibly thanks to her body's desire to expel the overdose, we feel that the original amount was intended to kill.'

Jim huffed the air out of his lungs like he had been winded. He shook violently and brought his hands to his face.

'Mr MacDuff, are you all right? I know this is a lot to take in. Can I get you a drink of water?' Dr Guzman asked.

Jim croaked, 'Thank you… yes.' Dr Guzman left the room.

The detective stepped forward. 'Mr MacDuff—'

'Call me Jim, please.'

'Okay, Jim… once we have ascertained the young woman's identity and if it *does* prove to be Ms Johnston-Hart, we'll need to ask you some questions, okay?'

Jim nodded. 'Yeah... whatever it takes. How... however I can help,' was all he could manage to stutter.

Dr Guzman returned and handed a cup of water to Jim. 'Now, once you're ready, we'll go. But I must warn you that the young woman is attached to a number of pieces of medical equipment to help sustain her. Please don't be alarmed. She is in the best hands here, and we're doing our best to make sure she's comfortable.'

Jim finished the cup of water in one gulp and stood. 'I'm ready.'

They walked along a long corridor flanked on either side by numerous rooms housing some seriously ill-looking patients. Shivers traversed Jim's aching spine as the tension in his skeleton ratcheted up a notch.

The doctor and detective came to a halt outside a room with a large window. Through the glass, Jim could see the body of someone lying on a bed, surrounded by large pieces of equipment, just as he'd been warned. Wires protruded from the body. *Oh god, surely that's not her?* His blood ran cold, and he placed his palms on the window.

Dr Guzman held open the door. 'Okay, Mr MacDuff, you can go on in. We're right here with you.'

Jim nodded. 'Please... call me Jim,' was his autopilot response.

Hesitantly, he walked into the room. An intermittent bleeping noise was audible, and situated by the bed was a large cylinder, which contained something resembling a concertina folded paper bag, expanding and contracting, hissing as it moved.

As if noting his concern, the doctor spoke. 'This apparatus is a ventilator. It's helping her to breathe at the moment, but don't worry, she's being kept in an induced coma while we assess any damage caused by the overdose of the drug she was subjected to.

The drugs have been stopped and all we need to do now is wait for her to wake.' Jim simply nodded again.

He approached the bed and inhaled sharply, almost stumbling backwards at the terrifying vision before him. He ran his hands through his hair and rested them atop his head, struggling to take things in. A wave of nausea hit, combined with dizziness. Someone placed a hand on his back to steady him.

'Jim, can you confirm the identity of this young woman?' Detective Rand enquired.

Jim's voice was almost a whisper as he replied, 'It's her. It's my Flick.'

30

Dr Guzman pulled a chair over and beckoned Jim to sit beside the bed. 'We'll leave you alone for a while, Jim. Please call if you need anything.'

Jim spun around. 'Wait! Can I... can I touch her? I want to... to hold her hand.' He looked pleadingly at the doctor.

Dr Guzman patted his shoulder. 'Of course, you can, Jim.' The doctor and the detective left the room.

Felicity had been lying here for almost a week. His poor, beautiful girl, no one knowing who she was. The thought yanked his heart into his throat and made his eyes sting. He reached into his pocket and pulled out his mobile phone.

He hit dial on Penelope's number and when she answered as if she had been waiting by the phone, he said, 'It's her Penelope. It's our Felicity.'

Penelope sobbed and the sound of relief tugged at Jim's heart. They weren't out of the woods yet but at least there was hope.

Jim took Flick's hand in his, and much to his relief, it was warm. Her face was pale and drawn, and her closed eyes were sunken and rimmed with dark circles, the lids had a distinct purple hue. A tube leading from the ventilator was taped to her skin, and disappeared between her once rosy lips, distorting her mouth at the corner. Her usually perfectly styled hair spread dully across the pillow.

At least her hand is warm. That must be a good sign, right?

Jim tried his best to eradicate the fear that was creeping over him, the feeling of dread that lay heavy in his stomach. He stifled the sob trying to escape his body as a nurse walked into the room.

'Hi, Jim. I'm Norah,' the kind-looking woman said as she smiled over at him. 'Dr Guzman tells me we have a positive I.D. on our pretty Jane Doe. I'm so glad. I'm one of the nurses who's been taking care of Felicity. If you need anything just holler. Oh... and talk to her. She may hear you.' She patted his shoulder and then proceeded to mark things off on the chart she held.

* * *

When Norah left the room, he looked back to Flick. She looked so frail and helpless lying there. He squeezed her hand.

Clearing his throat, he began, 'F-Flick it's... it's Jim. I don't know if what the nurse said is true but I'm here. I came as soon as I heard they'd found you. They will find who did this to you. I'll make sure of it.' Tears stung his eyes and he blinked them away. Gritting his teeth, he went on. 'I can't believe someone would do this to you. I just can't.'

He drew in a long, shaky breath. 'I have so many regrets, Flick. That last time I saw you... I should have been honest, but I was a coward. I was too afraid to tell you I still love you. I treated you so badly and I'll never forgive myself for that.' He rested his head on their joined hands for a moment to compose himself. 'That's the truth, Flick. I still love you. Always have, always will. I know I may have messed this up, but as soon as you're better, I'll tell you again. If you don't want me, I'll understand. But at least you'll know. I don't deserve you though. I never have. Your mum was right. The funny thing is – and if you were awake, you'd laugh – she's decided she likes me. Can you believe that? It's only taken thirteen years, a disappearance, and an attempted murder, but hey…' He smiled, wishing he could look into her sparkling eyes once again.

He squeezed her hand gently. 'I want you to come home. I want to take you to Scotland and look after you forever, Flick, if you'll have me. I want to set your easel up and watch you paint. I want to cook for you and go for walks with you and Jasper. I want to snuggle up with you and watch sappy movies and to feel you next to me in our bed. To wake up with you and bring you breakfast. To take you for long walks up to the viewpoint… our viewpoint. I just want to have the chance to be with you again.' His lip trembled and tears escaped his eyes once more. 'You should see what me and Julian have done for you, Flick. There's an exhibition of your amazing paintings in a real gallery. They look stunning hung there in Glasgow. Everyone loves them.' He glanced at her face to check for a response but there was none. 'Julian has worked so hard. He's a great guy. He said seeing as you discovered him, he wanted to discover you right back. He'll be so happy you're okay. You *will* be okay, Flick. Any time you want to open your eyes will be fine… there's no rush… I'll wait for you. I'll always wait for you.'

After a while Nurse Norah returned. 'Jim? Detective Rand would like to speak with you. And we feel it's best if you go get some sleep and come back tomorrow, okay?'

Jim shook his head. 'No, no I can't leave her. What if she wakes up and needs me?'

Norah smiled reassuringly. 'If she wakes, we'll call you. Please don't worry, honey. The test results were very encouraging, and Dr Guzman is the best in his field. She's in safe hands.'

Jim was too tired to fight. He followed Norah to the room where

Detective Rand was waiting. The detective shook his hand and offered him a seat.

Then he sat too. 'Okay, Jim. Is there anything at all that springs to mind that you can tell us that may lead us to who tried to kill Ms Johnston-Hart? Anything at all. No matter how small or insignificant it may seem. For example, do you know of anyone who may have held a grudge? Or anyone you know who may have been on the medication that was found in her system?'

'I'm sorry... I know nothing at all. We were divorced and didn't really keep in touch. Our last meeting was when she told me she'd been offered a job here. She wasn't on any medication herself that I know of, so I have no clue.'

'Okay, that's kind of what we figured, but we have to ask, you understand?'

'Sure, sure. Have you got any leads at all? I mean, is she still in danger from someone waiting for her once they know she's alive?'

'Well, apart from the obvious possibilities of organ damage, we presume that currently the perp presumes she's dead. Hopefully, it'll stay that way until we catch up with them. Our focus just now is to interview all the people at her workplace.' He put his pen and pad in his inside pocket. 'There's a guard posted on Ms Johnston-Hart's door from the time I leave, so please don't worry. No further harm will come to her while she's here, and we'll ensure that none comes to her once she's well enough to leave. It's my intention to solve this case before she's discharged and leaves for home. In my opinion, this was an amateurish murder attempt. I think we'll close in very soon on the culprit.'

Jim reached out and vigorously shook the man's hand. 'Thanks, thanks so much, Detective.'

* * *

A cab transported a rather dazed Jim MacDuff back to his hotel. Penelope had thought of everything, bless her.

Jim called her once he was in his room. 'It's me, Penelope. I've just got back from the hospital.'

'How is she? How's my darling girl?' Penelope's voice was filled with emotion.

'She's pale but she's... she's warm. The doctor says the signs are good so far.'

Her relieved sobs vibrated down the line, but her joy was short-lived. 'Oh, Jim, who would do such a thing to our darling Felicity? She didn't have any enemies that I know of.'

'I have absolutely no idea. But they will figure it out. They're already covering every possible angle. I spoke with Detective Rand today, and he seems to be determined to get it sewn up quickly. We must have confidence in them. They know what they're doing.'

'Oh, Jim, dear, I do hope so, I just want her home now.'

'Me too, Penelope, me too.'

The call ended and Jim decided to shower and, in spite of the late hour, order room service. He stood under the large showerhead as the soothing hot water cascaded down his back, relaxing his tense and aching muscles and washing his worries temporarily down the drain.

He vowed to himself that he would be back at the hospital first thing in the morning. His mind whirred with the events of the past two days, and he clambered to make sense of the knowledge that someone had tried to kill his ex-wife. Nothing made sense. After he had half eaten his dinner, he gave in to the need for sleep.

31

Jim arrived at the hospital at eight the following morning but wasn't allowed to go straight in to see Flick. She had been taken off the ventilator, and the next couple of hours were crucial, he was informed. He paced around the family room with a pounding heart, chewing on his nails and awaiting news.

Eventually, running out of nervous energy, he slumped into a chair and clasped his hands together. 'God, I know that I've never been a church person... and I know I've never really prayed before... and... and I know I swear rather a lot. Probably too much. But if you're watching over my Flick... please, please bring her through this. Please. I can't be without her again. I just can't. Please. I'll try harder, I promise. I'll do everything in my power to make her happy.' He rubbed his hands over his face and continued to wait for news.

At eleven o'clock the door opened, and Dr Guzman walked in. Jim went to stand and he held out his hand. 'Don't get up, Jim. It's good to see you again. I hope you managed to get some sleep.'

Jim's voice was weak as he spoke. 'I think my body just gave up, to be honest. I fought it though.'

'Well, I'm pleased to be able to let you know that Felicity is managing to breathe unaided.'

The news winded Jim, and although relieved, he leaned forward and rested his elbows on his knees, and his head in his hands as tears of relief welled in his eyes. 'Thank you, God,' he breathed.

'As you know we also have the test results. Because you're here as her next of kin, and as we've been given permission by her mother to discuss her condition with you, we're able to share those results with you. Is that okay?' the doctor asked, placing a hand on Jim's shoulder.

When Jim nodded, the doctor sat in a chair opposite. 'Okay, now, it's not great news but it's not as bad as it could have been,' the doctor began. 'Felicity has suffered slight liver damage, but the liver is probably one of the most robust organs with the ability to repair itself to a certain degree, and so we're hopeful that this won't be permanent, although there are, sadly, no guarantees. Her kidneys are functioning normally. Heart is good and strong. The only thing is...' The doctor paused.

Jim lifted his head. 'The only thing is what?' Dread washed over him, and he feared the worst.

'Well, at this stage, it's hard to say if there is any brain damage caused by what was, to all intents and purposes, an overdose of a mind-altering drug. We've done all the tests we can while she is unconscious, but... well, we won't know the full extent of any damage until she is fully conscious. We have to be prepared for what may happen, if and when, she wakes up, Jim.'

He sat upright and faced the dark-haired, olive-skinned man opposite him. 'If and when? Well, which is it?' Jim could hear the desperation as it reverberated through his own voice.

Dr Guzman's brow crumpled. 'We don't know at the moment. We just need to wait for her body to repair, and for her to gain consciousness. We *are* hopeful, Jim. But please try and understand that we can't say for sure at this stage of her recovery.'

This was not welcome news. Penelope was arriving tomorrow and hearing this would devastate her. But all they could do was wait.

* * *

Jim was allowed to sit at Flick's bedside once again. He sat in the same place as the day before. Seeing her now, without the venti-lator tube was strange. She was pale, and her eyes still had that same purple hue. But she was breathing.

He squeezed her hand and stroked his thumb over her knuck-les. 'Flick, it's Jim. I'm here again. No getting rid of me, eh?' He leaned and kissed her hand. There was bruising visible where an intravenous line had been removed. He hadn't noticed it yesterday. But then again, she had been surrounded by all sorts of machines. 'I... I spoke to your mum again. She's on her way. I'll bring her to see you tomorrow.' He was desperate for a response, but none came.

'Flick, come on. Wake up, eh? Show them what you're made of. You can fight this thing. I know you can. And I miss you, so, so much.' Emotions constricted his throat and words came out as a strangled whisper. 'I've missed you ever since you left Scotland. In fact, I've missed you ever since you left me three years ago, Flick. I want to see you smile again. You have the best smile. The first time I saw it I think my insides melted. You certainly made your mark on me.'

Norah came in and checked Flick's vitals. 'How are you today, Jim? Did you sleep?' she asked whilst she filled in numbers on the chart again.

'I did, thanks. I'm okay. But I'll be better when Flick wakes up.' He didn't shift his gaze from his sleeping beauty.

'Well, we're all hoping for the same thing, Jim. Just hang in there, honey.' The older lady smiled kindly and left the room.

* * *

After another restless night, filled with dreams of Flick, Jim met Penelope at O'Hare the following afternoon. She hugged him so tight he felt like he was going to pass out. As soon as they had dropped her bags at the hotel, and she had freshened up, they made their way to the hospital by cab. She squeezed his hand throughout the whole journey and Jim was still astounded by the change in their relationship.

On arrival at the hospital, Jim opened Flick's room door and Penelope stepped inside. She gasped and rushed to her daughter's bedside. 'Oh, no, no, no, no.' She turned to Jim with a pained expression, and he hugged her to him as she sobbed, her hands covering her mouth. 'I can't lose her, too, Jim. Not my baby. Not so soon after losing Edgar.'

He let her cry until her tears subsided, and then he pulled a chair next to the bed and helped her to sit. Her legs had apparently weakened through the shock of seeing her only child lying unconscious.

Once she was calmer and he felt better about leaving, he touched Penelope's shoulder. 'I'll leave you to have some time alone with her, okay? There must be things you want to say.'

She looked up at him with puffy, sad eyes. 'Say? But... she's not awake, Jim.'

'No, but the nurse said she may be able to hear you. Go ahead. I'll leave you to it.' He smiled reassuringly and left the room. He walked to the family room and pushed the door open. Thankfully, it was vacant. He pulled out his phone and called Euan.

He answered the call after one ring. 'Hey, bro, how's it going? Is everything okay?'

'Hi, it's not great. Flick's off the ventilator and breathing by herself. She looks so different though. She's pale, kind of grey and there's been no response from her. They say there could be brain damage, Euan.'

Euan fell silent for a moment. 'Aw hell, Jim, I don't know what to say. That's not good, eh? How soon will they know more?'

'When she wakes, I guess. It's all a waiting game. Penelope's here now, so at least I'm not alone. We can support each other.'

'Bless the poor woman. She must be devastated.'

'Aye. She's a bit of a wreck, pretty much like me.'

'Well, keep your chin up, eh Jim? Stay positive. And make sure you both eat and rest. Don't worry about shit here. Jasper is great, and I'm a big hit with the local ladies so the business is doing fine.'

Jim snorted. 'Euan, the average age of the ladies around there is sixty-five, so I'd be careful about bragging there, mate.' He couldn't help but smile and shake his head.

Euan chuckled down the line. 'Look after yourself. Love you, bro.'

'Aye, love you, too, you ugly swine.' Jim hung up.

* * *

The next few days followed the same routine. Hospital, eat, shower, sleep, etc. Monday of the second week came around, and Penelope was feeling unwell. She stayed in her room to get some rest, and Jim went to the hospital alone. He walked into Flick's room to find Norah going about her hourly checks.

'Hi, Norah. Any change?' His words were hopeful as always. But as always, Norah's words did nothing to fan the flames of his hope.

'Not yet, sweetie. But she's a tough cookie. We haven't given up and neither has she.' She patted his shoulder as she did every other time and left him.

He clutched a piece of paper to his chest. It was a printout of an email that Julian had sent him. It showed the front page of *The Glaswegian*, the headline of which read – *Mystery Artist Takes Glasgow By Storm*. He intended to read it to Flick as he sat with her.

'Hey, gorgeous. You're looking brighter today.' He spoke softly, leaning in close to kiss her forehead. 'I think you have a bit more colour to your cheeks. I've brought a newspaper clipping for you. Remember that exhibition I mentioned? Well, it's a massive hit. *You're* a massive hit.' He pulled up a chair and held her hand as he read the article to her. He watched for any response as he read but received none.

'Anyway, it sounds like the exhibition is still going down really well. People just love your work, Flick. I want to take you to see it soon, so you need to wake up. Flick? Wake up for me, eh? Please.'

Nothing.

Feeling lost and drained, he leaned his head on the bed beside her hand and eventually dozed off.

* * *

He dreamed about Flick again. This time they were lying on a bed in a white room. She was stroking his hair as he gazed lovingly into her eyes. He touched her cheek and feathered her forehead, lips and eyes with kisses.

'Please don't leave me again, sweetheart. I couldn't bear it,' he whispered. She didn't speak. 'I keep losing you. I don't want to keep losing you.' She simply stared into his eyes and ran her hands through his hair over and over. 'I love you,' he told her again.

But no sooner had he said that than she started to drift away from him. Tears trailed down her beautiful face, and she held out her hands to reach for him. He grabbed for her and managed to pull her back. Her hands found his hair again and he leaned in to kiss her. 'Don't go... please don't go, Flick... don't go.' But she began to drift away again. He tried to call after her, but his throat constricted, trapping the words before they could be spoken.

* * *

His eyes sprang open. His breath was huffing in and out in short, sharp spurts. It took a moment for him to realise he was still beside her in the hospital, lying with his face turned away from her. He could still feel her hand stroking his hair as if it had been real... *wait a second... that is real.*

He sat bolt upright and turned towards her. 'Oh, my god!' He jumped to his feet and leaned over her. 'Flick, it's me, Jim!' His voice was urgent and panicked. He stroked her cheek waiting for a response. Her eyes fluttered open weakly.

Shakily, she reached her hand to his cheek. 'Jim... please take me home.'

His eyes stung with the tears that threatened to overspill. Okay, she knew who he was, but did she know what had happened? Did she know where she was? Did she know what she was saying?

He took a deep calming breath. 'And where's home, Flick?'

'Wherever you are, Jim.'

32

Jim paced around the family room as he nervously chewed at the skin around his nails. Why had they rushed him out? It was a good thing that she had gained consciousness. This wasn't one of those scenarios where she suddenly wakes up to say goodbye and then dies, was it? *Shit! No, it can't be like that. It just can't. This is not a damned movie. This is real life!*

Penelope burst into the room and the anguish in her eyes tugged at his heart. 'Jim! They won't let me see her! What's going on?'

He pulled her into his embrace. 'I don't know, Penelope. She woke up, and then when I called for the doctor, they ushered me out and asked me to wait in here. It's driving me mad.' They hugged, clinging on to each other as they waited.

After half an hour, Dr Guzman finally came into the family room. He asked them to sit and that unsettled Jim further. It made him think the worst.

Dr Guzman smiled warmly. 'Jim, you look terrified.'

Jim wrung his hands together. 'I *am* terrified. Please, what's going on?'

'Okay, well she has regained full consciousness, which is marvellous. We've done the necessary tests, and we're very pleased to see that cognitive function appears to be unharmed. Felicity's just speaking with Detective Rand and telling him what she remembers of the events leading up to her being discovered in the restroom. She's a little upset as you can imagine now that she's aware of the implications of being in hospital. But all in all, she's very fortunate as it appears she may have escaped permanent damage. Now I know it's tempting to go in there all guns blazing, talking to her, asking questions, and so on. But I feel it would be best if you let her be for today.'

Jim stood, holding his hands up defensively. 'Whoa, no way, pal. I'm not leaving her. Never again am I leaving her.'

The doctor placed a firm hand on Jim's shoulder. 'Jim, believe me, I fully understand how hard it must be to hear this, but she's been through quite a traumatic ordeal both physically and now emotionally, and from hereon in, it may be a bumpy ride as she's learning about what's happened to her. She needs time to process it all, and to maybe let things sink in. She has a lot to come to terms with for now.'

Jim exhaled what felt like all the air from his lungs as he sat down again. 'Please, Dr Guzman. Please, you don't understand. I have to talk to her, even if it's just for a few minutes. And her mum will want that, too. We won't overcrowd her. I can promise you that. We'll even go in separately if that's better but please.' He pleaded and prayed that the doctor would understand.

Dr Guzman pursed his lips and for a moment it seemed like he was sticking to his guns. 'Fine. Five minutes each, and then you go and come back tomorrow. That's my final say on the matter.'

Penelope clung tightly to her handkerchief. 'Thank you, Dr Guzman. Thank you.'

Jim nodded his agreement. 'Aye, thanks for that. I can't tell you how much I appreciate your help, Doctor.'

Back in the room, Flick was slightly more elevated in her bed. Her face brightened as she saw Jim enter. He rushed to her bedside and leaned in to stroke her hair back and kiss her forehead.

He caressed her face lovingly. 'Hi, gorgeous. How're you feeling?'

'Jim, you came all the way to America for me?' Her lip trembled and a tear escaped the corner of her eye. He caught it with his thumb.

'Of course, I did. I couldn't stay away. I... I couldn't believe that you'd been found when I was told. When I heard that you were missing... I thought that I'd lost you. I had to come and see for myself that you were still here.' He stroked her cheeks, happy to be touching her again.

'Thank you for coming, Jim.' More tears were set free. 'It means such a lot to me that you came.'

He pulled her head into his chest and he smoothed her hair down, kissing the top of her head as she clung to his arms. 'Hey, hey... shhh. It's okay. You're okay. You're going to be fine. You're safe now. I won't let anything happen to you again. No one will get to you again. I promise.'

'There are so many things we need to talk about, Flick. So many things I need to explain.'

Norah knocked on the door. 'Jim, it's time to go so that Penelope can come in and see her daughter.' She left again.

He gazed down into Flick's eyes. 'We'll talk tomorrow, okay? Your mum has been so worried.'

'Wait, what? The two of you are here t-together? And you're both still alive?' She smiled.

He grinned and kissed her forehead. 'Oh, you'd be surprised what can happen whilst you're in a coma for a while. I'll see you tomorrow. I lo—' He stopped before the words escaped. 'I'll tell your mum to come in.' He turned to leave the room feeling relieved.

* * *

Penelope squeezed Jim's hand as she passed him in the doorway. A sob escaped her as she reached Flick's bedside.

'Hey, Mum, don't cry. I'm going to be fine. The doctor has said so. I'm so sorry for scaring you.'

Penelope leaned forward and kissed Flick's head. 'Felicity, darling, you're lying in hospital, thousands of miles away from home after someone tried to kill you and you're apologising for scaring me? My wonderful silly, silly girl. Felicity, sweetheart, it's me who needs to apologise.'

Felicity's lip trembled again. 'Mum, really—'

Penelope squeezed her hand. 'Felicity, please. I need to get some things off my chest, and I only have five minutes. Please. They're saying you need rest, and I promised to be brief. So, I'll just speak, and I want you to listen.' Flick simply nodded. Penelope took a deep breath. 'I have brought all of this on.'

'Mum—'

'Felicity, please. If I'd just stopped being such a busybody, you'd have had a long, happy marriage with that wonderful man out there, who adores every hair on your head by the way. You'd probably have children, and I would be a grandma. Your father would maybe have seen his grandchildren, too. This is my fault entirely. If not for me, you'd never have been over here trying to be a high-flying executive in the art world.

'You'd have stayed doing what you loved and what you were so good at. You'd still be painting, darling. But above all else, you'd be happy. Jim has been wonderful, Felicity. Despite my disgusting treatment of him, he's been so gracious, and I don't deserve that. He's been kind and warm. He's taught me what it means to really love someone. And that you don't need flashy cars and big houses or lots of money. He's been like a son to me over these past weeks, when we thought we had lost you.' She let out a sob and Flick squeezed her arm, her own tears now falling freely.

'Sorry, love... I want you to realise that it was *me* who caused your divorce. I put so much pressure on you to be successful and to marry into wealth. I will understand if you want me out of your life. I had some misguided opinion of what life should entail. Which is stupid considering I adored your father, and we had true love... hah... he must have really loved me because he put up with such a lot.'

'Oh, Mum.'

'I want you to know that you have my complete and utter blessing to be with Jim. You should have had it all along. You never really stopped loving him, and I have it on good authority that he feels the same. Once you're well, tell him how you feel. Promise me?'

Flick sighed as she touched her mum's cheek. 'I promise... and Mum?'

Penelope covered Flick's hand with her own. 'Yes, dear?'

'Don't ever say anything about me not wanting you in my life, okay? All I ever wanted was for you to be proud of me.'

Penelope sobbed. 'Oh, Felicity, darling, I've always been proud of you, so very proud.'

Norah opened the door and peeped her head in. 'Mrs Johnston-Hart? I'm sorry but it's time to go.'

'Okay, thank you, Norah dear. And please, call me Penny.' Norah smiled, nodded and left the room.

Flick smiled and raised her eyebrows. 'Penny, eh? That's what Dad and Jim always called you.'

Penelope looked thoughtful for a moment. 'Yes, I like the sound of it.' She kissed her daughter and left the room.

* * *

The following morning when Jim and Penelope arrived at the hospital, there was a buzz of activity outside Flick's room.

Detective Rand spotted them and came rushing over. 'Jim, Mrs Johnston-Hart, would you come with me please?'

Jim's heart rate increased, and Penelope's face paled. 'Why? What's happened? Is she okay?'

'Sorry, yes Felicity is fine. We have news and need to update you on what's happened.'

The three of them walked into the family room and closed the door. They sat, and Jim and Penelope waited expectantly.

'Okay, we've arrested a young woman by the name of...' He glanced down at his notepad, 'Ella Cole. She gave herself up late last night. She was in quite a state. It appears she was the one who added the drug to Felicity's drink.'

Jim frowned at the detective, trying to understand. 'But... she was helping me. She was trying to find Flick too? Why would she... There must be some mistake.'

The detective shook his head. 'I'm afraid not. It appears there was some art forgery going on at the gallery, and Felicity uncovered it.'

'Shit... art forgery? But... but... to try to kill her? Isn't that a bit extreme?'

'It certainly is. But there was a lot of money at stake... millions... Apparently, the former gallery manager, Chester Withers, was in a sexual relationship with Miss Cole. He had gotten her involved. She insists that she didn't want to do it and that she thought a lot of Ms Johnston-Hart, but her life was threatened if she didn't cooperate. I guess it was a difficult situation for her, *if* what she says is true, but she should've come to the police before taking such drastic action. Obviously, a warrant is out for Withers' arrest, and we'll find out if things add up there. It appears he may have fled, but my team are good at what they do, and I have no doubt they'll find him. Miss Cole insists that the drugs were those belonging to Withers. He had a nervous breakdown on account of all the stress connected to what he'd gotten himself into but had also been having other problems.'

With widened eyes, Jim exhaled noisily and ran his hands through his hair, resting them on his head. This was a real blow.

Penelope sat, open-mouthed at the news. 'But... what if Felicity's still in danger?' she asked, her hands shaking in her lap.

'Mrs Johnston-Hart, I can assure you we have posted a guard on Felicity's door, and we are investigating every single lead provided by Miss Cole. To say she was distraught is an understatement. She knows she'll do time for her involvement, yet she's determined to squeal on those involved, which is very helpful indeed. We've interviewed Felicity and have all the details from her that she can remember.'

Jim swallowed hard. 'Is Flick implicated in all of this? You know with the art forgeries?' He wasn't sure he wanted to hear the answer.

'No. We have no reason to suspect her involvement. She was trying to compile evidence about the forgeries and was going to inform one of the gallery owners, Mr Nilsson, while she was in the UK. What she says is corroborated by Miss Cole. Felicity just needs to get well and go home.'

Both Penelope and Jim sighed with relief.

'I'll update you again once we have more.'

'Great, thanks. Can we go see Felicity now?'

Detective Rand nodded and gestured towards the door. Penelope and Jim hurriedly made their way to Flick's room.

* * *

She was sitting up, still pale, but looking much improved. A smile spread across her face when her visitors walked past the burly-looking guard on the door.

Jim's grin felt a mile wide on his face. 'Hey, Flick, you're looking great.' He wanted to rush over and kiss her but held back and allowed Penelope to step forward. Flick, however, didn't move her gaze from Jim's.

Penelope looked from her daughter to Jim and kissed her daughter's head. 'Darling, I'm going to go and get a coffee. I sense that there are things that you two need to discuss.' She patted Flick's arm and turned to Jim. 'Hear her out, Jim dear,' she whispered.

He pulled up a chair to Flick's bedside and sat. His hands itched to hold hers, but now that she was fully conscious, he felt awkward and had no clue what the limits were. As if she read his mind, she reached for his hand.

'Jim… I need to… I want to… erm…' Her gaze dropped to her lap. 'I think we need to talk.'

'Flick, I know all about the art forgeries. Don't worry. They're on the case. It'll be fine. You're not implicated, and no one will get to you. I won't let them.'

She squeezed his hand. 'Jim, that's not what I meant. I think we should talk about… about us. There are things I need to say to you.'

Jim sat up straight, suddenly realising he was about to find out where the limits were, and whether there was a future for them. 'Yes… yes, I suppose you're right.'

She took a deep breath. 'I know this involves dragging up the past, but I want to apologise, Jim. I put you through hell because I thought I was lacking in my life. It turns out I was only lacking in myself. It was nothing you did. You were wonderful and supportive and stood by whilst I tried to achieve this amazing career that I was so sure I wanted. I lost you because I was trying to aspire to a lifestyle that my mother, at the time, convinced me was right, and I was stupid enough to listen. She admits it now. It doesn't excuse my behaviour, I know.'

Her words came out in a rush and her voice wavered. 'The truth is... I... I never stopped loving you. I just convinced myself that I had, but... seeing you in January was so hard. And then we made love, and I thought that maybe you felt the same.' Jim saw tears glistening in her eyes. 'I realise now that you're over me and our relationship, and that you care deeply for me as a friend, otherwise you wouldn't have come all this way. And I'm so grateful for that.' She swiped at an escaped tear. 'And I will learn to get over the rest. Having you as a friend is so much better than not having you in my life at all. You were my best friend, Jim, and I miss that.' A sob escaped the confines of her throat. 'I miss that so much. But I needed to say sorry and to tell you... I love you... that I'm still in love with you. I just needed to say it and... I thought you should know.' More tears escaped the corners of her eyes. She pulled her hand away from Jim and wiped them away.

His heart ached to see her like this and his own eyes stung. 'I know you still love me, Flick. I've known since you left Scotland. That manuscript your dad sent me... there was a letter with it. Ed told me everything.'

She nodded but avoided eye contact. 'Oh... I see. Well, now you've heard it from the horse's mouth, eh?' She smiled and laughed once but sadness clouded her eyes. 'I'm still glad I said it. I think it was important that you heard it from me. And, well, now I can try to move on.'

Jim grasped her hand again. 'But what if I don't want you to move on?' He rubbed his thumb back and forth over her knuckles.

She smiled wider.

It was Jim's turn to take a deep breath. 'Flick, I've never stopped loving you either. I let you go because I thought that I didn't make you happy. That was all I ever wanted, for you to be happy. So, I figured I loved you enough to let you go.' He leaned towards her and cupped her cheek with his free hand.

Her mouth fell open at his words. She was silent and her brow furrowed as she seemed to be allowing the news to sink in. 'Oh, Jim, what did I do?'

'Hey, stop that. It's over. Forgotten.' He waved his hand dismissively and then returned it to her cheek. 'It's what we do from now that matters.'

She nodded slowly. 'So, what should we do?' Her tears were relentless now, and she covered his hand with hers, leaning into his touch.

'Flick, I don't know if you remember but you said, when you woke from your coma, that you wanted me to take you home. My home is Scotland, I don't know whether that changes things.'

Another sob escaped her throat. 'Oh, Jim, you want to take me home to Scotland?'

'Sweetheart, there's nothing I would like more. Is, is that what you want too? To come home to Scotland to me and Jasper?' He blinked as his tears finally overflowed and he swallowed hard.

She couldn't speak. She simply nodded.

He stood and bent towards her. Tilting her chin up, he kissed her gently. Her hands snaked up around his neck, and she deepened the kiss. 'I love you so much, Jim.'

He wiped away the tears from her cheeks. 'I love you, too, no more tears, eh?'

33

The cab pulled up outside the restaurant where Jim had secured a table in a quiet area at the back. Glasgow city centre on a Saturday night wasn't known for its serenity or composure, and Flick was still panicky in crowded places. Since her release from hospital and the flight back to Scotland, she had recovered well and was now only on minimal medication. They had spent the first few days down in Surrey with Penelope and had travelled home on the insistence of Jim who had a surprise to share.

Investigations into the attempted murder of Flick had resulted in Ella Cole and Chester Withers being arrested, awaiting trial for this and several counts of forgery. The surprising thing, and the thing that had hurt Flick more than anything, was that Vitale DeLuca had been arrested for illegally supplying the drug that had almost killed her. DeLuca's pharmaceutical company didn't exist, the card had been a forgery. He was simply a courier that Ella and Chester had met through the gallery. If Flick had carried out that internet search she almost embarked upon, however, she would have discovered a very genuine-looking website, such was their intent to deceive her.

He, too, had been involved in the forgeries and had known both Ella and Chester. Initially, he was supposed to coerce Flick, by way of his masculine charms, into becoming involved in order to implicate her, blackmail her, or keep her quiet about the whole thing. Flick turning him away had clearly scuppered their plans, and she felt glad that she hadn't fallen for his apparent sensuality. He had seemed so sincere when they'd almost spent the night together, and she had thought he genuinely liked her. Discovering it had all been a ruse to acquire her cooperation made her feel ashamed and incredibly foolish.

It was now June, and Julian had been in touch again to ask her to view the exhibition of the artist he had discovered. She had explained that she had resigned from her job and had no interest in this any more. But had eventually agreed to go and look as a last favour to Nilsson-Perkins – they had been roped into it all following an explanation from Julian.

Jim and Flick met Julian at the restaurant with hugs and handshakes.

Julian held her at arm's length. 'Wow, you really look amazing, Felicity, considering what you've been through.'

'That's sweet, thanks Julian. I feel much better. I just want to get this evening over with and get home to Shieldaig with Jim and to see Jasper.' She gazed lovingly up at Jim standing beside her with his arm tight around her waist.

They chatted over dinner about Julian's latest work and enjoyed a wonderful meal together, and even though she had been a little reluctant to go to the exhibition as the time drew closer, she felt the excitement building.

* * *

They climbed into a waiting cab that took them to the gallery. Julian had arranged to show Flick the exhibition when the gallery was closed so that she would feel safer.

They walked through the large wooden doors and followed Julian to the exhibition hall.

'So, do I get to know the artist's name yet?' she asked.

Julian huffed. 'You will soon enough, don't worry. The exhibition is called *Through the Glass*. That will suffice for now.' He stopped at the double doors. 'Now I want you to close your eyes.'

'Julian, I'm not five. This is about art, remember?'

Julian laughed. 'Oh, shut up moaning woman, and humour me.'

With an eye roll and a sigh, she did as he requested and allowed him to lead her through the doors.

Jim whispered, 'I told you about this while you were sleeping but now you get to see for yourself.'

Flick's brow crumpled but she smiled all the same. 'Told me about what, Jim? What's going on?'

With his hands on her shoulders Jim whispered, 'Okay... open your eyes.' He released her and she heard him step away.

Flick fluttered her eyes open as instructed and gazed up at the first painting. Waves of confusion and recognition washed over her simultaneously. She spotted the stand, which showed the exhibition title and the artist's name, 'Flick MacDuff'. She gasped and her hands shot to her face.

She looked over to Jim who stood with one arm across his middle and his other elbow resting on it, his finger on his lips, watching her reaction. He was grinning widely, his eyes glistening.

Her focus shot back to the painting.

Slowly, she walked towards the next piece, took her time viewing it, and then moved on. Scenes she had encountered on countless journeys with Jim, with friends, and with her parents all hung before her. Scenes she had observed through the glass and had recreated first in pencil and then in paint.

What an unexpected situation to find herself in.

The colours, the brush strokes... all her own. Every mark remembered. Every memory so special. She walked on until she had viewed all but the last painting.

Standing before this final piece overwhelmed her, and a sob escaped as she gazed into the scene that had plagued her memory for many years until she was taken there by Jim. On that day the memory of looking through Jim's family holiday snaps came flooding back into her mind. The place was somewhere she had thought she had imagined. She had so desperately wanted it to be real and discovering that it was, had filled her heart with such joy.

She couldn't quite take it all in.

As she walked around again, a wide smile spread across her face and the butterflies set to flight inside of her.

Through the Glass... this is me... this is what I see through the glass... I understand now. All this time, I've been living a life that wasn't mine. The high-flying career, the status symbols... it all means nothing. It's like I've been watching myself through the glass instead of living. But I need to step back into my life... this life... the life I was meant to have. With Jim.

She glanced over to where he stood. He was leaning against the wall now with his arms folded across his chest, observing her like he always used to. But this time it was different. This time the smile on his face was genuine and full of adoration. This time she could see who she was through his eyes and it all fell into place.

Finally, Flick turned and looked at Julian. Her face damp with tears of happiness. 'How? Why?' was all she could manage to say.

Julian held his arms out to gesture towards her paintings. 'Felicity... you're such a talented artist. This is what you deserve. Your own exhibition. What do you think?' A mask of worry descended over him.

'It's... it's wonderful, Julian. Thank you... thank you so much.' She rushed towards him and flung her arms around him, burying her head into his shoulder.

'Erm... Felicity... I think your gratitude is aimed in the wrong direction, honey. It was Jim who did all of this.'

Slowly, she turned to look at Jim, who had stuffed his hands in his pockets and was watching as the realisation hit his beautiful Flick. Myriad emotions coursed through his body and the familiar feeling of unshed tears stung his eyes.

'You? You did this? For me?' Her voice was almost a whisper as she slowly walked towards him.

He cleared his throat. 'After you left to go back to London and I read that letter from your dad, I realised I needed to do something to get you to remember how much you love painting, and maybe that way you would come back to me.' He wiped at the dampness around his eyes.

'Oh, Jim. I wanted you to come after me, desperately.'

'Aye and I would have if Euan and Aisha hadn't turned up just as I'd arranged to do that very thing. Then I heard that you'd left for Chicago. I asked Julian for his help and he's being far too bloody modest if you ask me. I couldn't have done this without him. I just had the idea. He made it happen.'

She arrived to stand before Jim and locked her gaze on his, smoothing her hands up over the lapels of his suit jacket. He pulled her close as his heart pounded in his chest.

His lip trembled. 'This is who you are. This is who I love.' He leaned to kiss her. Brushing his lips softly over hers, he felt her melt into him.

'I get it now. I understand and you're right. I love you so much, Jim, thank you for reminding me.'

He stroked her face and ran his thumb over her lower lip. 'Flick?'

'Yes, Jim?'

'Please, can I take you home now?'

34

Being back at Sunset Cottage for the last few months had been wonderful. Flick had forgotten how much she had loved it there for those few short days at the beginning of the year. They settled into life back together with ease, but this time things were so much better. It felt like it did in the early days when they had first met.

Their long walks together with Jasper were so special, and she had been painting again, making up for lost time. Many of her pieces displayed in Glasgow had sold, some for quite staggering amounts, and she had interest from galleries all over the UK. She was now living the dream she'd forgotten she had.

Jim had admitted to her that he had written a book about them and she had read it with tears streaming down her face. It was a beautiful story and she had encouraged him to write part two.

'But we don't what happens yet,' he'd told her.

She had smiled. 'I think we do.' Once the book was finished, he had eventually acquiesced to Flick's badgering and submitted it to publishers. Back in October he had received the incredible offer of a four-book deal with a British publishing company based in London. He'd snapped up the offer and had been writing ever since. He had so many ideas and so many notes that they had built a structure in the back garden for him to write in.

Flick told Jim how much she loved him as often as possible and whenever she did, the happiness in his eyes made her heart skip and swell.

Christmas morning arrived and Flick was rather giddy. She had conjured up a surprise for Jim in secret, and she was eager for him to unwrap it.

'Jim... wake up, sweetie... I think Father Christmas has been,' she whispered, sliding her hand down his naked back. He murmured and rolled over, wrapping his arms around her.

'Mmm... Merry Christmas, gorgeous. I love you,' he said in his delicious, husky morning voice. His familiar Scottish accent sent shivers travelling the length of her spine, and she decided maybe the gifts could wait a while.

She had so much lost time to make up for.

Being in Jim's arms again was like coming home. She would never tire of their closeness and newfound passion for each other. This time was forever, and as he worshipped her body with delicate kisses and caresses, she lost herself in the bliss of his touch.

Once their breathing had calmed, she pulled on his T-shirt and went downstairs to light the fire that he had built in readiness before bed on Christmas Eve. She made fresh coffee, and he arrived in the kitchen behind her, sliding his arms around her waist and nuzzling her neck.

'Mmm, you smell delicious. Have I told you I love you this morning?' he mumbled into her hair.

She covered his arms with her own. 'You have... but I never tire of hearing it.'

After eating croissants and drinking their coffee in the kitchen whilst Jasper looked on hopefully, apparently waiting for their leftovers, they went and sat beside the Christmas tree in all its pine-fragranced freshness. Flick handed Jim a parcel.

He ripped off the red and green holly print paper eagerly and when he took out the canvas, he gasped. 'This is the painting of us that you did back in university! I wondered what had happened to it.'

'It is. I wanted you to have it. Well for us to have it on the wall, here at home.'

His eyes widened. 'I thought you must've got rid of it. But I'm so happy you didn't. This is wonderful. Thank you so much. It can go beside the one of our view.' He lifted his gaze to look at the canvas over the fireplace; the one Flick had painted from memory when she stayed with him in January.

She smiled as her eyes blurred a little with tears at his reaction. 'I thought the same. Two special pieces that mean the world to us both.'

'Flick, it's so beautiful, thank you so much. I've always loved it. It's perfect' He leaned over and kissed her deeply. His flushed cheeks and glistening eyes told of the emotion he too felt. He cleared his throat. 'Erm... here's your gift... Merry Christmas, gorgeous.'

Flick carefully unwrapped the golden-coloured parcel with its huge red bow, prolonging the surprise for as long as she could, and Jim laughed as he watched her. Taking out the gift she looked over the contents and began to sob quietly, her body shaking and tears flowing freely. She lifted her face and gazed into his eyes where she saw her own tears reflected.

Looking down again, she read the cover of the book – *Reaching Everest, a Biography of George Leigh Mallory by Edgar Johnston-Hart*. She shook her head and smiled. 'Oh, Jim... it's wonderful. I'm so proud of you. Of both of you.' She flung her arms around him and kissed him once again.

* * *

They prepared their Christmas lunch together and enjoyed a slow dance in the living room to Nat King Cole's 'Christmas Song' as the snow gently drifted to the ground outside.

In the afternoon they watched *It's a Wonderful Life*, snuggled up on the sofa together with Jasper sprawled out on top of them, snoring his head off. Once the film had ended, Flick lifted her head from Jim's chest. 'C'mon, let's take Jasper for a walk up to the viewpoint.'

'Awww, Flick I'm comfy and cosy right here with you,' Jim whined, nuzzling her neck.

Jasper had clearly heard his name and the word walk, and his ears had pricked up. His tail began wagging frantically in a rhythm all of its own against Jim's leg and he lifted his head to lick Jim's chin.

'Too late, Jasper's ready, too, and it's stopped snowing. C'mon… please?' She pouted and fluttered her eyelids at him, and he finally gave in to her feminine wiles.

After wrapping up warm, they trudged along the road in the biting air of the chilly December afternoon, once again dodging the snowballs being thrown by the village kids. Miranda was out with Jess and they stopped for a quick chat. Next, they spotted Max with a West Highland White Terrier puppy giddily getting lost in the snow that camouflaged the poor wee creature.

'Hey, Max, who's your new friend?' Jim called out.

Max lifted the puppy and jogged over to them. 'Oh, hi, you two. This is Freddy. isn't he gorgeous? Phil got him for me for Christmas.' Jasper wagged his tail and sniffed at the pup who was a little scared at first, but then began to wag his tail too. 'I know you shouldn't give a pet for Christmas, but he knows I've wanted a dog for so long. I absolutely adore him. Anyway, what do you have planned for Hogmanay? Phil and I thought we'd invite you round to ours for dinner and some silly games if you're up for it.'

Flick grinned as she fussed over the cute, little, white dog. 'That sounds amazing, Max. Count us in. Although weather permitting my mum will be here too. Is that okay?'

Max beamed. 'Oh, definitely bring Penny along. We adore Penny.' Max and Phil had met Penelope in August when they'd come to a barbecue at Jim and Flick's after the community fete, and they'd got along famously.

'Great, thank you. She's viewing a few houses whilst she's here so she may be a more permanent fixture.'

'Wonderful. Well, I'd better get going. You lovebirds enjoy your walk.'

Eventually, Flick, Jim and Jasper arrived at the viewpoint depicted in Flick's painting and the old photo from Jim's childhood. They stood and admired the view in silence, their arms wrapped around each other and Jasper sitting beside them.

As Flick glanced up at the sky, she gasped. 'Jim, it's snowing again!' The sparkling flakes cascaded from the sky and began to settle all around them, carpeting the bracken with a white blanket. The landscape was rapidly transforming into something of a winter dreamscape.

After they had watched the snowflakes flutter down for a while, Flick turned to Jim. 'I was wondering... why did you put my name on the exhibition as Flick MacDuff?'

He chuckled. 'Ah... It was mainly because we didn't want you to put two and two together if word got out about the exhibition... although looking back, I think it was a bit daft really.'

She smiled out at the view. 'It has a nice ring to it really, doesn't it?'

His responding smile was tinged with a little sadness. 'Aye, well I always thought it did.'

She pulled away from him and grasped his shoulders, turning him to face her. His brow creased in confusion.

Undeterred, she gulped in the cold air. 'Jim, I know that we've had a rocky relationship, and that I was stupid on more than one occasion. But… I want you to believe me when I say that it will never, *ever* happen again.'

'I know, Flick, you don't need to—'

'Jim, please let me finish. I have something I need to ask you but I'm a little scared of the answer. And I distinctly remember you saying that you were only going to ask once, so I figured… it must be my turn…' She rambled as bewilderment still clouded his eyes and the line between his brows deepened.

Flick continued regardless. 'The name, Flick MacDuff? I'm hoping it's still up for grabs?'

He shook his head. 'Flick, I don't understand, you want to change your name? But we can just change the name of the artist on the exhibition now that everyone—'

She rolled her eyes. *God, he can be so dense*. She stopped his words with her fingertips. 'How about you stop talking and listen to me properly, eh?'

He clamped his mouth shut and nodded his acquiescence.

She fumbled in her coat pocket and dropped to one knee; warm, salty tears now trailed a heated path down her chilled face as she held up the silver Celtic band towards him. 'Jim, I want to be her. I want to be Flick MacDuff. Please, will you marry me… again?'

He stared down at her with his mouth open but didn't speak.

Oh shit… 'I know it's sudden and I know that maybe it's too soon… but—'

He dropped to his knees before her and took her face in his hands. 'Flick?'

'Yes?'

'You took the words right out of my mouth… The answer's yes.'

They sealed their engagement on their knees in the deepening snow with a passionate kiss, surrounded by snowflakes falling like confetti – as if they knew there was something to celebrate. Jasper nuzzled in between them and proceeded to lick them both from chin to nose, as if he knew too.

This wasn't really a second chance at love. It was a first chance at being who they had always been deep down. Having had the chance to step back and view their own lives, like observers looking through the glass, they knew that this was who they were.

Flick and Jim.

Together, this time, forever.

EPILOGUE

TWO MONTHS LATER

Jim stared across the table at Flick. She looked stunning, his fiancée. She was letting her hair grow and had stopped attacking it with the straightening irons. It looked golden in the amber glow of the roaring fire, the natural waves falling just past her shoulders.

He couldn't help but stare.

Valentine's Day hadn't exactly been filled with good memories for them. But this one was going to be different. Jim was determined about that. He arched his mouth up into a smile without realising it.

She tilted her head to one side and looked at him through long lashes. 'What are you so happy about?'

'You,' he replied simply.

She placed her knife and fork down and rested her chin on her hands. 'What about me?'

'Just that, you're so beautiful, Flick. More beautiful right now than I've ever seen you look.'

Although the lighting in the pub was low, Jim could see her cheeks colour slightly. She reached across the table and squeezed his forearm. 'Oh, Jim, I do love you.'

'And I love you. I want this Valentine's Day to be special, Flick. I want the memory of this one to replace all the others. We've wasted so much time. All I want to do is take you home and make love to you all night.' He reached for her hand and trailed circles around the back of her arm.

She flicked her hair back exposing her long neck. 'That sounds like a wonderful way to spend the evening.' A flush of colour rose from her chest up her neck to her cheeks.

He cleared his throat and pulled at the collar of his shirt. 'So… was your meal good?' He changed the subject before ravishing her in public.

She giggled as if fully aware of what he was doing. 'Mmm. It was delicious. The combination of spices was amazing… I'm so glad we have this place on our doorstep. Having said that, what I would really like is to skip dessert and have that at home.'

'I couldn't agree more, sweetheart. I'll go pay the bill.'

He walked over to the bar where he briefly chatted with the owner. Once he had paid, he came back over to Flick. Gazing down at her, he caught himself staring again. *Wow… she really is stunning.*

Her attitude to life had completely changed. She was so enthusiastic about painting again. Her passion shone through when she stood at her easel. He could sit, pretending to read a book or make notes, and secretly watch her for hours, her paint-spattered face begging for him to kiss her. Every so often she would catch him, and a smile would play on her lips.

Sometimes she would just continue with her work but sometimes – the times he loved the most – she would walk over to where he sat and remove her paint-covered clothing seductively. He'd never really fallen out of love with her but giving in to what his heart really wanted had been scary. And *she* was what his heart truly desired.

But they had trust again. Only this time it was stronger. And

Penelope had accepted their relationship like she should have all those years ago. It felt good to be in such a positive place in their lives.

Snapping himself from his thoughts, he stood beside her. 'C'mon, lassie. I'm taking you home.' He held out his hand, and she slipped hers into it, intertwining her fingers with his.

As she stood, she stopped smiling and leaned on the table. 'Oooh. Went a bit dizzy.' She smiled.

'You okay?' He couldn't hide his concern.

'Yeah, I'm fine. I think I just stood up too quickly. Head rush.' She giggled.

'Well at least we can't blame the wine. You hardly touched yours.'

'No, I didn't fancy it. And anyway, I wanted to keep a clear head for later.' She raised her eyebrows at him.

He groaned, rolling his head back. 'Och, you're killing me. C'mon, let's go home... *now*!' He helped her on with her jacket and scarf. They didn't have far to walk, but the bitter chill in the air demanded appropriate winter clothing.

As they walked on the icy pavement back to the cottage, she began taking deep breaths. He looked to her and again worry washed over him. 'Are you sure you're okay?'

'Do you know what, Jim? I have an awful feeling that I'm coming down with something. I keep going dizzy.'

He rubbed her back. 'Oh no. I hope the food hasn't disagreed with you, sweetheart. That's all we need, eh?'

'No, it wasn't the food at all. It was cooked to perfection as always... I... I think maybe I'm getting the flu or... something. My immune system isn't quite as it should be yet after the... well, you know.' He watched as she lifted her hand to her head. They walked as fast as they could in the icy conditions.

Bloody typical. The one Valentine's Day that we get to spend together properly... Damn that witch for drugging her.

He felt selfish at his thoughts then. He was gravely worried about her.

When they arrived home, she rushed up to the bathroom. He heard unpleasant noises coming from up there. This wasn't ordinary flu. This was turning out to be something like stomach flu. He followed her up and sat on their bed, feeling helpless, running his hands through his hair in a bid to keep them occupied.

The urge to ring for a doctor was overwhelming, but he had to try to stop panicking every time she sneezed, coughed, or threw up. She never did like him to be there if she got sick. He'd offer to hold her hair, but she would shout at him and tell him to get out. So, this time he sat. Waiting. The sickness started again.

This is so bloody unfair. The poor wee girl. She doesn't deserve this. Oh god... what if it's her liver? I'm going to have to ring the bloody hospital. I can't just sit here and bloody do nothing. No... I'll wait awhile... If things don't calm down, then I am ringing a doctor... and she can complain as much as she likes about me being over bloody protective. Tough. I love her, and I won't sit by and watch her being ill. I can't stand it.

After pacing around the room awhile longer, he realised that everything had gone silent in the bathroom. She had been in there ages now. Had she fainted or something? Panic washed over him again, and he decided to go check on her. Just as he got to the bathroom door, he heard sobbing.

He tapped on the bathroom door. 'Flick, you're really worrying me now, would you please open the door?' The sound of retching came loud again from within the bathroom. 'Flick? Maybe I should call the doctor, eh?' He tapped again but the sobbing and sniffing continued. 'Stomach flu can be serious, Flick. If that's what it is, you should really see someone especially with your history. You could be dehydrated, and I'm really worried.' He tried the door; she hadn't locked it. She looked up as he walked in. Her eyes were bloodshot, and she was so pale.

'What's wrong Flick?' A terrible memory came back to haunt him, Flick crying in the bathroom, arguments, pain, hurt, and his own stomach lurched. Was history about to repeat itself right before his eyes?

Croakily she spoke. 'Jim, I've been unwell for a couple of days, but I just presumed it was a bug, so I didn't say anything. Then I started feeling sickly at the pub and put it down to the flu or the spices in the chicken—'

He squeezed his jaw tight and shook his head, bracing himself for the impact of her next words.

She stopped speaking and fixed him with a worried gaze. 'Hey, why do you look so sad?'

He shook his head again. 'Because I know what you're going to say.' His lip trembled. 'The look on your face... I've lost you over and over again and now this? Why can't things just go right, eh?' A sob escaped his throat.

Her face was filled with unreadable emotions but mostly bewilderment, which, in turn, foxed Jim.

She placed a hand on each of his arms. 'Jim, will you just stop thinking the worst for a second? This is not what you think.'

He widened his eyes. 'It's not?' He wasn't sure whether to be relieved or sad, but he plumped for relieved. He couldn't lose her again. If that meant no children, then he would learn to accept it.

'Jim... I have something to say. And I need you to listen, okay? Just hear me out... please, trust me?'

He folded his arms across his chest and braced himself for what was coming. His heart pounded against his ribcage. 'Okay,' was all he could force his quivering voice to say.

Confusion surged through him again as he saw a wide smile appear on her face.

Her hands moved to his cheeks. 'Jim, you know how you said you wanted this to be a Valentine's Day to remember?'

He inhaled roughly and nodded. 'Aye, I remember.'

'Well…' She handed him a little white stick. 'Happy Valentine's Day… You're going to be a daddy.'

ACKNOWLEDGMENTS

So much has changed since I first released this book as *Through the Glass* back in 2013, but one thing that has remained the same is the fantastic support I continue to receive from friends, family, readers and other authors alike.

I've met so many amazing people during my time as an author, and I want to thank each and every person who has been there for me. Whether it's been to offer advice, to kick my bum when I've been filled with self-doubt, or to read unfinished manuscripts and give opinions, every bit of your input has been invaluable.

The story was inspired by a wonderful place called Shieldaig on the west coast of Scotland, and specifically a tiny little coffee shack there that was once called Nanny's. Although these days the little shack is the most wonderful café on the site of the original building, it's a part of the world that stole my heart many years ago and I hope you enjoy reading about the place.

The story has had a re-edit to bring it into line with my other books and I'm so delighted with the results. Seeing this book republished by Boldwood as *Starting Over at Sunset Cottage* fills my heart with joy, and I'm so grateful to Caroline and the wonderful team there.

Thank you for reading my stories.

Printed in Great Britain
by Amazon